"Hilarious . . . moving . . . deeply disturbing." —*Mademoiselle*

"A page-turner . . . gritty, funny, sexy." —*Chicago Sun-Times*

"It all rings true." —*Pittsburgh Tribune-Review*

"O'Dell does a wonderful job of making the world of the Altmyers real . . . a unique voice . . . a fine effort by a writer of promise." —*Newsday*

"A strong, thoughtful first novel." —*Kirkus Reviews*

"O'Dell's storytelling has natural flair."
—*Los Angeles Times Book Review*

"Scorching. . . . O'Dell's characters fight free of stereotypes, taking on an angry, authentic glow." —*Publishers Weekly*

"*Back Roads* transports us to the hills of western Pennsylvania and introduces a wonderfully touching narrator, Harley Altmyer. Watching Harley grapple with his sisters, his jobs, and his lover is by turns comic and suspenseful. This is a fast, furious, funny novel." —Margot Livesey, author of *Criminals*

"A vividly rendered voyage of personal discovery."
—*Chicago Tribune*

"A wonderful book about family relationships. . . . It's nearly impossible to put down. With deft prose, authenticity of character, and sheer tenderness, O'Dell . . . is the absolute master of her craft." —*The Denver Post*

A Main Selection of the Book-of-the-Month Club

back roads

Tawni O'Dell

New American Library

New American Library
Published by New American Library, a division of
Penguin Group (USA) Inc., 375 Hudson Street,
New York, New York 10014, U.S.A.
Penguin Books Ltd, 80 Strand,
London WC2R 0RL, England
Penguin Books Australia Ltd, 250 Camberwell Road,
Camberwell, Victoria, 3124, Australia
Penguin Books Canada Ltd, 10 Alcorn Avenue,
Toronto, Ontario, Canada M4V 3B2
Penguin Books (N.Z.) Ltd, Cnr Rosedale and Airborne Roads,
Albany, Auckland 1310, New Zealand

Penguin Books Ltd, Registered Offices:
80 Strand, London WC2R 0RL, England

Published by New American Library, a division of Penguin Group (USA) Inc.
Previously published in a Viking hardcover edition and a Signet mass market
paperback edition.

First New American Library Printing, June 2004
10 9 8 7 6 5 4 3 2

For my sister, Bean

acknowledgments

To Jennifer Robinson for being the first person to go to the mat for me. Thank you for your faith and outrage.

To Liza Dawson, my genie in the bottle, for her counsel, wisdom, and sanity. Thank you for helping me realize my dream.

To Molly Stern, Lippy Goddess and Master of Minutiae, for her passion and devotion to this book and its author. Also for her remarkable ability to always be right. (So far.) Thank you for your guidance.

To Mike for his love and support through sleepless nights, dark days, and dictionaries in the fridge. A lesser man would have deserted the trench.

To my sweet pea, Tirzah, and my little man, Connor. Mommy loves you bigger than anyone.

And finally, thank you to my mom for her constant assurance that I could be whatever I wanted to be; and to my dad for his steady insistence that what I should be is a writer.

chapter 1

All those times me and Skip tried to kill his little brother, Donny, were just for fun. I keep telling the deputies this, and they keep picking up their Styrofoam cups of coffee and walking away only to return a few seconds later and heave their fat butt cheeks onto the metal-topped table in front of me and flash me sad, weary stares that would be almost tender if they weren't filled with so much hatred. They tell me they don't care about Skip and Donny. They're not interested in stuff I did when I was a kid. I'm twenty years old now. I will be TRIED AS AN ADULT. The words come out of their mouths in Skoal-flavored capital letters and hover against the fluorescent glare of the room. I reach out to touch them but before I can, they melt away again and one of the deputies slaps down my hands stained the color of a dead rose. They won't let me wash them.

They want to know about the woman. I laugh. Which woman? My life is lousy with women. All ages, shapes, sizes, and levels of purity.

"The dead woman in the abandoned mining office behind the railroad tracks," one of them says, making a face like he might puke.

I close my eyes and picture it. The roof with gaping holes.

The rotting floorboards scattered with broken window glass, rusted screws and bolts, and pieces of flattened iron that used to be part of something bigger a long time ago. When I finally took her there, she didn't ask me to sweep it out. She said she didn't want to change anything about it because she knew it was a special place for me. She said she loved the calm of decay and desertion that reigned there. She liked art and sometimes the way she talked sounded like a painting.

Rage starts building inside me, nicely and neatly, like a perfect pyramid of sticks being piled up for a fire. My hands start shaking, and I sit on them so the police won't see.

"Me and Skip used the mining office for our secret hideout," I answer, smiling, while the blaze roars to life inside me. Soon I will be nothing but a black skeleton of ash that the slightest touch will cause to crumble. But no one on the outside will know.

The deputies shake their heads and groan and snort at the mention of Skip. One of them kicks a folding chair across the room. Another one says, "The kid's in shock." The other one says, "We're not going to get anything RELEVANT or CO-HERENT out of him tonight." I reach for those words too and this time I get the side of my head smacked instead of my sticky hands.

"You better start talking," the sheriff says, pausing to spit a brown bullet of chew into an empty coffee can before adding, "son," to his suggestion.

He's the only one here I know. I remember him from my mom's trial two years ago. He testified that she gave herself up willingly after shooting my dad. He smells like a wet couch.

I do start talking but all that comes out is the same stuff about me and Skip again, how we used to spend hours in the old mining office eating bologna sandwiches and hatching our plans against Donny. We called it secret even though Donny knew where we were. It was secret because he couldn't get to it. He was too little to make it up the hill and through the vicious under-growth surrounding the place like nature's barbed wire.

We came up with some great ones. Once we bent down a birch sapling and anchored it to the ground with a tent stake and tied a rope loop to it, then lured Donny into the middle with a shiny foilwrapped HoHo. The tree was supposed to break free and fling him to his death by his ankles, but we realized too late we hadn't figured out a way to make it do this, and Donny just finished the HoHo and left.

Another time we spilled a bunch of marbles on the back porch steps and yelled at him to come outside, we had a box of Little Debbie Oatmeal Creme Pies for him. He came tearing out of the house but instead of slipping and falling on the marbles, he skidded to a stop and sat down and played with them.

Another time we promised him a box of Little Debbie Star Crunches if he would let us tie up his feet and hands and lay him on the railroad tracks but they were freight tracks—the same ones that run by the old mine—and we all knew a train hadn't been down them since before we were born. Donny got bored waiting to die and started wriggling toward home on his belly.

Our most ingenious plan was probably the time we put a pack of Dolly Madison Zingers beneath the open garage door, and we hid out with the garage door opener and clicked it on when Donny sat down to eat. He didn't notice or didn't care about the heavy door grinding down toward his skull. We watched in amaze-ment, unable to believe we were finally going to succeed, but I lost my nerve and ran and yanked him to safety. I saved him. I can't seem to make the police understand what this says about my character.

"That's the closest I ever came to murder," I explain, "up until my dad . . ."

The sheriff interrupts me. He doesn't want me to go into that again. He knows all about my mom and dad. Everybody does. It was in the papers and all over TV.

He was the one who was there, he reminds me. Not me. I wasn't even home. He was the one who walked in and found my mom with a bucket of red sudsy water calmly scrubbing the stains off her kitchen wallpaper while her husband lay a foot away stuck to the tile in a pool of tarry blood staring right at her with hunting trophy eyes. He was the one who found my baby sister huddled in one of the doghouses with vomit all over her because she had cried so hard she made herself throw up; and Jody never even liked Dad. He was the one who watched Dad get zipped into a body bag. Not me. I never got to see him again. It was a closed casket funeral. I'm not sure why. Mom shot him in the back.

It's been almost two years now, the sheriff reminds me. No one cares anymore. It's not RELEVANT.

"Define relevant," I say.

The deputy who keeps hitting me grabs me by the front of my dad's camouflage hunting jacket and pulls me out of my chair. He has big sweat stains under his armpits. Eighty-five today. Hot for the first week of June.

"Tell us about the woman," he shouts at me.

I don't know why they won't say her name. I guess they're waiting for me to say it. For me to admit I knew her. Well, of course, I did. They know I did.

He drops me back into my chair, and TRIED AS AN ADULT appears in front of my eyes bright and buzzing like neon. I don't know why I can't talk about her. Each time I open my mouth something about Skip comes out, and he's not even my friend anymore.

I always knew Skip would leave. His constant scheming never seemed a part of these quiet, wounded hills the way Donny's blind love of snack cakes did. Donny will be here forever. I see him every morning on my way to work at the Shop Rite waiting on the side of the road for the school bus like a stump.

"Skip's away at college now," I say.

4

I'm still staring at the words so I don't see the fist coming. I feel the warmth of blood gush down my chin before I feel the pain. Bright red droplets spatter onto the front of Dad's coat where her blood has already dried into a brown crust. They keep trying to make me take off the coat. People are always trying to make me.

I hear the sheriff say, "Jesus Christ, Bill, did you have to do that?"

I think the sheriff's up for reelection next year. I guess I'll be old enough to vote then if I want. VOTE AS AN ADULT. I think I would probably vote against him though. It's not that I dislike the guy, and I don't know anything about his stands on law enforcement issues so I can't say I disagree with him. My vote would be based solely on smell.

I touch my smashed nose and decide to tell them the TRUTH. Who's to blame. Who's at fault. Who should be locked up. I have nothing to be afraid of anymore. What will I be giving up by losing my freedom? What will the world be giving up by losing me?

I told her once I wasn't good at anything. She ran her thumb over my lips raw from kissing her and said survival was a talent.

chapter ② 2

When Skip left for college, he never even came around to say good-bye. I heard about it from Amber, who heard Donny talking about it on the bus.

He wrote me once during his whole first year at school. The next year I didn't think he was going to write at all, but he finally did and invited me to come visit him. We both knew I wouldn't go and that's why he asked. I read the letter a dozen times, then put it in my drawer with the Victoria's Secret catalogs I was always swiping from Amber's room.

I made the mistake the next day of telling Betty about the letter. Betty loved it when I talked about Skip. She especially loved hearing about the times we tried to kill Donny. I supposed I should have never told her that stuff in the first place, but she asked me to tell her a pleasant childhood memory once and it was the only one that came to mind.

She wanted to know how Skip's letter made me feel and why I wouldn't consider going to visit him. I pulled my stare away from the window where blue-gray tree branches crawled against the white sky like the veins on Betty's thighs. I had tried not to notice, but she wore her skirts way too short for an old lady.

I didn't look at her but the fact that I had stopped staring out the window was a signal between us that I heard her question but the answer to it was so obvious I wasn't going to say it out loud.

"I think I know what you're going to say, but why don't you tell me anyway," she said, smiling. "Treat me like I'm stupid."

It was what she always said to try and get me to talk. One of her textbooks must have told her teenagers could never resist this invitation.

"I have to work," I said finally.

"This weekend?"

"Yes."

"Next weekend?"

"Yes."

"Every weekend?"

I didn't say anything, and she leaned back in her chair.

"Do you have any other reasons for not going?"

I shifted around on the far end of the couch and tried to find something new in the room to look at, but nothing ever changed. Desk. Window. Chair. Table with lamp. Couch. Table with box of Kleenex. Door. Betty. She didn't even have a framed diploma or a bookcase here. I asked her about this once—I thought all shrinks had bookcases—and she said this wasn't her real office; it was just the place where she saw government cases. I could tell she regretted the way she said it, and I let her.

"Who's going to watch Jody and Misty?" I said after a while.

"Who watches them when you're at work?"

"I'm talking about overnight."

"Amber is old enough to watch them overnight."

"Amber," I snorted, and I was done talking.

I went back to staring out the window, and Betty reached into her blouse and adjusted her bra strap when she thought I wasn't looking.

"I'm going to assume from that reaction that you and Amber

7

aren't getting along any better," she said, and let me stew for a minute.

"Why do you think that is?" she asked.

A crow landed in the parking lot outside and started trying to peel a flattened earthworm off the blacktop. Early March had been warm and fooled everyone into thinking spring was here. The ground thawed. Worms woke up. Girls got out their summer clothes.

Every morning on my way to work, I drove past a yawning group of bare-legged ones in shorts and miniskirts waiting for the school bus with Donny the stump. In the past, I would've slowed down and watched from my rearview mirror until they disappeared around a bend in the road, but lately looking at girls shredded my nerves. It was a big part of becoming a man: discovering there was a difference between wanting sex and needing it.

"Amber says she's been trying," Betty persisted. "She's told me she's been helping out a lot more around the house."

"Are you kidding me?" I cried out.

"No, I'm not. Do you disagree with that?"

I laughed. A real laugh. A sincere Har Dee Har Har.

"Why would she tell me that if it isn't true?" Betty asked.

I pulled one of my feet onto my lap and started digging at a piece of gravel stuck in the tread of my Sears work boot. Amber made fun of their red laces. I didn't care. They lasted forever. Not like the Payless crap she bought with my money.

"Because along with being lazy and stupid, she's also a liar," I answered.

"How do I know she's the liar and not you?"

I got the gravel out and seriously thought about flicking it across the room at Betty, but instead I put it in the pocket of Dad's camouflage hunting jacket.

"I guess you don't," I said, feeling my face burn.

I dropped my foot back on the carpet with a thud.

"I didn't mean to upset you."

"Sure you did. You want me to get mad so I'll say something meaningful."

I had made that mistake before. Recalling things like the way my mom's eyes had sparkled with tears at my three-year-old observation that "I am person-shaped," or how my mom used to save the dogs' expired rabies tags because she thought they were pretty. I could always tell when I had accidentally said something meaningful because Betty would look at me like I was suddenly naked and surprisingly well-hung.

She smiled and caught a piece of her nickel-colored hair with a finger and hooked it behind one ear. Her hair was expensive-looking, cut on an angle and shiny solid like a helmet. It didn't go with the rest of her. It reminded me of the county fair pony rides and the brand-new, freshly oiled saddles sitting on top of the broken-down, shaggy old ponies.

"Everything you say in these sessions is meaningful, Harley."

I slumped down as far as I could go and still be on the couch. "Can I go?"

"Not yet. Let's try and resolve this problem. I think it would be good for you to get away for a day or two. If you don't trust Amber to watch your sisters overnight what about someone else? A relative or neighbor?"

"I told you before my mom doesn't have any family, and Dad's family won't have anything to do with us anymore."

"Why do you think that is?"

"I guess because we're related to Mom."

"You're related to your father too."

"Not as closely."

She smiled at me again and I fingered the gravel in my coat pocket and imagined it embedded smack in the middle of her forehead with a tiny trickle of bright red blood dripping from it. She would have gone right on talking if I did it.

"What about your Uncle Mike? I thought you said he's been helping out lately."

"He's been bringing me cases of Black Label. I guess that's helpful. Although Rolling Rock would be more helpful, in my opinion."

She gave me her concerned look. Clear young eyes peering out anxiously from a wrinkled face like a kid trapped inside a mask. I hated it when old people kept something young about them, like Bud who bagged with me at the Shop Rite and chewed bubble gum all the time. It was easier to think of them as always being old instead of being young and dying very slowly.

"Alcohol is not a solution to your problems," Betty announced, frowning.

"I didn't say anything about alcohol. I'm talking about beer."

"If your social worker found alcohol on the premises, the girls would be put in foster homes immediately. You're underage."

"I don't care."

"You don't care if your sisters are put in foster homes?"

"No."

"Well, you have a funny way of showing it."

"I have to go."

I stood up and pulled my Redi-Mix Concrete cap out of my back jeans pocket. Betty glanced at her watch and said, "We still have fifteen minutes."

I slapped the cap on my head and pulled the brim down to my eyes. "My apologies to the taxpayers," I said, and headed out the door.

The false spring had only lasted a week and then, as if to punish the worms and the girls for their optimism, the weather had turned brittle cold. I blew in my hands and rubbed them together, then stuck them under my armpits while I walked quickly to my truck. I didn't know why I was hurrying. The heater didn't work.

The county Behavioral Health Services office was in the same long, low, brown brick building as the DMV and the animal control office. Across the intersection was the Eat N' Park that had driven Denny's out of business (even Grand Slam breakfasts couldn't compete with Eat N' Park pies) and the strip mall with Blockbuster Video, Fantastic Sam's, the Dollar Tree, and a Chinese restaurant called Yee's. I always stopped at Yee's after my appointment with Betty.

Jack Yee, the guy who owned the place, bobbed his head and smiled deliriously when I walked in and his wife did the same, waving from a far corner where she always sat at a table reading a newspaper. I feared I was their best customer, and I only came in once a month and bought a two-dollar egg roll.

Jack tried pushing the General Tso's chicken on me.

"Spicy, spicy," he said, grinning.

"No, thanks," I told him, even though I was starving and all I was going to get at home was blue box mac and cheese and hot dogs. It was Misty's night to cook. She was twelve.

He gave me Jody's umbrella and cookie for free and asked about her. He and his wife had only met her once, but they were blown away by her. They couldn't stop touching her hair. It fell all the way down to her butt and was the same color as the gold letters stamped on church hymnals.

All the girls had long hair—including Mom—but Jody's was the most admired. Mom's was the reddest. Misty's the most neglected. Amber's the most likely to smell like a rank old blanket from the back of some guy's pickup truck.

I took the little brown bag and sat it next to me in my truck, then spent the half-hour drive from Laurel Falls to Black Lick watching the grease stain grow from the egg roll pressing against the paper. I wanted to eat it more than anything in life. I rolled down the window to try and get rid of the deep-fried smell, but I couldn't stand the cold. By the time I took the final bend leading home, I was driving so fast the old Dodge Ram was shuddering.

Ours was the only house on Fairman Road, an unpaved two-mile shortcut connecting two parts of a county road that doubled back on itself. Locals called it Potshot Road because before my dad had started piecing together our house at the top of it, so many deer gathered in the clearing any hunter hiding in the trees could take a potshot and hit something. Every hunting season, Dad had to lock up the dogs in the garage and Mom made us kids play inside for fear of getting shot. I never felt safer than those days Amber and I spent hiding beneath a blanket-covered card table playing war and listening to the crack of rifles outside and the calm blasted silence that always followed.

The deer had thinned out the past couple years though. Even the stupidest animal could sense when a place had gone bad.

The truck bounced over a rut, and the egg roll went flying off the seat onto the floor, where it landed on top of a bunch of empty fast-food coffee cups, crumpled McDonald's bags, and a cheap gray windbreaker with Barclay's Appliances written across the back. One of Jody's dinosaurs was down there too and my parents' wedding picture.

I had found the picture stuffed in the bottom of a garbage bag a couple months after the shooting. The sharp corner of the cheap yellow-gold frame had poked a hole through the plastic and scratched me on the calf while I was standing in my underwear putting on a twist tie. The rip got bigger and garbage spilled out all over the kitchen floor and I had froze, bracing myself for the flat of my dad's hand to connect with the base of my skull and for the tiny stars of light, like floating dandelion fuzz, to drift into my line of vision and pile up until I couldn't see anything but cold white nothingness. Then I remembered he was dead.

The girls were all asleep so I cleaned up the mess myself. I kept out the picture and was on my way to throw it in the outside can when something made me throw it in my truck instead.

I never looked at it. Whenever I happened to notice it by accident, I buried it under the trash but it always managed to surface again: Dad in a white suit and a glossy shirt patterned in jewel-toned splotches like a melted stained-glass window, way too much hair and collar, a Burt Reynolds mustache, a blood-red carnation in his buttonhole, grabbing Mom around the waist and grinning drunkenly at one of his off-camera buddies; Mom in a gauzy white handkerchief dress, a ton of eye makeup, long white feather earrings and ceramic Farrah hair, her shoulders kind of hunched together and her head tilted away from Dad's breath, looking like she was trying not to throw up. I gave her a lot of morning sickness.

I reached over with my foot and pushed the picture under the trash.

The first half-mile of our road was straight uphill and the trees grew together over the top of it making a tunnel of leaves in summer, and a tunnel of snow in winter, and a tent of bare branches like charred fingers the rest of the year. Our house sat at the crest. Across the road was the clearing, stretching out green and smooth, then disappearing over a slope into a rolling sea of hills the color of rust and soot and worn yellow carpet. The power lines and the smoke-belching twin coal stacks of the Keystone Power Plant in the distance were the only signs of humanity. Whenever people asked me how we could stand to stay in the house, I told them I liked the view and then they thought I was even crazier than before they asked.

Aside from Laurel Falls National Bank, the only thing that could have driven me away was the sight of the four empty doghouses. Every time I parked my truck and was greeted with silence instead of the barking chorus I had come to expect ever since I was old enough to put meaning to sound, I hated myself for failing them. But dog food cost a fortune. I managed to find homes for three and kept Elvis, my shepherd mutt. He was allowed to come inside now, but he was nervous about it. So were the girls. If anything could have brought my dad raging back from the dead it would have been the sight of a dog lying in the middle of his living room.

Misty opened the front door and let Elvis out. She followed him and stood on the front porch, silent and expectant, fingering the pink rhinestones on the grimy cat collar she wore around her wrist.

The collar had belonged to the kitten Dad got her for her tenth birthday. It only survived for two months before we found it shot in the woods.

I remembered Mom taking the death harder than anyone. She burst into tears when she saw what was left of the blood-matted fluffy white carcass Misty had dragged back to the yard by its tail.

She folded Misty into her arms and held her while Misty stood stiffly and stared at the body with her eyes a glazed brown like a medicine bottle. Then she knelt down and slowly unbuckled the collar and fastened it around her wrist while Mom's hands still clutched her shoulders. Later Mom said she had been in shock.

"Did you get my egg roll?" Misty called out, rubbing her thin bare arms at her sides and her stockinged feet against each other.

I threw the bag. Elvis stopped in his tracks on his way to meet me and watched its flight. It fell on the frozen mud next to the steps and he bounded over to sniff it.

Misty glanced at me, unsmiling, before she walked down to get it. I couldn't tell if she was pissed or hurt or couldn't care less. Her mask of freckles gave her the appearance of being more persecuted than she really was.

I started across the yard and paused at the patch of cement with a sawed-off piece of pipe sticking from it where Dad's satellite dish used to be. I tapped at it with the toe of my boot and reminded myself I needed to get rid of the rest of the pipe before someone got hurt on it. The dish had gone the way of the dogs, leaving us with only four channels. Jody lost Disney. Misty lost Nickelodeon. Amber lost MTV and Fox. At the time they had all been too depressed about Mom and Dad to care, but now they weren't and I had to hear about it every day.

I went inside and wiped my boots on the mat by the door, but I didn't take them off the way I used to have to.

"Did you get my fortune cookie and umbrella?" Jody asked from the living room.

On my way through, I told her Misty had the bag. I tossed the stuffed dinosaur over the back of the couch, and Jody's head popped up from the cushions.

"Sparkle Three-Horn," she cried. "I lost him."

"I know. I found him."

"Where?"

"My truck."

The head disappeared and the couch said, "Thanks."

I walked into the kitchen and found the Thursday pot of boiling water on the stove and five hot dogs laid out on a paper plate ready for nuking in the microwave. I opened a cupboard and grabbed a bag of pretzels. Misty came in after me, eating her egg roll.

I hadn't noticed from a distance that she was wearing some of Amber's purple eyeshadow again. Mom wouldn't have approved of her wearing makeup already, but I had surrendered control of everything female to Amber the day Misty came to me the year before and told me she was pretty sure she had started her period.

I looked at the hot dogs again and did the math: one for Jody, one for Misty, three for me.

"Isn't Amber eating?"

"She's got a date."

"What?"

Misty tore open the Kraft box, pulled out the cheese packet, and dumped the macaroni in the pan. The water foamed up, and she adjusted the heat.

"She said you'd be mad. But I can watch Jody. I'm old enough."

"That's not the point."

"I know. Amber said the main reason you'd want her to stay

15

home is because you want to ruin her fun. Not because of the baby-sitting."

I threw the bag on the counter, and pretzels spilled onto the floor. Elvis lunged for them as I stormed out. Misty pushed one aside with a blue-polished big toe and kept stirring the pot.

I pounded on Amber's door so hard her Indian dream catcher fell off the wall. She was holding it in her hand when she opened the door. She had on a red lace bra and hiphugger jeans, and her pinched expression of annoyance changed into a satisfied smile when she saw me looking at her.

"You're supposed to watch the kids tonight," I yelled at her over the music blaring from her radio.

She turned her back on me and walked with exaggerated hip thrusts over to her dresser, the top of her hummingbird tattoo peeking at me over the waistband of her jeans. He seemed to be waving a green wing at me.

She grabbed a brush and bent over.

"Misty's twelve. She can baby-sit a six-year-old," she said upside down from behind a curtain of reddish-blond hair.

"They shouldn't be alone in the house late at night," I said.

"What is your problem? Why is it okay to leave them alone during the day and not at night? I swear you're afraid of the dark."

She finished and stood up, tossing her hair behind her with her throat arched and exposed, a female gesture that always cut right through me.

I stood at the doorway not wanting to go in. Every inch of wall space and ceiling was covered with tie-dyed scarves and pieces of sheets done mostly in purples and blues. Her only window was hung with strings of midnight-blue star-shaped beads. The shelves behind her bed were packed with psychedelic-colored candles, most of them lit. The combination of the colors and the dim lighting gave the place a half-digested feel.

I walked through it quickly and arrived at her stereo sitting on a cinder-block shelf next to a stack of *Glamour* magazines worth at least two hundred pounds of dog food.

I turned off the radio.

She threw her brush back onto her dresser in protest where it clattered against all her makeup and hair stuff.

"What is your problem?"

"I can't hear."

"No, I mean what is your problem?" she said again, rolling her empty blue eyes at me. "Did Betty Wetty tell her Harley Warley he needs to have more wee-spect for himself? Did she tell him he needs to get more wee-spect from his girls?"

She made a kissy face. I didn't say anything.

"I don't need to stay home tonight," she added, and pulled a tiny, striped sweater out of her drawer that looked like something a schnauzer might get for Christmas. Amazingly, she squeezed her head into it and the fabric expanded, first taking on the shape of her face, then the shape of her breasts.

She caught me staring at her again and smiled triumphantly. "Admit it," she said. "You just hate the idea that I have a life and you don't."

"Define life," I said.

The smile flickered and went out. She retrieved her brush and gave her head a few vicious strokes, then started lightly slapping it against the palm of her hand the way Dad used to do with Mom's wooden cooking spoon before he took off after one of us.

"You know what your problem is? You're pissed off because you have to work. Well, you'd have to work anyway. It's not like you'd be going to college or hanging out with friends or doing anything meaningful. You don't even watch TV."

I laughed even though I wasn't feeling the least bit humorous. "Meaningful?" I repeated. "Like fucking guys in the back of pickup trucks?"

The brush flew out of her hand and hit me in the arm.

"You'd give anything to fuck someone," she hissed at me.

I wanted to pick up the brush and beat Amber senseless with it. I wanted to put big red welts on her pretty face and make blood gush from her ears. Not because I hated her. Not because she deserved it. Not because I wanted to make her fear me. Simply because it would feel good.

This must have been the same way Dad used to feel before he belted me, and I took some comfort in realizing the desire to hurt someone was nothing personal. The difference between Dad and me was that he always went ahead and hit one of us, and he was a much happier person.

I knew it never occurred to Amber that I might hurt her. She believed violence was an act of strength, and she thought I was weak. Otherwise, she would have never risked pushing me like she did. She hated getting hit.

I picked up her brush and gave it back to her. For a moment we both held onto it, and I felt it tremble.

She went back to preparing for her date. I went to get ready for work.

Amber had the best room in the house: mine. She used to have to share with Misty until Jody came along, then she got my room and I got kicked into the basement. I didn't want to go, and I never bothered to try and make the place homey. A twin bed with a naked lightbulb hanging over it, a chest of drawers, a stereo, a coat of leftover green bathroom paint on one of the cement walls, a square of purple shag carpet, and a couple of mousetraps were the only signs of life down here.

Most nights I lay on my back and imagined what it would feel like if the lightbulb crashed down on my forehead and a needle of glass pierced my eyeball or got in my mouth and I swallowed it.

Skip used to say if someone got a glass sliver under his skin and didn't take it out right away, it would get into his bloodstream and travel to his heart and kill him. We tried killing

Donny that way once—there was a ton of broken glass around the old mining office—but Donny wouldn't let us stick the glass in him, not even for a Tastykake Jelly Krimpet.

If the bulb ever did break and a sliver did kill me, I'd want to be buried with the white glass shards all over my face. People would think they were white rose petals unless they got up close.

I pulled the string and the light came on after a couple sputters. In a day or two, I was going to pull the string and the bulb was going to die with a hollow pop, and I didn't know where Mom kept the new ones. When she went off to prison she took all sorts of secret domestic knowledge with her: what drawer the envelopes were in; how to make Jell-O jigglers; which bubble bath brand made the longest-lasting bubbles; who was allergic to what, and who was afraid of what.

The closest I ever came to asking her for help was the time I needed the cupcake pan to make cupcakes for Jody's school birthday party. It had already been a year and a half since Mom's sentencing, and I hadn't heard anything from her outside of secondhand messages through the girls. Not a single phone call, card, or letter. Not a single attempt to mastermind a jailbreak or mount an appeal or tell her story to Oprah. Of course she hadn't heard anything from me either.

I knew it was stupid for both of us to be sitting around blaming each other for abandoning each other and trying to figure out who did it first. It wasn't any different from asking, "Which came first, the chicken or the egg?" knowing full well it didn't matter because God had to come before either one of them.

But no matter how hard I tried, I just couldn't see any reason to keep up a relationship with her. She wasn't ever getting out. She was done being our mother. I understood that completely from the moment I saw her take a seat in the back of the sheriff's car with a serene slumped relief like she was going off to bed after a particularly long hard day. The part I still didn't get was why.

It turned out Misty knew where the cupcake pan was and spared me from making the phone call to Mom. Misty used to bake blueberry muffins in it for Dad all the time. Mom wouldn't do it for him because she knew he was going to smother them in butter, and she worried about his cholesterol level. She told me once she envied women who lived back in the good old days who only had to worry about Indians and mountain lions killing their husbands. Something about those things being beyond a wife's control.

I changed into the black pants and blue polo shirt I had to wear at Shop Rite, put my dad's coat back on, yanked off the light, and started bounding up the stairs two at a time. Then I turned around and went back for Skip's letter and stuffed it in my pocket.

Misty was already eating. Jody had a full plate, but she was busy writing in her red notebook covered with stickers. About twenty dinosaurs were lined up on her side of the table. Sparkle Three-Horn sat in a place of honor in the very middle with the fortune cookie. Elvis whined and scratched from outside the back door.

I reached for the loaf of Town Talk.

"No buns?" I asked.

"We're out," Misty said.

"Why aren't you eating?" I asked Jody.

I slapped three slices of bread on my plate, put a hot dog in the middle of each, squirted mustard and ketchup on them, rolled them up, and was done eating two before Jody answered me.

"I'm making my list of things to do. I don't like hot dogs anyway."

"Since when?" Misty asked.

"Since always."

"You always eat hot dogs."

"Not like that."

We all looked at her Lion King plate and her hot dog cut into pennies and the puddle of ketchup she dunked them in.

"I like them long now," she said. "Esme says cut-up hot dogs are the number one cause of choking deaths among children in the United States. She wasn't sure about the world. She told me on the bus today."

"Live dangerously," Misty replied.

"I won't eat it."

"You have to."

"I do not."

"Harley," Misty commanded me. "Tell her she's got to eat it."

"I don't care if she eats it," I said, and emptied the pan of macaroni and cheese onto my plate.

"I'll eat it if you fix it."

"How am I going to fix it?" Misty asked, narrowing her eyes until they became two purple slits in her speckled face.

"With glue," Jody stated in all seriousness.

I smiled across the table at her. She cracked me up sometimes.

Misty looked back and forth between the two of us. "Eating glue will kill you," she instructed us.

"Then make me another one," Jody asked.

"I don't want to."

"Make me another one."

"Eat Harley's last one."

"No way. I want it," I said.

"Trade with her," Misty said.

Jody looked at my hot dog skeptically. "There's mustard on it," she said. "Wipe it off."

Misty's hand suddenly shot out. She grabbed my last hot dog, scraped off the bread and mustard with her blue fingernails, and plunked it down in front of Jody. Then she picked up Jody's plate and dumped the sliced hot dog onto mine.

Jody studied the situation for a moment, then gave Misty a

shit-eating grin and asked her for a juice box. Misty stared back at her blankly, the lack of expression on her face betraying a storm of emotion underneath.

"We don't have any," she said slowly.

"Then I want milk."

"Get it yourself."

"I can't pour the big jug. I always spill."

I closed my eyes and imagined picking up the empty pan and swinging it with all my might, catching Jody in the head first, knocking her off her chair, and then hitting Misty and watching her spit up bloody macaroni and cheese.

Instead I went and poured Jody a glass of milk and brought it to her. As I sat it down, her list caught my eye.

FEED DINUSORS

CULOR PISHUR FOR MOMMY

GO TO SCOOL

GO TO PRISUN

WACH TEEVEE

PRAY FOR DADDYS SOWL

GO TO BED

I hadn't told her yet that I wasn't going to take her to see Mom tomorrow. Our last visit had been three months before, but I still wasn't ready to brave another drive home. They were always the same: all four of us crammed into the cab of my truck; Jody crying; Misty telling her to shut up; and Amber swearing at me because I wouldn't go in and see Mom.

Jody's handwriting reminded me of a map Mom had drawn as a kid to help her find her way back home to Illinois after an ancient great-aunt and -uncle she had never met before drove her to Pennsylvania where she was going to live from then on because her mom and dad and infant brother had been killed in a car accident.

Mom only showed me her map once. I was having problems with a map of my own I had found in a school library book, traced, and brought home. The book claimed the map would work starting from any kid's bedroom, and I spent days trying to figure out how to get to the amazing dragon-shaped island crowded with volcanoes spewing rainbow-colored lava.

Finally I gave up and went to Mom with it. She took me to her room and let me crawl up on her bed while she went and got her Bible out of her top dresser drawer. Mom read the Bible a lot, but she never went to church. She said she didn't like Christians.

She brought it over and held it out to me, holding it closed, and let me run my thumb along the scarlet-edged pages the way I always did. Squeezed together, the pages looked and felt like a red satin ribbon, but apart they sliced like razors. She turned to the back and took out a folded piece of paper.

"This is what you call an antique," she said, smiling. "I drew it when I was about the age you are now. That's about eighteen years ago."

She opened it up. It was a crayon drawing beginning at a yellow house detailed with a pink roof and ruffled curtains and a flower garden and a tree with a smiling squirrel. Then a stark straight black line cut across the paper until it suddenly broke off into a downward angle and ended at nothing. On top of the line was written HI WAY 80.

"Maps," she explained while I studied it, "only work if the place you are trying to get to exists."

I felt Jody's grip on my wrist. She tugged on my arm, and I saw Mom's quiet insistence in her face, a look that used to make me want to do my best or act my worst depending on how strong I felt at the moment. She asked me if I wanted to hear her fortune.

"I've got to go to work," I told her. "Tell me tomorrow."

"No," she said.

She let go of me, cracked open the cookie, and gently pulled out the strip of paper.

"'Worry is the interest you pay on trouble before it's due,'" she said, smiling up at me.

"Great," I said.

Elvis almost knocked me over when I stepped outside. I kicked him out of the way and got in the truck, turned on the radio good and loud, and locked both doors. I wasn't afraid of the dark; I was respectful of it. Out here it was so thick, it swallowed headlight beams.

I tried to make my mind a blank during the drive, but Jody's list kept popping into it, and Skip's letter, and Amber fucking some guy in the back of a pickup truck.

By the time I swung my truck into the Shop Rite lot, I had worked myself into a fairly foul mood. Fortunately, weeknights were dead ever since the 24-hour Super Wal-Mart had gone up. I knew people who did their grocery shopping there at 3 A.M. just because they could.

I parked and put my keys inside Dad's coat pocket and found Skip's letter. Against my better judgment, I took it out and read it again and right in the middle of Skip's description of his fraternity I suddenly realized our entire friendship had only happened because we were two boys who lived within walking distance of each other and nobody else.

Funny how something like that only occurred to a person during his lowest moments. I couldn't have figured it out when I was happy.

chapter 3

Like I said, I was in a bad mood. Fortunately, Shop Rite was empty by nine o'clock. No more mumbling "Have a nice night" to customers who didn't care what I wished for them anyway. Usually, I snuck off the first chance I got and went and stocked shelves so I didn't have to listen to the cashiers talk about every unemployed husband and ovarian cyst in the tristate area.

When I first took the job, me and my family were a hot topic of discussion. Especially around Mom's trial. Sometimes I thought that was the only reason I was finally able to get someone to hire me.

Most employers looked at me as coming from an unstable family environment and didn't want me around which cracked me up because the only difference between my environment and everyone else's around here was that mine had been revealed on the eleven o'clock news.

I think Rick, the manager here, saw me as a way to get his fat face on TV—he had visions of reporters in short skirts and high heels saying, "I'm standing here with Rick Rogers, manager of the Shop Rite where convicted husband-killer Bonnie Altmyer's son works"—and he saw me as a drawing card for new customers. People would come by to get a look at me and then have to buy something so they didn't seem like jerks. I didn't know what they thought they were going to see. A slobbering mental case? A guy who broke down and cried every couple minutes?

Either way I was a freak show, but it was better to be a freak with a paycheck than one on welfare so I jumped at the Shop Rite job. A couple months later I got a job at Barclay's Appliances too.

It was tough knowing everybody was staring at me and whispering behind my back, but I preferred the gossip over direct confrontation. The worst was when people tried to talk to me about it, and they were always women. Some were well-intentioned but most were looking for a phone conversation to have with their girlfriends that night.

I never knew what to say to them. Sometimes I was tempted to tell them what really happened.

One day you're a guy who's happy he managed to survive high school and get that almighty piece of paper, and you're thinking you might try and get a job at Redi-Mix Concrete where your dad's worked since the beginning of time or maybe Sharp Pavement. Good pay and good bennies, your dad's always telling you. Blue Cross Blue Shield: none of that HMO crap. Good pension plan. Good workman's comp: he knew a guy who threw out his back moving his brother-in-law's pool table and blamed it on a job pouring a 7-Eleven and got full pay for three months of couch time.

In the meantime, it's summer and the hills are every shade of green and you can take your dog and walk for miles and not see another living soul and if it gets too late, you can sleep on the ground and wake up covered in dew, surrounded by sparkling grass and the smell of wet dirt and wet dog.

On those mornings you try not to think about the rest of the world. You try not to think about the fascinating lives people lead on TV and how even bad shit seems exciting on TV and better than what you're doing.

You try not to think about the models in your sister's Victoria's Secret catalogs and how you will never have a woman who even remotely resembles one of them. You try not to think about how you will probably never have any woman and how the one shot you had, you messed up so bad you don't even want to think about trying again yet all you can think about is trying again.

You try not to think about how you're about to lose your only friend to college, and how you've already lost a sister to puberty.

You try not to think about the fact that you're eighteen years old and people are always telling you you've got your whole life ahead of you, but you already feel like you've done all the living there is to do around here and you're too much of a chickenshit to go somewhere else.

But at least you've got a family you can stand, even if they are all sisters. And at least you've got two parents, two married parents living in the same house with you. One day you're that guy, and the next day you're assigned a social worker and a therapist and given the choice of either being a LEGAL ADULT with three DEPENDENTS or an ORPHAN with NOBODY.

Sometimes I felt like telling them this, but I knew they would think it was boring.

Only three baggers worked weeknights, and we were two too many. Rick knew this and always scheduled me with Bud and Church because they couldn't handle busy hours. They were agonizingly slow: Bud because he was old and never shut up; and Church because he was retarded. A lot of people didn't like that word, but it was the word Church preferred so I used it too. He hated terms like "handicapped" and "challenged" and "special" because he wasn't any of those things in his opinion.

He had looked up the word "retard" in a dictionary once and was pleasantly surprised to find out it was a verb and not a noun.

The definition said, "To delay the progress of," and he felt this described him perfectly.

"Like when cars slow down for a PennDOT crew," he had carefully explained to me, using a can of Green Giant baby peas as a visual aid.

I understood. He didn't think of himself as a complete stop.

Church had a difficult time stocking shelves—he questioned the placement of every product—and Bud had arthritis in his knees, but I loved a straightforward task I couldn't possibly screw up. I loved wheeling out a stack of boxes into a quiet, deserted aisle and filling up empty space. And I never thought twice about why the bouillon cubes were with the condiments and not the soups; and if the CheezIts were more snack than cracker or more cracker than snack. I told Church he was going to drive himself crazy dwelling on other people's biases.

I slipped away from the registers and left Bud talking to the cashiers and Church sitting on his bench picking at a scab on one of his knobby elbows.

On my way to the storeroom, I counted three shoppers. None of them were near the pet food aisle so I loaded my dolly with eight-pound bags of Meow Mix and set off.

I was heading past Canned Vegetables and Ethnic Foods when I saw a woman in jeans and a short gray sweater pushing her cart slowly along the shelves. At first, I thought she might have been more of a girl. I hoped she was because then I might have been able to get up the nerve to talk to her. She was perfect from behind.

I stopped and watched. She was swaying her head back and forth, sort of keeping time with the sway in her walk. I couldn't tell if she was grooving to the song on the Lite FM station Rick made us play. I hoped not. It was "Muskrat Love."

She stopped in front of the Chinese food and reached for a soy sauce on the top shelf and while I was staring at the section of exposed skin right above her jeans where her sweater had pulled up, I realized she was Esme's mom. I felt my face flush and checked around to make sure no one had seen me. Then I remembered no one could see my thoughts.

The Mercers lived about two miles east from where Potshot met Black Lick Road, making them our second-closest neighbors next to Skip's family. There were four of them: Esme; her little brother, Zack; her dad; and her mom, Callie.

This wasn't the first time I had noticed Callie Mercer's body. I saw her here at the store now and then, and whenever Jody played with Esme and I had to pick her up afterward. She had brought us a lasagna the day of Dad's funeral and a stuffed chicken the day of Mom's sentencing, and she used to come by the house to check up on us but eventually Amber's hostility and my total lack of conversation skills put an end to that.

I even discussed her with Skip once. The summer of our senior year we were out walking the railroad tracks and decided to cut across her property, and we saw her splashing in the creek with her kids in a pair of soaked cutoffs and a pink bikini top and I breathed out, "Look at that."

Skip thought I was joking. He said I was sick. He said wanting to nail someone's mother was like wanting to nail your cousin.

And I told him if she walked over and pressed her wet shorts against him and whispered in his ear that she wanted to fuck him, he would shoot off in his pants before he could say anything back.

He gave me a strange look and said I was really sick.

"Hi, Harley."

She had spotted me. Not that I minded. But I never knew what to say to her. I wasn't sure if I should talk to her like she was Esme's mom, or Mrs. Mercer with a lasagna, or a chick in a pink bikini top.

"Hi," I said back.

"How have you been?" she asked in a softly urgent voice that made me feel like she had been looking for the answer to this question for days.

"Okay."

"The girls?"

"Okay."

She smiled a little. "Jody told Esme that you won't let Amber get her driver's permit."

Just the mention of Amber driving made me want to kick something, but I tried to stay reasonable.

"I told her she can get it once she gets a job and can pay for her own insurance," I explained, angrily. "The insurance company's going to put her on my policy the minute she gets her license whether I let her drive my truck or not. Just because we live in the same house. It's like a thousand bucks."

"Harley." She laughed and touched my shoulder. "You're great," she said.

I didn't know what that meant, but it made the anger melt away and my mouth feel dry.

"You have definitely become a full-fledged Head of the Household," she said, still smiling. "Esme's been bugging me to invite Jody over for dinner again. I was thinking about Monday. Would that be okay with you?"

Monday was Jody's night to cook, but I guessed we could all pour our own bowls of cereal.

"Sure," I said.

She added a can of bamboo shoots and a packet of dried mushrooms to her cart. I must have been looking at her funny because she smiled again and explained that she was going to make hot and sour soup.

"Do you like Chinese food?" she asked, her voice full of a stirring sincerity again.

I pictured her writing down my responses to all her questions so she could pull them out later and remember them fondly.

"Yeah," I said.

"Well, the recipe makes a ton. I'll send some home with Jody for you."

She tucked a few stray brown curls behind one ear. She had most of her hair pulled back in a clip, but it was thick and wild and always looked messed up no matter how she wore it.

"I'm having the best time shopping tonight," she said, sounding astonished by her own words.

"What?"

"No kids. I left them at home with Brad."

"Uh, right."

She gave me another big smile and brought both hands together in front of her, clenched into fists, like she was begging for something. Then she slowly spread her fingers like the opening of a paper fan.

"It's so wonderful shopping by myself and shopping at this hour. There's nobody else here. It's the most relaxing thing I've done in weeks." Her eyes traveled appreciatively over the shelves as if she had just discovered an art behind food placement. "God, that sounds pathetic. Coming to a grocery store for kicks."

"It's not as pathetic as working in one," I said.

Her smile disappeared with a stricken suddenness that made me think the condition might be permanent. The hands closed up like dying flowers. She plucked them from the air and shoved them into her jeans pockets.

"It's a lot more pathetic," she said, her voice hardening from a liquid to a solid. "I have to finish up," she added. "If I take too long Brad will be pissed when I get home and then the whole reason for going by myself in the first place will have been wasted."

"Sure," I said, nodding.

"Remember to send a note with Jody on Monday so she can get off the bus with Esme."

"Okay."

"Bye," she said.

"Bye."

I wheeled on past, in a sort of shock at the unexpected transformation in her. I had thought only kids acted that way: deliriously happy one minute, deeply depressed the next over stuff nobody else cared about. I hated myself for ruining her good mood.

After a while, I thought about taking a break from stocking and going back to the registers so I'd be there when she checked out, but I wouldn't have been able to talk to her in front of other people and even if I had been able to talk to her, I probably would have made things worse.

When I did finally wander up front, she was long gone. Bud was talking to the cashiers about a rabid skunk he had spotted staggering around his place that morning.

"That warm spell woke everything up too early," he told them.

One nodded her agreement and said, "I must have passed four dead groundhogs on the side of the road today."

"There was a dead cat by our house once," Church interrupted from where he sat on the bench. "My mom said not to touch it."

I walked over and sat down beside him. He turned his head toward me and settled his small gray eyes on me. He wore the thickest glasses I had ever seen. Sometimes I wondered if he really needed them or if some cruel doctor had prescribed them for him just because he was retarded and they completed the look.

"My mom said not to touch it," he repeated for my benefit.

"That's good advice," I said.

"So did you shoot it?" the other cashier asked Bud.

"Hell, no," he said, blowing a quick pink bubble and snapping it back inside his mouth with a loud crack. "I'm not going to shoot a skunk and stink up the whole hill."

"But you said it was rabid."

"Harley," he called over to me. "Would you shoot a rabid skunk?"

The question had barely left his lips before the two cashiers realized the potential for scandal by mentioning guns around me. They both perked up and gave me their full attention, something I could never get them to do when I had a question about a price check.

I didn't know what they expected me to say: "No, but I'd shoot a family member." Or, "Come on, Bud. You know the sheriff's department confiscated all of my dad's guns after my mom used his Remington to blow a hole through him."

Someday I was going to give them what they wanted.

"I guess not," I said.

Church slapped his skinny thigh like I had just told the best joke in the world. I watched his face and saw his whole unavoidable life summed up in its parts: the flecks of spit spraying from his mouth when he laughed, the zits on his chin, the scar on his forehead where a kid had thrown a Tonka truck at him in second grade, the smooth gray eyes rolling around behind the glasses like pebbles in a jar.

"That's telling him, Harley," he hooted.

I envied him.

The house was dark when I got home. No one had thought to leave the porch light on for me, but I didn't care. I remembered once getting into an argument with my mom about her not leaving the light on for my dad on the nights he stayed out drinking. I told her a man driving up to his own house at night deserved to see a light burning no matter what he had done. She said if the man had done something that needed forgiving, a burning porch light was the last thing he wanted to see.

At the time I disagreed with her, but now I understood what she meant. He didn't want to be reminded he had dependents.

Elvis came flying out of the woods at the sound of my truck door slamming shut. He ran up, put his paws on my chest, and sniffed me all over. Sometimes I brought him scraps from the meat case. He gave up and followed me to the house, hovering for a second in the doorway as if he still expected one of Dad's boots to catch him in the chest, then he came inside. Mom's sheers on the front window were getting snagged and ripped around the bottom from him jumping on them.

Misty was asleep on the couch with a TV show flickering across her face. An empty Mountain Dew can and an open bag of barbecued chips were spilled on the floor. I went and got a beer out of the fridge and collapsed on the end of the couch near her feet and tried to watch some TV, but I got bored.

I took Skip's letter out of my dad's coat pocket, opened it again, and searched out the part where he said he'd been laid by two different girls since he'd been at school. I believed him. That was only a girl a year, and he did okay with girls. He wasn't a virgin when he went away. He had a girlfriend for a while during our junior year. She was a friend of Brandy Crowe's, the girl I almost made it with.

Brandy was married already. I had seen her wedding picture in the Laurel Falls *Gazette* a month before. A Valentine's Day wedding. She and her husband probably lay in bed at night after a successful screw and made fun of me: the only guy in America who didn't know how to use a rubber correctly. I didn't care. He was from Penns Ridge, and they were all a bunch of grass-chewing rednecks over there.

The night I messed up with Brandy, I went and slept at the old mining office. I couldn't stand the thought of going back to my basement bed unchanged when I had seriously believed I was going to return physically and spiritually altered. I stretched out right on top of the broken glass and rusted bolts and didn't feel any of it. The humiliation had made me numb.

I woke up once in the middle of the night to the smell of rotting wood and bologna and yellow mustard but I must have imagined the sandwich part. A huge white moon shone through the ragged tears in the roof and covered me in this eerie silver glow and made me think about my mom reading from her Bible at Christmas about the angel Gabriel showing up at the Virgin Mary's house and explaining how the Holy Ghost was going to come upon her and the power of the Highest was going to over-shadow her and then she would be pregnant with Christ.

Each year when Mom read that to me, I pictured a serenely beautiful naked girl bathed in the same kind of silver, her eyes big and scared but her lips smiling; God crawling all over her but she thinks it's moonlight.

The moonlight was what drove me back home that night. I didn't want God on me. Even by accident.

I folded Skip's letter and put it back in my pocket, then closed my eyes and allowed myself one quick fantasy about horny college chicks before finishing my beer and going out back to make sure the garbage can lid was locked against the raccoons.

Waking a hibernating bear was easier than waking Misty. I didn't even bother trying and scooped her up like a bride and carried her to her bed.

I laid her down and her arm wearing the cat collar slid off and dangled. I picked up her hand and placed it on her chest. She still had bread and mustard caked beneath her fingernails.

Her side of the room had changed a lot the past year. She had packed away most of her stuffed animals and all of her Bar-bie dolls. A Spice Girls poster had replaced the one of gallop-ing horses, and her dresser top was littered with nail polish and lipsticks now instead of toy ponies with pink and purple hair.

A framed photo of her and Dad sat on the nightstand between her bed and Jody's. The two of them were smiling next to a wide-eyed, gutted buck lying tangle-legged across the hood of the Dodge. It was Misty's first clean kill. She had turned the picture completely around to face her side.

I noticed a folded scrap of paper tucked behind it. I picked it up and recognized Jody's painstaking boxy letters.

35

ITS AGENST THE LAWS OF NACHUR.

I smiled and turned it over to see if she had written anything else. It sounded like a controversy involving her dinosaurs. I looked over at her and all I could see was the golden top of her head poking out from a mountain of her stuffed ones.

Her latest paper umbrella had been added to the Dixie cup where she kept all her other ones. She kept all the fortunes too, flattened and smoothed out and tucked neatly into an envelope marked FORJUNS.

She had been about three the first time I brought her a fortune cookie. Yee's had just opened up and Skip and I went and checked it out on the way home from school. Mom showed Jody how the cookie worked. She cracked it open and let Jody pull out the slip of paper. Jody asked Mom what it said and Mom winked at me and said, "It says Barney loves you."

Jody was way into Barney back then.

The look on Jody's face killed me. She totally believed in the cookie's power. Mom and I had swapped smiles. Hers was full of a selfless, satisfied joy. Dad was there too, but he was watching TV.

I had never seen Dad smile sincerely the way Mom did. Happiness to him was just another violent emotion as far as I could tell, something he turned into backslapping and arm-punching and used for an excuse to get drunk and destructive.

As a kid it seemed to me it was the same for all men, and I worried that maybe men could only feel anger and every other emotion had to grow out of it. When I asked Mom about it, she said I was probably right. Sometimes Mom's honesty got in the way of her parenting skills.

I folded the note and put it back.

I switched off Jody's Noah's ark lamp that had once been mine then Amber's then Misty's. Most of the pastel colors had flaked off Noah and the animals, leaving them faceless and ghostly.

I waited for my eyes to adjust to the dark. A weak spill of

moonlight slowly seeped into the room. Enough to make Misty's wrist sparkle; everything else stayed black.

I left and headed down the hall, passing Mom and Dad's room on the right. No one had been inside it since the day Dad's sister, Diane, had come over to strip the bed and pack up his clothes and personal effects. That's what she called them: effects. She taught third grade and thought she knew everything.

I cracked the door sometimes and looked inside at the glaring flesh-pink mattress that used to feel so soft to me, and the framed poster of a Lake Erie honeymoon beach that used to look so exotic to me, and the empty ballerina-shaped bottle of a perfume called Moonwind that used to sound so beautiful to me. Now I knew it was all crap. It was like visiting Dad's grave.

Down in my own room, I undressed and checked the pilot light on the heater—it was giving me trouble lately—and got into bed. Elvis circled the rug a couple times and lay down with a sigh. The last thing I remembered was staring at the vague grayness of my unlit bulb against the pure black of the basement, and the next thing I remembered was the sound of Amber and her date on the couch.

At first it was just random body shifting and muffled voices. I looked at my clock: 2:35 A.M.

I sat up and swung my feet onto the floor. I heard a moan. I heard a giggle. Then a rhythmic furniture thumping started up.

I didn't know how long I sat there on my bed with my ears strained and my fists clenched before I accepted the incredible fact of what they were doing. It must have been awhile because when I opened my fists I had dug bloody little crescents into the palms of my hands with my chewed-off nails.

Amber knew she wasn't allowed to bring it in the house.

I got up and slipped back into my jeans, threw Dad's coat on, and went to get the .44 magnum Ruger Uncle Mike had given me. The sheriff's department did take all of Dad's guns, but

Uncle Mike felt I needed at least one. I never knew when a rabid skunk might happen by.

The shells were in my drawer with the Victoria's Secret catalog.

I snuck quietly up the stairs. My plan was to go out the back door and shoot up his truck like Bonnie and Clyde's getaway car, but I had forgotten that the kitchen looked right into the living room and right at the end of the couch.

I saw him above her. He wasn't even looking at her. He had his head back and his eyes closed. All I could see of Amber were her naked legs wrapped around his bare ass.

I stopped and aimed the gun at his head.

It would have been so easy. It should have been so easy, but it wasn't. It wasn't easy to shoot someone no matter how much you hated him or hated what he did. No matter how angry you were or how much you hurt inside. It wasn't easy. How had she done it?

I turned away and walked across the kitchen, banging into a chair on the way, no longer caring if they heard me. I slammed out the back door, took a stand in the front yard, and started pumping shots into the air.

I had decided not to shoot his truck because then he couldn't get the hell away from me which was my main goal by then. I wasn't crazy, I told myself, feeling a little relieved. Crazy people didn't think ahead.

Amber's date came lurching out of the house trying to get his pants up. It struck me that he wasn't a very bright boy or he would have been running away from the gunfire, not toward it.

Amber came out behind him in panties and her tiny sweater.

"You said he was a sound sleeper," her date screamed at her.

"Stop it, Harley!" she screamed at me. "You son of a bitch! You prick!"

Her date grabbed her by the arm and shook her. "What are you doing?" he cried.

"You fucker! I hate you!" she kept screaming.

"Don't you have any parents?" I asked the boy as I stopped to reload.

"Huh?" he said.

"I hate you!" Amber shrieked at me.

"Shut up!" he yelled at her.

"Do you know what time it is?" I said.

My voice sounded amazingly calm and sane, but I didn't feel that way. My insides were heaving and my hands had started shaking again. I was glad I didn't have to aim at anything.

"It's a school night," I explained to him.

"He's fucking nuts," the boy said, fumbling with the zipper on his jeans.

"You don't have to go," Amber told him.

He gave her a crazy laugh. "Yeah, right," he cried.

I noticed Misty and Jody standing in the doorway behind Amber. I didn't care if they saw me ready to shoot someone, but I didn't want them seeing Amber half-naked and thinking about what she'd been doing.

"Get out of here," I said to the boy, and started walking back to the house.

He darted me a frantic look and bolted for his truck.

"Go back to bed," I told the girls as I pushed past them.

A dozen questions sprang to their lips, but I silenced them all with a look.

"You fucker," Amber was still screaming at me.

I walked into the living room and leaned my gun in a corner, then got down low to the floor and started pushing the couch toward the front door with my shoulder.

"Keep it out of my house," I grunted at her.

"Harley, what are you doing?" Misty asked me.

"Go to bed."

"It's not your fucking house," Amber screamed.

"Harley, what are you doing?" Misty tried again.

39

"Get out of my way."

I propped open the front door. Getting the couch turned on its side so I could angle it out the door was difficult by myself but I managed.

"What are you doing?" Now Amber wanted to know.

"Were you using something?" I asked her.

"What?"

"I didn't see a rubber hanging off his dick or did he have time to take it off?"

"Fuck you, Harley."

"You get pregnant and you're on your own."

"I'm already on my own, you fucker!"

She threw herself at me and started hitting my back. I got rid of her with a good shove and finished dragging the couch down the front steps into the yard.

I couldn't remember if I had filled the extra gas can at the end of last summer. Dad was always on me about that. He hated starting up the tractor for the summer's first mow and running out of gas.

I went and opened the shed door. A blacksnake as long as my leg slid slowly from one side to the other. He didn't even have the energy to coil up once he stopped. He had been fooled into waking up too early like the worms and Bud's rabid skunk. Now he was freezing to death. Taking the hoe and lopping his head off might have been a more humane end for him, but if he lived he'd keep the rats out of the garage and the moles from tearing up the yard.

I left him alone and got the gas can. I gave it a shake. There was enough to douse the couch.

I went to the kitchen for a box of matches.

Amber was gone when I got back out front. Misty and Jody were on the steps. Misty started to ask me again what I was doing but fell silent when a ball of yellow flames roared up from the cushions. The blood drained from her face, making her freckles stand out against her skin as dark as coffee grounds. She flashed me a furious look and ran inside with angry tears spilling from her eyes. I didn't know why. It was a shitty couch.

Suddenly, my whole body ached. Probably from moving the couch on my own. Dad had needed Uncle Mike and Aunt Diane's husband, Jim, to help him carry it in after Grandma died and he inherited it.

I took a seat on the grass and watched it burn. Jody walked over and stood on the other side of the flames, her little body in one of my old white T-shirts wavering in the heat ripples like a ghost.

She didn't ask me why I did it, and I was glad for that. She came and sat down beside me and laid her head against my arm.

"I can't wait to see Mommy," she said.

"Great," I murmured.

She looked up at me, her smooth forehead puckered with adult concern. "What's a rubber?"

"Hey," I said quickly, glancing around for a distraction greater than a burning couch. "Where did Elvis get to? I haven't seen him since I went to bed."

Her face brightened. "I bet I know."

She jumped up and ran over to one of the doghouses with my shirt flapping around her legs. She stuck her head inside, then pulled it out again, smiling and making a Vanna White hand gesture. Elvis slowly appeared, sniffed the air, and lay down in the dirt with a yawn.

chapter (4)

I ended up taking Jody to see Mom after all but only after Misty and Amber agreed not to go. I realized the problem had always been taking the three of them together so I asked Misty at breakfast if she'd mind not going this time. She was still mad about Dad's couch. She gave me a quick, dark glance and said I couldn't pay her to spend two hours in a truck with me. Amber never came out of her room.

Before I picked up Jody at school, I put in two hours at Barclay's unloading refrigerators, scrubbing them out, and setting them up in the showroom, and another three hours in their truck delivering washers and dryers and stoves with Ray, a guy who spent all his time bitching about his wife and kids.

I was in another foul mood and I felt bad about it because I knew Jody was going to need me to spout a bunch of phony optimism after she saw Mom. That was usually Amber's job; and I admitted—no matter how much I hated everything else Amber did—she was good at comforting Jody.

Jody was standing by the school office window when I pulled up, wearing her backpack and carrying her pink spring coat that was too small for her this year. She had on a flowery dress, and tights with snags around the knees, and the silver, little kid, army boots that Amber had got her for Christmas last year.

A lot of the kids dressed up for their prison visits. Some of them were forced by an aunt or grandma, but some of them made the choice on their own like Jody did. They were easy to spot. They were always preoccupied with keeping themselves wrinkle-free.

I didn't understand the rationale behind it except to say to their moms, "Look at me. Look how cute and pathetic I am in my little dress. Look what you gave up." It was probably the same kind of fanatic neediness that drove some of their moms over the edge in the first place.

Jody spent most of the drive prattling on about the Easter Bunny coming soon, and some girl bringing in a platypus Beanie Baby with the tag on and telling everyone how her folks were going to sell it in a couple years for a million dollars, and how the cafeteria served corn dog on a stick for hot lunch. She had developed into a real chatterbox lately, and I was glad despite how annoying it could get.

She didn't talk for a long time after Mom shot Dad. She started wetting her bed and wouldn't eat anything except red Jell-O jigglers. She had a different shrink than Betty. A guy with a beard who knew exactly nothing about everything. He wanted to put her away for observation. Amber freaked.

For the next month, every time I came home after another futile day of scouring the county for a job, there would be Amber on the couch with Jody on her lap, not doing anything or saying anything, just holding her. Then one day I came home and they were playing dinosaurs and eating a bowl of popcorn, and everything's been fine since.

Through trial and error, I had discovered Fridays were the best time to go see Mom. Hardly anyone else showed up. Only an idiot wanted to start out his Friday night with a prison visit.

Weekends were the worst. The visitor's parking lot was an endless trickle of dressed-up little kids clutching homemade draw-ings and schoolwork.

I bet a man's prison didn't get as many children. I bet they didn't have special visitation rooms—called Hug Rooms—where they could go to touch their kids. I bet their cafeteria walls weren't covered with stick figure families in front of crayon houses, and spelling tests with stars on them. (Jody said Mom said they used oatmeal to stick stuff to the walls since they weren't allowed to have things like tape or tacks or string. She said the tapioca pud-ding worked too.)

I imagined the visitors at a man's prison to be mostly lawyers and whores.

It would make sense. Prison was a reflection of real life, and it had always seemed to me that once a woman had a kid noth-ing else mattered about her. Being a dad might describe a man, but being a mom defined a woman.

Jody didn't stop talking until we approached our exit. The prison was easy to see from the interstate. It sat at the bottom of the kind of valley pictured in every local bank calendar except the calendar photos always had a big red barn in them instead of an enormous angular gray cement building that cast a stark shadow like a scar against the soft hills behind it. I was sure when the government built it they were just looking for an iso-lated area and weren't trying to make a statement, but they had done a great job pointing out the difference between Man's ug-liness and Nature's beauty.

I hadn't been paying much attention to what Jody was saying but I was enjoying the excitement in her voice, the same way I had enjoyed listening to Callie Mercer at the Shop Rite. I found it soothing and distracting, like the hum of Mom's vacuum, and once she stopped doing it, I felt strangely panicked.

I caught her staring out the window and tried to come up with a topic of conversation to distract her but before I could think of something, she said, "What's a lethal injection?"

"Where'd you hear that?" I asked roughly.

"Tyler Clark at school. He said Mom's going to get one."

I glanced over at her. She was still looking out the window.

"Mom's not going to get one," I said.

"Esme said it's what the vet gives old dogs when they're having trouble dying. She said people don't get them because they don't need them. They die on their own."

"She's right."

"Mom's not going to die, is she?"

"No."

"I don't want her to die. Even if she killed Daddy."

My hands cut the steering wheel. Sometimes they did stuff like that; acted on their own. The truck swerved to one side, then jerked back into the right lane. Jody braced herself against the dashboard.

"I can't talk about this shit while I'm driving. Okay?" I said to her.

"Okay," she said back. "What's the matter with you anyway?"

"Nothing."

"You're in a bad mood."

"No, I'm not."

"Yes, you are."

"No, I'm . . ." I stopped myself. There was no way to win this particular argument with a six-year-old.

"You are," she added.

"Jody," I started grumbling. "You can't understand."

"Don't tell me I'm too little," she complained. "I'm not too little."

"Yes, you are."

"No, I'm not."

"Yes . . . never mind."

"You want to hear a joke?"

"Sure."

We got off the interstate and started down the county road.

The field on the right-hand side was empty now but by the end of summer it would be covered in sunflowers for as far as the eye could see. The inmates couldn't see them from inside, but Mom was arrested in August so she would know they were out there.

"What does a vampire say when you do him a favor?" Jody asked.

"I don't know."

A big smile spread across her face before she even answered. "Fangs a lot."

I laughed. It was a pretty good one.

She waited for me to open her door after I parked and when I did she said, "Fangs a lot," and burst into giggles again. She grabbed the picture she'd made for Mom: a kaleidoscope of neon marker-colored fruit with the words FROOT IS GUD FOR YOU written at the top. She was studying the food groups in school. At the bottom she always signed them YUR DODR, JODY. She headed across the parking lot, throwing smiles at me over her shoulder. She wasn't scared of anything.

I hadn't been planning on actually seeing Mom this time. I had planned to sit in the waiting area like I always did and read a worn back copy of *Outlaw Biker*. It was either that or *Better Homes and Gardens*. But Jody latched onto my arm and insisted I had to come too. She didn't want to go by herself. I started giving her all kinds of excuses, and the guard who was standing nearby waiting to go over us with a metal detector said to Jody, "Don't waste your breath, hon. Some people can't handle it."

And that was the reason I broke my vow never to see my mother again for as long as I lived. Because some stranger in a polyester uniform and rubber shoes made fun of me. Sometimes I hated being a guy.

Jody eagerly submitted to the detector after I said I'd go. The first time she had been subjected to one, she thought they were looking for candy.

The year before there had been talk about starting up body cavity searches for visitors going into the Hug Rooms after a woman had used her ten-year-old daughter to smuggle in pieces of a gun.

I didn't believe in capital punishment as a rule but when I heard about where that woman made that little girl put pieces of metal all I could think was someone should take her out back and shoot her in the head. The ACLU could take a flying leap. Some shit was just very straightforward.

Instead they put in more surveillance cameras.

We went in first. The room had four chairs. One of them was a rocking chair. I knew right away it must be for women with babies. I should have left then but the door opened and there she was in a crappy cheap smock like a hospital gown. And it was yellow. Faded sunflower yellow. Somebody's idea of a joke.

Jody went running up to her. The guard stepped away and closed the door behind him. Mom bent down and scooped Jody into her arms before she noticed me.

She didn't recognize me at first or maybe there was a part of me that didn't want her to recognize me, a part that wanted her to mumble an apology for the misunderstanding so I could go back to not knowing her anymore.

"I'm sorry," I wanted her to say. "For a second there, I thought you were my boy." "That's okay," I would say back. "I could've sworn you were my mom."

Actually, she didn't look much like my mom at all. Not at any age or stage in her life I could remember. Not the anxious girl in the wedding picture fighting off dry heaves. Not the pretty, untroubled, ponytailed mom from my baby years. Or the exhausted, short-tempered mom she became later. Or the skittish, worried mom she became recently. Or the untroubled mom—back again—driving away from her home forever with her wrists in handcuffs and her clothes stained with her husband's blood.

She was thinner now. Older. She looked disturbed but not in

47

a bad way. A sort of worn haunted calm hung about her as if she had finally reached some divine female plane where concern and disappointment were necessary and good. Her rusty hair was chopped short like mine. I couldn't believe Amber hadn't freaked out and ranted for days about her hair.

"Harley?" she said.

It was a statement of fact even though it sounded like a question. I had been identified. Spotted. Caught in her sights.

She released Jody and slowly stood up.

"Harley," she said again, and her eyes filled with tears.

She came at me. I thought she was going to hit me. I didn't know why. She had never hit me before. I stepped back but she cupped my face in her hands, gazed at it like it belonged to a newborn, then hugged me with all her might.

"My baby," she said against my exposed neck without sounding stupid or sappy or phony. Another statement of fact.

The voice was what got to me. I could convince myself I was looking at a stranger or being held by one. But the voice was the only voice that had ever been kind to me without wanting anything in return. I had absorbed it into my consciousness before I had even formed ears.

I tried but my arms wouldn't rise to hug her back or push her away. All feeling left me except for a dull pain between my eyes. My free will had been crushed to bits between the rush of love I felt and the wall of hate that rose up to meet it. It occurred to me too late that seeing my mom for the first time since she started serving a life sentence in prison was probably a big deal.

She finished hugging me without seeming to notice or to care that I didn't hug her back. I was a grown man after all. I had never seen my dad hug anyone back besides Mom and Misty.

She moved aside and Jody came up between us and put her arms around Mom's middle.

"You cut your hair," I said, surprised at how easily I found my voice.

"Awhile ago," she told me, looking as pleased at my ability to speak as she had been at my ability to finally hit the potty without spraying the wall behind it. "Do you like it?"

I squared my shoulders like she was a beatable foe.

"No."

She just laughed. Jody held up her picture to her, and Mom took it and raved about it, then her eyes traveled quickly around the empty room before landing on me, full of concern. I thought she was going to touch me again but she asked urgently, "Where's Misty?"

The question stumped me for a moment with its irrelevance. I shrugged. "She decided not to come," I said.

"Why not?"

"Harley asked her not to come," Jody corrected me.

I glared at her.

"Well, you did."

"Why?" Mom asked.

"Because they fight," I blurted out, and then felt stupid. "They fight in the truck and it drives me crazy."

Mom smiled warmly at my confession, her obvious pride and fondness for me robbing me of all the hard-ass points I had earned over the past year and a half. I was glad Amber wasn't there to see it.

"Well, how is she?" Mom persisted.

"Who cares?"

"Harley," Mom lightly scolded. "What's wrong with you?"

What's wrong with you? I repeated to myself, trying not to laugh out loud. My aching head filled with irate four-star generals stepping onto body-strewn battlefields and asking survivors the same question.

"Nothing," I answered her.

"Why would you say, 'who cares'?"

"Because I'd like to know."

"I care about her," Mom said firmly. "And so do you."

49

"And me too," Jody piped up.

I looked from Jody to Mom and back again. I thought about Misty and Amber being here too and how the four of them had been meeting here together for a year and a half now, privileged members of a Hug Room secret society. I could picture them laughing and gossiping. Talking about clothes and hairstyles and Beanie Babies. Never once bothering themselves with the facts of where they were and what had happened. Not caring about blame and shame and paying bills.

Then it suddenly hit me: the girls hadn't taken any of this shit personally. They didn't feel abandoned by her.

It shouldn't have surprised me. They had always been more accepting of Mom's screwups than I was: more willing to forgive her for mixing up who liked strawberry jelly and who liked grape, or who got her the good birthday present and who got her something stupid. They defended her on occasions when I expected an apology.

I assumed their leniency came from being the same sex. It was just one more woman thing I would never understand like how they didn't want you to bug them but if you didn't bug them for too long, they came looking for you wanting to know why you weren't bugging them. Or how all they cared about was looking good but whenever you told them they looked good, they got insulted because you were implying there was something else wrong with them. Or how they were obsessed with proving they were as good as men by trying to do things only men did, when what made them better than men in the first place was that they weren't naturally good at those things.

These were a couple of the things I had learned about them during my captive years among their kind. The only thing I had ever learned about men from watching my dad was how to settle for less.

"Don't you want to know where Amber is?" Jody asked.

"Amber's a big girl now," Mom replied.

She flipped her head the way women with long hair do to keep it out of their eyes. Then her fingers darted to her head, disappearing briefly into her short cut, and came out disappointed.

"I figured maybe she was busy with something else," she went on, hugging herself like she was cold and walking a couple steps across the room. "I know she's started dating."

The innocent way she said it made me think of a boy in a suit holding a car door open for a girl in a dress while her dad puffed on a pipe and called out, "Be home by ten, honey." It also made me realize that I had no idea what the girls had been telling Mom about our lives and about me.

"Define dating," I said.

Mom gave me a look that said she didn't have the time or energy right now to decipher the hidden meanings of Teen Speak, and she took a seat in one of the chairs with the unthinking ease of someone plunking down on her couch. Jody instantly hopped into her lap and laid her head against her chest and started chattering. Mom gradually began to stroke Jody's hair, her presence next to her body acting like heat applied to a strained muscle. She kissed the top of her head and smiled and nodded at her string of sentences. I had seen the same scene played out a hundred times at home. Nothing was different here.

I turned my back on them and walked over to one of the cameras hanging near the ceiling and peered up into it. I wondered how much video the state penal system possessed of people doing this. While I stood there, I tried to decide what to do next.

I knew Betty would advise me to pop the big question. Go ahead and do it right now. She was always telling me I would never have closure until I asked Mom why she did it. I asked her once what the hell "closure" meant, and she said, "Peace."

I told her I already knew why Mom did it. Even Mom's attorney and the state prosecutor agreed on the reason why, the only difference was one presented it as a mother's love and the other presented it as a mother's hatred. The question was, How could she do it? and I didn't want to know the answer to that.

The next thing I considered was getting into a big fight with Mom. It didn't matter what the fight would be about, but I decided against that too. Mom and I didn't fight well with each other. Neither one of us had ever been able to put our hearts into confrontation. Betty called it "internalizing." I called it being lazy and chicken.

I always thought Mom and Dad were made for each other when it came to fighting. Mom was the perfect opponent for him because she took everything he could dish out, matching the intensity of his anger with the intensity of her patience, until eventually he got tired and retreated and she could go about her life.

One time Dad got in a big fight with her while she was making Sunday breakfast. He got so mad he took an entire carton of eggs and started whipping them one at a time around the kitchen. Gobs of yolk oozed down the walls and made sticky pools on the tile floor.

Misty was just a baby in a high chair, and she laughed and clapped. Amber cut and run. Being a kid I thought what Dad was doing was pretty cool, but being his son I realized I might be the next thing that hit the wall with a splat. I stayed in my chair, waiting.

After he depleted his arsenal, he came raging back to the table and brushed the breakfast dishes onto the floor with a big swipe of his arm, then he went stomping out the door.

We waited to hear what he would do next before deciding what we would do next. We waited for a dog to yelp, or the mower to roar to life, or the truck to start, or for ominous silence.

Eventually, we heard the truck. I started eating again. Amber came back to the table. Misty craned her little head around and pointed out the door and said, "Da Da."

Mom grabbed a dishrag and glanced around at the dark yellow carnage dripping everywhere like the sun had bled all over her kitchen. Then she walked over to her grocery list and wrote EGGS.

I turned back around and stared at Mom with Jody on her lap. She caught me watching.

"You look like you want to say something," she said.

"Where do you keep the extra lightbulbs?"

"Below the bathroom sink, way in the back, on the right-hand side," she answered without missing a beat.

"Do we have any?"

"I don't know, Harley." She sighed. "It's been a long time."

She said it too easily and I understood all at once that she had accepted our new lives while I had only adjusted to them. I had never known there was a difference, but now it seemed clear to me that the first had been done willingly while the second had been done in order to survive.

I didn't want to be there anymore. I started noticing how small the room was. There weren't any windows. The chairs were bolted to the floor. The rocker was chained. There weren't any pillows. Or pictures on the wall. The cameras were made in Japan.

"I know, honey. It's very nice," I heard Mom say.

"Harley thought my banana was a crescent moon." Jody giggled.

I swallowed a bunch of times but couldn't get any moisture into my mouth yet I had a ton of it collecting at the top of my forehead and dripping down the sides of my face. I touched some with a fingertip and brought it to my mouth. Salty. Sweat. Claustrophobic: that was the word. A perfectly normal reaction to a tiny room without windows. I was not crazy. A crazy person would have killed that boy. A crazy person would have lived with that couch.

"It's funny you sign your pictures the same way Harley used

53

to," Mom said to Jody. "Of course he didn't sign them 'your daughter.'"

Jody giggled again.

"He signed them 'your son.' Amber and Misty never did that. I guess they assumed I knew who they were."

"Harley used to draw you pictures?"

"Of course he did. I could've sworn I showed some of them to you. I've got them all in a box in the basement along with Amber and Misty's school papers. He used to love to draw."

She lightly kissed the top of Jody's head again and then gently grazed her cheek across it. This was the gravy part of motherhood. She still got it even though she no longer had to deal with the bad stuff. The fights. The fevers. The bills. The spills. The nightmares. The questions. The future.

She still had us kids but we didn't have her.

"Your daddy didn't like it though," Mom explained to Jody. "He thought Harley should be more into sports and hunting. Typical man."

"That's dumb," Jody said.

"Yes, it is. I remember how he used to drag Harley outside and throw footballs at him. How he used to hit him if he . . ." Her voice trailed off, and she cleared her throat. "Oh well, what do I know? Your Uncle Mike used to do the exact same thing to Mike Junior and now he's at Penn State on a football scholarship."

She laid the picture upside down on the floor, and I imagined it smeared with tapioca.

"You want to be here," I said, hoarsely.

Mom's head jerked up. "Harley, that's ridiculous."

I saw her map in my head. I felt myself being dragged along the black line to the place where it ended at nothing. I looked behind me and instead of a little yellow house, I saw Mom done in crayon the way I used to draw her. A smiling stick figure in a dress with pale gray eyes and burnt orange hair. I still remembered the names of the crayons: Timber Wolf and Bitter-sweet.

"No," I said. "You want to be here."

She nudged Jody from her lap and stood up.

"Harley," she said fearfully, and took a step toward me.

The sweat had started dripping into my eyes. I blinked it away, but I still couldn't see her well. My hands started shaking like a palsied old man's. I looked down at them and saw sweat beads as big as raindrops forming on them. My breath came too fast for me to use it.

"Harley!" she said again, forceful this time.

She lunged at me. I heard her cry out my name again. It unfurled from her lips, violent and sudden, like a whip snap.

My knees buckled and I collapsed to the floor. Her hands were on my face. They were shaking as bad as mine. She told me to be calm. She laid her head on my heart.

I screamed. I scraped her off me and got to my feet, choking for air. I ran for the door and tried to yank it open but it was locked. I pounded with my fists and screamed for someone to let me out.

Two guards rushed in and went straight for Mom. I watched Jody run to save her picture before running behind a chair. Jody had adjusted too.

I sank back down to the floor.

The guards pushed Mom into a corner. She held her hands up in front of her face and cried, "I didn't hurt him."

That was the first time I saw words in the air. They hung in front of my eyes like a camera flash.

YUR SUN, HARLEY.

chapter 5

After my visit with Mom I decided my biggest problem in life was getting rid of that piece of pipe in the yard left over from Dad's satellite dish, not ACCEPTING.

I spent the weekend studying it. I could saw the pipe off fairly close to the ground with a hacksaw but that would make it more dangerous because the grass would hide it, and Jody never wore shoes in the summer. She could tear open her foot on the jagged metal, and we didn't have any health insurance. We would if we were on welfare. Or if I disappeared and the girls were put in foster care then they'd have insurance. Social Services had made this very clear to me.

I could try digging out the cement plug but that would take forever. I could dynamite it but that might collapse our well. Probably the best thing to do would be to cut the pipe down as low as I could get it and put something big and noticeable on top of it.

On my way to the truck Monday morning, I decided the couch would work until I found something better.

Misty had covered the blackened carcass with an old scab-brown bedspread. The smell of gasoline, burnt foam padding, and other flammable man-made materials still lingered in the air. I gave it a kick to see if anything had crawled up inside it yet. I pushed it over, and I felt better.

I put in a full day at Barclay's, then decided a Froot Loops dinner wasn't worth driving all the way home for when I had to drive all the way back afterward for my shift at Shop Rite. It was a warmer night. I decided to grab a bag of chips and a Coke at the store and go hang out at the self-service car wash across the road in the hopes a car full of girls would come through. I was halfway there, thinking about cutoffs and soapy thighs, before I remembered I had to pick up Jody at Esme Mercer's house.

I could have called. Esme's mom would have run Jody home for me. But I drove out there instead.

The Mercers' house was a strange one by local standards because the front faced away from the road toward the hills and because it was all windows, and because they had built with expensive cedar, not siding, and left the boards natural. Six years later, everybody was still wondering when they were going to paint it.

I had never been inside the house but from the driveway I could see into the front room jammed with plants and wicker furniture. Jody said they called it the jungle room, and Esme's mom went and sat there every night after she finished washing dishes and before she gave Zack his bath.

Lights were burning even though it wasn't dark yet. The days were getting longer. Only one more week until daylight savings time. I wasn't looking forward to the extra hour or the hot weather on the horizon. I didn't particularly like the cold, but I liked being covered up. Last year, retiring Dad's jacket to the closet felt like giving up my skin.

I pulled in next to Callie's blue Celica. The Jeep Grand Cherokee was gone. Her husband, Brad, drove it. He was vice president of something at Laurel Falls National Bank. Callie's dad was the president. It was a very small world.

Their two dogs barked and strained at the ends of their chains until I got out of my truck and they recognized me, then the blond collie mix started whining, and the black Lab started tearing in circles around his doghouse. Dogs never forgot the bearer of affection no matter how infrequently he came by.

I walked over and untangled the Lab and scratched them both on the chest until their eyes glazed over.

The front door opened and Jody ran out. The dogs started barking again. She saw me and scowled and went running back inside, yelling, "It's him. I don't want to go."

I took a moment to appreciate the view. The Mercer property dipped down to a circular pond sitting in the middle of a lawn the color of pool table felt. A twisting section of clear, pebble-shiny creek lay at the foot of their hills; and they were their hills. They owned them. Not like our hills. We just lived on ours.

Callie's grandfather had willed her fifty acres along with the mineral rights, which meant the old man never sold out to the coal companies while everybody else around him let their land be stripped raw.

Besides the Virgin Mary, he was a dead person I would have really liked to meet.

Through the hillside trees I saw the railroad tracks, the same tracks that led to the mining office behind Skip's house, the same ones we used to fantasize about following out to California after we bumped off Donny.

Zack Mercer ran out next. He grinned at me and whirled around to go back in and ran into his mom's legs. She grabbed him gently by the shoulders and told him to slow down.

She looked up and gave me a slow female smile. "How are you, Harley?" she said.

"Okay," I said back.

Then she whipped her head around in the direction of the dogs and gave them a steely, military stare. "Shut up," she yelled harshly.

Esme and Jody exploded from the house and took off for the swing set. Zack tore after them.

Callie composed herself and walked toward me, smiling in a stirring way again. I remembered our meeting at Shop Rite and how she had gone from a childish excitement to a deep depression with the quickness of a finger snap.

"I just got off the phone with Misty," she said.

She didn't have any shoes on, but she crossed the sharp gravel driveway without flinching, making me wonder what the bottoms of her feet felt like.

"I called to tell you Jody could stay for a while and then I'd run her home for you," she went on. "We should have planned on that in the first place."

"That's okay," I said.

"It turned out to be a beautiful day. Aren't you hot in that coat?"

"No."

She moved closer to me. "Did you have dinner?"

"Yeah."

"But you haven't been home yet."

"I ate in town."

"Oh."

I got the feeling she was taking notes again. Not out of nosiness but because she wanted to reconstruct me later at her convenience, piece by insubstantial piece, like a house of cards.

She lifted one of her bare feet and brushed the top of the other one with it.

"Well, I have something for you anyway. You want to come in for a minute?"

"In?" I said.

She turned away from me again and shouted at Esme to quit pushing her brother so high on the swing.

"In the house," she finished.

"Sure," I said.

I tried not to watch her walking in front of me, but her jeans fit like someone had rubbed the color on with a piece of powder-blue chalk. They had been worn and washed so many times, I bet the denim felt like a puppy's ear. I tried not to think about that while I tried not to watch.

The inside of the house was all wood too. Even the floors. Except for the kitchen floor. It was made of stones of all different shades of gray set in mortar and polished to a high gloss.

It was one of those open houses where the rooms weren't really divided off with walls and the downstairs ceiling went all the way up to the upstairs ceiling. A big stone fireplace separated the kitchen from the living room, and a wall of glass shelves covered with knickknacks and framed pictures separated the living room from the jungle room. There was nothing but air between the shelves making it seem like the plants were in every room.

I didn't see a TV so I guessed the big room with the fireplace was a formal living room, something we didn't have and my mom always wanted. She said any decent house should have one room for the TV where the family hung out and another room without a TV for people to visit in. I never saw the point in that because everyone I knew preferred to visit in front of a TV.

The room didn't look formal though. The furniture looked beat-up and there were toys everywhere. Through the doorway at the end of it, I saw a mirror over a chest of drawers and in the mirror an unmade bed.

"You want to sit down?"

Her voice brought me back from the bed. I was grateful for that.

She glanced at the table and chairs. The chairs were bamboo and had sawdust-colored cushions and the table had a glass top. The dinner dishes were still sitting on it.

"We bought that table before we had kids," she explained

when she noticed me looking at it. "So far no one's thrown a dish through it although Zack's been practicing."

She came over with a dishrag and wiped off the tray on Zack's high chair. Their dinner smelled great, like apples and honey and charcoal.

I couldn't even remember what real food tasted like. My mom wasn't the greatest cook in the world, but these days I would have given just about anything for a piece of her bland meat loaf or one of her overcooked chickens.

"You have a nice house," I announced.

The sound of my words made me cringe. I couldn't have come up with a more uninspired thing to say if I had spent all day trying. The worst character on the worst TV show would've come up with a better opening line.

I knew people on TV were fake but that didn't stop me from wanting to be as smart and funny as they were; and there was nothing like constantly falling short of unrealistic expectations to make someone feel like giving up on real life completely.

"Thanks," she said.

"I never saw anyone use rocks for a floor before," I added. "I saw brick once."

"It's terrible if you drop something breakable," she said. "Stuff shatters like you wouldn't believe. But it's pretty. I love this rock here."

To my amazement, she dropped to all fours, still holding the wet cloth, and motioned for me to join her. I got down there with her, and she pointed out a pale silver-gray rock full of glittering black and ivory chips.

"If you look very closely, you can see a tiny vein of pink going through it. You don't notice it if you just glance at it. You really have to look."

I did, and she was right. I couldn't help looking at her too. I wondered how much time she had spent staring at her kitchen floor to notice something like that.

She sat back on her feet, and her arm brushed against mine. I had on my coat. Skin didn't even touch skin but a flash of heat went shooting to my crotch, giving me a serious boner. It wasn't a good feeling though. I realized it was supposed to be, but it ripped through me too fast like fire eating up a trail of gasoline.

I practically jumped up and took a seat at the table. She was still staring at her rock. She hadn't felt a thing.

"Do me a favor, Harley," she said, standing up and taking a couple plates with her over to the sink. "Eat that last pork chop for me."

I adjusted myself inside my jeans. My zipper was killing me. I had pitched my last pair of underwear that morning. The money I was going to spend on new stuff I had ended up spending on a Happy Meal and a new dinosaur for Jody to keep her mouth shut about what happened with Mom.

"No, thanks," I said.

"Oh, come on."

"I already ate."

"A big guy like you can't polish off that one little pork chop?"

I didn't say anything. I waited for some big guy to answer.

"Please," she said. "Otherwise it's going to the dogs."

"What about your husband?" I asked.

"He won't want it," she said, kind of irritated. "He went out to dinner."

"Okay," I said.

I stabbed a fork through it like I was afraid it might escape and plopped it onto the dirty plate in front of me.

"You want a beer?" she asked.

"Sure."

She came back with a Michelob. I almost had it in my hand before she asked, "Wait. You are old enough to drink, right?"

"Well, not legally."

"How old are you?"

"Nineteen. Well, twenty. Just about twenty. I'll be twenty in a couple months."

"That's it?" she breathed out, and took a seat across from me. "My God, you're a baby."

I couldn't believe I didn't lie. I might as well have told her about Brandy Crowe too, and how I had freaked out at the prison with Mom, and how I used to pee my pants when Dad hit me too hard, and any other embarrassing thing I could think of that might help her figure out I was a total idiot.

"I thought you were older," she added.

"I'm old for my age," I said with my mouth full of pork chop.

She laughed. I didn't mean it to be funny. I was dead serious. But it was okay with me if she thought it was a joke. Ask any woman what was most important to her in a man and she would say a good sense of humor. Of course, they were all lying but a sense of humor must have counted for something or they wouldn't have always been bringing it up.

"This is great," I said about the pork chop, and I wasn't sucking up to her. It was the most tender, juicy, flavorful thing I could ever remember putting into my mouth.

"Thanks," she said, smiling.

She seemed to like the compliment about her cooking more than the one about her house.

"Jody loved them too. She ate two whole chops by herself."

The door banged open and all three kids came running in. Callie's kids were vanilla-skinned with big dark eyes; Esme with blue-black, Snow White hair and Zack with a fawn-colored mop.

They skidded to a stop and stood beside each other. Esme leaned into Zack, and he gave her a two-handed shove. A pink tongue popped out of Esme's angel face, and Zack grinned like a soldier who's seen too many battles.

"You forgot to close the door," Callie told them.

"Can we have something to eat?" Esme asked.

"You just had dinner," Callie said. "Go close the door."

"We want dessert."

"We want dessert," Zack echoed.

"I haven't even cleaned up the dishes yet. Maybe later."

"Did you eat these pork chops?" I asked Jody.

"Yeah," she said. "I loved them."

"You hate pork chops."

"I hate your pork chops. They taste like napkins."

"It's probably just the marinade." Callie laughed. "It's a very simple one. Apple cider, lemon juice, honey, soy sauce. I could give you the recipe."

"And your macaroni and bean soup recipe," Jody added, eagerly.

"That's an easy one too," Callie said, then gasped, "Where are your shoes?"

They were all barefoot.

"Outside," they answered.

"It's not summer yet," she scolded them. "Go get your shoes back on. Right now."

"Cruz wore shorts today to school," Esme argued with an imperial tilt to her chin.

"Which Cruz?"

"Cruz Lewandowski."

"Do I care what Cruz does?"

"His father's an educator," Esme pointed out.

Even Callie rolled her eyes. "His father's a gym teacher. Now go get your shoes, and Zack, it's time for you to come in."

They all went tearing out again, their pounding feet on the wood floor sounding like a tiny fleeing army.

Callie sat down across from me and opened the beer for herself, sighing.

"There are five Cruzes in their class. Do you know what that's all about?" she asked me. "The only Cruz I know is Santa Cruz and I have a feeling that's not what people around here are naming their kids after."

"I think he's some guy on a soap opera," I answered.

"Oh. Okay. That would make sense."

She took a swig from the beer and stared off into space. I finished the pork chop. I didn't think she had noticed, but she reached out and pushed a bowl of potatoes in my direction without looking down at them. All mothers had that empty plate reflex.

"Funny how you can like a name and then find out the reason for it is stupid and then it's ruined," she said, kind of absentmindedly. "And vice versa. A name might seem really dumb and then you find out the reason for it is interesting or sentimental and then you like it."

I wasn't listening to her but I heard her. I was busy shoveling potatoes in my mouth and staring at her because she wasn't looking at me so I didn't have to worry about eye contact. She had one perfect black freckle in the hollow of her throat like a speck of pepper.

"I always wondered about Misty," she said. "Did your mom just like that name, or was Misty born on a misty day?"

I swallowed the last spoonful of potatoes. They had a ton of garlic in them. They were great too.

"My dad picked out Misty," I answered her. "She's named after some chick on *Hee Haw* from when he was a kid. I think she was a centerfold too. Dad never got over her, I guess."

Again, I was being serious but Callie laughed. She brought her beer bottle to her lips and giggled around the neck. I could see her tongue inside the brown glass.

I started feeling hot again but it was a slow melt this time, not incineration. I realized we were having a conversation.

"Where did you get Esme from?" I asked.

"It was the name of a model and mistress of one of my favorite artists. A French Impressionist."

She held up a finger signaling for me to wait before slipping out of her chair and out of the room. She came back lugging a big, glossy book. She set it down in front of me and flipped it open to a sloppy picture of a vase of flowers, a bottle of wine, and an artichoke, then she sat down again and went back to her beer. I studied the page out of courtesy.

"He paints like Pierre Bonnard," I said.

She gasped. It was the only time I had ever heard a real one outside of bad TV.

"You know who Pierre Bonnard is?" she asked.

"Sure," I said.

"You must have a wonderful art teacher."

"I don't have any art teacher," I told her. "I haven't had art since third grade."

She put her beer down, frowning. "I can't believe it. Don't tell me they've finally cut the art program," she said angrily. "I know they've been threatening it for years. They've got some nerve saying there's not enough funds when they just budgeted all that money for new football uniforms and a bunch of videos so kids can watch *Moby Dick* instead of reading it."

I didn't bother telling her the only movie about a whale in our school library was *Free Willy*. I couldn't believe how mad she was getting over art and books. I knew she had gone to an out-of-state egghead college that no one around here had ever heard about because it didn't have a good football team. I hoped she wasn't the intellectual snob type who thought she could venture out into the real world and bring civilization back to the natives, and we were all supposed to crowd around her with our jaws hanging open while she dangled her enlightened views in front of us like shiny beads.

I wanted to tell her this and see if she would get madder. I thought about what it would be like to get her mad enough to try and take a swing at me. Then I would have to grab her and restrain her. I pictured her struggling and screaming for

66

help, and me clamping my hand over her mouth. She would open her mouth to try and bite me, and I would stick my fingers inside. She would start gagging, but I'd push them down deeper and deeper into her throat until she fell to her knees. Then I would turn her over and press her face against her favorite rock.

"That really upsets me," she went on. "I feel like driving over to the superintendent's house right now just to put him on the spot and hear him stammer through the ridiculous justification for this."

I almost didn't hear her over the blood pounding in my ears. My hands were killing me under the table, and I looked down at them. They were white-knuckled and clenched. I slowly, painfully unfolded my fingers and saw tiny new welts near the crescent scabs where I had broken the skin Friday night listening to Amber fuck a guy who was too stupid to run away from gunfire. I should have shot up his truck for that reason alone. That would have been my JUSTIFICATION.

I blinked. The word hung where Callie's face had been. I blinked again and she was back.

She was looking right at me and for a moment I was sure she had read my thoughts. I swallowed and hoped sweat wasn't pouring down my face.

"Nobody cut the art program," I confessed. "Art's an elective."

"Oh." She gave me a quick embarrassed smile. "Why don't you have it?"

"It interfered with a study hall."

She took another gulp of beer. "Then how do you know who Pierre Bonnard is?"

I pressed my throbbing hands together. Nothing hurt worse than a human scratch except for a human bite. My dad only bit me once, and it was because I bit him first. My mom said I was the only one of us kids who went through a biting phase.

"My mom had a set of note cards that used to belong to her

mom," I explained. "She got them as a souvenir from the Art Institute of Chicago. Mom's from around there originally. They had one of his paintings on the front. 'Table Set in a Garden.'"

"So you're familiar with his work?" she asked eagerly.

"I'm familiar with his note cards."

I watched her throat pulse as more beer slid down it. I pulled my eyes away and dropped them back to the book.

At first glance, I hadn't liked Callie's artist nearly as much as I liked Mom's. The painting on Mom's cards had lots of warm green light and soft smudged colors and a tablecloth with a bright pink stripe: the kind of table I would have liked to sit at with Jody.

The painting in the book was set in a shadowy corner of a room. There was an open window and it was day outside, but no light was coming in. The flowers were a glaring white but looked waxy and dead. The bottle had been opened but was still filled to the top with a weak brown wine. But the thing that really bothered me was the artichoke. Its sharp leaves were outlined in blue-black and each tip had a dot of red so bright it looked wet.

Looking at it again I realized the reason I didn't like it the first time was because it gave me the creeps, but that was exactly why it was a better painting. It was probably a lot harder to scare someone with an artichoke than it was to tempt someone with a sunny garden.

"I like Impressionists," I said.

Right after I said it, I regretted it; realizing immediately that I had to add something to it.

I fumbled around inside my head, not trusting any of the observations I came up with. Until a couple minutes ago, I thought Impressionism was Dana Carvey doing Ross Perot.

"They don't seem to care about what things really look like," I tried. "It's like they care more about how looking at something makes a person feel."

She smiled at me. It was a beautiful smile: one she made with her eyes, not just her mouth; one that came from her heart, not just her head because I had touched something inside her that no one else ever did anymore. I didn't know how I knew that but I did and even though I wanted to violate her a hundred different ways physically, I didn't want to go anywhere near her soul.

"That's the definition of Impressionism," she said softly.

"Yeah, I know," I lied.

I got up from the table.

"I'm going to be late for work," I told her. "I've got to go."

"I'm sorry," she said, getting up too. "I didn't realize you were on your way to work. Wait a minute."

She left and came back with a sloshing Rubbermaid container.

"Hot and sour soup." She held it out to me. "You said you liked Chinese."

I stared at it but didn't take it.

"Please," she urged. "Esme and I are the only ones who like it. I have so much extra."

I took it. I didn't even say thank you. I never thanked her for the dinner either. I didn't think about it until I was in the truck. I should have gone back and said it.

Driving away, I caught myself staring at her hills and wondering if her grandpa gave them to her before or after she got married.

"Where's Esme's dad?" I asked Jody.

She pulled some school papers out of her backpack. She wanted to show them to me now in the truck since she would be asleep by the time I got home from work.

"Her mom said it's his night out with the boys," she answered me. "She said her night out is going grocery shopping. She said that's marriage for you."

I looked at the star at the top of Jody's addition and subtraction work sheet and nodded.

If I had a pretty wife who could cook, I would never leave the house except to go to work so I could keep her. The rest of the time I would spend having sex and eating, and I would be deliriously happy.

I didn't know how happy she'd be, though. I wondered if I would care.

chapter 6

I went ahead and told Betty about my visit with Mom at our next appointment a month later. At first I wasn't going to because I didn't want to talk about it, but Betty wasn't all bad so I did it for her sake. Sort of a personal favor. Boy talks to mother for the first time since she killed his father: it was a shrink's wet dream.

She almost fell out of her chair when I told her. It got her more excited than the time I told her about how Dad used to take Misty hunting with him instead of me and every time he'd say to me, "She's more of a man than you'll ever be."

Shrinks loved it when dads cut down their sons. Verbal emasculation, she called it. I didn't care what it was. He was right.

It wasn't that Misty was butch. She was slight and freckled and had a glossy ponytail the color of an acorn and long, thick eyelashes like tiny feathers from a baby bird's wing. But she was definitely a tomboy. Especially around Dad. They watched pro wrestling together and worked on the tractor mower together, and he took her to the Penns Ridge Speedway to see the stock car races. And she was definitely more of a hunter.

Betty got up and left her office and came back with a glass of water for me when I started talking about Mom. She had done the same thing when I told her about Dad and Misty. I figured it was something she had read in one of the psychology textbooks she kept at her other office where she saw real patients instead of charity cases. There was probably a whole chapter in one of them about water and Kleenex and when it was appropriate to offer them.

I left some things out of my description of my prison visit, but I didn't make up anything. I was beginning to think I should because Betty was looking pretty disappointed. She kept tapping her forehead with the eraser on her pen and saying, "So you didn't really discuss anything of substance," and she kept asking me why I thought the sunflower fields outside the prison bothered me and I kept saying, "I don't know."

"When are you planning on seeing her again?"

"I don't know," I said.

"You are planning on it, aren't you? This was a very big step for you, Harley. You need to keep moving forward."

I needed to keep looking out the window. I was glad Betty's office was at the back of the building instead of the front where the view would have been the Eat N' Park. The parking lot wasn't much to look at, but the maples bordering it were nice. They were covered with bright, new leaves now and drooping with seed helicopters.

"Are you sure you don't want to take off your coat?" she asked me.

"I'm sure," I said.

She sighed and crossed her legs and looked at her notes. She started tapping her forehead while tapping one toe in the air. I noticed her shoes. They weren't her usual scuffed black pumps that gapped at the sides when she walked. These were a soft silver-green like the wrong side of a leaf. Not a mark on them. Not even on the soles.

They didn't go at all with the coarse, putty-colored dress she was wearing. It wasn't just the color that was wrong. I thought of Cinderella finding herself in rags again with one glass slipper still sparkling on her foot.

Betty saw me looking at her shoes, uncrossed her legs, and tucked her feet under her chair like she was concealing an accident.

"Let's go back to the comment you made about feeling that your mother is more concerned about the girls than she is about you. Why do you think that's true?"

"I know it's true," I corrected her.

"Then why is that? Why is she more concerned about them?"

"Because they're girls."

"Why should that matter?"

"Parents are always more concerned about daughters than sons."

"Let's not generalize. Why is your mother more concerned about your sisters than she is about you?"

"There's more to be concerned about," I said.

"Such as?"

"They can get pregnant."

She raised her eyebrows at me.

"Not all of them right now," I added, frustrated.

"Your sisters getting pregnant is something you worry about?"

"No."

"It's something you think your mother worries about?"

I slumped down on the couch while trying to think of an answer I could give her that she couldn't respond to with another question. I finally gave up.

"No. It's just a fact."

"Okay." She nodded. "And what else is there to be concerned about?"

"They can get hurt easier."

"Do you mean physically? Or emotionally?"

"Both, I guess."

"You think Amber's feelings get hurt easier than yours?"

I could barely keep my eyes open and my stomach kept growling. I was getting the egg roll for myself today. Screw Misty.

"Amber doesn't have any feelings," I said.

"Then you're not making sense."

She waited for me to say something, and I didn't. She started messing with her dress. It went all the way down to her knees, covering her thighs. I thought about complimenting her so she might start wearing longer ones all the time, but I had never said anything remotely nice to the woman and she probably would have thought I was having another breakthrough and run off to get me more water.

"Let's get back to your mother and what you were saying earlier about how comfortable she seemed in the Hug Room. You denied that this bothered you, but it seemed to me that it did bother you. Why? Shouldn't you be happy that your mother is coping well?"

I didn't want to talk about Mom anymore but not talking about anything never worked at getting Betty off my back. I threw out a different topic, hoping to take her mind off Mom the same way the ketchup-stained end off a bun made Elvis forget about the hot dog he didn't get.

"Parents do worry more about daughters than sons just because they can get pregnant," I insisted roughly.

"That might be true in some cases," she allowed. "Why don't we talk about this some more after we finish talking about . . ."

"It's true in all cases," I pushed.

"Well, I don't know about that."

"It is."

"It's true a girl can get pregnant, but it takes a boy to get her that way. Don't you think parents worry about their sons being sexually active too?"

"It's not the same thing."

"Why not?"

"A guy can walk away from it."

"A girl can have an abortion."

"It's not the same thing."

"What would you do if you got a girl pregnant?"

I wiggled my toes around inside my boots. I was going to have to break down and start wearing gym shoes. My feet were roasting.

"Marry her," I said.

"That's interesting."

"Why?"

"Because you answered so quickly and so confidently, yet you don't know anything about the circumstances. For instance, what if you didn't like the girl very much."

"I had sex with her, right?"

"Yes. So you're saying you would only have sex with a girl you liked."

"If she would have sex with me, I would like her."

"Harley." She laughed and her nickel-plated hair shimmered a little.

I turned back to the window, disgusted and embarrassed. I was serious.

"All right," she said. "What if you didn't love her?"

She was starting to piss me off. I wondered if I should take her low opinion of me personally or if it was only something else she had read in a book: "Teenagers have no morals and will fuck anyone." Someday I wanted to visit her real office and go through those books. I was willing to bet I could find everything stupid and mean she had ever said to me written down in one of them. I bet she had hundreds.

"What if a wife and child would interfere with your plans for the future?" she kept at me. "What if you had no source of income?"

"If I got her pregnant," I burst out angrily, "it would mean I was being stupid."

I snapped my mouth shut and went back to staring out the

75

window but I could feel her staring at me. I knew she was going to ask me why. WHY? WHY? WHY? WHY? Why would it mean you were being stupid? Why do you feel that way? Why do you think your mother shot your father? Why do you think your father didn't like you?

"There's no excuse for it," I answered her before she could ask me to explain. "You know it can happen unless you do something about it. I have no sympathy for people who get accidentally pregnant. They're all idiots just like that idiot woman who sued McDonald's because she burned herself with their coffee."

"Some people don't think that woman was an idiot. She won a lot of money."

"Yeah, I know. And O.J.'s walking around. All that proves is the courts are fucked. What I'm talking about is people being responsible for their own fuck-ups."

I didn't usually say the F-word around Betty. I could tell it bothered her, and she wasn't sure what to do about it. Give me water? Offer me a Kleenex? Pat my hand? She had tried patting my hand once. I had been talking about getting rid of the dogs and started to cry. It was the only time I had ever cried around her.

I remembered her old hand feeling cool and dry and I liked her touch for a split second but then I felt more hatred for her than I had ever felt for anyone in my life. I jerked my hand away and went running out. I stayed away for two appointments after that, even after I realized the reason I hated her was because I didn't hate her.

She made a fist and coughed into it.

"So you would marry her out of responsibility?" she asked me.

"I guess so."

"Could I go so far as to say you would marry her as a form of self-punishment?"

"I guess."

"Do you hear what you're saying, Harley? You would commit

76

yourself to another human being for the rest of your life as a
form of punishment. Do you think that's what a marriage should
be based on?"

"I don't know."

"You don't know?"

She leaned back in her chair and glanced at the untouched
Styrofoam cup of water sitting on the table next to the Kleenex
and my Redi-Mix cap.

"What about your parents?" she asked. "They were married
because your mother got pregnant. And they were very young.
Were they stupid?"

"Yes."

"Yet despite feeling this way, you would intentionally do the
same thing if you got a girl pregnant?"

"Yes."

She looked at me with her young eyes in her old face, and I
looked away. She was trying to figure me out. That always made
me nervous as hell. I preferred it when she stuck to her job,
which as far as I could tell was getting me to talk mindlessly
about myself.

"Did your parents have a good marriage in your opinion?"

I had to hand it to her, not many people could ask that question with a straight face.

"I thought so."

She nodded again. "What made you think that?"

I gave the question a lot of thought. I didn't know why. I usually said the first thing that came into my head. "They got along
well," I answered.

"They liked each other?"

"Yeah. I mean, they didn't paw each other or write love letters or anything like that."

"How could you tell they liked each other?"

"Well, Mom almost always went out to the truck to meet him
when he came home even though she knew he was coming

straight in the house anyway. And she would touch him all over. Not grope him or anything like that. It was more like the way moms touch their kids when they find them after they lose them in a store."

"What about your father? How did he act toward your mother that made you think he liked her?"

I thought some more.

"Well, when Mom talked about her day while she fixed dinner, Dad had this way of closing his eyes and making his whole face look peaceful. Kind of like he was listening to a poem. Except he would hate listening to a poem, but that's the way it made me feel."

Betty smiled. "That's one of the few things you've ever said about your father that makes him sound human to me."

"What do you mean?"

"You've always described him as if he were a cartoon villain. A type of person; not a person. It's a very common way for abused children to describe their abusive parents. They see them as monsters or saints."

"He was a type," I said, suspiciously.

"You don't think he was more complicated than he appeared on the surface?"

"Define complicated."

"Having a variety of emotional and psychological factors influence a reaction to a situation, unlike a dumb animal who responds purely to physical stimuli and instinct."

"The second one," I said, getting annoyed. "That was my dad."

"What about what you just described to me?"

"Forget it."

"Did you like your father, Harley?"

Every couple months she asked me this same question and I always answered it the same way.

"I didn't know him well enough to know if I liked him."

"Your gut reaction to him?"

"He was a swell guy."

"You respected him though. Didn't you?"

I shrugged. "He did everything he was supposed to," I said.

She raised her eyebrows at me. "Including beating his children? Was he supposed to do that?"

"He thought he was."

"Good," she said firmly. "What makes you think that?"

"I don't want to talk about my dad," I said flatly, and went back to staring out the window.

She gave me a little time to stew, then got out of her chair and walked over to the old gray metal desk even principal offices had abandoned years ago. She opened her chocolaty leather-bound planner and touched her finger lightly to something and closed it again.

I asked her once where she got the date book from because it looked a cut above what Hallmark sold at the mall. She had looked a little startled at my question, then explained she bought it out of town and that sometimes a person needed to splurge on herself.

"Have you given any more thought to visiting your friend Skip?" she asked, still standing.

"I just bought new underwear," I said.

"I'm afraid I don't see the connection."

"I'm so strapped for cash, buying underwear is a big deal." She still didn't get it.

"I can't afford it," I explained further. "I'd need gas money, and money for food and beer and shit. I don't have it."

"I see," she said, even though I knew she didn't.

Then I noticed her hand resting on the cover of the date book. She probably thought I should splurge.

"I haven't asked about your financial situation in a while. How are things going? Certainly your father's estate is through probate by now."

My father's estate. That cracked me up. I was wearing my father's estate.

"I told you before all he had was some life insurance through his job. The government took a third and the rest went to back taxes on the house, Mom's lawyer, the funeral home . . ."

My voice died before I could finish the list. The cost of funerals had been as big a shock to me as the cost of dog food.

I decided I'd had enough. I reached for my cap sitting on the table and knocked over the water. I knew I was supposed to say I'm sorry and offer to help clean it up, but I couldn't move. The water spread in a glossy puddle across the dark brown tabletop and started dripping onto the carpet reminding me of something that made my stomach heave, but I couldn't focus on the right memory.

A bunch of them rushed in and out of my mind. Every spill I had ever made and every punishment I had ever received. Smacks in the head. Swats across the face with the wooden spoon. Belt whippings and backhanded slaps. Dad responding spontaneously, without feeling. The beatings coming, violent but impersonal and necessary, like cloudbursts. If Betty had ever been a witness, she would have agreed they were instinctual.

She jumped up from her chair and tried wiping up the water with Kleenex that kept falling apart in her hand. I heard her tell me not to worry and not to go, but I found my legs again and ran. I ran all the way to my truck and screeched out of the lot. She followed me outside and stood next to the building, a young-eyed old lady holding a handful of soggy white strands of my guts.

I was so rattled I almost forgot to stop at Yee's. I must have looked bad because Jack Yee's grin faltered and he asked me if I wanted a glass of water. I laughed until I cried.

For the first part of the drive home, I felt like puking. Everybody and his brother had a trash fire going in his yard since it was a nice night. The smell of burning plastic, grass clippings, and shitty diapers filled the truck along with the hot egg-roll grease.

A lot of people still had their trees and shrubs hung with Easter eggs. Some would keep them there until Halloween. Some people had started bringing out their lawn ornaments and would keep them there until hunting season, when they would have to take them back in again so they wouldn't get shot up.

I saw a woman I didn't know by name but had been driving by all my life, polishing a peacock-blue reflecting ball with a green rag. I waved and she waved back.

I noticed she had put her Virgin Mary out next to the bird-bath and behind some oversized yellow-polka-dotted red mush-rooms with two elves perched on top. Her Mary wasn't one of the gray stone statues everybody bought nowadays, the one where she's staring at the ground like she's not worthy. This Mary was one of the old-fashioned plastic kind, dressed in sky blue, look-ing toward heaven, a slight smile on her painted pink lips. Those were Mom's favorites. She loved the colored robes and serene white faces. She had never seen one until the drive from Illinois after she lost her family, and she thought they were a sign from God that this was going to be a good place to live. She spent the whole drive through our valley counting Madonnas.

I was completely calm again by the time I bounced over the final ruts in our road. My heartbeat had returned to normal. My hands were behaving. I could pick a thought and stick to it. I wasn't even bothered when I glanced down at the floor of the truck and noticed Mom and Dad's wedding picture had surfaced again through the latest layer of trash. I just put my boot on it and pushed it back under.

When I pulled in the driveway, Elvis raised his head from where he was lying on the char-broiled couch. Once the worst of the burnt smell had disappeared, he had claimed it for his own.

The girls hadn't made any mention of replacing the couch

indoors. They had covered the living room floor with pillows and sat on those when they watched TV. Every once in a while, I got a point across.

Misty didn't appear wordlessly on the porch waiting for her egg roll. Jody didn't come rushing out begging for her cookie and umbrella. I didn't think much of it until I had my hand on the front door handle, then all of a sudden I was absolutely certain they were all dead. Someone had gunned them down and put them in a pile in the middle of the living room where the couch had been. I couldn't tell one from the other until I noticed the eyes, open and vacant, staring out of surprised bloody faces. Jody's gray eyes like Mom's. Misty's dark eyes like Dad's. Amber's blue eyes like mine. Then I knew who they were. Who they had been. They weren't anybody anymore. They were a tangled heap of sticky red arms and legs and hair. Lots of hair. Gold and rust and brown.

Elvis started growling. I hadn't seen him there. He had his muzzle low to the ground and his haunches in the air, his ears flattened against his head and his lips drawn back over his teeth. The black fur on his back stood straight up like the bristles on the brushes that used to brush all that hair. There was blood in his fur. Somehow I knew that he hadn't been shot. It was the girls' blood. He had been standing too close when the shooting started. So had I. He was growling at me. I looked down and saw blood spattered on my boots, on my jeans. In my hands I saw Uncle Mike's gun.

I dropped it and the crash from it hitting the floor made me jump. I looked down again and saw the bag from Yee's sitting on the porch floor outside our front door. Elvis was growling at me. For real.

"What's the matter, boy?" I asked shakily.

He stopped growling immediately at the sound of my voice. He perked up his ears, cocked his head at me, and went trotting off with his tail waving.

I bent down slowly and retrieved the bag and checked to make sure Jody's cookie hadn't cracked.

Maybe one of these days I would ask Betty about these scenes that played out in my head. They were probably nothing but sometimes they bothered me because they seemed real. Not the way dreams seemed real but the way life seemed real. The only reason I'd bring them up to her would be on the chance there might be a cure for them—a pill I could take—because, like I said, sometimes they bothered me.

I opened the door. Normally I never announced my presence but tonight I shouted, "Where is everyone?"

Jody came running out of the kitchen, her eyes huge with excitement.

"Where have you been?" she asked me. "Why are you so late? We couldn't wait any longer. We got too hungry."

She paused to make a sound I had only ever heard little girls make; it was a sort of a cross between a shriek, a gasp, and a moan.

"You didn't forget. Amber said you would forget. She said whatever it was that made you late would make you forget."

She ran up to me, snatched the bag, and hugged my legs. I touched the top of her silky head.

"You seem happy," she said, and took my hand.

"I'm not," I assured her, and let her lead me into the kitchen.

"Where have you been?" Amber bitched at me. "You could have called."

"I haven't been anywhere," I said.

"And why are you wearing a coat? Every guy I know is wearing shorts today and you're stomping around in Sears work boots and a hunting jacket. I swear to God, you're a headcase. I hope you're a headcase. 'Cause if you're not then you're just the biggest dork on the face of the earth."

I took off Dad's coat and hung it over the back of my chair, not to please Amber but because the kitchen was too warm.

"It's better to be insane than unfashionable, is that what you're saying?" I asked, and reached for the buns.

"You're so funny," she huffed.

"You're wearing my shirt," I said.

All three of them wore my T-shirts to sleep in. Half the time I got dressed by going through my sisters' drawers.

"Take it off," I finished, forgetting who I was talking to.

She gave me a terrible grin and before I could tell her to stop she had stood up and was starting to pull it over her head. She had on only panties underneath. String bikini ones with butterflies on them. She had the shirt pulled up far enough that I couldn't see her face anymore and for one guilt-free moment, I stared dumbly at the tiny triangle of fabric where her thighs met, then the hips, the tummy, the curve of her rib cage before the welcomed repulsion overtook me.

I jumped up from my seat, grabbed her roughly by the arm, and pushed her back into her chair.

"You said take it off," she yelled at me.

"Where were you?" Misty asked.

We both turned at the sound of her voice. She was chewing her egg roll with mechanical disinterest, holding it slightly away from her face with her elbow resting on the table. I noticed how the kitten collar didn't slide down her forearm anymore. It stayed tight on her wrist.

"You're an hour late," she said to me.

I looked at the clock on the microwave and forgot about Amber. Misty was right.

"I don't get it," I said. "How can I be an hour late?"

"Maybe you were abducted by aliens," Amber suggested snottily, "and they gave you some kind of drug to make you forget what happened. Too bad. Your first sexual experience and you won't be able to remember it."

She laughed hysterically at herself. I didn't blame her for once. It was a smart insult for Amber.

"Maybe you got lost," Jody said, opening her umbrella and twirling it between her fingers. "I needed another purple one," she said, smiling. She had about six hundred purple ones.

"I was hoping you'd finally decided to split permanently," Amber told me when she got done laughing. "Then I could get my license."

I paused in the middle of fixing my hot dogs. It was my turn to laugh.

"It's not funny, Harley," she fumed. "You can't stop me forever. I should just go ahead and borrow one of my friend's cars and get it. The only reason I haven't done it yet is 'cause I know you won't let me get anywhere near the truck so what's the point?"

"I thought the only reason you hadn't done it was because you know I'd kill you."

"You don't have the guts to do anything to me."

"You just don't get it, do you?"

"What don't I get?"

I looked around the table. Mom and Dad's chairs were still here. One at each end. We hadn't bothered moving them somewhere else just like we hadn't bothered cleaning out their room. That would have been too much ACCEPTANCE.

Misty sat directly across from me, still chewing. She watched me and Amber, back and forth, superior and patient, like she had already reached the end of our argument and was waiting for us to catch up.

Jody was working on her list of things to do. Most of the instructions were short except for a big one at the bottom I couldn't make out.

"I can't afford it," I said slowly to Amber. "Which word don't you understand?"

"I understood all of them," Jody said.

"Even if I was the greatest guy on the face of the earth who only cared about making you happy," I went on, "I don't make

85

enough money to give the Good Hands People a thousand fucking bucks. Do you understand me?"

Amber puckered her lips and blew air out her nose in frustration. "I don't get it," she said. "How did Daddy do it?"

"Dad made good money."

"Driving a cement mixer?"

"Yes," I cried.

"Why can't you drive a cement mixer?"

"I can drive a cement mixer. I can't get a job driving a cement mixer. There's a big difference."

I finally made out the last thing on Jody's list. PUT TUTH UNDR MY PILLO.

"Did you lose another tooth?" I asked, not very enthusiastically.

"Yeah," she said, and pointed out the hole in her smile.

"I suppose you can't afford a quarter," Amber sneered.

"Harley doesn't pay for my teeth," Jody assured us all. "The tooth fairy does. Except I don't understand why the tooth fairy only gives me one quarter and gives Esme two quarters. Esme says it's because I use Aquafresh instead of Crest."

"Speaking of Esme," Misty said to me. "Her mom brought you a present."

Amber glared at her. "I wouldn't call it a present," she snorted at me.

"What are you talking about?" I asked.

"She stopped by this afternoon and left you some recipes and a book," Amber explained, practically spitting the words "recipe" and "book" at me. "Are you turning into a fag or something?"

"Something," I said.

"What's a fag?" Jody asked.

"I guess you might as well be a fag since you can't get a girl to make it with you."

"What book?" I asked.

"A gigantic book," Jody gushed before Amber could open her mouth again. "As big as a phone book."

"About what?"

"The Art Institute of Chicago," Amber said in amazed disgust.

"There's a Post-It note on top with the page numbers of some pictures Mrs. Mercer thought you'd like," Misty offered indifferently.

Amber shot her another outraged look.

"Since when do you know anything about art?" she asked me suspiciously.

"I know a lot of shit you don't know I know."

"Well, I'm sorry," she huffed. "That's just too weird and gross, Mrs. Mercer bringing you recipes and an art book. It's like she thinks you're a woman or something."

"Or something," I said again, and Jody laughed. I smiled at her.

"Go ahead and laugh," Amber said, tossing her hair around. "But that woman needs to get a life. I thought she was done coming around here. I can't believe the way she dresses."

I wasn't sure which comment to address first. I picked the one I was most interested in. "What's wrong with the way she dresses? I've never seen her wear anything but jeans."

"Yeah, but they're always way too tight for someone her age."

"Her age?"

"You should have seen what she was wearing this time."

"What was she wearing?" I asked.

She screwed up her face in disgust. "These low-rise pink denim shorts and a tie-dyed crop top. It was embarrassing."

"You're just jealous because those are the shorts you wanted at Fashion Bug," Misty said.

"Why was it embarrassing?" I asked, slowly chewing a mouthful of mac and cheese, and picturing Callie Mercer in low-rise pink denim shorts and a tie-dyed crop top.

"Because she's old. Women like that are so pathetic. Do they really think guys want to look at them after they hit thirty?"

"Yeah, that poor Kim Basinger," I said. "She's a real eyesore."

"Who's Kim Basinger?" Jody asked.

"You know what I mean," Amber said.

I finished eating. It took me about ten seconds. I went and got a Coke out of the fridge and walked back to the table but didn't sit down again. I was running late now. I took a couple long gulps from the can and belched.

"I can't wait to see you in your thirties, Amber," I said.

"You won't know me in my thirties. I'll be so out of here."

"You'll be living down the road in a trailer with five kids and no husband."

She fixed me with an acid stare. "You know what, Harley? I was going to do you a big favor and now you can go fuck yourself."

"A favor?" I laughed. "The only favor you can do for me is get a job."

"What if I knew someone who wanted to go out with you?"

My mind jerked back to the book and the recipes and the pink shorts. I turned away from the table. I was sure my face was red. "I'm not interested," I said.

"You don't even know who it is."

"If it's someone you know, I'm not interested."

I started to walk away. I needed to change my clothes. I was going to be late for work. Amber jumped up from the table and ran around in front of me.

"What if I knew someone who wanted to—" she paused and touched her upper lip with the tip of her tongue, "fuck you," she whispered.

"Get away from me."

"I'm serious."

"Get away."

"Ashlee Brockway. Her brother Dusty was in your class. She has a thing for you. I don't know why."

"How old is she?"

"My age."

"Sixteen? Forget it."

"What's the big deal? You're only nineteen."

"I'm almost twenty."

"So? She'll be seventeen someday."

"Forget it."

"Where do you get off being so high and mighty? It's not like she's a kid."

"She is a kid."

"And what are you?"

The phone rang. I asked Misty to get it.

"Do you want to hear my fortune?" Jody asked.

"Fine, Harley," Amber said, moving so close to me, her nipples beneath my T-shirt were almost brushing against my chest. She wasn't wearing a bra. If I hadn't stopped her at the table when I did, she probably would have flashed me. That was a sight I desperately wanted to see and I desperately wanted to avoid seeing; like Dad inside his closed casket.

"Be that way," she said, narrowing her eyes into bright blue creases in her face. "Just remember, beggars can't be choosers."

"That's what my fortune says," Jody squealed.

Amber turned and walked off to the shower with her butt twitching under my shirt.

"That was Mrs. Shank," Misty said, coming back from the phone.

"Who?"

"The Shanks. They live out past the Malones. Before you get to the bridge. The people with the birdbath and the blue ball. Doug and Cruz ride our bus."

"Who?"

"She said she saw you pull your truck off the road and just sit there for about an hour. She said she didn't want to bother you because you looked like you didn't want to be bothered, but she wanted to be sure you got home okay."

"What?"

"You didn't have to lie about something like that," Misty said, sounding disappointed in me. "She would've understood."

"What?" I said again. "Who?"

She walked out of the kitchen too. I looked over at Jody, who was writing again. Suddenly, I couldn't figure out what I was supposed to do next.

Sounds bombarded me. My sense of hearing became painfully keen. I heard the scratch of Jody's pencil on her list of things to do, and I knew she was writing PRAY FOR DADDY'S SOWL. I heard Misty punch a pillow as she settled down to watch TV, and I knew it was the flattened, musty, denim blue one that Dad used to take on overnight hunting trips. I heard Elvis outside nudging his nose around his food bowl, and I knew he was still hungry. I heard the driving water splash against Amber's naked soapy skin, and I knew where she was touching herself.

I wished Betty could have had the same experience. Maybe then she would have understood why some questions should be left unanswered.

I went to Amber's room and got out her yearbook. I looked up Ashlee Brockway. She was not repulsive.

chapter 7

I couldn't remember the first time my dad hit me, but I remembered the first time he hit Amber. She was three years old and a major cramp in my lifestyle. I couldn't watch my *He-Man* cartoons around her because Mom said Skeletor was too scary. I got yelled at for leaving my Legos out because they were a choking hazard. I had to let her play with my Hot Wheels but if I went anywhere near her kitchen set, I got my head smacked. There were plenty of times when I wanted to hit her myself, but I didn't because I didn't want to get hit and the punishment for hitting was hitting.

Dad hit her for knocking over his beer. One minute he was calmly watching TV on the couch; the next minute his big hand shot out and clamped around her little arm, easy and familiar, like he was reaching for the can. He yanked her toward him, making her head snap back, and he hauled off and slapped her.

The crack of his hard grown-up hand meeting her soft baby cheek was the loudest sound I had ever heard. Even louder than her screams.

I watched the bewildered terror cloud her eyes, and I saw myself in them. Not my reflection but proof of my existence, just the same. I knew Dad had destroyed her courage.

Mom came rushing from the other room and stopped in the doorway to take in the scene. Then she stared at me, begging me for an answer I was too little to give her. I wanted her to leave him because he hurt us, but I needed for us to stay because we belonged to him. I was a kid and nothing seemed more unjust to me than somebody taking your stuff.

Finally she grabbed up Amber and left, murmuring things in her hair.

That night Amber had a bad dream. She came and crawled into bed with me instead of Mom and Dad. I couldn't get back to sleep with her snuggled up next to me. I lay there until dawn, thinking about Dad, and feeling the same useless frustration I had felt the first time I had seen him piss on a sparkling white drift of pure new snow.

Amber set up the date for me. I never talked to Ashlee, and I never wanted to. I did want to put a part of my body inside her body and I was willing to go hungry for a week so I could scrape together enough money to take her out and try and convince her to let me, but I didn't want to know anything about her. I didn't care what kind of music she liked or if she loved her parents or what she wanted to be when she grew up. Common sense should have told me that was a bad sign.

I stayed awake the night before staring at my lightbulb in the dark wondering if it was the last night I would lie there as a virgin. I tried not to think about it too much because it was the exact same thing I had thought about the night before I screwed up with Brandy Crowe, but I couldn't stop myself.

Excitement. Dread. Desire. Disgust. I made myself sick with confusion. How could I feel opposite emotions for the same act? How could I feel so strongly about a girl I had never met? How could I want to love someone without getting personally involved? There was something evil about feeling that way. Something too arrogant. Even for humans.

Eventually, I cleared my mind enough to sleep. My main concern was my sanity. I had begun to secretly cherish it lately the way most guys did their hard-ons. I sorted out my feelings for Ashlee a final time and strung them out in a nice, neat mental line.

I didn't want her to talk. I didn't want her to judge or feel. But I did want her alive. I wanted her warm.

Rick wouldn't give me Friday night off, but he said I could leave early. He asked me if I had a date. I said no, but that didn't stop him from telling the cashiers and Bud and Church that I did.

On his way out the door at the beginning of our shift, he announced very loudly that I could help myself to a box of rubbers in the pharmacy section, free of charge, because that was the kind of guy he was. And he was right. That was exactly the kind of guy he was.

"Ignore him," Bud said to me. "He's just jealous 'cause even his own wife won't go near that fat ass."

The cashiers laughed. One of them said it was true. What else could explain their lack of children? Everyone knew his wife didn't have fertility problems ever since she had that abdominal pain checked out last year.

"Didn't she have one of those laparoscope operations?" another one asked.

The other one nodded. "They make a cut in your belly button and snake this tube down inside you with a laser and a little telescope on the end of it so they can see your ovaries."

"That's what my sister-in-law had done when she had her miscarriage."

"They wouldn't do that for a miscarriage," the third one broke in. "She would have had a D and C to clean out her uterus."

"Is that the one where they suck out the stuff with the little vacuum or the one where they scrape it out with a knife?"

A woman wheeled her cart up to one of the registers and the

conversation ended, but the damage had already been done. Ashlee's female parts had temporarily lost their mystical appeal. This wasn't the first time the cashiers had ruined women for me. They were like English teachers taking all the pleasure out of a perfectly good book by breaking it down into themes and sentence structure.

Church got up from the bench to go bag but paused, looking puzzled, and said, "If it was going to rain my mom would've told me. She always makes me wear my slicker."

I glanced up at him but only for a second. Eye contact with Church was like seeing his soul through the wrong end of a telescope.

"She doesn't want me getting wet," he said.

"Right," I said.

"One time I got sick from getting wet. I'm not kidding you."

"I believe you."

"It's a red slicker. You've seen it."

"Right."

"Yellow's for girls." He suddenly barked a laugh and turned in Bud's direction. "I don't care what you say, Bud," he cried, pointing at him. "Yellow's for girls. I don't care what you say."

Bud winked at me. "But I always thought yellow was for girls, Church."

That sent Church into lurching hysterics. "Shoot, you're funny, Bud," he said once he calmed down. He took off his glasses and pulled out a handkerchief from his baggy black pants to wipe at the tears in his eyes. "You and Harley," he said, shaking his head. "You're funny."

He finished, carefully positioned his glasses back on his nose, and folded his handkerchief into a perfect square before cramming it back in his pocket.

"I better call my mom and tell her to bring my slicker. And my rubbers too. I got sick once from getting wet. I'm not kidding."

He walked off to the pay phone by the ATM machine. Bud held his breath until he got out of earshot, then busted a gut laughing.

My shift went smoothly, and my thoughts gradually improved from the night before. Stocking shelves and fluorescent lighting usually had that effect on me. I tried looking on the bright side. I might actually like Ashlee Brockway. Maybe she was mature for her age. And I had to keep reminding myself: she liked me— or thought she did—and for girls, thinking they liked a guy was just as important as actually liking him.

I finished unpacking eight boxes of Toaster Strudels, closed the freezer door, and stepped back to take a look at myself in the glass. There was nothing wrong with me. No glaring errors. But there was nothing incredibly right about me either.

My hair wasn't any definable color. People called it brown and strawberry blond and even auburn. Jody once told me it was the color of a pile of raked-up leaves.

My eyes were blue but not a startling gas-flame blue like Amber's. When I was a kid, I used to think they looked like blue construction paper when it got wet, and I used to think that was good.

I had an okay body. I didn't pump iron, and except for some amazing midlife crisis I never would; but heavy lifting was one of my vocations so I had strong arms and a good chest. Dad probably knew what he was doing, thinking I could have been a football player.

Admiring my adequateness got me all fired up. I went straight from the freezer section to the pharmacy. The prescription counter had closed at eight and no one was around. I grabbed a box of condoms. The sight of it in my hand made all my concerns about Ashlee fly right out of my head. She could still have her baby teeth for all I cared.

I stuck the box in my pants pocket. I only had fifteen minutes left on my shift. Rick wasn't around to make me work them

95

so I decided to go change out of my Shop Rite clothes early. I headed for the storeroom, dragging my dolly behind me, and had to pass by the produce section. I stopped in front of the bananas.

I had practiced putting rubbers on countless bananas ever since the night with Brandy Crowe when I had unrolled one before trying to put it on. And I did try to put it on. A little thing like that wasn't going to stop me.

Unfortunately, Brandy didn't try to stop me either. At the time I thought that meant she was as inexperienced as I was, but it turned out she was just stupid and horny and cruel. She told me I could go ahead and do it anyway even though the thing was barely on and so full of air it looked like a balloon some clown might twist into a wiener dog at a kid's birthday party. I tried, and I think I achieved about a half-inch of penetration with my dick feeling nothing but inflated latex, then the rubber fell off. At that point I was willing to risk pregnancy, disease, and even death but Brandy put a stop to everything including the alternatives I suggested that couldn't result in pregnancy. I knew right then she didn't love me like she had been saying ever since she let me unfasten her bra. If she had loved me she would have wanted to put me out of my misery the way a tortured wife gives a cancer-racked husband a suicide dose of pills. A mercy hand job—that's all I was looking for.

I wasn't going to let any of that happen again. Practice made perfect and I had some time. I eyed the bananas but grabbed a good-sized cucumber instead. My optimism was running at an all-time high.

I put it in my pocket along with the box of rubbers, made a wide berth around the artichokes, and wandered toward the meat and seafood counters.

We were having a sale on salmon fillets. $4.99 a pound. Jody loved salmon. Not the taste. None of us had ever eaten it. She loved the shiny silver scales.

I remembered her when she was real little sitting in the front of the cart pointing at the bright pinkish-orange and silver layers stacked on ice chips in the display case and babbling baby talk. Mom would smile and tell her it was too rich for our blood and try and get her interested in a slab of something colorless or the trout and catfish with their eyes still in their heads. It never worked, and Mom would end up laughing and telling Jody how she hoped she would always stick to her convictions like that. How she might grow up to be a Supreme Court judge.

I could see it now. A copy of Jody's first decision from the bench stuck to a prison cafeteria wall with tapioca.

Sometimes I wished Mom would get that lethal injection. She'd make a better ghost than a spectator.

"Hi, Harley," a female voice said.

My heart jumped. My head was crammed full of women: Mom, Jody, Ashlee, Brandy, the cashier's sister-in-law with her scraped-out uterus; it could have been any one of them and I wasn't prepared.

Callie Mercer came up beside me. She was wearing the pink shorts but not the crop top. She had on a T-shirt instructing the world to save the tigers.

"Hi," she said again.

"Hi," I said back.

She gave me a funny look, then a smile crept onto her lips. She tilted her head and glanced at me from the corner of her eyes. "Is that a cucumber in your pocket or are you just glad to see me?"

"Huh?"

"I'm sorry." She laughed. "I had to say that. There's a cucumber in your pocket."

I looked down, panicked, forgetting if I had put the rubber on it or not.

"I found it on a shelf," I explained in a hurry. "I was just putting it back."

"What else would you be doing with it?" she said.

"Right," I said.

"So how are you?" she asked with a throaty hopefulness that made me think of random destinations on long, lean, gray highways.

"Fine."

"I stopped up at your house last week. Did Amber tell you?"

"Yeah."

"I wasn't sure she would. I don't think she likes me very much."

"Why?" I asked. "Did she say something to you?"

"Let's just say she wasn't very hospitable. It's not a big deal. I don't blame her for thinking I was snooping around."

"Snooping around? Is that what she said?"

"Don't worry about it, Harley."

She started to reach out her hand to touch me but stopped. "It's okay. I understand. It must be very hard to deal with people sometimes after . . ." she struggled to find the least alarming words, "after what happened."

"No, you're wrong," I answered sharply. "What happened doesn't give us an excuse to act any way we want. It's not an excuse for anything."

"Well, let's just forget about it."

She stared into the display case, checking out the salmon. They probably had it once a week, sale or no sale. She probably had some remarkable marinade she would write down for me if I asked. I could smell that night's dinner in her hair and on her hands: ginger, garlic, and brown sugar.

Then I realized she was staring at her reflection in the glass. She studied it, confused and irritated, like she had been handed a bunch of parts and instructions in a foreign language.

"Thanks," I thought to tell her. "For the stuff you brought."

She turned back around. "Did you look through the book at all?"

"Yeah. I checked out that Pierre Bonnard painting. 'Earthly Paradise.' They were supposed to be Adam and Eve, right?"

"Right. What did you think?"

"It was pretty accurate, I thought. Eve stretched out sleeping in the woods like she wasn't worried about anything. Adam standing at the edge of the woods looking like he's trying to figure out where to build a house."

"Why do you say that's accurate?" She laughed.

"I don't know. I guess because women seem better at accepting things the way they are and dealing with shit while men are always trying to figure out ways to change things and when they can't they get pissed."

She watched me like she wanted more. I searched my brain for something else I could offer her.

"Like in the Garden of Eden," I went on. "I always felt like, even after Eve became enlightened and realized she was naked, she would have been fine with it. Adam was the one who got embarrassed and couldn't deal with it."

She smiled deeply and gave me a familiar sparkling appraisal with her dark eyes. I pictured her giving the same look to her husband and him totally missing it and giving her a dry peck on the cheek on his way out the door for his night with the boys.

"A lot of people think that's one of the things Bonnard was trying to show in his painting," she said. "That Eve reveled in her natural state while Adam became awkwardly aware of his nakedness. He's standing alone because his consciousness has separated him from her."

She paused.

"I'd be curious to know who you think was to blame for their fall from grace: Adam or Eve?" she asked, kind of joking.

"Both," I said with a nod of my head. "They were both selfish."

"Selfish?"

"I always felt like that's why God wanted rid of them. Not because they broke a rule. Because they turned on each other. I bet they could have smoothed things over if they had just gone to Him and admitted they were both stupid instead of trying to blame it on each other. If He thought they loved each other, God probably would have given them a second chance instead of damning the entire human race for all eternity."

She was smiling at me again. I glanced down at the cucumber sticking out of my pocket.

"So what does your husband do on his night out?"

I asked it kind of snotty. There was a part of me that didn't care about offending her. What would it matter? She was as much a fantasy as a lingerie model; the only difference was I could smell her and I knew where she lived.

The question was absolutely none of my business and I half expected her to tell me but she answered me.

"I don't know," she said, fanning her fingers in the air. "He has a couple friends from work he goes out with. They went through a racquetball phase a couple years ago. Then a basketball phase. I didn't mind those so much because at least he was getting exercise. Now I think they just sit in the country club for hours on end complaining about how their wives and kids make so many demands on them and how they can't golf at night."

She stopped, bit her lower lip, and spit it out like it tasted bad.

"That didn't sound too bitchy, did it?"

"No," I said.

She put her index finger lightly on her lips. She seemed to like the taste of it better because she slipped the tip in her mouth and started lightly chewing on the nail.

"What would you rather be doing on your night out?" I asked her. "Besides grocery shopping?"

"Besides grocery shopping," she said, giving me a sly smile

around the finger before hooking it into an empty belt loop in her shorts. "That's a tough one. Well, I suppose on a warm, clear night like tonight, I'd take a book and a blanket and a couple beers and go to this clearing behind my house on the other side of the railroad tracks. It's this huge open field surrounded by trees about a mile up the hill. You feel like you're in a completely secluded world up there. I bet tonight it's as bright as day with that big full moon."

"You'd take beer?" I asked.

She nodded.

"Not a bottle of wine?"

"I like beer."

"I kind of had you pegged for a wine drinker."

She laughed. "Somehow I don't think that's a compliment."

"Why can't you do that?" I wondered. "Go read in the woods?"

"I suppose I could if I lobbied hard enough. It's just not worth it." Her face fell and her mood with it.

"Well," she sighed, "I should let you put your cucumber away. By the way," she started as she positioned her cart to leave, "what happened to your couch?"

I thought about it for a moment. "It caught on fire."

"My God. You're lucky the whole house didn't burn down. Was someone smoking on it?"

"Yeah. One of Amber's friends."

"Thank God you were home."

"Yeah, thank God."

"Well, I'll see you around."

She started to go.

"I'm sorry about Amber," I called after her. "I'll have a talk with her."

"No." She stopped dead in her tracks and shook her head at me. "Please don't. It's okay. Really."

I waited for the pink shorts to make a turn down the cereal aisle and went and put back the cucumber.

I didn't want Callie Mercer or anyone else cutting Amber slack because our family had experienced a tragedy. People were always making excuses for stupidity and a lack of basic decency. They were always looking for someone else to blame.

Mom's lawyer blamed Dad for his own murder. He practically came out and said he deserved it for beating us kids. He painted Mom as the ultimate martyr who sacrificed her freedom to save her children, but anyone looking at Mom sitting stunned and dry-eyed staring at her wedding ring knew even she didn't buy it.

The lawyer purposely left out some very important facts like Dad married Mom when she got pregnant instead of running out on her, and he worked hard every day of their married life to provide for us.

He didn't talk about the PHYSICAL STIMULI that shaped Dad's world. How he didn't like his job, but he went to it every day. How he didn't like to shave, but Mom couldn't stand stubble. How he didn't like Bill Clinton, but he had to vote for him anyway. He wasn't a monster. He was a flesh-and-blood man who couldn't stand it if you spilled something.

I tried explaining these things my day on the witness stand, but the judge kept telling me to stick to the questions. Even the prosecutor, whose job it was to convict Mom, wasn't interested in making Dad look good so Mom would look worse. He didn't care at all about the individuals involved. He latched onto the big philosophical questions, "Is it ever right to take the law into our own hands?" and "What happens to the fabric of society when we do?" I thought he was crazy trying that argument with a jury box full of people who all had gun cases in their living rooms instead of bookcases but I had forgotten the reason they did was because they loved killing, just not their own kind. The prosecutor hadn't forgotten. He twisted his line of reasoning into a big knot of paranoia.

Where do you draw the line? If it's okay to shoot him for

beating the kids, is it okay to shoot him for staying out too late drinking? Today it's a wife shooting her husband for beating the kids, tomorrow it's a stranger shooting you in your car because he doesn't like your bumper sticker. By the time he was done, everyone in the courtroom believed freeing my mother would be signing their own death warrants.

My good jeans and a clean blue T-shirt were waiting for me in the storeroom. I changed my clothes behind a stack of Heinz ketchup boxes, put on my cap, and transferred my box of condoms.

Callie was already checking out when I strolled up front. I hung back and watched. She was chatting up a storm with Bud. He knew everybody, but he seemed to know her on a personal level.

I waited until she left. I hadn't been planning on talking to anybody on my way out, but I had to walk past all of them to get to the doors anyway. I slowed down as I neared Bud. He blew a bubble at me.

"Ready for your big date?"

"I guess so."

"Where you going?"

"Movie."

"That's a good idea, Harley," Church commented.

I stepped up closer to Bud. I didn't want the cashiers hearing me mention Callie and launching into the history of her reproductive organs.

"How do you know her?" I asked him.

"Who?" he said. "Callie Mercer? I used to work with her."

"She buys too much peanut butter," Church volunteered. "I told her so. I'm not kidding."

"Where?" I asked Bud.

"At the *Gazette*. She used to work there summers when she came home from school."

"You used to write for the newspaper?"

"Don't look so amazed," he told me, popping his gum. "Writing for it's only slightly more impressive than being able to read it."

"Peanut butter's full of fat," Church said. "People don't believe you when you tell them, but it's true. Just like olives. Full of fat. People never believe me when I tell them."

"Why'd you quit?"

"Well, one day I was going through my clips and realized the most important story I had ever written was 'Man Dressed in Groundhog Suit Assaulted.'"

"Was that the Roebuck boy who got jumped up in Punxsy during Groundhog Days?" one of the cashiers asked.

My attempt at being discreet hadn't worked.

"Up on Gobbler's Knob, wasn't it?" another cashier chipped in. "He was the groundhog who worked the crowd in town. The other one worked the mall, but he didn't have the big top hat."

"Yep, that's the one," Bud said. "They caught the guys who beat him up. I still remember the quote they gave me: 'We got that damned groundhog.'"

"So you quit because you got disgusted?" I said.

"I quit because they made me. Mandatory retirement. But I like to think I would've quit anyway."

"Why'd Callie quit?" I asked. "Because she had kids?"

"Well, let's see. She worked there summers during college." He paused and brought an age-spotted hand to his chin and rubbed it thoughtfully. "And then she worked there for a couple years after she came back here to live permanently. Yeah, I guess she did stop after she got married and started having kids."

"Why would she want to come back here and live?" I wondered. "Doesn't seem like she'd want to."

"Why do you say that?"

"She seems different. That's all."

"I don't know," Bud said. "You might be confusing different with dissatisfied."

Church stepped up between us. "She buys too much peanut butter." He gaped. "She doesn't even buy it for her kids. She buys it for herself. I'm not kidding. She told me she likes it." He shook his head. "It's full of fat. I told her so."

"If she grew up here," I went on, ignoring Church, "she had to know what this place was all about. She had to know she'd be dissatisfied with it. Why would she stay?"

"I'm pretty sure it was simply a case of love."

"For her husband?" I asked, feeling a pang of disgust at the question.

"For her grandpa," Bud answered me. "She came back to take care of him after he had his first heart attack. He lived for another year, then had the big one that killed him. She inherited his land and stayed on it."

"She must have really loved him."

Bud nodded. "Callie's a little intense. When I worked with her I always felt like she was being pulled in a hundred different directions. Her grandpa was sort of her compass from what I could tell. Once he passed on—" he paused and tapped his temple with a finger, "her needle started spinning, if you know what I mean. I think she stayed on his land hoping to find some peace."

"Did he give her the land before she got married?"

Bud stopped and gave me a searching look. "I don't think I've ever heard you talk so much. Getting all keyed up about your date, huh?"

"Did he?" I asked again.

"I think so."

"Why'd she get married then?"

"Well, I can't say for sure but I don't think land ownership factored into it one way or the other."

"I'm just saying if she had all that land and a job, she wouldn't have to get married."

"There you go again. Who said she had to get married? I

imagine she loved the guy. You got something against Brad Mercer?"

"I don't even know him."

I lost interest in the conversation once her husband came back into it. I was going to be late for my date anyway.

I said good night to everybody and started for the door. I was standing on the mat when I heard Church yell at the top of his lungs, "Harley, my mom says you won't need any rubbers tonight."

The doors slid open and I got out of there as fast as I could, their laughter ringing in my ears.

I was supposed to meet Ashlee at the fountain in the middle of the mall. I hadn't given much thought to why she wanted to meet me instead of making me pick her up but as soon as I turned the corner past the fabric store and heard girls laughing, I knew. I would have left, but one of them spotted me and whispered to Ashlee. She looked over and waved and went back to her girlfriends. They whispered and laughed some more, then eyed me up and down with leering, smirking smiles.

Ashlee had snagged herself an older guy, a real man who paid taxes and bought his own underwear. She didn't like me. She didn't want to know me any more than I wanted to know her. She just wanted to show me off to her friends.

I deserved it considering the reason I was there. I couldn't think of a more even exchange: my dignity for her pussy.

She slid off the bricks surrounding the fountain and walked over to me. I couldn't take my eyes off her. There were certain things you couldn't tell from a yearbook picture.

"Hi, Harley," she said.

"Hi," I said back. "I hope I'm not late."

"I don't care," she said.

She stepped up in front of me and stood perfectly still like an offering.

"I mean, I don't want us to be late for the movie," I explained.

"I don't care," she said again. "I've seen it."

"You want to see something else?"

She waved her hand in the air, then slipped it into one of mine.

"I've seen them all," she said, and started leading me to the fountain to introduce me to her friends.

There were four of them, but they were interchangeable. Same fluffy hair. Same doe-eyed makeup and berry brown lipstick. Same clingy halter tops and fringed cutoffs and stack-heeled sandals.

I looked at them sprawled on the brick around the fountain, the bare legs and bellies and throats begging to be handled. It should have been a crime. Premeditated arousal. I should have been able to call Security and have them dragged off. All except Ashlee, who I wanted to keep for myself.

It turned out she didn't talk much. She flashed me a lot of adoring looks and kept reaching down to adjust her sandal buckle after we took our seats in the theater. Each time she did, her halter top pulled away from her shorts and I glimpsed the start of a shadow at the base of her spine. I wanted to kiss that spot more than I wanted to kiss her lips.

The movie was lost on me. I couldn't have cared less about a bunch of screaming teenagers getting ominous letters and finding dead bodies in the trunks of their cars. Ashlee had claimed she'd already seen it but that didn't stop her from being terrified. She grabbed my arm whenever something scary happened. She had become permanently latched there by the time the credits rolled. I barely noticed her. I was thinking about how much money I had spent on a lame movie and popcorn and Cokes. Being the breadwinner took the joy out of a lot of things.

We left the theater holding hands. Ashlee kept looking around for anyone she knew. In the parking lot, she headed straight for my truck. I couldn't figure out how she recognized it. If she had ever been over to our house, it was while I was at work. Then I remembered that sometimes the cars and trucks that dropped off Amber in the middle of the night were full of girls.

I got a strange feeling imagining Ashlee walking past my truck in the dark, slowly dragging her fingertips across the dirty hood, and thinking about me while I was asleep not thirty feet away in my ratty underwear. I liked her thinking about me as long as she didn't know me, but I didn't like her touching the truck. I opened the door for her and watched her crawl inside.

"You want to get some pizza or something?" I asked her after I got in too.

"You don't have to do that," she said.

What she meant was "I know you don't have any money." I must have let my anger show because she quickly added, "I'm not hungry is all I mean. It's kind of late."

"Do you have to get home?" I asked, almost hopeful.

"My mom don't care what time I get home."

"What about your dad?"

"My folks are divorced."

She said it with a pinched dignity as if she admired the act but disagreed with the principles behind it.

"What about Dusty?"

"Dusty? Why would he care?"

She reached down into the trash on the floor of the truck. I had forgotten to clean it out. She brought back Mom and Dad's wedding picture.

"This your folks?" she asked.

"It came with the frame," I said.

She giggled. "You look like your dad," she said, and gave me a hesitant smile. "I'm sorry about all that."

ALL THAT. The letters floated in front of my eyes, soft and puffy, like the caterpillar in *Alice in Wonderland* had blown them from his hookah. I blinked them away.

"Yeah, ALL THAT really sucked," I said.

"I know it's been real hard on Amber. It really changed her a lot."

"Yeah, she used to be human."

She laughed again, letting it trail off into another giggle. "Amber says you're real funny."

She was still holding the picture. One of her purple polished thumbnails covered Mom's face. I thought about grabbing the back of her neck and smashing her face into the glass.

"You don't want to go home yet?" I said, looking away from her and the picture.

"Not really."

"What do you want to do?"

"I don't know. It's such a hot night for this time of year. We could go over to the reservoir. You got a blanket in the truck?"

"I've got a coat."

The glass shards embedded in her forehead would twinkle in the moonlight when I laid her down on it.

"Okay," she said.

We weren't the only couple out on a Friday night who had come up with the reservoir idea. The sight of all the cars and trucks—some of them solitary and rocking, others covered with kids sitting on the hoods and trunks smoking and drinking and laughing about shit they weren't going to find at all funny in a couple more years—irritated me. I suggested to Ashlee we try the township park.

Except for a couple making out on the slide and another one on the swings, the place was empty. I parked my truck facing away from the playground and toward the softball field.

"You want to go there?" Ashlee asked, staring out the windshield at the pitcher's mound.

I wanted to wash her face. She wore too much makeup. I knew she did it to look older but it had the opposite effect. She reminded me of all those child beauty queens that were on TV and the tabloid covers after that one was murdered. Little Miss

Lovely. Little Miss Physical Stimuli. Little Miss Pedophilia. That was Skip's joke. And if she was from Philly, she'd be Little Miss Philadelphia Pedophilia. And we tried to say it ten times fast sitting in the mining office, all grown up now, with beers stolen from our dads instead of bologna sandwiches made by our moms.

"What are we going to do when we get there?" I asked her, glancing at the mound.

"What?"

"What are we going to do when we get there?" I asked again, slower and louder, like I was talking to a dim-witted Girl Scout.

"Whatever you want," she said.

"Whatever I want."

Maybe she had misunderstood. Maybe she thought I was talking about a choice between tag or hide-and-go-seek. Maybe this was all a big joke. Why had Amber set me up on a date in the first place? Since when did she do me favors? Was Ashlee going to turn me down? Was that it? Or was she going to make it with me and tell Amber all about it? Were they going to sit around with the Interchangeables and crucify me?

"Do you think I'm ugly or something?" she said in a low personal tone like she was discussing the possibility with herself.

"No."

"I'm on the pill," she added with holiday eagerness. "Most guys get real excited over that."

A sharp pain stabbed me above the eyes.

"You know what that means?" she said, lowering her voice to a whisper. "No rubbers."

My hands started shaking, but I smiled anyway. I was torn in two by a violent desire to be like MOST GUYS and a helpless need to be me.

"Aren't you kind of young to be on the pill?" I asked her.

"My mom put me on it. She says she doesn't want me ending up like her."

She put one of her hands on my leg and moved toward me.

I let her kiss me. It wasn't much of one on my part. She pulled away, mildly stunned, and fixed me with the straining, empty eyes of someone who had been recently blinded.

I pushed her away. Maybe too hard. She crashed into the passenger side door and gave a small wounded cry when her naked shoulder hit the window handle. She stayed perfectly still in the corner, staring at me, frozen not by fright but by glaring disbelief.

I started the truck. At the first cough of the engine, she tried to kiss me again. I saw her lips coming at me with the deadly intent of a charging bull. The back of my hand met the side of her face and I heard her head make a hollow clunk against the window glass. She broke into sobs.

"I lied," I said. "I think you're ugly."

It was for her own good.

I didn't know how I ended up at Callie Mercer's house. I couldn't remember where I had left my truck. If I had gone home first. If I had left it parked on the side of the road somewhere. Mrs. Shank had told Misty I sat in front of their house for an hour. I didn't believe it then but now I wasn't so sure.

I had taken a roundabout way, following the railroad tracks, crossing her creek, approaching the house from an angle where the dogs couldn't see me. A light burned in the jungle room.

The worst part about tonight was not having anyone to talk to. No Skip. No Dad. I was old enough now I could have talked to Dad about sex. We had come close once. The first time I went out with Brandy he had been home and as I was leaving he told me to remember, a few seconds of ecstasy wasn't worth a lifetime of driving a cement truck. He had said it laughing and my mom had called out, "Thanks a lot," from the kitchen. All I heard was "a few seconds of ecstasy."

Callie was sitting sideways on a white wicker couch, wearing a big T-shirt and nothing else, with a mile of bare leg draped over one of the armrests. She was reading a book and had a beer sitting on the floor next to her.

I changed my mind. The worst part about tonight had been finding out I didn't want the one thing I was counting on to make me feel good. There would be no relief from living.

Her husband came into the room. He walked over to her and his lips moved. She looked up from her book and I thought to myself, If he touches her, I will die.

chapter 8

All those times me and Skip tried to kill Donny were just for fun. At least they were for me. I never wanted to kill Donny. The truth be told, I kind of liked him although I would have never told Skip that.

Donny radiated contentment, a sleepy lying-in-the-sun kind of mental bliss I had never known. Even when Skip yelled at him or pushed him around, he seemed okay with it. One time we barricaded him in a closet for a whole day trying to suffocate him. I broke into a cold sweat when we went back and knocked on the door and didn't get an answer, but Skip didn't get scared at all. We moved the chairs away, opened the door, and a couple seconds later Donny slid out on his belly, blinking, saying he was a night crawler.

I was sure my fondness for him was nothing more than little brother envy since I only had Amber: a chattering shadow who turned cartwheels for no reason and left every room smelling like watermelon Lip Smacker. I thought the best thing about having a little brother would have been the luxury of occasionally forgetting he existed.

I was thinking about Donny because I had noticed Skip didn't mention him in his letter. I had it sitting on the counter next to

Callie Mercer's recipe for bean and macaroni soup. I couldn't imagine writing anyone a letter without mentioning the girls even if I was living away from them. They would have been there in my thoughts whether I wanted them to be or not.

Skip's letter had seen better days. Some of the words were beginning to rub off and the creases were gray and shiny from being folded and unfolded too much. I would have gone to visit him that very minute if I had the money. I thought about my schedule, searching for an extra chunk of time where I could stick in a part-time job. The ice cream places, the drive-in, the miniature golf courses would all be hiring soon. Some already were.

Weekdays I worked nine to five and seven to midnight. Weekends I sometimes worked the same, but every once in a while I had a day off like today. I could be handing ice cream cones to Ashlee and MOST GUYS and getting paid for it instead of making soup and getting abuse for it.

The bacon in the pot sizzled and popped. I was supposed to be sautéing it with a finely chopped onion and two minced garlic cloves in olive oil which we didn't have. I wasn't sure what sauté meant, but I was pretty sure it didn't mean burn the crap out of it.

I gave the brown mess a stir with Mom's wooden spoon. Most of it stuck to the bottom of the pan. I turned down the heat and added the can of whole tomatoes. The recipe said to chop them up so I started ripping at them with the spoon, thinking about Ashlee again.

I sensed Jody standing behind me.

"You're not supposed to burn it," she said.

"Are you sure about that?" I replied without turning around to look at her. "It says right here in the recipe, 'be sure to burn it.'"

She darted up next to me and left a note on the counter.

114

back roads

I hadn't been in a very good mood when I finally rolled out of bed that afternoon. I didn't look too good either.

I knew Jody was still in the room with me.

"What?" I shouted.

"You're supposed to put little leaves in with the tomatoes."

"Sorry. We're fresh out of sage."

"Esme's mom grows it in her garden."

"Good for her."

I kept stirring. Misty joined Jody. They lurked in the doorway and talked in whispers.

"Did you get my note?" Jody asked me.

"Yes," I said.

"I really meant it."

"Thanks."

"Can we go to the Lick n' Putt?"

"Can you get a job?"

"Told you," Misty grunted as Jody slumped back to her.

Add salt and freshly ground pepper to taste. Simmer for ten to twelve minutes.

"Freshly ground pepper," I muttered to myself.

I grabbed Mom's pepper shaker shaped like an Amish guy and dumped a ton in. I set him back down next to his wife in a black bonnet carrying a basket of apples. Men were always pepper; women always salt. Black. White. Evil. Virtuous.

"You prick," Amber seethed.

I heard her bare feet pad across the kitchen tile. She sounded naked. I glanced at the front of the microwave to catch her reflection in it. She had on a crocheted bikini top and a pair of cutoffs decorated with lace. I didn't know how I was going to

115

survive another summer of her lounging around in a bathing suit. The one she wore last year was chiseled into my brain with the cosmic permanence of the Ten Commandments on stone.

"I figured something might go wrong like you wouldn't be able to get it up or you wouldn't know where to put it," she said, "but I never expected you to hit her. You never hit me."

"What are you talking about?"

I whirled around and spattered tomato juice all over her bare belly. She flinched at the sight of it and at the sight of the spoon, her blue eyes showing a moment of pure depthless fear before she came splashing back to the surface to find her rage floating reliably above her like a life preserver.

She took hold of the bottom of my shirt with a yank and wiped off her belly with it.

"I just got off the phone with Tracy. She said Ashlee said you hit her."

"Who the hell is Tracy?"

"You met her last night at the mall."

"Right. Was she the slutty-looking one? Or the slutty-looking one?"

She eyed me with weary disgust. "Where do you get off with that attitude? Everyone's too stupid or slutty or lazy for you. Who do you think you are?"

"God."

"You do." She laughed drily. "You probably think you're better than God. If you ever met Him, you'd probably tell Him to get a job."

She walked over to the kitchen table still covered with last night's dinner dishes and straddled a chair.

"You're so fucking stupid, Harley. Ashlee really likes you."

"She doesn't even know me."

"She's known you her whole life."

"I'm not talking about riding the same bus."

I heard the chair legs drag across the tile. She came up beside me again and I automatically stepped away. Her body had the power to repel mine without touching it. We were like the wrong ends of magnets.

Add chicken broth and cannellini beans, I read off Callie's recipe card. Be sure to rinse and drain beans first.

"How do you think people get to know each other?" Amber asked me, her voice sounding almost pleading. "You think God's just going to drop a woman in your lap? You're going to wake up one day and there's going to be some smart, beautiful virgin living down the road who works five jobs and has a thing for loser headcases?"

"What are cannellini beans?"

"That's probably what you're always mumbling about in your sleep," she murmured.

"What?" I said.

Her eyes darted in my direction, then she walked back to the table and started clearing it with a determination she usually reserved for channel surfing.

She clattered the two plates into the sink. Neither one of us had been home for dinner the night before. I spotted a piece of crumpled notebook paper on the top plate. It had to be Misty's. It was licked clean.

I opened up the note and showed it to Amber.

ESME SES THE BABYS WILL BE DEFEKTIV.

Amber crinkled her nose. "What is that supposed to mean?"

I shrugged.

"That little Esme gets on my nerves," Amber said, crushing the paper back up and throwing it in the garbage can under the sink. "She thinks she knows everything. She's so promiscuous."

I felt a sudden surge of big brother protectiveness when I heard her mistake. Like I wanted to kill a spider or carry a heavy box for her.

"Precocious," I corrected her.

"Right," she answered, curling her lip skeptically. "You're just telling me that so I'll use it sometime and sound stupid."

I wondered if she even remembered that she used to trust me. My mind flashed back to a time we were fighting over my crayons. I wouldn't let her have any of them, and she went and tattled to Mom. Mom said I had to give her at least one so I gave her white.

I waited for her to figure out what I had done while I silently busted a gut and applauded my evil genius. But she had walked off contentedly and sat down at her white piece of paper to draw me a picture of sugar, salt, and snow.

Outside, Elvis started barking up a storm. I heard a truck coming up the drive and from the other room Jody squealed, "It's Uncle Mike." Amber ran out of the kitchen to go put some clothes on.

Jody and Elvis were already bouncing around the truck before he put it in park. He got out, resting a case of beer against one hip, and surveyed the place. He hadn't been out since February and everything had been covered with snow then. The only thing he could find to criticize was the lack of firewood stacked next to the house. Fortunately, he never went inside.

He and Dad had been close.

He reached down and gave Elvis a scratch between the ears and handed Jody a Butterfinger. She hugged his legs and skipped back to the house. I knew Misty wouldn't put in an appearance. She didn't like Uncle Mike because one time he told Dad he should spend more time with me and less with her.

"Those for me?" I asked about the beer.

They were Rolling Rocks. Not the piss water he usually brought.

"Well, they're not for Elvis. Here, take them. You look like you're going to kiss me for Chrissakes."

I took the case from him. He spit a bullet of tobacco in the

118

yard and helped himself to one of the beers. I set the case down and opened one too.

"You get a new couch?" he asked me, looking at the carcass.

Elvis had ripped open one of the cushions and little pieces of blackened upholstery and yellow foam were spread everywhere. He had pulled off the bedspread too and dragged it to his dog-house.

"Thinking about it," I said.

"Most people wait until they get the new one before they burn the old one."

"I guess I was overeager."

He gave me a sideways glance. His eyes were hard to read hidden in shadow beneath the brim of a brown and gold PennDOT cap.

"You being smart with me?"

"No."

"That was your grandma's couch."

"That had nothing to do with my decision to burn it."

"You are being smart with me."

Dad's mom had always been a sensitive topic with the kids. There were three of them: Mike, Diane, and Dad. None of them could stand to be around her and behind her back they called her a drunk and groaned about visiting her but in person they waited on her like she was the Queen of England. When she died, they acted like they were going to crawl in the grave with her. Then the next day they were whistling and joking around while they boxed all her earthly belongings and drove them off to the nearest dump.

I never felt like I knew her well enough to form an opinion on her. She was either very nice or very mean and neither side of her personality seemed to be her real self.

Grandpa, on the other hand, was always mean. He did nothing but sit in his recliner and rant about the environmentalists in Congress who had shut down all the mines. He had already been retired before his mine closed but apparently he resented that his sons and grandsons didn't have a job waiting to kill them too.

His cough terrified me. A harsh, wheezing hack that always made me think he was going to spit up one of the black lungs his disease was named for. He kept an empty coffee can with him all the time half-filled with his tarry phlegm.

They were a pair, Dad's folks, but they were the only grandparents I ever had since Mom's folks were killed when she was a kid. She hadn't been close to the great-aunt and -uncle who took her in. She never said anything bad about them but sometimes when she talked about marrying Dad, she said he had saved her from them.

I chugged my beer, crushed the can, and dropped it on the grass. It gave me a nice buzz. I hadn't eaten anything since my popcorn with Ashlee.

"I'm sorry," I apologized to Uncle Mike. "I'm not feeling so hot today."

"Now that you mention it, you look like hell." He dropped his gaze to my shirt. "Were you gutting something?"

"I was making dinner."

"Why don't the girls do that?"

"They do. We take turns."

"You bring home the paycheck. You shouldn't have to go anywhere near a kitchen."

"They shouldn't either. They're just kids."

"Amber's not a kid. Where is she anyway? Out running around with a boy, I suppose."

"She's inside," I told him. "Scrubbing floors and doing laundry. She doesn't have much time for a social life. She's so busy helping out around the house."

"Amber?"

"Mm Hmm." I nodded over my beer can.

He finished his beer and reached for another. I had noticed

a rattle in my truck earlier I would have liked to ask him about but if he stayed to fix it, he would drink all my beer.

"When are you going to mow?"

"Today," I said emphatically.

"You're going to need to get to that soffit and fascia this year. And the trim on those windows. That wood's going to rot right off there if you don't put a fresh coat of paint on. Did you ever clean out your gutters?"

"Today," I said. "I'm going to do it today."

Amber came out of the house in a prim pale-yellow T-shirt dress sprinkled with little blue flowers and her hair pulled back in a ponytail with a ribbon. She still managed to look like a slut.

She said hi to Uncle Mike and gave him a hug. He told her she got better looking every time he saw her, and she acted like she didn't know what he was talking about, like she had never seen a mirror. I knocked off my second beer and belched.

Amber looked over at me.

"How's Mike Junior doing?" she asked Uncle Mike, slyly, and watched for my reaction.

Amber and I didn't agree on much, but we both hated our cousin Mike. I didn't know why she hated him so much but my feelings were fairly straightforward. My whole life I had been forced together with him at every family gathering, and he had used every opportunity to out-throw me, outrun me, out-eat me. He never showed up anywhere without a football trophy, or a Polaroid of his latest buck stretched out dead across the hood of his truck or his latest girlfriend stretched out drunk across a friend's couch.

"He's doing great," Uncle Mike gushed. "They're starting training already. He's raring to get back out there. He was their third leading rusher last year. He's hoping to be number one this year."

"I'm sure he will be," Amber said, smiling at me. "Mike's the best."

"He sure is," I said, reaching for another beer.

The ground came rushing at me too fast, and I thought I was falling but I kept my balance. I straightened back up and heard Uncle Mike tell Amber we should try and make it up for one of the home games this year.

"Notice how he just said try and make it up," I muttered to Amber. "It's not like he'd want us inside the stadium with them."

She started giggling.

"What's so funny?" Uncle Mike asked, smiling too.

"I was just telling Amber how much I'd enjoy that."

"Mike could show you around," he said to Amber. "You could meet some of the players."

"Maybe I could meet a cheerleader," I added.

Amber grinned at me. She reached for my beer and took a sip off it.

"Mike's dating a cheerleader," Uncle Mike volunteered.

"Really?" I said.

Amber burst out laughing, and Uncle Mike's smile faded.

"Well, I guess I'll leave you two to your private joke," he said.

"We're sorry," I said.

"No, it's all right," he replied angrily. "I'm used to it. A lot of people are jealous of Mike's success. The only way they can handle it is to make fun of him."

"Is that why they do it?" I whispered to Amber.

She collapsed against my arm, laughing.

"Okay. All right." He shook his head and backed away. "I guess I'll be going. I was only trying to help out a little."

"As little as possible," I whispered to Amber again, and we both started howling.

Uncle Mike got in his truck and slammed the door. The sound cut through my drunken fog and made me realize what I had done.

"Hey, we're sorry, Uncle Mike," I called out, running over to his truck.

He started backing out.

"Really. We're sorry. We're just kidding around."

He raised his hand in a wave and shook his head at me disappointedly.

Uncle Mike had been the only person at Dad's funeral who spent any time with me one-on-one. He took me for a walk after the burial, with his arm around my shoulders, the two of us strangers to ourselves and each other in our dark suits and stiff shoes with our heads bare and the dirt missing from beneath our fingernails.

He led me silently down row after row of polished headstones. Every once in a while, I'd notice a small flat gray stone engraved with the word BABY. I couldn't figure out what they were supposed to mean. I thought parents always picked out a baby's name before it was born, so how could a baby die nameless? The only answer I could come up with was after the baby died, the parents took the name back because they didn't want to waste it.

Even my dad being lowered into the ground didn't seem as big a betrayal as that. I imagined all these dead babies without names going up to heaven and being put in a big holding pen like livestock before slaughter while the angels tried to figure out who they were supposed to have been.

Suddenly, I couldn't handle all the injustices in life and how a lot of them didn't even seem to end with death.

I started shouting, in short explosive bursts, about what a joke Dad's funeral had been. How he had lived here his whole life and knew a ton of people, but hardly anybody showed up.

Uncle Mike waited for me to get it out of my system. For me to kick a tombstone and hurt my foot because I was wearing shoes instead of my steel-toed work boots. For me to finally start crying and for me to finally stop crying.

I eventually took a seat with my back up against a big speckled gray slab. Uncle Mike's voice came to me from above and behind.

"From the moment people heard, they made a choice," he instructed me. "You and your sisters are either the children of a murdered man or the children of a murderer. If you're one you deserve sympathy. If you're the other you deserve hatred. But you can't be both because people can't feel both."

I let his words sink in while I thought about how Mom had asked Uncle Mike to buy Dad a new suit to be buried in even though we couldn't afford it, and how Uncle Mike had done it but then the funeral was closed casket. I thought about how Mom had sent a condolence card from her prison cell to Aunt Diane. I thought about how even now—after seeing my dad in the ground and seeing my mom in handcuffs—I still couldn't shake the feeling that he was the criminal and she was the victim.

"Awkwardness kept them away today, and it's going to keep them away tomorrow," Uncle Mike finished before he walked off. "You better get used to it."

I stayed there until Aunt Jan finally came looking for me talking about the glaze hardening on a baked ham and the perils of spoiled potato salad. I wasn't sure which revelation had stunned me more: the fact that something as trivial as awkwardness could destroy something as powerful as decency, or the fact that Uncle Mike had been the guy who figured it out.

I waited until his truck disappeared, then I started pitching rocks at the empty dust cloud.

"Who needs him?" Amber said.

"He was my beer connection," I moaned, and lay down in the middle of the dirt.

"Maybe Betty could start getting it for you," Amber suggested.

That one killed me. I lay on the ground and laughed until every muscle in my gut hurt. I had tears in my eyes when I looked up and saw Misty standing over me, wearing oven mitts, and holding a smoking, black-bottomed pot. She dropped it.

"What the fuck?" I cried, rolling away just in time to keep it from hitting me square in the forehead.

"I'm not washing that," she said, and went back inside.

The girls had frozen pizza for dinner. Around my sixth beer I started feeling antisocial and decided I didn't want to eat with them. I took two more beers, a bag of chips, and Elvis, and went off down the road.

My plan was to hike to the railroad tracks and follow them to California like Skip and I used to fantasize about, but I had to stop about a quarter-mile down Potshot to take a leak. While I did, I stared into the black woods and they stared back.

Even drunk in the dark, I could find my way around them. They were my woods. I didn't own them but they belonged to me because I had taken the time to get to know them. Ownership was about power. Belonging was submission. I wasn't even sure who owned this land along the road. For all I knew, Callie Mercer did.

I wasn't going to be able to pay the real estate taxes this year. They were due the first week of June, and I had nothing saved. If the bank took my house, I wondered if Callie would let me live on her hills. I could be one of those wild-eyed mountain hermits with mice nesting in my beard. I could pull down some of the boards from the mining office and build a lean-to in her clearing. I could hunt and fish and season my kill with sage stolen from her garden. One moonlit summer night she might appear with her book and her beer and her blanket and her mood swings.

The effort of pissing away a six-pack tired me out. I whistled for Elvis and staggered back up the hill. He came tearing over to me as I sat down next to my truck and gave me a couple rowdy licks on the face. I grabbed him by the ruff of his neck and pushed him to the ground. He let me lie on his softly thudding chest for about ten seconds before he jerked up with his big paws flailing. But it had been enough comfort to put me to sleep.

I woke up a couple hours later cold and damp; my mind numb and blank. I didn't dream anymore. I had told Betty this and she said I just wasn't remembering any of them, but she was wrong.

I was sure something had been breathing in my ear but it turned out to be my own hair blowing against it. A breeze had kicked up. The air was heavy with an incoming storm. Across the yard the night grass shivered in ripples of silver and black.

It took me two tries to find my feet. I steadied myself against my truck with one hand and inched my way around it.

Elvis was at the side of the house, growling and shaking a limp gray body so hard it kept smacking him in his own head. I had to kick him to get him to drop it.

I knelt down over the torn, bloody body. It was a groundhog. A baby one.

"Git!" I hissed at him.

He jumped away like he'd been kicked again and sat down a couple paces away from me.

I went to the shed, casting glances over my shoulder, and pausing every couple steps to make threatening lunges back in his direction. The shovel was right inside the door, but he was at the body again by the time I found it. I chained him up.

I buried what was left of the groundhog near the tree line. After I was done, I stabbed a stick in his grave and slipped an upside-down beer can over it. I named him Rocky.

Elvis strained at the end of his chain and gave me a final hopeful bark as I walked past him to the porch. I ignored him. He looked first at me, then at the grave, then stretched and lay down in the dirt with the calm surrender of a creature who knows he will eventually be set free.

I only made it as far as the living room. The sight of a floor covered in pillows was too tempting. It called to me like a lake on a scorching hot day. I held my arms out to my sides and fell into them, face first, and drifted down to the bottom.

I woke up to the sound of breathing again. This time I was sure it was Mom. She had fallen asleep with me in my race-car bed, her arms wrapped around me and her hands clamped together like a padlock.

Then I was sure it was Jody back in the red Jell-O days. She used to have nightmares and Amber and I took turns lying with her while she tossed and turned and mumbled and wrung Sparkle Three-Horn like a wet washcloth. When she finally calmed down and fell into a deep sleep, I always did too even though I knew she was going to pee the bed.

Then I relaxed into the certainty that it was Amber. She had crawled into my bed again, sleeping behind me with her body pressed against my back and her arms and legs wrapped around me. Most nights I hated it but some nights I gave in and let the warmth and weight and smell and softness of her overwhelm me. I belonged to someone.

I took her hand and pulled her tighter against me. Her breath tickled my neck.

"Harley," she whispered.

We were alone beneath my covers. We were alone beneath our card table fort listening to gunshots.

"Harley. Are you okay?"

"Huh?"

"Harley. Wake up."

I was still on my stomach. I hadn't moved a muscle from when I fell into the pillows. My eyes flew open and I lay perfectly still as reality sank in. I wasn't a kid anymore.

Amber squeezed my hand and leaned over to see if I was awake. Her hair brushed my face like a spray of perfume.

"It's not such a big deal what happened with Ashlee," she whispered in my ear. "You could have talked to me about it instead of getting shitfaced."

I rolled away from her and sat up. The motion made my head spin.

"Were you afraid? Is that it?" she asked.

"Huh?" I said, groggily.

"I was afraid my first time," she told me. "That's why I picked out Ashlee for you. I wanted you to be with someone who loves you. So she could help you."

My eyes began to make her out in the dark. She knelt next to me in a stretch lace chemise. Victoria's Secret had done wonders for my female undergarment vocabulary.

"Help me how?" I asked in a croak.

"I don't know," she said quietly, "but that's what I always feel like I'm looking for when I fuck someone. Help."

I couldn't make out the expression on her face but I could make out the lace pattern against her skin and the absence of anything beneath it.

I started backing away from her in a crab crawl and bumped into a wall.

"What's wrong?" she asked, and started toward me.

"Don't," I suddenly shouted.

"Don't what?"

"Stay there."

I got to my feet and held out my hands, praying for the power of a crossing guard.

"Are you freaking out again?" she asked.

She started to stand, and I dropped my head and squeezed my eyes shut.

"Jody told me what happened when you saw Mom."

Great. Just great. I laughed out loud. A dinosaur and a Happy Meal. Ten bucks. Ten wasted bucks. Twenty wasted bucks on Ashlee.

"Why don't you ever tell me anything?" She kept at me. "You could've told me that. I wouldn't have made fun of you."

She was coming. Getting closer and closer. I could feel her even though I couldn't see her.

"You were afraid of her. Weren't you? You were afraid to touch her," she said in a trembling voice. "You can touch me."

She took one of my hands in both of hers and started to raise it. Then she stopped suddenly, blocked by her own intentions.

I opened my eyes. She stared back at me without seeing, her jaw lifted in defiance but her face tranquil.

I ripped my hand out of hers. I whirled around and stumbled over my feet trying to get away.

"What's wrong?" she said, frantically. "What are you doing?"

I didn't waste time trying to stand. I scrambled across the floor on my hands and knees.

"You prick," I heard her say. "You bastard. You fucker. You son of a bitch," she chanted like a teacher calling roll.

"You prick," she said again, coming up behind me.

Anger had returned to her voice. Once she was completely hidden behind it, I could usually be fooled into facing her again.

"You're supposed to take care of me too."

An unseen force yanked me to my feet, but it pushed me too fast. It was dark. I ran into a wall but I kept my balance. Amber's breath seared my neck.

"What about me?" she screamed.

The front door was a dream door: an arm's length away but impossible to reach. I gathered all my strength but it was more than I needed. The momentum threw me outside. I tripped down the porch steps and hit the ground face first. White light burst in front of my eyes and the salty-sweet taste of blood filled my mouth.

Amber came out on the porch crying harsh, bitter sobs.

I raised up on all fours. Beneath me was a round gray rock jutting from the grass like a wart. Tiny black splashes of blood hit it with a steady raindrop rhythm. A sticky warmth crawled down my chin.

"I don't love any of them," she screamed at me. "I hate all of them. I want you to know that. I want you to think about it all the time."

I staggered to my feet and took off at a run. Behind me in the dark front window, I saw a sparkle. Mom's sheers danced and it was gone.

I didn't slow my pace until I came to Black Lick Road. I walked down the very middle knowing if someone came around a blind curve at this hour they would have no choice but to kill me.

My lungs burned. My face throbbed. I checked my mouth with two fingers to make sure I still had all my teeth and found a dent on my bottom lip where the skin had been parted. I wiped my fingers on my jeans and left a long dark smear.

There was no light to guide me or lead me. I looked up at the black sky patched with cast-iron storm clouds. The moon was distant and milky gray like an old man's sightless eye.

I kept walking. I didn't know where I was going but I knew what I was leaving and that was enough motivation. When a house materialized out of the gloom, my first thought was to pass it by but instinct pulled me toward it. Not to use as a form of refuge but to use as a target for my building rage.

I stopped and filled my hands with roadside gravel. Dogs started barking, ruining my plan for a sneak attack on the house, but I was already halfway down the driveway so I started whipping rocks at them instead.

An outdoor light went on. The dogs barked louder. I threw harder. A door opened and Callie Mercer peered out.

"What . . .?" she started to say.

She stepped outside barefoot and bare-legged in a short white nightshirt that said WORLD'S GREATEST MOM.

"Harley, is that you? My God, what happened to your face?"

I looked down at the rocks still waiting in my hands and I wondered for a moment, Was it me? She started across the driveway, not feeling the sharp stones beneath her feet. I searched the horizon for an escape route, over the dark sloping yard, past the onyx glint of the pond, through the wall of hills, to a fierce black line with no end in sight.

I dropped the rocks and started running again, slipping on the dew-slick grass and swearing at the pain that flared from my lip each time my foot connected with the ground. When I got to the creek, I stopped. It was only five feet across but it stretched out before me as wide as any river.

My knees buckled and I collapsed on the muddy bank, beaten.

I was lying on my side staring at the rustling water when I heard her heavy breathing and the crack of a branch. She got down in front of me on her knees and put her arms around me. I thought about resisting out of pride but I couldn't remember if I had any.

"I'm not going back there," I said, and started to cry.

I circled her waist with my hands and buried my face in her lap.

"You don't have to," she said quietly, and held my head against her. "I never understood how you could stand to stay there in the first place."

She didn't make me feel better. I felt worse. I sobbed harder. Hoarse, ugly sounds like my grandpa's cough.

"It's okay," she said.

"It's not okay. It's not ever going to be okay."

"Not so hard, Harley. Don't hold me so hard."

I moaned.

"Shh," she murmured.

I clutched her tighter, rubbing my face all over her like a blind pup. My cheek brushed across her nipples, and she took in a sharp breath. They felt too hard to be part of the rest of her.

"You're right," she said, her voice catching in her throat. "It's not okay. I can't make it okay. Do you understand that?"

I slipped my hands down over her hips, along her legs, up under her nightshirt. She was naked. The feel of her made me lose my mind. I couldn't tell what parts I was touching and I didn't care. They were all the same. They were her.

I pushed her down in the mud. I kissed her belly with my torn lips. I kissed her thighs. I kissed her everywhere. That's all I wanted to do. Kiss her. I kissed her breasts. Her nipples weren't hard at all. I felt like I could crush them with my lips. I tried and she cried out, and I jerked back, panting. She was smeared with my blood.

"It's all right," she said.

She reached beneath my shirt. Her fingers stroked my stomach and chest, then slid into the waistband of my jeans.

I made some kind of noise, a cross between a war whoop and a death rattle. She didn't seem to understand that in about thirty seconds, I was either going to come or throw up.

"I can't—" I groaned.

"What?"

"Wait," I finished. "I can't wait."

She pulled her hand out and rushed to undo the button on my jeans and unzip my fly. I just watched. I was way past handling small manipulative skills.

I wasn't afraid at first. I wasn't afraid when I pushed inside her and felt my mind, body, and soul twist themselves into one raw nerve. I wasn't afraid when she gasped and called out to God and I realized there were two people having sex here, not just me. I wasn't even afraid when I realized I wasn't going to last long enough to bring her anything but frustration.

The fear came when I realized my dad had been wrong. It was worth a lifetime of driving a cement truck.

It was worth a lifetime.

The end neared and my hands started trembling so hard I couldn't hold onto her anymore. All my efforts to bring her to me were like grappling for a handhold in crumbling earth. I gave up and let go and let her hold onto me. I came with my fists clenched above her.

chapter (9)

When I opened my eyes again, I felt like I had been asleep for a hundred years. I was so sure of it, I was afraid to look around. I thought I might find an alien world without trees and grass, where the houses were built in the sky and shiny silver people flew around with jet packs on their backs.

I didn't want to look at my body either. I didn't want to see a gray sunken chest and a withered old pecker. I didn't want to see Bud's brown-spotted hands or Betty's white thighs with inky veins like windshield cracks.

I remembered my grandpa on his deathbed hooked up to a respirator cursing environmentalists. His skin had lost all its color by then, paling until I could see every pearl-blue vein beneath its surface. All I could think of was worms and how he looked like he was already being eaten by them from the inside out.

The last time we visited him in the hospital before he died, Dad told him he was looking better. I remembered glancing over at the two of them, wondering if they were seeing something I couldn't see. Grandpa had nodded and his bony hand, sprouting with tubes, had jerked up like he meant to touch Dad but before he could, it fell crumpled onto the sheet like a bird shot from the sky. Dad explained later it had been a muscle spasm.

They didn't talk after that. Dad sat in the chair next to him unable or unwilling to look anywhere but out the window.

I started getting mad at him. This was his big chance to pour out his soul without being afraid or embarrassed because Grandpa was dying and couldn't hold anything over him anymore. I knew they had a lot to talk about because they never did. They communicated solely through pace and posture.

I knew Grandpa still hit Dad and that had to bother him. If a kid outgrew his dad's piggyback rides, it seemed only fair he should outgrow his punches too. But I had witnessed it. I saw Grandpa cuff him once out in his backyard. He caught him in the side of the head and Dad took a few faltering steps backward before finding his balance and shaking off the blow like an athlete shaking out a cramp in his leg.

I had been shocked more by Grandpa's nerve than what he did. Dad was bigger than him in height and weight, and in my mind they were equals since they were both adults. But Grandpa had a skinny fierceness about him and chipped eyes as black and blunt as the coal he missed mining.

While Dad had traded attitude for endurance. Except for when he was beating his kids, his personality was insignificant.

Back in the hospital room, remembering that day, I began wondering if the way Grandpa treated Dad explained a lot about the way he treated me. Maybe if Grandpa had never hit him, he would have never hit me. Maybe it was that simple. But it might not have been Grandpa's fault either. Maybe his dad had hit him.

Then I started thinking about Mom and how different her life would have been if that trucker hadn't dozed off on his way from Sheboygan to Chicago with a trailer full of bratwurst and wiped out her family. She would have never moved here. She would have never been looking for someone to save her from an old aunt and uncle who didn't want her around. She would have never screwed my dad and got pregnant.

Was that how life worked? Was that nameless, faceless trucker from my mom's past responsible for me getting smacked every night? Or was it the fault of a great-grandfather I never knew staring at me from a black and white family photo with eyes like my own? Or did I need to go back further, hundreds of years, tracing dozens of generations, back to the first guy who hit his kid, back to the first random act of God that made a child an orphan?

It got too complicated for an eight-year-old. All I knew for sure was Dad blew his chance to work things out with Grandpa.

It wasn't fair he got the chance and I didn't. I wouldn't have wasted it. If I had known Mom was going to kill Dad that night as I went off to Skip's house to drink contraband beers and bull-shit about horny college chicks, I would've stopped first and cleared some things up. I would've asked him why he didn't like me. I would've apologized for being a disappointment to him. And I would've told him I loved him—because I did—in some joyless, unsatisfying way that hurt instead of healed, but I knew it was still love.

It wasn't enough love to keep his memory alive, though. Or maybe it was the wrong kind. It hadn't even been two years yet, but I already had a hard time picturing Dad's face. I found it easier to conjure up the cast of The A-Team.

Still, sometimes I could see him and sometimes I could hear his voice. I could replay certain events like the day in the hospital with Grandpa. I could recite facts about him the way I could about certain historical figures: he supported his family, he gave excellent piggyback rides; he remembered his anniversary, kept his yard mowed, and hunted and drank with his buddies. He wasn't too smart, but he didn't need to be. He wasn't enlightened, but he didn't want to be.

But I couldn't remember his presence in my life.

A stick started digging into my back. I reached under my shoulder blade to pull it out. My arm moved slowly, heavy with sleep or old age. I started thinking about the shiny silver people again and then an episode of *The Flintstones* popped into my head, the one where Fred takes a nap at the company picnic and when he wakes up he has a white beard down to his knees and Pebbles is off marrying Arnold the paper boy. The same panic he felt suddenly rushed over me along with the certainty that I had slept through my sisters' lives.

Twenty years later and they were all still living at the top of the hill with the roof sliding off the house and the porch sagging badly to one side. The grass was three feet high, all four doghouse doors choked with goldenrod and Queen Anne's lace, the rusted frame of my old truck home to a family of possum. The couch was missing and I knew Misty had dragged it back inside, and I also knew she sat on it at night and thought about Dad.

She was the only one who had a job. I didn't know what it was but it didn't matter. She hated it the same way I hated my jobs because she knew she was worth more, but she also hated herself so there wasn't much point in trying to do better. A lousy life for a lousy person; the punishment fit the crime.

Amber was pushing forty in stretch pants and too much makeup, bitter and scared, realizing too late that most of her life would be lived after thirty, but she never was good at math. At least she didn't have a bunch of illegitimate kids running around. She had a scraped-out uterus instead, and her dreams were plagued by dead babies who always had names.

But Jody was the worst. She had returned to the red Jell-O days. I could see her, but I wasn't with her. She sat at the kitchen table, mute and useless, the little-girl gold gone from her hair, the bottoms of her feet in bloody tatters from that piece of Dad's satellite dish I never got around to ripping out of the ground.

I tried calling out to her, and I found myself in Bedrock with Fred running from one stone chapel to the next, chasing after Pebbles's doomed giggle.

I came awake with a jolt. The storm clouds had scrubbed the night clean, leaving behind a fresh black sky pinpricked with stars. Night bugs chirped, and the creek made a sound like a snake gliding through grass. The air was chilly, but my skin itched and tingled. If flesh could simmer, this was how it would feel.

My body wasn't old after all. My arms and legs weren't feeble. I felt stronger than I ever had in my life yet nothing about me seemed solid anymore. I thought of pictures I had seen as a kid of swirling galaxies and how I used to wonder what held them together; refusing to believe in gravity, wanting to believe the planets all stuck around because they knew it was where they belonged.

Something big had happened. Maybe God had come looking for me again—appearing this time in the form of Fred Flintstone since the moon was too distant tonight to supply the silver light. It looked man-made: like a small ivory button.

I turned my head to one side and saw the Virgin Mary standing naked in the creek, more beautiful than I ever imagined. She bent down and splashed water over herself, then stood again and tilted her face toward the trees, wearing her shy waiting-for-God smile.

Her lines made me ache. I watched her hands rub her arms and throat and move in circles over her stomach and breasts, and enlightenment was mine. God made them that way on purpose. Getting kicked out of the Garden of Eden and being forced to earn our bread by the sweat of our brows wasn't man's punishment. We were damned the minute God decided to make women beautiful. And women were damned for the same reason.

She finished washing and walked to the water's edge, where she stopped to pick something out of her hair. She glanced my way and I squeezed my eyes shut. It was a reflex reaction like she might possess the same powers as that mythology witch with the snakes on her head who could turn men to stone. God had turned Lot's wife into a pillar of salt. Who knew what He'd do to some guy spying on His girlfriend?

I waited to see if she'd come to me again. If I would feel her breath on my face and her fingers on my chest. If she would take my hand and lead me to a better place.

Instead I heard a very human "Shit!" and the sound of her sucking in her breath in pain. I looked over and saw her hopping around on one foot, all her grace and innocence gone; and I remembered everything. Who she was. Who I was. What we had done. What I had run away from. What she probably was running away from in order to fuck around with me. I understood perfectly that there was no way she could love me. Enlightenment sucked.

She placed her foot gently back on the ground and reached down for her nightshirt. She had her back to me and the sight of her bending over brought me to a sitting position. She probably could have brought me to a floating position if she had stayed bent over long enough but she stood up and slipped into her shirt, checked the bottom of her foot once more, and went walking off into the grass without looking back.

I wanted to yell after her, but I couldn't figure out what to call her. Mrs. Mercer? Esme's mom? She had never given me permission to call her Callie.

My heart started beating too fast. I lay down and closed my eyes again and tried to sort out what had happened. I had always thought if a guy did a good job at sex the woman was left limp and breathless, purring maybe, gazing at him with dumb animal love the way Elvis looked at me while I scratched his chest.

She had taken a bath in a freezing cold creek and left.

A terrible sinking feeling came over me as I realized I might have already blown it. I couldn't buy her nice things or take her places or provide her with witty conversation. All I could do was fuck her well. That was the only way I could keep her.

It was cold now. I would've given anything for Dad's coat. I didn't know where my shirt was, but I could feel my jeans down around my ankles. I thought about wearing them that way for the rest of my life. "You show them, Harley," Church would have said.

I started to shiver, but my crotch stayed warm and sticky. There in the dark with my eyes closed, a woman's pussy juice didn't feel all that different from blood.

Dawn was breaking when I finally started on my way up Potshot Road. The woods were noisy with birdcalls. A raccoon scurried across the road in front of me, hurrying back to his dark den with a vampire's urgent need to avoid the coming light. His thick shaggy body and delicate black hands and feet looked like they belonged on different animals, like God had been in a hurry to finish him off and just slapped on the first set of paws He could find.

I took my time walking the hill. A gray mist had settled over everything, absorbing the weak morning light, and giving the air substance. I stuck my bare arm out into it and brought it back covered in shimmer. I breathed it in deeply, letting its feather weight fill my lungs and roll over my tongue. It tasted sweet and empty like purity should.

I approached the top and slowed down even more in case deer were grazing in the clearing. The biggest flock of wild turkeys I had ever seen were spread out over the grass eating, their dark darting bodies rippling with copper glints. There must of been thirty of them. Good-sized ones too. Instinct made me pause by the tree line waiting to see if a gun was going to pop.

They didn't notice me at all. I walked past them and sat down in our front yard where I had a good view of them and the green hills dropping away behind them like folds in a blanket.

The sun had risen into a patch of clouds and turned them golden pink. Their color made me think of peaches, and how peaches would be in season soon and we'd be selling them at the Shop Rite for a dime apiece during our annual ten-cent produce sale, and Jody would be walking around, barefoot, with her face buried in one, juice dripping down her chin and wrists, and me yelling at her to go eat over the sink.

School would be out in a month, and Amber would be saddled with the girls all day long again. This summer wouldn't be as bad as last summer since Misty and Jody were more ADJUSTED now and older too.

The first school year was the worst time we had been through so far. Jody only had a half day of kindergarten and no one could watch her in the afternoon. Amber and Misty were in school. Aunt Diane taught school and had three little kids of her own. Uncle Mike's wife, Jan, never volunteered and none of us liked her anyway. We couldn't afford a sitter or day care.

For a while I dragged Jody around with me looking for a job. She was always good. That was back when she wasn't talking. She would sit quietly staring at her fingers while I filled out job applications and talked politely to guys in Dockers with sticks up their asses because they were the almighty assistant managers of shoe stores and discount warehouses. One guy asked me if I had brought along my little sister to make him feel sorry for me so he'd give me the job. After that, I made Jody wait in the truck.

My hours at Shop Rite were pretty flexible. I was able to work a lot of nights and weekends and still watch Jody, but the money wasn't enough. I had to get another job—the one at Barclay's Appliances—but I was able to sneak Jody along with me some days.

She loved playing in the warehouse behind the store, where she made caves out of the empty refrigerator boxes and hid with her dinosaurs. Whenever Ray and I had to go on a delivery, she rode with us. Ray was okay with it—not because he was a swell guy, but because he loved the idea of pulling one over on the boss. We must have violated a hundred different insurance laws having her in the truck with us, he constantly reminded me, clutching the steering wheel and grinning at me like we were driving away from a bank robbery.

Even with me taking Jody to work now and then, Amber still ended up cutting a lot of school to stay with her the days I couldn't. Eventually a truant lady came out and had a talk with us. She said it was a shame that Jody wasn't Amber's child because then we could have put her in the free day care school provided for teen mothers who could demonstrate need.

I asked her to define "need."

She said financial need: girls who couldn't afford real day care and would have to drop out of school to take care of their children instead.

I pointed out we couldn't afford real day care and Amber was probably going to end up dropping out of school to take care of Jody.

She said we couldn't participate in the program because Jody wasn't Amber's child.

I said she was my child. I had signed the papers making me the legal guardian of all my sisters. My mom had signed them too.

She said I wasn't a student anymore. I had graduated. The school couldn't do anything for me.

And I said, "So you mean if Amber did something stupid like get pregnant and have a baby, you guys would cut her a break and help her out, but we can't get any help?"

The woman had stared back at me with flattened lips and a stony look in her eyes and I could tell she wanted to say, "You don't deserve any." Those people were out there. I had encountered them before. Ones who read the newspaper stories or saw the news reports and decided to not only condemn my mom but hate her guts as well. Some of them even seemed to think we should be punished too.

I kind of flipped out a little after that. I started ranting about how teenaged girls who have babies should be expelled from school. How anyone that stupid wasn't ever going to be a productive member of society anyway. How the school shouldn't be wasting their time with day care; they should be tying down every girl in a halter top and stabbing that birth control implant under her skin. How I didn't care if it was a violation of her civil rights; the ACLU could take a flying leap.

I meant all of it too. That's what I hated most about what was happening to me. I couldn't feel sympathy anymore.

The truant lady waited patiently until I finished. My behavior didn't faze her at all. She dealt with much worse around here. At least we weren't filthy or starving or lice-infested or drunk. We weren't covered in bruises anymore either. And I wanted the girls to stay in school, and they did too.

She said she'd get back to us. Maybe Jody could be an exception. I stood at the front window and watched her walk across our yard in her wrinkled plaid skirt and gray blazer and thought about all the women I had dealt with recently wearing Wal-Mart workday separates from the Kathie Lee Collection and all the men in suits from JCPenney's.

The first couple weeks after Mom's arrest we were shuffled from one official-looking government building to the next. We talked to detectives, lawyers, shrinks, bill collectors, correctional facility personnel, undertakers, reporters, social workers, bankers. We buried Dad and said good-bye to Mom through Plexiglas.

The last place I went was Laurel Falls National Bank to talk to a guy who worked for Callie Mercer's dad about getting a break on our mortgage payments for a month or two. He said the bank would like to be able to help—like the bank could think and feel—but if they gave an extension to one customer they would have to give extensions to everyone.

I argued that maybe they could only give extensions to kids who lost both their parents unexpectedly and simultaneously and had no money and no job. That would probably limit the amount of people who would qualify.

He smiled and made a very small laugh and said yes, it probably would.

Then I asked him if maybe I could talk to the bank instead of him. Maybe the bank knew our house socially.

The guy looked at me like I was certifiable. That was right after the shooting and the whole gory mess was still fresh in everyone's mind.

I got up and walked over to the Pennsylvania Scenic Wonders calendar hanging on his office wall. The month of August was a bright red barn sitting in the bottom of a bright green valley surrounded by bright blue sky. I had lived in this southwestern corner of the Allegheny Mountains my entire life and I had never seen a barn or a day that color.

I motioned at the barn with my thumb and asked, "Any relation to the bank?"

I swore I saw him reach under his desk and press a silent alarm. He had me figured for a definite TYPE.

When I got home, all three girls were sitting on the porch waiting for the verdict. Looking at them, I had one of my flashes of enlightenment and it was this: nobody knows we are here.

I had the same thought watching the truant lady leave. She did get back to us though, and Jody was allowed to go to the school day care but I wouldn't let her. We were not going to be EXCEPTIONS.

We survived that year without anybody's help, and I was proud of us. Amber passed ninth grade. Jody started talking again. I paid our bills. At our lowest moments, I got my strength from concentrating on the anger and terror I had felt coming back from the bank when I realized we had been forgotten.

Forgotten but not alone. I knew there were a ton of kids like us out there who had gone through the same thing. Eighty percent of the women serving time for murder in Mom's prison had killed a husband or live-in boyfriend. I mentioned that statistic to Betty once. I said that really told you something about women and she said no, it told you something about men.

Watching the turkeys and the sky made me drowsy. I couldn't

remember what day it was or if I had to work but I didn't care. I had to get some sleep.

I got up from the grass and turned toward the house and froze in my tracks. Misty was on the front porch with the Ruger aimed at my head.

I screamed and dove for the ground. Thirty turkeys broke and ran for cover, gobbling and clucking.

"Why'd you do that?" Misty shouted.

"What are you doing with my gun?" I cried.

"I was going to shoot a couple turkeys."

"Jesus."

I got shakily to my feet. My forehead had broken out in a sweat. I walked over to her. "Don't ever do that," I said, taking the gun roughly from her hands.

"I figured you'd be happy about it," she said. "Free food."

She had already attacked her young freckles with two bold strokes of purple shadow like a slash-and-burn farmer.

"Why are you looking at me like that?" she asked.

"Like what?"

"Like you're surprised to see me."

"Sometimes I forget you're just a kid."

"No, I'm not," she replied. "I started my period."

"Don't tell me that." I winced.

I followed her eyes. They were looking at the rock I must have hit the night before. It had four perfectly round blood-brown spots on it.

"Don't call me a kid," she said.

I gingerly touched my lower lip. I had washed my face off in Callie's creek, but I hadn't been able to find my reflection. The lip was probably cracked and swollen. It still hurt like hell.

"I was just thinking I want you to go to college and get a good job when you grow up," I said without knowing where the thought had come from.

"College?" She laughed. "I can't even go to the Lick n' Putt."

"I just mean, I don't want you to work at Shop Rite. You can do whatever you want."

She gave me a quick dark glance. "No, I can't."

"Yes, you can."

"You have to be smart to go to college."

"No, you don't."

"You have to be rich."

"No, you don't."

"You have to be something," she persisted, in her determinedly empty voice. "I'm not anything," she added so low I had to lean over to hear it.

"That's not true," I said.

"Okay." She sighed, openly appeasing me. "You know what I am?"

"What?"

"A good shot."

I looked down at her. She looked back with a challenge in her eyes.

"That's something," I said.

"That doesn't count with anyone. Except Dad."

I didn't know what to say. Misty never talked about Dad even though we all knew his death had left a bigger hole in her life than it had in any of ours.

"It's kind of like the way you don't count with anyone except Amber," she further explained when I didn't respond.

"Huh?"

Her lips twitched into something like a smile, then went back to normal again. She turned her back on me and walked away. She was done talking. Getting her to start again would be like prying open ancient cathedral doors.

I left her there on the porch fiddling absentmindedly with her collar. She stared across the yard that had become sprinkled with small yellow flowers overnight, past the ginger-brown road and the green hump of a clearing to the blue-gray smudge of hills against a pink sky, but I knew all she saw was a failed kill.

I went straight to the basement hoping for sleep. I set my gun back in its corner and walked over to my bed, took off my clothes, and lay down. I didn't want to get under the covers, but the room was about ten degrees cooler than outside. I went and got Dad's coat off the back of my desk chair.

Skip's letter was sitting on the desk. I finally had something to write back to him about. Dear Skip. What's new with you? I nailed Mrs. Mercer.

He would have shit reading that. He wouldn't have believed me though, and I couldn't blame him. But I did. Nail her. With all my might. If she had been a board, she would have cracked down the middle.

I got an instant hard-on thinking about it. Not a nice one I could dispose of at my leisure with the ladies of Victoria's Secret. An urgent one. A maddening one like a bad itch.

I had never been good at not scratching. I used to scratch mosquito bites until they bled. Sometimes Mom would see me and blame the blood on Dad and I would let her not because I wanted her sympathy or because I wanted Dad to get in trouble but because when they figured out I had been lying, they were united in their anger toward me.

I wanted to beat off until I bled but even then I knew I wouldn't get the relief I craved. A hand wasn't going to do it for me anymore. Friction wasn't going to be enough. My dick had been enlightened too.

Peaches again. An overripe peach before it started to rot. That's what she felt like inside.

I went back to bed and stared at the white circle of my light-bulb and thought about her ass in a white T-shirt growing dimmer and dimmer in the black night as she walked away from me.

I didn't know if she had enjoyed it. I had been too preoccupied with what was in my hands and between my lips to pay much attention to her as a whole. Even if I had paid attention, I'm not sure I would have known what to look for.

I once overheard my cousin Mike talking to a buddy about his latest girlfriend. He said they had to be real careful fooling around if there was anyone else in the house because she was a screamer. The way they both grinned when he said it, I could tell they thought this was great. I supposed it was if while you were having sex with someone you wanted to think you were killing her too.

Screaming would have made me a nervous wreck. I didn't want a screamer. I didn't want someone to talk dirty either. I wanted someone who would look at me.

At least that's what I always thought. Then when I got to be with a woman, I couldn't look at her. Seeing her eyes, like saying her name, would have been unbearably human while I was pumping away at her like an animal.

I didn't know what I was going to do if it turned out she left because I wasn't good enough. I wouldn't be surprised. I wasn't good at anything. But knowing there was something wrong with you didn't make it any easier to accept even if you knew it your whole life. Fat people never grew fond of their fat. Poor people never felt good about their crappy houses.

I went ahead and jerked off anyway.

The TV was going full blast and Amber's radio was blaring when I woke up. I spent as little time as possible in the kitchen finding something to eat. There were two pieces of leftover frozen pizza sitting on the stove. I scarfed them down and grabbed the last Mountain Dew.

I slipped out the back door. The day had turned out as nice as the morning. Not too hot; not too cool. Blue sky and fluffy white clouds. Bank calendar weather.

I walked around front and surveyed the place. It wasn't a bad house as cheap little prefab vinyl-sided shitboxes went. The original house was kind of cute: gray with brick-red shutters and a front porch Dad had built for Mom as a first-anniversary present with white wooden railings and green shingles on the roof.

When Mom got pregnant with Misty, they decided to build on another bedroom. Mom had been promising me one anyway because Amber and I were getting too old to share a room, and I was too young for them to already be thinking about kicking me into the basement.

Dad and Uncle Mike and Uncle Jim decided to do it on their own. Between the three of them, they had the know-how and the tools. What they lacked was an attention span. They were like kids together. Shaking up their beer cans and squirting each other. Having belching contests. Quitting in the middle to go fishing or watch a Pirates game.

It took them two years to finish it. The first winter they covered the insulation with plastic sheeting. The next winter with fiberglass. Dad finally got a deal on some used siding he couldn't pass up. It was brown but he promised Mom he would paint the whole house the same color some day. He never did.

My folks gave me the room on my ninth birthday. Mom stretched a big red ribbon across the doorway and had me cut it with a pair of scissors like it was the grand opening of a new county dump. My bed was already in it, made up with a new set of Teenaged Mutant Ninja Turtle sheets. Dad had sacrificed the chest of drawers he used in the shed for his odds and ends crap, and Mom had fixed it up and painted it green to match the turtles. On top of it stood the pencil holder Amber had made for me out of a soup can, construction paper, and glitter.

They all stood there waiting: Dad with his hand resting on Mom's shoulder; baby Misty on Mom's hip; Amber grinning from ear to ear in her pink ballerina Halloween costume she had insisted on wearing to my birthday dinner. I could see chocolate cake crumbs caught in the tutu netting.

They were expecting me to be thrilled even though they knew I wanted a Stretch Armstrong and the Graverobber, a remote control monster truck from Radio Shack.

My eyes filled with tears. It wasn't that I didn't want the room. I did. It's that I thought the room was owed to me.

I was too stunned to speak at first, but I finally found my voice and shouted something about every kid in America getting the Graverobber for Christmas except for me, and how this was the worst birthday any kid ever had. I didn't care that I was going to get the shit kicked out of me for doing it. I tore out of the house, ran across the road, through the clearing, and into the first belt of trees.

To my surprise, Dad followed hot on my heels. He wasn't a chaser by nature. If he didn't catch you on his first couple lunges, he settled back into the camouflage of his couch like a big cat lowering himself into the high grasses of a savanna, and he waited for you to forget.

And I wasn't a runner. I always stayed and took my punishments because I liked getting them over with and because it was easier to withstand a beating when you weren't winded. This time was different though and we both knew it. I wasn't running away from Dad. I was running away from my life, and Dad was chasing me because I had felt the need to.

I did a good job of staying ahead of him until I suddenly conveniently tripped over my own feet like some idiot in a horror film. Dad caught me easily by the arm and threw a roundhouse punch which missed my face but hit me square in the chest and knocked me on my butt. I landed on a bed of black lick: what the natural salt licks are called around here because they're tainted black by the coal in the ground.

I looked down and saw the dark salt showing through in a big patch like a dried-up scab on the hillside. I used to wonder if the black licks were safe for the deer since there was so much coal in them. I used to feel sorry for them because they were dumb animals until I came to realize instinct would always drag them back even if they were smart enough to understand that what they were doing was slowly killing them.

Dad pulled me up and hit me once more. I knew he was going to have to do it. I knew he needed to hit me in the face successfully before he could relax since that had been his original intention. I didn't take it personally. I wasn't his son or even a person at that point; I was a task.

Then he grabbed me by the arm and escorted me home. He opened the door of the truck and pushed me inside. I sat perfectly still except for the violent shaking going on inside me.

Mom came out on the porch and started screaming at him. They yelled back and forth for a couple minutes. None of it was about me. Mom went on about how hard she had worked on my dresser, and Dad shouted back that he was the one who built the whole fucking room and if she wanted to live in a goddamned palace she should have never married him in the first place. Then Mom started screaming about how the ice cream was melting and the cake was drying out.

Amber was hiding somewhere because she didn't have any courage left, but she would crawl into bed with me that night to make up for it. I didn't like it when she slept with me because Dad had hit her, but I didn't mind it when it was because Dad had hit me.

Dad ended his side of the argument suddenly and slammed into the truck. Mom looked scared as we drove away. I remembered calmly thinking, Dad's going to drive me down a back road and kill me and bury me in the woods. The idea didn't shock me, and the fact that it didn't depressed me even more than my shitty birthday or the thought of dying.

He didn't say a word during the drive. He didn't seem to notice his surroundings at all until we rounded a bend in the road and off to one side was a small city of rust-streaked, iron-gray buildings standing grim and empty in the middle of ten contaminated acres. A chain-link fence ran for a mile along the road posted with bright orange HAZARD signs and bright yellow NO TRESPASSING signs, all of them shot full of bullet holes.

"The Carbonville Mine Water Reclamation Plant," he announced, his voice making me jump after the silence.

I knew about it, of course. Everybody did. It had been designed to treat the acid mine water coming from the abandoned #9 J&P complex nearby and make it safe for human consumption again. I knew all about #9 too. It was the first mine Grandpa worked in and he brought it up a lot, talking about its tunnels like they belonged to a woman.

The plant only served its original purpose for about a year before something went wrong and the DER shut it down, but its remains had lived on for another twenty-five as a monument to the folly of trying to clean up a region that was poisoned from the inside.

Dad pulled the truck off the road and parked by the fence. He got out and started walking. I automatically followed.

He stopped when we came within view of a couple dozen small, gray, Insul-brick houses scattered along the outside of the chain-link like the plant had shook and showered its perimeter with tiny replicas of failure.

Dad squatted down so he was lower than me and pointed at one or all of them.

"That's where I grew up," he said.

I glanced at him to make sure he was being serious. I had always assumed he grew up in the house where my grandparents lived now. It wasn't anything to get excited about, but at least it was a decent size and completely nailed together.

I couldn't read his expression at first. I expected him to be torn up or pissed. Or he could have been happy: one of those ass-backwards people like Grandpa who only felt fondness for terrible places and bitched like hell if he had to go on a picnic. But I didn't see bitterness or self-pity or some warped nostalgic wistfulness in his face. What I saw was something like pride but pride without ego, something like acceptance but acceptance without ever being allowed to consider any other options. I didn't figure it out until I was back home lying on my sore butt on my new sheets in my new room, feeling the familiar ache spread through my chest and face where Dad had hit me, that what I had seen was a gracious loser.

That was the year birthdays stopped being about cake and presents for me and started being about survival.

Dad started another addition about four years ago after he got it into his head that he needed his own TV room away from us kids. He and Uncle Mike never finished that one at all. Eventually they built a new wall to replace the one they had ripped out and left the wood frame hanging off the side of the house and a couple rolls of pink insulation in the yard. I pulled the thing down about a month after Mom shot him and sold the lumber.

Uncle Mike was right. The eaves and the trim needed painting. The wood around the windows was starting to rot. I noticed two shingles missing from the roof. Even from the ground, I could see clumps of wet leaves sticking out of the gutters. And I had to do something about that piece of pipe.

I saw Jody sitting on the front porch steps writing in her notebook. Sparkle Three-Horn and Yellowie the yellow helmet-head I had bought her to keep her mouth shut sat on either side of her. She looked up at me looking at the house.

"What are you doing?" she asked me.

"Making a list," I said. "What are you doing?"

"I'm making a list," she answered emphatically. "You don't have any paper."

"I'm making one in my head," I explained. "Can I see yours?"

She held it out to me.

Tawni O'Dell

FEED DINUSORS

CLEEN MY SIDE OF ROOM

FOLD LONDREE

MOE YARD

I gave it back to her smiling. "I went to school with a Moe Yard," I said.

"What?"

"Never mind. It was a joke."

"'Fangs a lot' was a better one," she said.

"I agree." I sat down next to her on the steps.

"What happened to your lip? It's all puffy."

"Nothing." I brushed her off. "Since when do you mow the yard?" I asked.

She drew a heart on her list. "Last night Amber told us you were upset because Uncle Mike said you need to mow the yard and do a bunch of other stuff and that's why you drank beers and went for a walk with Elvis. I thought I could help out." She paused and drew a couple more hearts. "Why do you and Amber fight all the time?"

"You heard us fighting?"

She nodded.

"What did you hear?"

"Amber screaming swear words mostly."

"Yeah, well," I started. "Just ignore that stuff."

"I guess it's not so bad," she said. "Esme says it's unhealthy to bottle up emotions. She says it's good to get your feelings out in the open."

"Is there anything Esme Mercer doesn't know?"

"She doesn't know who Confucius is."

"Confucius?" I gave her a look out of the corner of my eye. "You know who he is?"

"He's the guy who writes the fortunes," she answered, nodding.

I laughed. "Who told you that?"

"Mommy."

I swallowed my smile. She watched me patiently, waiting to see if I was going to dispute Mom's facts. I flaked a couple pieces of paint off the step with a fingernail.

"Esme says her mom and dad fight all the time," Jody went on, "and when she asks her mom about it, her mom tells her it's better for parents to fight than keep it bottled up."

"Her parents fight a lot?" I asked.

"I guess so. Her mom screams at her and Zack too and then she hugs them and cries and says she's sorry. I've seen her do it." She glanced up at me to make sure I was paying attention. "Esme's mom is nice and pretty and she can still do cartwheels but . . ."

"You've seen her do a cartwheel?" I interrupted.

"Yeah."

She kept studying my face. I tried to keep it composed.

"She'd do one for you I bet," she said.

"That's okay."

"Anyway," she went on, hunching up her little shoulders beneath her faded rodeo Minnie Mouse shirt. "I think she's nuts."

"She's not nuts," I explained. "All parents have to yell at their kids sometimes."

"Why?"

"'Cause they do bad things and 'cause they drive them crazy."

"Do we drive you crazy?"

"Yeah."

"You hardly ever yell at us."

"I'm one of those unhealthy people."

"Oh. So why does she cry and say she's sorry later?" she asked.

"She probably feels bad because she loves her kids and doesn't like yelling at them so she apologizes."

"Daddy never apologized to us for hitting us. Does that mean he didn't love us?"

155

"Dad loved us."

"Mommy never apologized for shooting him."

"Jody," I said quickly, and stood up to leave. "I got a lot of work to do today."

"Does Mommy love us?"

I closed my eyes wishing with all my might that she'd disappear along with the house and the guilty joy I felt knowing Esme's parents fought all the time.

"Doesn't Mom tell you she loves you every time you see her?" I asked her slowly.

"Actions speak louder than words," she announced. "I read that in one of my fortunes. I can go get it for you."

"No," I said. "I believe you."

I walked away from her and our conversation and felt instant relief. Two years ago before I knew any better, if someone had given me a list of all the things I was going to have to do for Jody and asked me to pick the hardest one, I probably would have picked "Clean up her puke when she gets sick in the middle of the night." If they had asked me to pick the most important one, I would have picked "Put food on the table." Now I would answer both of them the same way: Talk to her.

I headed for Dad's shed, trying to decide if I wanted to mow or scrape first, when I noticed Elvis off to the side of the yard with something clamped in his jaws, shaking his head wildly from side to side.

One of the girls had unchained him.

I ran across the yard to Rocky's grave but before I even got there, I saw the empty hole.

"Shit," I said, and took off after Elvis.

He saw me coming and thought we were playing a game. He went tearing into the woods. I gave him a good chase, but I had to stop and catch my breath after a while.

I sat down and leaned back against a tree trunk. Elvis suddenly burst from the undergrowth in front of me, his tail wagging, wondering why I had given up so soon. Something dangled from his mouth but it wasn't a groundhog. Up close, it looked like a crusty old rag.

"Come here, stupid," I said, and made a soft whistle between my teeth. "You're not in trouble."

He watched me skeptically for a moment, the tail stopping in mid-wag.

"Come here," I said again.

He made one more playful lunge. When I didn't respond, he came trotting over and shoved his face in mine. He dropped the rag in my lap and gave me a couple licks.

I picked the thing up. It wasn't a rag. It was a girl's shirt: a red one with a big sunflower in the middle, covered with a big brown stain, stiff and mud-encrusted like it had been out here for a long time.

I scraped off some of the dirt and smoothed it out a little. It looked familiar, but it looked too big to be Jody's and too small to be Misty's. The stain was huge. It could have been chocolate or paint, but I knew blood when I saw it.

chapter 10

I waited a couple of days before asking anyone about the shirt. I didn't know why. There wasn't anything terrible about me finding a little girl's bloodstained shirt in the woods as long as I didn't find a bloodstained little girl too.

I asked Jody about it first since she wouldn't ask me why I was asking. She told me she never had a sunflower shirt, but she used to have a pair of pink overalls with daisies on them.

I asked Amber next. She did most of the laundry and all of the patching, mending, hemming, and unhemming. A lot of Misty's and Jody's clothes were hand-me-downs from her, and she never forgot an outfit and how it made someone look. Too fat. Too geeky. Too seventies. Too eighties. Too obvious.

The moment I mentioned a sunflower shirt, she perked up. Things had been pretty tense between us since Saturday night. We hadn't talked much, but clothing was a topic she couldn't resist.

Of course we had a sunflower shirt, she told me. How could I forget it? It was hers. It came with red-and-white checked bike shorts. She never wore it much. Too hillbilly. But she gave it to Misty, and Misty wore it for a while. Not the shorts. She thought they made her look fat.

Come to think of it, she hadn't seen that shirt in years. Misty would have outgrown it by now, but Jody might want it. Did I know where it was? What did I care about a sunflower shirt anyway?

I started to tell her the truth—that Elvis had dug it up in the woods and it had blood all over it—but I changed my mind. Amber didn't deal well with blood. She used to faint at nosebleeds. I told her I had a dream about it instead.

She narrowed her eyes at me in disgust, but she bought the explanation. It was easy to accept coming from her brother the loser headcase.

My next step should have been talking to Misty, but I never got around to it.

The shirt bothered me though. I wasn't sure why. During Amber's Wednesday night dinner, I finally came up with an explanation. A bunch of Misty's sloppy joe fell out of the bun and got all over her shirt. Amber freaked and started ranting about how hard it was to get greasy ketchup out of clothes and how Misty couldn't afford to ruin a perfectly good shirt because God only knew when she'd be able to get any new clothes. She sounded just like Mom except Mom would have said it calmly.

Dad would have smacked her. Not hard. He never smacked hard in front of Mom or at the dinner table. He would have reached out and cuffed her on the side of the head just enough to make her teeth click together and her ears ring for a second or two.

I remembered Dad popping her in the mouth once, and Misty watching silently as penny-sized drops of black blood fell from her split lip and soaked into her new jeans. She hid those jeans from Mom to protect him. She threw them in the garbage can, not the best of hiding places but she was only five or six. Mom found them, of course, and she and Dad had a big fight.

Misty had probably hidden the sunflower shirt too. The explanation made sense, but it gave me the creeps thinking about what he must have done to her to make her bleed that much.

Betty would have told me to ask her. She would have told me to ask Jody what she saw the night Mom shot Dad and to ask Amber why she hated me so much. She would have told me to drive over to Callie Mercer's house and burst in on the amazing dinner she'd be serving to her banker husband and her perfect kids on her glasstopped table on her polished stone floor and ask her why she fucked me. She was always telling me to ask Mom why she did it.

I could never have CLOSURE until I got the answers.

All week long I worked eight-hour days at Barclay's, came home, asked if I got any phone calls, ate dinner, scraped trim for a half hour, asked if I got any phone calls, drove to Shop Rite, worked till midnight, came home, and woke Jody to see if I got any phone calls.

I told myself I wasn't being unreasonable. Callie could've called me if she wanted to. We knew each other. We were neighbors. Our kids played together. They rode the same bus. There were all sorts of excuses she could make. She could have come up to the house with another book or a recipe.

I wasn't completely without an ego though. Once I got through the first five or six hours Saturday and I hadn't heard from her, I started to worry maybe someone or something was keeping her from me. Maybe her husband had found out. Maybe their house had burned down. Maybe she had hit her head and had amnesia. Maybe there had been a family emergency. Maybe she had been attacked by a rabid skunk.

But as the week dragged on, I knew none of those things had happened because I questioned Jody every night at dinner and found out that Esme's mom put Esme on the bus every morning and met her at the bus every afternoon, and she looked happy and healthy.

I did my best to get Jody to go play at Esme's house or invite Esme to ours but for the first time in the history of their friendship, Esme was booked solid for a whole week. She had a dentist appointment on Monday, her dance class on Tuesday, a Brownie meeting on Wednesday, and plans to play at Cruz Battalini's house on Thursday.

I finally decided Callie Mercer thought I was a joke.

I couldn't sleep at all Thursday night. I gave up and went upstairs around 5 A.M. and sat at the kitchen table, staring at the phone. I knew she would still be asleep. I closed my eyes and made myself dizzy thinking about her stretched out naked in bed and me lying beside her. I knew what she felt like now. That was the worst part. Even if I could get her out of my mind, I couldn't get her off my fingers.

I sat there for about an hour, until I heard the girls opening and closing dresser drawers and the bathroom sink running. I went out the back door with Elvis at my heels and started walking.

I stayed on Potshot Road for a while, then turned off into the woods. The morning was cool and misty and the woods were thick with wet spring undergrowth. Briars tore at my jeans and low branches swatted at my face, but I still went at a pretty good pace.

It took me longer than I thought to cover the three miles to the Mercer house. I came out on the bank across the road just as Brad Mercer's Jeep pulled out of their driveway.

The bank was a steep one. More of a hill. Elvis and I took a seat on the damp ground back in the trees. We were about twenty feet above the road with a good view of the back of the Mercer house and their driveway curving around to the front. The bus stopped at the end of it to pick up Esme before going on to pick up Jody at the bottom of our road.

I waited and watched, holding tightly to Elvis's collar so he couldn't bolt and give away our position.

Esme came down the drive first, slipping her arms into her backpack. Zack ran after her, clutching a juice box in one hand.

Callie came next, walking slowly so she could sip at the steaming mug of coffee she had cupped in both hands. She was wearing shorts even though it was still chilly, and she had on a big gray sweatshirt. She called out to the kids to stay away from the road. I heard her voice clear as a bell.

She didn't look or act any different. Esme lectured her about something and she shook her head at her. She smiled at Zack when he brought her a handful of gravel. She turned her back on them for a moment and looked at her hills while she drank her coffee.

The bus came rumbling up the road and groaned to a stop below me, temporarily blocking my view. When it pulled away again, Esme was gone and Callie and Zack were waving.

She reached down a hand for Zack. He took it and they walked back down the drive.

I stood up. My jeans were soaked from sitting on the ground for so long and from tromping through the wet woods. I stared at her, willing her to turn around and see me, to look at me with pity or ridicule or indifference but to at least look at me. I was beginning to think I had imagined everything.

I ended up getting to Barclay's an hour and a half late and got chewed out royally for it. I had to stay and work an extra hour to make up for it so I didn't have time to drive home for dinner. Friday night was Jody's other night: scrambled eggs and Bac-O's.

I got to Shop Rite starving and dead tired. I bought two Milky Ways and popped a couple of NoDoz tablets from the box I had ripped off the other night. It was the first thing I had ever stolen. I was planning on buying them until I saw the price.

Rick was usually long gone by the time my shift started, but tonight I saw his fat face behind the glass of his manager's cubicle. He always stayed inside when he talked to one of us. Up there no one could tell he was short and fat and useless. He was an all-powerful head like the Wizard of Oz.

He motioned me over. I was sure he had found out about the pills, and he was going to fire me.

I didn't get upset. I felt kind of relieved. We couldn't survive on the shit wages I made at Barclay's. I wouldn't be able to get another job because Rick would tell everyone I was a shoplifter. We would have to go on welfare. I could sit back and let the government take care of us. Or the girls would go to foster homes and I would only have to take care of myself.

"I had a complaint about you," he said, without looking up from the papers he was pointlessly shuffling.

Here it comes, I thought.

As soon as the girls found homes, I was going to hit the road with Elvis. We could go anywhere. I'd start by visiting Skip. Then maybe my cousin Mike. That would be worth it just to see the look on his face when I showed up at his jock fraternity.

"A customer complained you packed a hair care product in the same bag with produce."

"Huh?"

"You heard me. And you didn't put it in a separate plastic bag before you put it in a regular bag."

"Am I fired?" I said.

"Christ, Altmyer. Could you be any stupider?" He sneered. "No, you're not fired. Just don't do it again. And one other thing." He stopped me before I could walk away. "There's some shelving sitting on the left-hand side when you walk in the storeroom door. I want you to set it up at the end of the cereal aisle and stock it with bananas."

"Bananas?"

He blew out his nose in annoyance. "Some people want bananas to go with their cereal and this way they don't have to walk the whole way to Produce if that's the only item from Produce they want. Or maybe they weren't planning on buying bananas at all but seeing them next to the cereal reminds them they like them sliced up on their cornflakes. So they buy them. Understand?"

"Should I set up a shelf of celery next to the peanut butter too?"

He gave me a flat stare. "They do it at the Bi-Lo and they sell a lot of bananas."

"Okay," I said.

I walked back to the cashiers. Church was busy bagging and talking to a woman about the superiority of Heinz pickles over Claussen. Not only were they cheaper but you didn't have to rush them home to the refrigerator. You could put them in a cupboard and keep them there for months. He knew because his mom did it all the time. They had jars of pickles in their cupboards from last Thanksgiving. He wasn't kidding.

When I passed by him, he fixed me with a serious look.

"Something wrong, Church?"

"What did the boss want?" he asked.

"He wants me to put bananas in the cereal aisle."

Before the words were out of my mouth, I regretted them. Church's jaw dropped open. He set down the jar of spaghetti sauce he was about to bag and started shaking his head. "Why would he do something like that?"

"People like to eat them on their cereal," I answered him. "Rick thinks it'll make money."

Church dropped his stare to his hands and concentrated. "It's wrong," he said. "Bananas can't go with cereal."

"Don't let it bother you," Bud said from his register. "Sometimes it makes more sense to think about what something's used for instead of what it is."

"No," Church insisted.

"Think about people for instance," Bud continued. "If we divided up people by what they were instead of what they did, none of us would be working together. I'd be stuck with a bunch

164

of old fogies and Harley'd be working with the other boys. He'd have to get his head shaved and start wearing an earring."

He winked at me.

"No," Church said again. "There's nice people and mean people and that's all. Right, Harley?"

"Sure. I guess so."

He wandered slowly away from his station, with his skinny arms pressed to his sides and his skinny shoulders hunched forward looking like a closed umbrella, and sat down on his bench. Bud finished with his customer and started bagging for him. He didn't look like he was ever coming back.

I tried to slip away unnoticed but Church spotted me.

"Don't do it, Harley," he shouted after me. "It's wrong. I'm telling you."

I took my good old time putting the shelves up. They were cheap metal crap with about a hundred screws. I kept getting distracted thinking about Church and how I was violating his world order, and Rick and how I was doing his bidding, and all the boxes of PopTarts and granola bars sitting a few feet away from me and how I'd kill for just one. When I finished, I wanted to tear the whole thing down.

I crouched down to pick up my screwdriver off the floor and heard a female voice from the next aisle over.

"I said if you were good, you could pick out one snack."

"But Mom, that's not fair," Esme explained. "Every snack I pick Zack likes too so he actually gets two snacks. But he always picks Doritos and I hate Doritos so I only get one."

"Life isn't always fair," Callie growled.

I couldn't believe I had forgotten she did her grocery shopping on Friday nights.

This was a perfect opportunity. I could see her but she had her kids with her so it would be safe. I could make polite small talk with her. I'd be obligated. She was a customer. And if she gave me one of her honey-dipped smiles, I'd know I might still have a chance. But if she looked at me like a school budget cut, I wouldn't know what to do.

I stood up and turned around so fast, I fell into the Wheaties and knocked a couple boxes on the floor. I put them back and raced to the opposite end of the aisle and waited there until I was sure she wasn't coming toward me. Then I jogged to the front of the store, grabbed the orange reflective vest off its hook near the magazines, and headed for the door.

"Did you do it, Harley?" Church cried after me.

Once I got outside, I stopped to catch my breath.

There weren't many carts to bring in. I gathered up the few strays and took a seat on the cart return's metal railing to try and calm my gut. I felt like I was going to puke. I probably wasn't supposed to take those pills on an empty stomach.

The sun had just gone down. The sky was gray tinged with blue. Across the road, the hills beyond the car wash looked even bluer. They rolled away from me like an ocean's waves but without the violent motion.

Technically they were mountains—part of the Allegheny foothills—but mountain was too colossal a word for them and foothills was too humble. Hills, on its own, sounded solid and comforting which is what they were most of the time.

Laurel Falls was a nice enough town. Named after pink flowers and crystal waterfalls. Sitting at the bottom of a small cup of a valley. It was the county seat so it had its own fairgrounds and an old-fashioned red brick courthouse with big white pillars and a gold clock tower. It had a hospital, two malls, a drive-in, the new Super Wal-Mart, a YMCA, and a Planned Parenthood clinic that was always hopping. But it was too big. Eight thousand people last census.

I didn't mind working here but I was glad I lived in Black Lick, which was a town named after a poisoned chunk of salt. Population: 118. Me and the girls were 3 percent of our town. We were almost significant.

166

A woman pulled in and parked her car and gave me a dirty look on her way into the store. She was probably going to complain I was a loafer. I didn't care. I would have set there all night except while I was doing it I forgot the reason why I was out there in the first place until it was too late and Callie Mercer came wheeling her cart toward me.

Esme saw me before I could do anything about it.

"It's Jody's brother," she announced, beaming at me and giving a royal wave. "Hi, Harley. Hi. It's me. Esme."

"Hi, Harley," Zack chimed in. "It's me too."

Callie came to an abrupt stop in the middle of the lot when she saw me. Zack went lurching forward in the cart seat, then snapped back. A roll of paper towels tumbled out onto the blacktop. She bent down and picked up the paper towels.

"I wondered where you were," she said to my feet as I came up next to her. "I mean, I know you work here but I didn't see you. Not that I was looking for you."

She wedged the paper towels back in the cart.

"Not that I wasn't looking for you either. I mean, if I had seen you I wouldn't have minded seeing you."

She straightened up and pushed her hair away from her face. She finally looked at me and I looked at her. I imagined what it would have felt like to look in her eyes when I was inside her. I started thinking about Amber fucking that boy on the couch and how he hadn't been looking at her. I wondered if she had been looking at him.

I went back to that night in my mind and instead of lowering my gun and going outside, I blew his head off. It exploded like an overripe pumpkin, but it didn't stop him. His body kept pumping away at Amber. The stump between his shoulders jerked back and forth sending blood spraying everywhere. Then he shuddered and collapsed from coming or dying or both. Amber pushed him off her and rose up from the couch, naked, spattered in his blood and brains, and she thanked me.

167

"Do you need help with your groceries?" I asked Callie.

"You don't have to do that," she said.

I glanced down at my orange vest. "It's kind of my job," I said.

"Oh, right." She made an embarrassed laugh. "Sure. Thanks."

I started loading bags in her trunk while she leaned into the car to buckle Zack in his seat. I watched and put a bag, heavy with canned goods, on top of her loaf of bread.

"Is Jody at home?" Esme asked me.

"Huh?" I said.

"Is Jody at home?" she repeated, firmly.

"Sure."

"Mom," she called out. "Can I play with Jody when we get home?"

"It's almost nine o'clock," Callie responded with her head still stuck inside the car. "You're going straight to bed when we get home."

"Brad had this business dinner tonight down in Latrobe," she started explaining to me after she finished with Zack, "and tomorrow he has a golf game with the same people so he's just staying there. I forgot about it so I didn't have anyone to stay with the kids." Her voice trailed off. "I'm sorry. You don't care about any of this."

I finished loading and closed the trunk lid. Callie walked over and stood next to me and stared at her rear bumper. Her forehead was creased with concern. I knew what she was going to say to me.

I wished I could be MOST GUYS. I wished I could just come out and ask her if she wanted to have sex with me again and if she said no, I would figure it was because there was something wrong with her and I wouldn't let it bother me. Or I wished I could have kissed her. I never got around to kissing her mouth. I was pretty sure I was a terrible kisser so I wished I could kiss her like MOST GUYS and when I stopped she'd be wet and pliable.

168

But I wasn't MOST GUYS; and she wasn't the Virgin Mary. She wasn't a ruthless whore either. She didn't want to hurt me, but she couldn't fix me either. It was too big of a job. I think I scared her.

"Harley," she started.

I didn't want to hear it. I couldn't stand to hear it.

"I really like that artist Francis Bacon," I blurted out.

Her forehead smoothed out again except for two faint lines that were permanent. She gave me a silky smile. My ace in the hole. Every woman had her weakness. My mom's was Valley Dairy's maple walnut ice cream. Whenever Dad brought her some home for no reason, he was golden for days.

"You liked 'Figure with Meat'?" she asked a little uncertainly.

"That's the one with the Pope sitting between two bloody sides of beef, right? Yeah, I liked it."

"Huh," she said. "Did you read the description?"

"Sure."

"Which explanation do you believe? That the artist was saying the Pope is a butcher, or that he was saying he's as much a victim as the slaughtered animal behind him?"

"I thought the Pope was laughing."

"Laughing?" she said, startled.

She slipped her hands into her jeans pockets. I watched them go, remembering how they had given me gently brutal strokes.

She leaned back against the trunk.

"He did a series of paintings around the same time of screaming figures wearing business suits. Some critics say he was trying to show the anguish experienced by people in authoritarian roles. I think he was saying they're evil."

"Maybe they were dancing?" I tried.

"Maybe," she said, smiling and nodding.

"Is he dead?" I asked.

"Who? Francis Bacon?"

"Yeah."

169

"Mom!" Zack shouted. "Esme's touching my car seat!"

"I think he passed away in '91 or '92."

"Good."

"Good?" She laughed.

"I want to put him on my list of dead people I'd like to meet."

"Do you have a list of living people you'd like to meet?"

I shook my head. "I figure I have a better chance of meeting people I'd like when I'm dead."

She laughed again. I was being serious.

"Is it a big list?"

I shook my head. "I'm just starting it."

"Mom!" Esme stuck her head out the back car window. "He's singing the Barney song! Make him stop!"

Esme's shrill words affected Callie like a whip cracked behind her. She jumped around and rushed at the window and Esme's head instantly disappeared. Callie's head followed and a heated buzz came from the car.

Then she walked back to me, smiling calmly, and announced, "I have to go."

"Sure."

"No, wait," she said suddenly.

She took a deep breath with her whole body the way kids do and began an earnest discussion with herself.

"I want to apologize to you for the way I left. For everything, really. Not to imply that it wasn't wonderful. But I'm not sure it should have happened. Actually, I know it shouldn't have happened. I feel like I took advantage. But I wanted to help. You were so upset. Of course, there are better ways to help a person. Or maybe not. I guess I wasn't thinking too clearly."

The only word I heard was wonderful. It was a word to describe tea parties. When I thought of our night together, I pictured fire-ravaged buildings.

"It's okay," I told her.

"No, it's not." She brought a hand to her forehead with a

worn-out air. "I tried waking you and I couldn't. You actually had me worried there for a minute or two. I thought maybe something had happened. Kids have heart attacks too. Then I realized you were just sound asleep. I know that's no excuse for leaving you there. Outside. Alone. At night."

She laid each word down then paused and considered them like a card hand before carefully adding, "In the mud," and, "Near the water."

"It was a terrible thing to do," she finished.

"It's okay," I said again.

"It's just that"—she hadn't finished—"while I was waiting for you to wake up I started thinking about all the awful things you might think about me."

"What things?"

"My God, Harley. I'm married with two little kids." She said it with a fearful awe like it was a rare medical condition. "I couldn't stand the thought of you thinking I'm some pathetic, bored housewife on the prowl for boys to corrupt."

CORRUPT. It appeared one neon letter at a time across the trunk lid. Once it was all there, I stared at it for a moment, letting it burn into my brain, then I snuffed it out with a blink of my eyes.

"And I'm so much older than you. Do you know how old I am?"

"Twenty-eight?" I guessed.

"I'm thirty-three," she corrected me simply.

I was glad to see she wasn't one of those women who turned into a gushing, giggling mess because some guy told her she looked younger than she really was. I hated that.

"Amber thought you were over thirty," I said.

She raised her eyebrows. "Oh, she did?"

"I don't want to hurt your feelings," I said, changing the topic from Amber, "but when I think about you, I don't think about personal shit like you being married or having kids or how old you are."

"What do you think about?"

"You really want to know?"

"Yes."

Zack started wailing.

"Your butt, mostly."

"My butt?" she repeated, her lips melting into another smile. "Do you think about my butt a lot?"

"Define 'a lot.' "

"Once a day."

"Yes."

The car started rocking. Through the rear window, I could see stuffed animals and small hands and feet flying around.

"Look, Harley," she said in an aggravated rush. "This obviously isn't a good time to talk about all this. I've got to get these two home to bed, and I'm sure you need to get back to work."

"Right," I said.

"If you'd like, you could stop by tonight after you're done with work. Brad's out of town, and I usually stay up pretty late."

"Sure," I said.

She looked pleasantly stumped. "Okay." She gave me a final smile. "Then I'll see you later."

"Later" echoed in my brain. I couldn't move my legs until I heard her car pull out of the lot and drive off down the road. I prayed she hadn't seen me in her rearview mirror standing stiffly with my eyes glazed like the first time I had been combed with a metal detector.

chapter (11)

I went straight there. I never even thought about going home first and doing stuff like changing my clothes or brushing my teeth or picking her a bouquet of my mom's daffodils. I showed up in my blue Shop Rite shirt and Dad's coat with my hair sweating beneath my Redi-Mix cap.

I was prepared though. I kept the art book in my truck and I studied a couple more pictures under the parking lot lamps before I drove out. I showed up with my head crammed full of "impassioned brushwork," and "bold composition," and "carefree lines of great verve and fluidity."

She answered the door, smiling, wearing a short black tank top and drawstring pants that hung low on her hips. I was pretty sure Victoria's Secret would have called them loungewear.

"Hi, Harley," she said. "Come on in."

The floor inside the door was made of the same polished stones as the kitchen floor. The walls were a varnished gold wood. On a row of black iron hooks hung Esme's backpack, a Tweety Bird umbrella, two little coats, a purse, and a man's flannel shirt.

"You want to take off your coat?"

"No," I said. "I mean, yes."

I took it off and handed it to her. She hung it next to the shirt. I took off my hat too and messed up my hair with my hand so it wouldn't be flat. I wished I could see a mirror but I reminded myself if she was the type who cared about hairstyles, I would have never made it this far.

She turned and walked into the house, calling over her shoulder, "Do you want a beer?"

"Sure," I said

Her bare feet padded over her stones. I followed her, glancing around me nervously, not fearing the bad but fearing the good. I felt like I could stand my ground if her husband burst out of the bedroom waving a shotgun at me or if I found a freezer full of body parts from other boys she had CORRUPTED and then decided to dispose of. But I felt like I would go running screaming from the house if she slipped her fingertips into my pants again.

She opened the refrigerator door and leaned into it. I could tell by the way her pants stretched and clung to her ass that she wasn't wearing anything underneath.

All of me went stiff. Not just my dick. If Francis Bacon could have seen me he would have painted me standing rock-hard and purple-faced in a sideshow tent. He would have called it "The Amazing Erection Boy."

"Here."

She held out a beer bottle to me. She took one for herself too, but I already smelled something harder on her breath. So she had to get a little trashed to be able to do it with me again. I didn't care.

I tried to twist off the cap and it wouldn't come. She giggled at me. She was very trashed. She handed me a bottle opener, a gold one shaped like a stag. His antlers fit over the cap.

"I like your bottle opener," I said, handing it back to her, and cringing at my words.

"Thanks," she said. "It belonged to my grandfather."

I had lucked out. Instead of sounding like an idiot, I had complimented someone she loved.

"You never told me what happened to you Saturday night," she said, pausing to sip from her bottle. "I was worried about you. You were so upset and your mouth was bleeding."

"I fell."

"You fell?"

"Yeah."

"Everything's all right at home then?"

"Yeah."

I glanced at the bottle opener sitting on her kitchen counter and thought about my own grandfather and how my dad had blown his chance with him. If he had been honest with him at the end, he might have had some CLOSURE. He might have felt like he accomplished something and then maybe he might have been able to accomplish something else.

"No," I said suddenly, my face burning. "Everything's not all right at home. Everything sucks at home."

She watched me, not with pity or curiosity or even concern. It took me a moment to figure out what it was since I had never seen it before. It was respect.

"Is there any way I can help?" she asked.

"You can fuck me again."

I almost didn't get the words out before a sob blocked my throat. She dissolved in front of me behind a blur of tears. I wiped them away with the back of my hand, then I felt the hand being pulled away from me. She placed it on her throat like she wanted me to strangle her.

I took my thumb and pressed it against the perfect black freckle in the hollow of her throat. Her hands went under my shirt and her mouth went to my mouth. Her lips, the weight of her against me made me drop my beer.

The bottle exploded when it hit the stone floor. Glass shards and beer foam sprayed everywhere. I jumped back and held up my hands in front of my face, knowing I was going to get hit and knowing there was nowhere I could hide, but I had never learned to take my punishment like a man.

Not like Misty. She always closed her eyes and tilted her head up like she was waiting for a kiss. I admired her bravery. All those times Dad dragged her off to her room, slamming the door behind him, I never heard her cry or scream.

"I'm sorry," I cried.

"It's all right," she said.

She took a step toward me. I heard the crunch of glass beneath her feet, but she kept coming. My hands were shaking. I was crying like a baby. I just wanted to go home.

She kissed me again. I felt her hands behind my neck and in my hair and her tongue in my mouth.

I thought it was going to be different this time. I wasn't hysterical tonight. I wasn't stupid with need. But it was the same. My hands crawled blindly over her body, trying to hold her, but she kept sliding through my fingers like she was made of oil.

I wasn't equipped to deal with the agony of anticipation. I wanted to be inside her. That was all I cared about. If I could be inside her, everything would be all right. I told her so.

She led me to the glass-topped table and pulled out a chair. She pushed me down into it, then slipped out of her pants. I was right. There wasn't anything underneath. There wasn't anything under her shirt either.

She knelt down on her knees naked between my legs to unzip my fly. The soles of her feet were bloody. Like Jody's. From that piece of pipe. I had to get rid of it.

She took me in her hand and climbed on top of me.

It hadn't been real.

And guided me inside her.

Jody's feet were fine.

I did even less this time. I didn't do any of the things I had promised myself I would do if I got a second chance. I didn't look at her. I didn't pay attention to her. I didn't care if she enjoyed it. I let her ride me while I held her around the waist and felt all my rage and grief being sucked from me each time she raised and lowered her hips.

By the time we finished, she had emptied me of everything. Good and bad.

When I opened my eyes, I had the swirling galaxy feeling again. She hadn't left me this time though. She was still sitting on top of me, resting against me, with her head on my shoulder and her breasts against my Shop Rite shirt.

She kissed my neck, then my lips, and shifted in my lap. I felt myself slip out of her. She studied me like she was going over her notes and was happy with them.

"You look like you could sleep for days," she said quietly, and kissed me again. "Even in this uncomfortable chair."

She smiled and pulled back, holding me by the shoulders, still clamping my legs between her thighs. I stared dumbly at her body and wondered if I could touch her now without losing my mind.

"Come here," she said.

She crawled off me and held out a hand. I took it and held it for a moment before I could stand up.

She walked out of the kitchen, tiptoeing on the ball of one foot because she had cut her heel on the beer glass. I followed and stood in front of the glass shelves with the jungle room behind them while she bent over to fluff the pillows on the couch for me.

"Lie down," she said, patting the cushions.

I didn't move and she made a funny look with a questioning smile.

"Something wrong?"

She didn't seem to know she was naked. Or if she did, she didn't know she was beautiful. Or if she knew that too, she didn't know being naked and beautiful made her mind-numbing.

"Huh?"

"Are you okay? Come here."

She sat down on the couch. I went and sat next to her. She pushed me down gently on my back, then turned and started taking off my shoes. I was glad I hadn't worn my boots to work today after getting them wet during my trek through the woods. She probably would have thought they were stupid. Amber was right about them.

"Your foot's bleeding," I told her.

"I know," she said, glancing down at it. "I need to go put something on it. I need to clean up that mess in the kitchen too."

My fear came rushing back. I started to sit up. "I'm sorry," I said, urgently.

"It's all right."

"I'll help you clean it up."

"No." She pushed me down again and leaned over to kiss me. I grabbed her and starting kissing her back. She pulled away and told me to calm down and slow down.

"I'm sorry," I said. "I'm a rotten kisser."

"No, you're not. You just need to relax and not think about it."

She climbed over me, pushed up on all fours, and bent her head down until our mouths were almost touching, then she started running her tongue back and forth over my lips.

"I'm thinking about it again," I said, swallowing hard.

She stopped and gave me a look that was pretty close to the way I thought a woman should look at a guy if he had done a good job.

"You need to go to sleep," she told me.

"Are you coming back?"

"Yes."

I watched her limp out of the living room. She left a trail of tiny bright red drops on her gold floor. I wanted to tell her, but I still didn't know what to call her and I was already falling asleep.

She woke me in the morning. Weak gray light filled the room. I looked around trying to figure out where I was. I saw a big stone fireplace and a jungle behind glass shelves holding framed family portraits of somebody else's family. I had slept so deeply, I didn't feel like I had slept at all.

"Harley."

She was hovering over me in the cleanest, fluffiest white bathrobe I had ever seen. I wanted to rub my face in it. I reached for her.

"No, Harley." She brushed my hands away. "We can't. I let you sleep too long. Zack's already awake."

I woke up a little more.

"I'm sorry," She stood up and tugged on my hand. "But you have to go."

I hardly recognized her from the night before. She was irritable and all business. I was familiar with mood swings—I had spent my life in a house full of females—but Callie didn't seem to swing as much as she switched.

She hurried me to the front door and piled my shoes, my Dad's coat, and my hat in my arms.

"Chances are Zack wouldn't say anything but you can never be sure with three-year-olds."

"Right."

"I'm sorry." She sighed and dragged her hand through her hair. "I hate to rush you off like this. Like you're some sort of criminal."

"It's okay."

"I don't know when I'll be able to see you again," she went on, "between the kids and Brad, and you working two jobs."

"I can quit one."

She looked up at me. The creases on her forehead were more noticeable in the morning light. Two lines beginning and ending at nowhere. She was standing sort of lopsided. I noticed the end of a Band-Aid on the outside of her heel.

"Very funny," she said, frowning.

I was being serious.

She sent me off with a promise that she'd call me. I walked to my truck turning her words over in my head, savoring them at first, then ripping them apart looking for hidden meaning. I decided to believe her.

It was early when I got home. The clock in my truck didn't work, but I figured it was about 6 A.M. I had left Jody and Misty alone all night. Amber had gone out. She was right about me being paranoid. If Jody and Misty could stay by themselves during the day, they could do it at night too. Betty had been right too, saying I was using it as an excuse to avoid visiting Skip.

Maybe I would go visit Skip after all, I thought to myself as I crossed the yard. Maybe I could get Callie to come too.

The idea was brilliant, so brilliant I had to stop and take a seat on the couch carcass.

I wondered if she ever got to go away overnight like her husband did. She could make up a story and meet me there. She could meet me anywhere. It wouldn't even have to be overnight. It could be more realistic. An hour. Fifteen minutes.

Summer was just about here. The nights would be warm. I thought about how easily she slipped out our first night together. How her husband and kids never even knew she was gone. We could meet in the woods. We could meet in her clearing.

We could meet at the old mining office.

The front door opened and Elvis ran out. He went straight to the woods without noticing me. Amber stepped out on the porch.

She wasn't wearing one of my T-shirts like she usually did. She had on a short, silky red robe. Beneath it I saw the black lace nightie she had worn the night we had our last big fight. She reminded me of the times Mom put on slinky stuff waiting for Dad to come back from the bars after a bad fight. She only did it when she knew Dad had been right.

It was way too early on a Saturday morning for Amber to be

up already. Maybe she had stayed out all night too and just got home. She had done that twice before. Both times we had a big fight about it. I didn't feel like fighting right now so I wasn't going to ask.

"What are you doing?" she shouted at me.

I made myself more comfortable on the couch.

"Where have you been?"

I ignored her. I was busy thinking about the office. I could clean it out. I could fix it up. I could put curtains on the windows.

She came over and snapped her fingers in front of my face. "What is with you? You look stoned. Are you stoned?" She bent over and sniffed me. "Where were you all night?"

"I fell asleep in the woods again."

"The woods." She rolled her eyes at me. "I swear to God, you are so fucked in the head. Do you know what kind of people sleep in the woods?"

"Campers?"

"Psychos," she said, sharply.

I glanced at the hills. The sun was coming up pink again, spreading a peachy-gold stain over the tops of the hills.

"Well, while you were off communing with nature last night," I heard Amber go on, "we had a crisis."

I sat up. "Is Jody okay?"

"Yes."

"Misty?"

"Yes. They're fine. Nothing like that."

"The gun. Where's the gun?"

"I don't know," she said. "Probably where you put it. Harley, what's wrong with you?"

She reached out to touch me and I pushed her away. I got up from the couch. "Did somebody call? What day is today? Did somebody call about the house?"

"What are you talking about?"

"You said there was a crisis." I grabbed her by the arm and shook her. "What's the fucking crisis?"

"Harley, stop."

"You said there was a crisis. Do you know what a crisis is?"

"What's wrong with you? You're scaring me."

"Define crisis."

"Something bad," she said, breaking into a sob.

I squeezed her arms until I saw her skin between my fingers turn white. "The last time someone told me there was a crisis in my house it was a state trooper standing in Skip's driveway with all those fucking blue lights going everywhere," I shouted at her. "'There's been a crisis in your household.' Who the fuck talks like that?"

I started shaking her again. Her crying went from wild and terrified to steady and defeated, the way it always did with Dad. I never wanted to make anybody feel that way about me. I used to have nightmares about it before I stopped dreaming.

She broke free of my grip and walked away rubbing at the finger welts on her arms. "What did you want him to say?"

"The truth," I shouted back. "Why can't anybody ever say the truth?"

"You wanted him to say your mom killed your dad? That would have been better?"

"I wanted him to say your life is going to suck every minute of every day from now until you die. That's what I wanted him to say."

She sat down hard on the ground, wrapped her arms around her bent legs, and buried her chin in her knees.

"You think you're the only one whose life sucks?" she asked the empty space in front of her. "You think you're the only one who has a right to be miserable just because you have a job?"

"I have two jobs."

"Big deal," she said flatly. "I'd rather have a job than go to school and have to hang around this house pretending to be Mom."

182

I had one of my flashes of brotherly obligation. I wanted to tell her she had her whole life ahead of her, but it would have been like tossing her another white crayon.

She straightened out her legs in front of her and started pulling up the grass between them.

"What's the crisis?" I asked defeatedly, all my anger and fear spent.

She took a deep breath and blew it out through pursed lips. "I probably shouldn't have called it a crisis." She lay back on her elbows and arched her neck so she could look up at me. "I didn't realize you had a thing about that word. It's not such a big deal, I guess. Maybe it's actually good."

"Tell me," I said, impatiently.

"I found almost a thousand dollars in Misty's room last night."

"What?"

"It belonged to Mom. It was her secret stash. She had been saving up for a long time, I guess."

"Secret stash for what?"

"I guess she was going to leave Daddy. Isn't that wild? I never had any idea things were that bad. Did you?"

"How did Misty get it?"

"She found it and stole it from Mom. I couldn't get her to tell me anything else. She clammed up the way she does. You know what that's like."

I couldn't think straight. Every thought I had ever had about my parents rushed into my brain. Every thought I had ever had about Misty followed. But the one that stayed the longest was the thought of a thousand dollars sitting in my house for almost two years.

"How much money?" I asked.

"Nine hundred and seventy-three dollars and fifty-four cents."

It was my turn to sit down hard.

"Where did you find it?"

"Do you remember that sunflower shirt you asked me about?"

The sunflower shirt. I blinked at her. The bloodstained sunflower shirt was in my desk drawer with Skip's letter and the latest Victoria's Secret catalog.

I nodded. I felt kind of sick. I tried to remember the last time I ate.

"Well, you got me thinking about that shirt and how much Jody would like it. It would go perfect with that little wraparound denim skirt she has with the eyelet trim. Right now she wears that old pink shirt of Misty's with the furry white bunny head on it. It's way too small and the bunny is missing an eye and it has a mustard stain on it. She looks so Appalachia in it."

I put my head in my hands. I was getting a headache on top of feeling like I was going to throw up.

"When Misty outgrows things, she usually gives them to Jody right away but sometimes she packs stuff in a box in her closet to save for her own kids someday. I've seen some of it. It's not special stuff like Christmas dresses. It's shit like that Joey Chitwood Thrill Show windbreaker she got at the fair and that ratty old T-shirt of Dad's that says, 'Old Hunters Never Die. They just Lose Their Bang.' Most of it's really old and crappy and weird so I thought maybe she kept the sunflower shirt."

I looked over at her. "So you found the money in a box of old clothes in her closet?"

"No. When I went in her closet, I found my Easy Bake oven. Do you remember how much fun we used to have with that? Do you remember the king and queen game? I was the Queen of Hearts and I made you pink cakes."

"I remember," I urged her along.

"Anyway, I opened it up to look at it. You know, for kicks. And I found an envelope stuffed inside the oven."

"I can't believe this."

"You were the King of Pain. Remember?" She was still reminiscing. "After that one song you liked so much. They used to

184

play it on the radio when we were kids. It was a hit or something. What was it called?"

"'King of Pain,'" I said. "Where's Misty now?" I asked.

"She's probably still sitting on her bed guarding her money. She stayed up all night doing it. Jody slept with me."

I got up slowly from the ground. The pounding in my head, the sloshing in my stomach, the fear and confusion in my heart were nothing compared to the anger I suddenly felt.

"She thinks she's going to keep it?" I asked, my voice shaking with disbelief.

"Yeah." Amber nodded. "That's what she said."

Misty was wide awake and sitting cross-legged on her bed just like Amber said she would be. She had on one of her own nightshirts—a big tie-dyed one that was mostly blue and purple—and the envelope full of money sat in the pouch of material draped between her knees.

She gave me an odd, close-mouthed smile when I walked into her room.

I walked right up to her. I wanted to hit her more than I had ever wanted to hit anyone in my life. I looked down at the envelope stuffed with bills and felt like I was going to faint. Her face was a deadly calm mask of superiority.

"It's mine," she said. "I'm the one who found it."

I couldn't unclamp my jaw to make words. "Where?" I managed to choke out.

"In Mom's underwear drawer," she answered me. "That's all I'm telling you."

My hand shot out so fast, I didn't realize it had left my side until I felt something warm and living in its grip.

Misty's head hit the wall behind her bed with a hollow thud. Her hands flew to my hand clenched around her throat, and she started clawing at it with her blue fingernails.

"You're going to tell me everything," I said.

"Or what?" She coughed, trying to pry my hand free.

I let go all at once, as quickly as I had grabbed her, and walked to the other side of the room holding the hand at arm's length in front of me like it might attack me next.

I heard her gagging. My hands started trembling. The right one had mean red marks dug into the skin. It already throbbed.

I wanted to say I was sorry but all I could do was stare at the wall. It needed a fresh coat of paint.

"You can't do anything to me," Misty said, her heavy stare numbing me from behind. "You can't hurt me. You can't kick me out. You're my legal guardian. You have to take care of me."

I couldn't look at her. I didn't want to go near her. I was afraid of myself.

"I'm not going to do anything to you. I don't even want you to tell me about the money," I said as calmly as I could. "I don't want to know another goddamned thing about Mom or Dad for as long as I live."

I turned around and saw Jody's empty bed. She had taken all her dinosaurs with her. It must have taken them forever to lug them all over to Amber's room.

Misty was rubbing her neck. She hadn't changed her position except to take the envelope and push it deeper into her lap. In order to take it from her, I would have to touch her between her legs.

"I had to take the money to stop her," she said. "She was going to take us away from him. Don't you understand?"

The confession didn't bring any satisfaction into her eyes but it livened them a little as if she had begun to eat after days of hunger.

"I don't care," I said. I held out my aching hand. "Give me the money, Misty."

"No."

"I don't get it. Even if you don't care about the rest of us, you could have been spending the money on yourself. What are you saving it for?"

"College," she said, triumphantly.

The urge ripped through me again. I imagined slapping her would feel like coming.

CORRUPT flashed across her chest, the letters molding the new little breast bumps beneath her shirt. I shook my head, but the word wouldn't leave.

Tears started spilling out of my eyes like blood, calm and steady and without emotion. They tumbled down my cheeks and dripped off my chin and made dark spots on my Shop Rite shirt.

"Give it to me," I said hoarsely.

"It's mine."

"It's not yours. It's Mom's. She doesn't know you have it, does she?"

She didn't say anything.

"We'll ask Mom what she wants us to do with it."

"She can't have any visitors thanks to you freaking out."

"She can have calls," I said.

Misty put her hands on the envelope.

"Give it to me now, Misty," I said. "You know I can take that money from you. I might have to hurt you to do it, but I can do it."

"No, you can't," Amber announced.

Her voice surprised me. She had been silent the whole time. I had forgotten she was still in the room.

"You can't hurt anyone," she added. "But I can."

She hauled off and smacked Misty, open-handed, full across the face. The impact threw her sideways off the bed, and the envelope went with her. Amber walked over, picked it up, and left the room waving it at me.

Misty glanced my way. Her eyes sparkled with tears in a face full of deliberate emptiness. "She did that because of you," she said.

"You brought it on yourself."

"No. That's not what I mean. She's not ever going to behave until you take care of her."

A chill curiosity kept me from moving.

"I want you to take care of her," she repeated.

I wanted to get out of there, but her eyes held me the way a stagnant well forced me to stay and drop stones in it.

"You'll be happy and Amber will be happy," she further explained. "Then me and Jody can be happy too. It's hard living with you guys."

Her one cheek blazed red.

"I just want us to be happy," she said before disappearing into her preferred silence. "That's all."

It sounded like a threat.

"Don't look at me like that," Amber said when I joined her in the kitchen. "I knew you wouldn't be able to do it. We'd have to spend the rest of our lives trying to get ownership by signing the proper legal documents."

She paused and brought her palm to her lips and blew on it.

"God, that hurt," she said.

I took a stunned seat at the kitchen table. The envelope sat in the middle of it. I had never seen so much money in my life.

"I guess things were worse between Mom and Dad than I thought," Amber said, "if she was going to leave him."

I looked over at her. She was pouring water in the coffeemaker. She hated coffee.

"Are you making me coffee?" I asked.

She turned around smiling in her skimpy robe, caught in a lazy shaft of white sunlight coming through the window, holding the coffeepot out to one side like a newlywed in a Folger's commercial.

"Don't you want some?"

She flipped on the machine and came and sat down across from me.

"I guess it all makes more sense now," she said. "I mean, what happened."

"It makes less sense," I told her. "Why shoot somebody you're going to leave?"

"She couldn't leave. Remember? Misty took her money."

The brewing coffee smelled great. I wished I had a big greasy breakfast to go with it: bacon, pancakes, sausage gravy over biscuits, home fries. My stomach rumbled and my dick stiffened a little. I bet Callie Mercer could do incredible things with an egg.

"Anyway." Amber sighed. "Now I can get my license."

"Huh?"

"You said we needed a thousand bucks, right?"

I laughed at her. "Are you nuts?"

Our hands shot out at the exact same moment. I was faster. I scooped up the envelope and backed off from the table.

"That's mine," she said, lunging for me.

I shoved it into the waistband of my pants. "We need it for taxes on the house."

"What are you talking about?"

"Eleven hundred dollars," I explained. "It's due in two weeks and we don't have any of it."

"Whose fault is that?" she cried.

"Fuck you, Amber."

"No. Fuck you."

"Hi," Jody said, coming into the kitchen, frowning, and rubbing her eyes with a little fist. "What are you guys fighting about now?"

"Nothing," I said. I closed my eyes and slumped back into a chair.

"Nothing to you," Amber shot back.

Jody took a seat at the table and set down her notebook, pen, Sparkle Three-Horn, Yellowie, and a pink plastic tyrannosaurus she won at the fair the year before, picking a duck.

"You just don't want me to ever get my license," she went on.

She leaned over the table toward me when she realized I was done fighting. I thought she was going to sniff me again. I wondered if she could smell a woman on me.

"Something's wrong with you." She said it with authority.

"Nothing's wrong with me. I just don't have the energy for this right now."

I put my head down on the table the way I had seen smart kids do my entire life when they finished their tests early.

"Will you play with me today?" Jody asked.

I heard Amber's chair being dragged out from the table and being pushed in again.

"She's asking you," she said.

"Sure," I mumbled into my arm. "Will you get me a cup of coffee?"

"I'm not allowed," Jody said. "I can only get the cup."

Amber made a persecuted snort and got up from the table. A cupboard door banged open. A plastic mug slammed against the countertop. I heard the click of an OFF switch and the *glug, glug* of coffee being poured.

The smell pulled my head up. I circled the mug with my hands. The heat felt good. I took the hand Misty had hurt, turned it upside down, and held the scratches over the steam. Across the table, Jody was working on her list. So far she had written:

FEED DINUSORS

EAT BREKFIST

BRUSH TEETH

Amber sat down with a box of Pop-Tarts. "You know, I was just thinking," she said, ripping open one of the foil packets. "How did Misty know for sure Mom was going to leave Dad? Mom could have been saving that money for lots of reasons."

"We heard her talking about it," Jody volunteered.

"What?" Amber said.

I put down my coffee cup.

"You know about the money?" Amber asked slowly.

"I think so," Jody said, without pausing in her work. "You mean the money Mommy was saving so she could move away from Daddy. She said she had a whole bunch hid in the house somewhere. Misty said she was going to look for it after we heard Mommy talking about it, but she couldn't find it."

Amber and I looked at each other.

"Who was Mom talking to?" I asked.

"Uncle Mike."

The pen in the little hand kept moving carefully across the paper.

"He was going to help her out," Jody went on. "He said she had to get Misty away from Daddy before it was too late."

"Too late for what?" I asked, feeling the skin on the back of my neck tighten.

"I don't know," Jody answered.

She finished writing PLAY WITH HARLEY and looked up.

"Misty didn't know either," she said.

chapter (12)

Skip and I were juniors in high school when that asteroid—1994
XL1—came within sixty thousand miles of hitting Earth. I remembered it happened around Christmas because we had a
crappy old wreath Skip's mom had thrown out hanging in the
mining office.

I heard about it on the news and before I could call Skip, he
called me. We were both blown away by the thought of a 100,000-
ton rock the size of a barn exploding above us and flattening the
United States. An Earth-crosser, one of the scientists on the news
called it: an asteroid that cruises through our orbit.

The next day I got off the bus at Skip's house and we grabbed
a bottle of the rum his mom stockpiled so people could drink
her homemade eggnog and we headed for the railroad tracks.

We talked the whole way there about all the cool disaster
movie facts: how scientists estimated there were one thousand
Doomsday Earth-crossers out there that could end life on our
planet as we know it; how the dust and smoke from impact would
block out the sun for years and there'd be a "nuclear winter"
and an ice age and giant tsunamis that would drown half the
world; how the only safe way to get rid of one would be to explode a nuclear bomb in front of it and nudge it off course with-

out shattering it, but scientists would need five months' warning to do it. XL1 wasn't spotted until it was fourteen hours away, and it was considered small. We'd see a Doomsday about six seconds before it hit.

Then we built a fire in the snow and got trashed and philosophical.

Why go to school if the whole planet could be destroyed tomorrow? Why get a job? Why take shit from your parents? Why take shit from anybody? The only thing we couldn't rationalize away was trying to get laid. Neither one of us had had any luck yet, but we instinctively knew it wasn't a pursuit we should give up just because we might only have six seconds left to live.

We were sure we were the only people around who appreciated the magnitude of what had almost happened. Hardly anyone we knew seemed to care. Not our parents. Nobody at school. Even the science teachers didn't get all that cranked up about it.

The only person I knew who cared was Jody. She got excited when I explained that a giant asteroid was probably what wiped out the dinosaurs, even though I knew she was too little to really understand. And Skip said Donny got interested when the news showed a futuristic computer graphic of a comet being made into a steam-propelled rocket by melting its ice core with nuclear power. We howled over that one saying it was because the comet looked like a flaming Zinger.

But everyone else went on with their stupid little lives without even glancing at the sky that night. My dad even bitched at me to change the channel when I found a late-night special on asteroids.

I tried making him see the terror but also the relief in knowing we were insignificant as a race; how it made the simplest acts more important and the monumental ones pointless.

He sank deeper into the couch and told me I had a better

chance of getting hit by a truck than an asteroid and to give him the goddamn remote.

I waited until I was sure he wasn't watching me, then I snuck a notebook out of my backpack and wrote down the definition of an Earth-crosser. It was probably the only educational thing I had ever done outside a classroom except for going to the library after Mom's arrest and looking up the differences between homicide, murder, and manslaughter.

I wrote: "Chance of a collision is small but if it did happen it would occur without warning and could cause total annihilation."

Just like the TRUTH about Dad and Misty. I knew it was out there. I also knew if I ever had to face it, my world wouldn't survive. All I could do was ignore it and hope it passed right out of my orbit. In the meantime, I started living my life with a little bit more urgency.

I gave Callie Mercer four days to call me. I didn't plan on it being four. It was a random number. But after I made the decision to walk away from the Hotpoint dishwasher I was supposed to be loading onto the Barclay delivery truck, and I got in my own truck, studied another painting, and started driving to her house, I realized the number four had a lot of significance for me.

There were four kids in my family. Jody was four years old when Mom killed Dad. Skip would be in college for four years. We only got four channels now that Dad's satellite dish was gone. There used to be four basic food groups before the government switched to a Food Guide Pyramid much to Church's relief; he hated having fruits and vegetables lumped together and it drove him crazy how eggs used to be with the cheese. Misty had left four scratches on my hand. There were four empty doghouses in my yard. I now had four artists I liked: Pierre Bonnard, Callie's artichoke guy, Francis Bacon, and this abstract artist named Jackson Pollock.

He was one of those guys who laid down canvases on the floor and squirted paint all over them. I always thought those guys were idiots until I saw "Greyed Rainbow." I recognized it right away. The black mess with gobs of gray and squiggly white lines. The smears of rust and fleshy yellow like dried blood and snot. It was the same kind of stuff I used to see in my head when Dad hit me.

I didn't know what Jackson Pollock meant for it to be but if his own dad had hit him when he was a kid and that's what he had been trying to show, then he was a genius. If the painting was really just supposed to be a defective rainbow, then he was an idiot. I decided to give him the benefit of the doubt and hoped his dad had hit him.

Callie's dogs started barking when I turned in her drive. I was going to go pet them, but I didn't get the chance. She was outside with Zack, playing in the sandbox near the house, and she saw me right away.

She stood up and brushed sand off her legs and the back of her shorts. She was wearing the pink bikini top.

I walked as far as her front door and waited for her, uninvited, in broad daylight, in front of her kid, without an excuse.

She crossed her yard, giving me her concerned look, and I realized I was getting sick of that one. I knew it was the same way she looked at Zack and Esme. Probably her dogs, too.

My mind started racing through all the looks I thought would be better. The way Ashlee Brockway had looked at me when I threw her against my truck door. The way Mom had looked at me when I started screaming in the Hug Room. The way Church had looked at me when I went to put the bananas with the cereal. The way Amber looked at Dad that first time he hit her.

"Is something wrong?" she asked. "Shouldn't you be at work?"

"You said you were going to call me."

"I haven't had a chance," she started to explain.

"Bullshit," I said.

She opened her mouth to say something but stopped. I tried to figure out what was the same about all those other looks that made them better. It was fear. Fear that I might hurt her. Fear that I had lost my mind. Fear that I was going to tamper with the universal order of things. Fear that there can't possibly be a God.

"Does your husband listen in on all your phone calls or something?" I kept at her. "You could have called me anytime. You could have said you wanted to talk to me about Jody."

Concern vanished but it wasn't replaced with any kind of fear. Her face paled with anger.

"When are you home, Harley?"

"Huh?"

"When are you home?"

I didn't answer. It felt like a trick question.

"Don't you work two full-time jobs?" she asked.

"Yeah."

My answer enraged her. She fought to keep her anger in check, but I could sense her helplessness. She didn't have much control over her emotions. They seemed to control her like a puppet at the mercy of a hidden hand. My own mom had been more of a bare hand.

"The problem is not when can I call you," she said, and took a troubled breath. "It's when can you be there to talk to me."

"I usually come home for dinner."

"Well, that's just great," she said in a brittle voice.

She took a step back and put her hands on her hips.

"Dinnertime is when I'm cooking and dealing with two hungry, whining kids while my husband sits in the middle of it all having a drink and bitching about his day. Should I just interrupt him at some point and say, 'Excuse me, dear. I need to call the nineteen-year-old neighbor boy and see if he'd like to come over later so I can fuck his ears off.' Is that what I should do?"

She was yelling at me by the time she finished. She was breathing hard too. I stared at her breasts moving up and down. There were sweat beads between them. Her nipples were hard. When I looked up again, she was watching me.

"Yeah," I said. "That's what you should do."

She shook her head and made a harsh laugh. "Do you know what would happen if I did that?"

"Your husband would divorce you and you wouldn't have to be married to a guy you can't stand?"

A menacing stillness came over her. Even her breathing seemed to stop. She was going to explode or she was going to transform again. I wondered what it would be like to be inside her when she had one of her sudden changes of heart.

My hand shot out the way it had done with Misty, without my consent, and hooked into the top of her shorts. It yanked her hard and she stumbled into me. I smashed my mouth against hers. She didn't want me doing it. It wasn't the kind of kiss she liked. It was more like a tongue fuck.

She got loose and pushed me away.

"What are you doing?" she gasped, darting a frantic look at Zack in the sandbox.

He was busy pouring a shovel full of sand into a dump truck.

I grabbed her again. This time around the hips. She held out her hands and braced herself against my chest, but I could still reach her throat with my mouth. I chewed on her thinking about Elvis chewing on dead baby groundhogs, and I felt her give a little. I went lower until I was sucking her nipples right through the bikini top. She made one of those shrieking, gasping, moaning noises I thought only little girls made.

"Zack," she breathed, and tried wiggling away. "He might see us."

"Let's go inside."

"I can't."

"Hey, Zack," I yelled over to him. "I'm going to go inside with your mommy and get a drink. That okay with you?"

"I want Kool-Aid," he shouted back.

"You got it, buddy."

I caught her wrist tightly and pulled her along behind me the way Dad used to drag Misty to her room to be punished. I untied her top as soon as we closed the door behind us, and she had her shorts off by the time we reached the kitchen. I laid her out on her glasstopped table and dropped my pants around my ankles. When I pushed inside her, she made that little girl sound again.

I pumped away at her. That's all I could do until she started screaming things and gripping me tighter with her legs and her hands. I wasn't sure what to do then so I pumped harder. I wasn't creative or skilled, but I was diligent.

I was pretty sure I made her come. It felt like a bunch of explosions going off inside her flesh. When it was over, I sat down in a chair and left her smiling, with her eyes closed, spread-eagled on the glass.

I was drenched with sweat, but I couldn't stop shivering. I pulled Dad's coat tighter. I was glad she hadn't asked me to take it off.

Afterward, she was calm as a puddle. She took Zack a sippy cup of Kool-Aid and walked me to my truck. As we were about to say good-bye, she remembered something and went back into the house.

She brought me a folded piece of notebook paper. I knew it was a note from Jody before I opened it.

"I found this in Esme's backpack," she explained. "She and Jody write notes back and forth all the time but this one concerned me a little. I thought maybe you should know about it."

The words didn't mean anything to me at first. Then they did.

"I asked Esme about it and she said it was just Jody trying to gross her out," I heard Callie go on. "Jody comes up with some wild ones. A month or so ago, she and Esme were writing back and forth about brothers and sisters getting married and having babies. I had a little talk with the two of them about that. Jody told me Misty said it was okay. I'm sure Misty was just messing with her mind. Big sisters do that, you know."

I kept staring at the note.

MISTY KILLD A KITTIN WUNS.

"I suppose this makes me a snitch, but I care about Jody. And Misty too. If this kitten thing is true, it's kind of disturbing."

"I'll take care of it," I said, crumpling up the note and shoving it in my pocket.

"When can I see you again?" I asked.

We made plans to meet a week later at the mining office. She liked the idea, especially after I told her how it had been my hangout since I was a kid.

She knew all about the place. It had already been abandoned when she was a kid but there were still cool things in it back then like ledgers noting tons of coal shipped, and yellowed receipts for mining equipment, and old Mountain Dew bottles with a barefoot hillbilly on them and the slogan, "It'll tickle yore innards!" Even a pair of work gloves and an old metal lunch bucket like my grandpa used to have. They had to use metal because the tunnels were so damp, a lunch in a paper bag would be soaked by the time they sat down to eat it.

I asked him once what was the worst thing about the mines: the dark, the cold and damp, the claustrophobia, the poison gases, the dust from blasting, the fear of explosions or cave-ins or flooding? He said Management.

I didn't take care of Misty right away like I said I would. I had to avoid thinking about her for a while the same way the wife of a wounded soldier had to shut out the first time she witnessed him strap a fake leg onto his stump.

I took care of the real estate taxes instead. I paid them early.

In person. In cash. The courthouse clerk who gave me my receipt said she wished her son was more like me.

I had to drive past Yee's on my way home so I stopped and got Jody a surprise umbrella and fortune cookie even though I would be having my appointment with Betty the next day. My intentions were good, but my hunger was stronger and I ended up eating the cookie.

The fortune said, "The bold man is free from fear, but the virtuous man is free from anxieties."

I decided to add Confucius to my list of dead people I'd like to meet. It was up to FOUR now.

I kept my head full of pointless thoughts—like my dead list—to help keep my mind off the family shit constantly crossing my earth's orbit, but sometimes I had too many pointless thoughts and they came too fast and I couldn't get my brain to shut down at night so I could sleep. It got so bad I found myself longing for the good night's sleep I'd get after getting fucked as much as I longed for the fuck.

We both decided to walk there. Callie didn't have a choice. Driving off in the middle of the night would have been too hard to explain to her husband if she got caught. I didn't want to have to explain to Amber either. She wasn't buying into my "nowhere" excuse anymore.

We would be coming from opposite directions so we didn't plan to meet and walk together. She assured me she'd be fine walking through the woods by herself even though I didn't ask her. They were the same woods she used to hang out in with her grandpa and she knew them like the back of her hand, she told me. And once she hit the tracks, she couldn't get lost.

I got there first and waited. I even started to worry about her. I knew there weren't any animals around that could hurt her— Bud's rabid skunk would be dead by now—but I couldn't help thinking about Amber's psychos.

I took a walk down the tracks looking for her. About a half-mile away from the office was the mine it serviced: a small single-shaft one with an entrance no bigger than an attic trap-door. Now it was almost completely blocked off by rocks and weeds and fallen metal support beams.

Across the tracks stood the tipple that used to sort and load the coal into the train cars. All I could see at night was the tallest section of the splintered wood skeleton, jutting out from the tree-tops thirty feet above me like the rotting head of a dinosaur. The rest of it—the hundred-pound gears, the massive iron funnel, the chutes and rollers and sorting screens—were all brittle with age and coated in blood-brown rust.

The companies never tore down the tipples or closed off the shafts when they bugged out. They just left them there the same way people threw garbage on the side of the road. Moms always told their kids to stay away from them and kids always ignored them but after a couple times crawling around one and getting your hands and knees full of splinters and rust flakes, the thrill was gone.

Skip tried to figure out a way to kill Donny on the tipple, but there were so many ways for him to accidentally get killed it took all the fun out of planning his death.

The mine was a different story. We came up with a plan to lure him inside it with snack cakes, then plant some cherry bombs around the shaft opening, explode them, and cause a cave-in. I didn't think it would work because I couldn't imagine anyone brave or stupid or hungry enough to allow himself to be swallowed up by a black hole in the ground but as I watched a grinning Skip toss individually wrapped Hostess fruit pies into the shaft and Donny obediently follow them, I realized those reasons didn't have anything to do with it. I finally understood Donny. He endured the indignity and the fear because it made Skip happy.

We didn't get to light the cherry bombs. I dropped the matches in a ditch of standing water, and Skip bitched me out for days about what a fuck-up I was. I never bothered telling him I did it on purpose.

I gave up and walked back to the office. I was thinking about leaving even though I knew I wouldn't, when I heard gravel crunching. I went to the door and she was coming up the tracks carrying a backpack and a Little Playmate cooler. She unpacked a blanket, a couple roast beef sandwiches, four beers, a flashlight, mosquito repellent, matches to start a fire, and stuff to make s'mores. There were some definite advantages to screwing a mom.

She asked me how my week went and I told her fine. I apologized for the condition of the place since I was the guy and I had asked her to meet me here. She said she didn't mind. She said she loved the calm of decay and desertion that reigned there, and I told her she sounded like Shakespeare. She smiled and asked me what I had read of his and I said nothing but I knew how he talked.

"Stand over there," she told me.

I could hardly see her in the dark, but I saw the blanket being snapped and floating down to the floor.

"Don't you want me to sweep out the place?" I asked her. "There's all kinds of shit on the floor. Even glass."

"I don't mind," she said.

She didn't waste any time. She came right at me and pushed Dad's coat off my shoulders and down my arms. When she touched the coat, my instinct was to grab a handful of her hair and smash her head into a wall so hard, it would break her neck and crack open her skull. I could cover her shattered face with the blanket and if I fucked her fast enough, she would still be warm. But warm wasn't good enough. I wanted to make her come again. Feeling her do that was almost as good as the rest of it.

I took a deep breath and let the coat fall off my arms onto

the floor with a dead thud. She pulled my T-shirt out of my jeans and over my head and kissed me on my mouth and my neck. Then she stepped back and stripped.

I still could hardly see her. She was just a pale form without details like someone had cut the shape of a perfect woman out of a piece of black fabric. I went for her and knocked her down.

We hit the floor kind of hard. I should have asked her if she was okay, but I already had my hands on her ass and a nipple in my mouth. She made a groan that could have meant she was hurt but then I felt her hands in my jeans and knew she was functioning.

"Lie on your back," she told me.

"Huh?"

"Roll over."

I did and she straddled my chest.

"I want to ask you something, and I want you to be honest with me. I don't care what you say. There's no right or wrong answer."

Jesus Christ, I thought to myself. She was talking in complete sentences.

"Sure," I panted.

"Was I your first?"

"Huh?"

"Was I your first?"

"First what?"

"Woman."

"Huh?"

She slid a little lower and leaned over until her breasts were in my face. She stuck her tongue in my ear, then whispered, "Was I the first woman you ever had sex with?"

I wasn't in any condition to try and figure out what I should have told her. All I heard was a question and I answered it.

She sat up on my chest again. I couldn't see her face in the dark. I ran my hands all over her body while she talked some more.

"I wasn't sure. I thought maybe I was, but you are nineteen. I didn't think about it until after it happened. I'm sorry your first time was in the mud. I hope it was still memorable. Was it?"

"I remember it," I said.

I felt her get off me. She kissed my mouth and neck again and my chest and stomach. Each time she kissed my stomach, I felt her breath near my dick. I dug my fingers into the rotting floorboards and prayed to God to let it happen. I didn't even care that I was praying for something perverted, that I was breaking Commandments, that He was probably pissed at me because I never prayed for Daddy's SOWL or Mommy's SOWL or any of our SOWLS anymore but now I was praying for this. I prayed harder than I did to shut up Brandy Crowe. I prayed harder than I used to pray every night for my dad to love me.

She stopped kissing.

"Harley." I heard her voice come from the darkness. "Has anyone ever given you head?"

The question alone almost made me lose it. I tried thinking about disgusting things to help me hang on. Rick's fat ass waddling out of Shop Rite. Mike Jr. running for a touchdown. Betty's thighs in a short skirt.

"No," I answered.

"Would you like me to?"

"Sure."

She took me in her mouth and at that instant I believed in God again. I had been doubting His existence ever since my mom killed my dad, not because of what it did to me but what it did to the girls. I couldn't believe He would hurt innocents. I knew God wasn't merciful. I knew He wasn't reasonable or far-sighted. But I never thought He was a bully. I decided I'd rather not believe in Him at all than believe in that.

But now I knew He was out there and He was good and kind. He had given me her and she was the answer. If every man had her, there would be no wars, no crime, no contact sports.

I was still in her mouth when I fell asleep.

She was gone when I woke up. I probably should have expected it. She left me a note this time, two beers and a sandwich. She said I was sleeping so soundly she didn't want to wake me, but she had to get home and it was a long walk. She'd meet me here next Wednesday.

Every bone in my body ached from lying on the wood floor, and my hands were on fire from digging them into the splintered boards. Everything bothered me all of a sudden. The night was too cool. The night was too dark. I had a three-mile walk ahead of me, a lot of it through the woods. But she bothered me most of all. I wanted her to suck me again. I wanted to make s'mores. I wanted a Rolling Rock, and she had brought me Miller in a can.

I put my clothes on and took my beers and sandwich outside to eat. She had left me the flashlight too. I sat in the middle of the rusted tracks and stared down the length of them wondering where they really did end up. It wasn't California. I bet they just stopped somewhere in a field of junk metal.

A noise cracked in the woods behind me. I jerked my head around.

"Callie?" I called softly.

I flicked on the flashlight and swept the trees, hoping to catch a velvet-eyed deer in the beam. Nothing.

I turned it off. Then I heard a rustle. It sounded too big to be a skunk. Too clumsy to be a deer. Too hurried to be a coon. Too decisive to be a dog.

Then one of the trees shook with a hiss and a human scream. I fumbled with the light but before I could turn it on again, a ghostly figure escaped from its branches and took off flying. It let out one more scream and turned its pale, heart-shaped face downward as it passed overhead.

A barn owl, I thought with relief. An owl that doesn't hoot.

I went back to eating, forgetting for the moment that there was something out there. It hadn't been the owl. Whatever surprised me the first time had been tragically earthbound.

chapter 13

Betty was very friendly when I got there, probably because our last appointment had ended with me freaking out and she didn't expect to see me for a while.

I slumped onto the end of the couch, stared out the window, and only gave her grunts and shrugs for the first half-hour.

The parking lot was busy with people going in and out of the DMV. A lot of people were going in and out of Behavioral Services too. Most of them women. Must have been the summer rush. They were all psychologically traumatized by the thought of putting on their bathing suits. They should have been too. They were cows. Except for one. She was good-looking. Wearing white shorts and a black T-shirt. She had nice legs and shiny gold hair like Jody. She already had a tan.

I watched her come out of the building and walk to her car. A brand-new dark-green Camaro. I wondered what her problem was. Fear of heights? Fear of breaking a nail? Fear of Wal-Mart? Maybe she was getting fed up with the characters on her favorite soap opera.

I didn't know her, but I hated her. I didn't even care that she was hot. If she had come on to me, I would have thrown up. I only wanted Callie.

I couldn't figure out if I loved Callie though. I thought about her all the time. Most of it was about fucking her, but some of it was about how she made me feel just talking to me or looking at me: not special or impressive or needed; accepted, maybe. She was one more thing that was wrong with me that I liked about me anyway.

I watched the woman stop at her car door and fish for her keys in her purse. She had a nice rear end, but it was nothing compared to Callie's. Hers could have been an altar.

"Harley, did you hear what I said?"

Lately, I had started thinking about marrying her. What that kind of life would be like. Sex every day. Blow jobs on my lunch hour. Someone to cook and clean and care for me.

It didn't matter if I loved her. From what I had seen of marriage, the woman had to love the man but the man only had to love what the woman did for him.

"Harley?"

I wasn't going to make it until Wednesday. Maybe I didn't have to. I didn't have to be married to her to go visit her on my lunch break. I could do it tomorrow.

"Harley, are you in there?"

She could blow me in my truck.

Fingers snapped in front of my face. I swiped at them before I realized what they were. Betty drew her hand back.

"I'm sorry," she said. "I didn't mean to upset you."

"I'm not upset."

She edged back in her chair, uncrossed her legs and recrossed them the other way, then fixed her skirt. It was a short one today. Just my luck. Mint green with white flowers on it. All pleated like a window blind.

"Did you find that woman attractive?" she asked me.

"What woman?"

"The one you were staring at so intently."

"I wasn't staring at her."

The veins on Betty's legs looked like scribbling to me. They could have come in handy being a shrink. Her patients could have read her thighs instead of ink blots.

"All right. You weren't staring at her," she said to humor me. "But you did notice her. Did you find her attractive?"

I pulled the brim of my cap down over my eyes. "No."

"Why not?"

"I just didn't."

"I thought she was attractive."

"Then I guess you're sorry she left."

She had a big purple twist on her right thigh that the hem of her skirt didn't cover. I studied it. I saw spaghetti. I saw a pile of night crawlers. I saw a baby strangling in its umbilical cord.

"Come on, Harley," she urged. "Treat me like I'm a person, not your therapist. We're just two people hanging out talking. I thought she was attractive. You didn't. Why not?"

"She had a tan."

"You don't like tans?"

"It's only the last week of May. A tan that good means she just got back from a vacation or she goes to a tanning place."

"And I take it you don't approve of either."

"It means she's rich or stuck on herself."

"I see. And you don't feel you're making broad assumptions and generalizations?"

"Yeah, I am."

I saw the Monongahela, Susquehanna, and Allegheny rivers meeting on a road map.

"Do you think that's fair to her?"

I shrugged.

"Would it be fair to you for someone to look at the way you're dressed and assume you're a redneck?"

I almost laughed at her saying the word "redneck." She said it like it was two words, like she could have replaced red with blue or green and it would have meant the same thing to her.

"Would that bother you?"

"No."

"But is that a fair summation of your character? Are you a RED Neck?"

"It doesn't matter," I told her. "People have to judge other people by the way they look. We don't have a choice. We can't smell personalities the way dogs can."

She smiled at me. I dropped my gaze from her face and fixed it back on her leg. I saw groundhog guts.

"True. But we can talk to each other," she said. "Wouldn't that be a better way to judge someone?"

I turned back to the window, scowling. Her pen eraser started tapping on her notepad. I wished I had the balls to take it and stab it in her eye.

"What do you find physically attractive in a woman?"

"What kind of question is that?"

"Just a question."

"Her body," I answered.

"What about her body?"

"That it's a woman's body."

"No, I mean specifically."

"That's it."

"So you like any female body. You don't care if it's overweight or elderly or . . ."

"No, no," I interrupted, shaking my head at a mental picture of all the Shop Rite customers shopping naked. "I mean if she's got a good body, I don't care about one part more than the others."

"What if you had to choose one part? What would it be?"

I looked over at her. She was leaning forward waiting for my response. I thought she might be turning kinky on me but then I remembered an article I had read once in a woman's magazine in the waiting room at Mom's prison about how men revealed a lot about themselves by what body part they liked best.

The article used nicer words but basically it said men who were obsessed with asses—even female ones—were closet fags. Men who were obsessed with breasts lusted for their mothers. Men who were obsessed with women's legs wished they could be women themselves. No men were obsessed with pussies because we were actually afraid of them.

Betty had probably read the same article. It was probably a chapter in one of the books at her real office.

"Her mouth," I said.

"Her mouth," she repeated, surprised.

"Can we stop talking about this crap?" I blurted out. "I don't want to talk about crap."

"Fine, Harley. What do you want to talk about?"

"I knew you were going to say that."

"It's your session, not mine."

"It's the state of Pennsylvania's session," I said angrily. "Don't they give you guidelines about what we're supposed to talk about?"

She leaned back in her chair and contemplated me. "In a sense, they do. But I'm willing to bet you don't want to talk about any of that either."

My scalp was sweating. I took off my hat and set it on the table next to the box of Kleenex. It was the first time I had taken my hands out of my coat pockets.

"What happened to your hands?" Betty gasped. "They look like you put them through glass."

I glanced down at them. Misty's scratches had faded, but the palms were a mess.

"I got a bunch of splinters," I explained. "I guess I didn't do a very good job digging them out."

"Splinters? What were you doing?"

I thought about it. "Ripping up floorboards," I answered.

"Did you put something on them so they won't get infected?"

"They're okay," I said.

She couldn't stop looking at them so I put them back in Dad's pockets. Then she kept glancing at my pockets. She was making me nervous. I was ready for her to go to the desk and whip out a first-aid kit. Would it be a cheap plastic one like the one my mom kept in the medicine cabinet? Or would it be a chocolate leather doctor's bag to match her datebook?

"Okay, there's something I want to talk about," I said to get her mind off my hands.

She gave me a pleased look of surprise like she had discovered a bud on a plant she expected to die. "Go on," she said.

"How can a kid like someone who beats them up? You know. How can they like hanging out with them?"

"Did you like hanging out with your father?" she asked.

"I never hung out with my dad. He didn't like ME."

A big flock of ME exploded in front of my eyes. They rose up from Betty's lap and fluttered around the room like butterflies. I tried keeping track of them, bobbing my head and blinking, but there were too many.

"This isn't about ME," I went on, watching them zip around the room. "I just want to know as a broad assumption or generalization how it can happen."

"Well," she began, tapping her pen on her forehead twice, "every child reacts to abuse differently. Some become withdrawn. Some openly hostile. Some self-destructive. But some embrace the abuse. They thrive on it. It's what they get from their abusive parent instead of love and they come to need it."

"So you're saying a kid can actually want to get hit?"

"In a sense."

"Can they start to think that it's okay? Morally okay?"

"Did you think it was okay for your father to hit you?"

"This isn't about ME," I stressed again.

"You can still answer the question."

I let out a shaky breath. I didn't want to lose it. I didn't want Betty running off to get me a Styrofoam cup of water. I didn't want to have a BREAKTHROUGH. I wanted it to be lunchtime tomorrow.

"I didn't think it was okay," I said bluntly, "but I thought it was normal."

I could tell she was going to ask me to explain my comment further so I rushed ahead with another question. It was a hard one to ask. I had to concentrate on something else and let my voice say the words without me understanding them.

"What about sexually abused kids?"

I watched one ME after another land on the windowsill, all packed together, making a colorful cluster like feathers in an Indian headdress.

"Can they think that it's okay?"

"Okay but not normal?" Betty asked.

"No." I shook my head in frustration. "Can they think it's normal? Can they think it's right?"

"Are you talking about Misty?"

Her question hit me like a sucker punch. I struggled to find my voice and then control it. "What do you know about Misty?"

"Very little since I treated her for such a short time," she replied, frowning.

Misty and Jody dropping out of therapy was a sore spot with Betty; but it got too hard. I couldn't get time off work to drive them to their appointments plus they both hated going. Misty used to disappear into the woods, and I used to have to carry Jody kicking and screaming to the truck.

Amber wanted to go to her sessions. She even made arrangements with friends to drive her and pick her up afterward.

Betty went on, "But in the few sessions we had, I did get the feeling Misty believed your father's abuse toward all of you was warranted. She felt it was right, if you want to call it that."

I fell silent, and Betty tapped her pen on her notepad.

"Who was sexually abused, Harley?" she asked with the detachment of a person filling out a form.

"None of us," I answered, startled.

"What about Amber?"

"Amber?"

My throat clamped shut the way it used to when I saw Dad listening to Mom's day.

"They were never alone," I protested. "When she was home, she made sure someone else was always in the room with her. She was terrified of Dad. She hated him."

"What about at night?"

"Amber hated him," I said again, ignoring her question.

"Did she?"

"Yeah," I answered, amazed she could even ask.

"How do you know? Have you ever talked to her about it?"

"I don't have to talk to her. I was always there when he hit her. I saw."

"How did you feel toward your father when he hit Amber?"

Tears filled my eyes. I couldn't figure out where they had come from. "I felt sorry for him."

Betty moved forward in her chair. "You felt sorry for your father, not Amber?"

I nodded.

"How did you feel toward Amber?"

"What do you mean?"

"Did you get mad at her? Did you think she deserved it? Did you want to help her?"

"I wanted to make her feel better."

"How do you think she felt when she saw your father hit you?"

"I don't know."

Her questions felt like rocks being thrown at my head. I covered my face with my mangled hands. The salt from my tears stung the gouges I'd made with my pocket knife.

"She probably didn't like it," I cried into them.

"Do you think she wanted to make you feel better?"

Six seconds. The scientist on TV had said the sky would light up like a thousand suns and by the time we turned to look at it, it would have hit with the power of ten thousand Hiroshima bombs.

I saw it coming, rushing at me. My head filled with a harsh white light obliterating the image behind it. I didn't have a chance to recognize it. To know if it was a memory or a dream. I was blind but I could feel. Amber. Her soft weight against me. Her surrender. The smell of watermelon Lip Smacker.

It hit before I could figure it all out. I came to huddled on the floor, trembling and sobbing, but I had survived, and like any survivor of a Doomsday strike I thought I was lucky. No one could have convinced me that I would have been better off dying instantly.

Betty was kneeling in front of me. I couldn't make out her face through my tears, but I saw her young eyes. I saw her whole young life in them. She was glad she was old now. She was relieved.

I felt her hands on my arm.

"It's all right, Harley."

Did Dad have six seconds? He didn't know it was coming. Mom snuck up behind him and let him have it. She didn't have a choice. It was a big gun. She couldn't have whipped it out and surprised him. She couldn't have faced him down either. If she had tried, she would have stood there with the gun shaking in her hands, and he would have walked right up to her and taken it from her like it was one more bill they couldn't pay.

"It's all right," she said again.

I got up from the floor and stumbled blindly around the room looking for my hat and a ME.

"Harley, please calm down. Don't go rushing off again."

I grabbed my hat off the table. I couldn't find a single ME.

"You need to talk about this."

"No, I don't," I cried.

"It will make you feel better."

"I don't want to feel better."

I bolted for the door.

"Please, don't go, Harley," she called after me.

But I was gone, and this time I knew better than to look back.

Yee's had three customers, the busiest I had ever seen it. Jack Yee didn't look as glad to see me as he usually did. The customers didn't look too glad either. Jack's wife glanced up from her newspaper, then buried her face in it again without waving.

I ordered Misty's egg roll and got myself an order of General Tso's chicken. I was supposed to be saving money—I still needed a hundred dollars to finish paying our taxes—but I couldn't shake the Doomsday feeling I had had in Betty's office. Every meal could be my last and I didn't want it to be hot dogs and mac and cheese.

Jack Yee went back in the kitchen and packed up the order himself. I had to ask him for Jody's fortune cookie and umbrella. On my way out, I checked myself in the front door glass to see what everyone had been staring at. I could have used a shower and a shave and a good night's sleep but other than that, I was still ME.

I got back in my truck and ripped into the chicken box right away. He had given me six plastic forks, three sets of chopsticks, and about twenty packets of soy sauce and sweet and sour sauce. I could almost smell his nervousness in the greasy-bottomed bag.

The chicken was good but not great. I was sure Callie could do better. If I was married to her, she would cook for me all the time too.

I finished eating and crushed the box before tossing it on the floor. It bounced off the Chicago Art Institute book and landed next to Mom and Dad's wedding picture. I had never thought about it before but it was pretty pathetic if that was the best photo they had from their wedding: Mom sick because she was pregnant with me, Dad falling down drunk because she was pregnant with me. I had always assumed Dad was grinning at a buddy. Now I wondered if it was Uncle Mike, and Uncle Mike already knew it was a bad idea. Or was he looking at Grandpa? Was he saying, "Look at me, you nasty old cocksucker. I got a job and a wife, and you were always telling me I'd never get either?" I was going to keep the picture buried there in the trash for the rest of my life. It was too fucking symbolic to mess with.

I took my time driving. I wasn't in any hurry now that I had a full stomach, and I definitely didn't feel like seeing the girls.

I hadn't seen any of them that morning. I didn't get home from the mining office until five. Elvis went nuts in the front of my truck where I had locked him so his barking wouldn't wake them when I left and when I got back.

I let him out, gave him a good scratching, and took him inside with me. We shared the leftover sloppy-joe meat Amber had left sitting out on the stove from the night before.

I didn't even bother trying to catch an hour or two of sleep. I went for a drive and counted Madonnas. They looked best at breaking dawn, gazing peacefully at the dew-soaked grass around their feet. They were always surrounded by a bunch of crap—ceramic deer with chipped noses, birdbaths, lawn jockeys, a kaleidoscope of reflecting balls, ducks with windmill wings, wooden cutouts of women bending over showing their underwear—but they always seemed to be standing alone.

I counted seven. The only old-fashioned plastic one belonged to the Shanks. On the way home from Yee's, I slowed in front of their house like I had done in the morning and admired her sky-blue robes and petal-pink lips. She was the only one of the Madonnas who had the nerve to look up at God, and she was happy with Him. Her smile gave me hope.

Driving up Potshot Road made me feel even better. The trees made a quiet leafy tunnel. Shafts of sunlight poked through them, striping the air and covering the rutted dirt road with white spots of dancing light. Freaking out with Betty faded into the furthest reaches of my mind. Everything did. My full belly, the bouncing of the truck, and the green calm almost put me to sleep.

I drove slowly as I neared the crest, hoping to see a deer bound away or the shimmer of a pheasant's tail. What I saw was a pickup truck parked in our driveway. It wasn't Uncle Mike's. The only other people who ever came by our place were either sent by a government agency or drawn here by Amber's ass.

A kid with two-tone hair wearing three earrings, a hemp bracelet, and a beaded choker sat on the hood drinking a can of Red Dog and smoking a cigarette. He looked in my direction but didn't nod or smile or acknowledge me with a wave. I considered that impolite.

I hadn't noticed Jody and Misty on the porch. When I got out of my truck, Jody tore across the yard, her face streaked with tears, and threw herself at my legs. Misty didn't follow her, but she stood up and allowed our eyes to meet which was the most contact we'd had since the day I took the money.

"What's going on?" I asked, putting my hands on Jody's shoulders but staring at the kid on the truck.

"Amber's running away," Jody bawled.

"Who the fuck are you?" I yelled at him.

He slowly took the can away from his mouth. He had the stale eyes and rehearsed smirk of someone who spent a lot of time in dim, smoky rooms thinking about himself.

"Who the fuck are you?" he yelled back.

I started toward him but Jody had wrapped herself so tightly around my legs, I couldn't move.

"Don't let Amber go," she cried. "Please, Harley. Don't let her go."

"Don't worry, she's not going anywhere," I said.

I pried her off me and stalked over to the kid. "I asked you who you are."

He finished his beer and tossed the can in my yard. "I'm a

friend of Amber's," he answered, poking the cigarette back between his lips. "You must be her brother the bag boy."

I waited for my hand to explode from my side like it had been doing lately but nothing happened. I stared dumbly at it.

"Don't hurt him, Harley," Jody said, coming up beside me.

"Hurt me?" The kid laughed.

"Just make him go away."

"Hurt him," Misty shouted from the porch.

The front door slammed open and Amber stepped out lugging a suitcase and carrying her pillow. She stopped when she saw me. All the blood drained from her face and her eyes turned black from some unspeakable outrage brewing inside her.

"Come on," the kid yelled at her. "I'm hungry. Let's go."

I walked toward her, without thinking. "What are you doing?"

"I'm leaving you."

"What did you say?"

"You heard me."

I grabbed her arm with my throbbing hand. She ripped it away.

"Don't touch me," she said, savagely.

"Amber, what's going on?"

"I won't live with you anymore," she turned around and hissed at me. "You're disgusting."

Jody came and squeezed in between us. She hugged Amber around the waist. "Don't go," she whimpered.

"I'm sorry, Jody. I don't want to go but I have to. It's all Harley's fault. Be mad at him."

"What did I do?" I cried out.

She grabbed up her stuff and took off running for the kid's truck. He didn't make a move to help her. He should have been carrying her stuff. He should have been comforting her. He should have been opening the door for her. He was blowing smoke and watching her tits bounce.

"You know what you did," she turned around and screamed at me.

"Harley." Jody tugged on my arm. "Shoot his tires," she pleaded.

"It's okay, Jody."

"No, it's not."

Amber threw her suitcase in the back and climbed into the cab with her pillow. She slammed the door shut and bowed her head, crying. Her friend took his good old time getting down from the hood.

"Stop her," Jody begged.

"She'll be back."

"No, she won't."

I put my arm around Jody's shoulders. She was crying so hard, she shook.

"That kid wants one thing from her and once he gets it, he's going to dump her in a parking lot somewhere."

"Does he want her pillow?"

I looked down at her, at all the love and trust shining in her eyes. I was never going to have a kid. I had too much respect for them.

"Yeah," I said.

"Will you go get her in the parking lot?"

"Yeah, I'll go get her."

"Okay." She sniffed. "Are you sure?"

"Yeah."

She plunked down on the top porch step. "This is all Misty's fault," she grumbled.

Misty was standing at the far end of the porch. She didn't show any sign that she had heard Jody. I told her her egg roll was in the truck. She didn't show any sign that she had heard me either but then she walked to the porch railing, swung herself over it, and started across the yard.

I didn't want to ask Jody what she meant. I had survived one

Doomsday strike. I wasn't ready for another. But I made the mistake of checking on Misty. She had the bag from Yee's in her hand but all I saw was the cheap sparkle of the fake pink stones around her wrist. It struck me that I couldn't remember seeing her without the collar since the day she had put it on.

She came walking back. She handed Jody her fortune cookie and pink paper umbrella and took the rest of the stuff inside. Jody cracked open her cookie.

"'Good news will come to you by mail,'" she read, and wrinkled up her nose. "That's a dumb one. Confucius didn't say that. They didn't even have mail when he was alive. They only had voices."

"I think you're right," I said, sitting down next to her. "I don't think Confucius wrote all the fortunes. Just the good ones."

She kept it just the same. She folded it in half and carefully slipped it into a pocket in her jean jacket with the Pocahontas fringe.

I still didn't want to ask about Misty but I saw the collar in my mind, sad and ugly in its necessity like a bad wig. She was my responsibility now.

"Why did you say Amber leaving was Misty's fault?"

Her eyes turned thoughtful and she studied one of Amber's clunky sandal footprints hardening in the mud.

"She told Amber something today when Amber got home from school and it made her really mad. The kind of mad where you cry."

"What did she tell her?"

"I don't know. They went into her room and closed the door. It was about you though. I heard your name a bunch of times."

She stood up all of a sudden and walked over to where a tulip was sprouting from the ground like a purple bullet. She knelt down and bent her head toward it like she meant to kiss it.

"I asked Misty to tell me but she said it was a secret," she told me, walking back to the steps. She sat down with a big deflated sigh. "Misty keeps secrets better than anyone. She told me I wouldn't be able to keep it."

"You kept the secret about Mom's money," I reminded her.

"Misty said if I told, Mommy and Daddy would get in the biggest fight ever and get divorced."

She glanced up at me. People always commented on her Sleeping Beauty hair, but her eyes were her most striking feature. They were a soft, downy gray and gave everyone the benefit of the doubt.

"Do you think I should've told?" she asked me.

"I don't think it would've made any difference." I leaned back and stretched out my legs. I crossed them at the ankles, doing my best to appear casual. "Have you kept any other secrets for Misty?"

"Maybe."

"You know, when Misty tells you you can't tell anyone, she's not talking about me."

"Yes, she is."

"She tells you not to tell me?"

"She tells me not to tell anyone. You're anyone."

"Did she ever ask you to keep a secret about getting lots of blood on a shirt?"

"You mean the night Mommy shot Daddy?"

One of my hands jumped at my side. The surprise started my heart thumping too fast.

"She got blood on her shirt that night?" I asked, conversationally.

"Yeah, but it wasn't a secret. Mommy knew."

I stood up. I could hear my heart pounding in my ears. I could feel it in my throat. My fingertips quivered. Six seconds. TICK TOCK.

"How did she get blood on her shirt?"

"When she hugged Daddy. She told me he was going to be okay, but I saw him and I knew he wasn't okay."

"Misty never hugged Daddy," I said cautiously. "The ambulance had taken him away by the time the state trooper and me brought her back from the mall."

"I know."

"She was at the mall. I saw her with my own eyes."

"I know. Mommy drove her there."

"Of course Mom drove her there. How else would she get there?"

I walked over to the railing. I put my torn-up hands on it and squeezed. The pain affected me like being pinched out of a dream. I suddenly understood the other question I needed to ask.

"When did Mom drive her there?" I asked.

"I don't know. I can't tell time yet."

"Was it before or after Mom and Dad had their fight?"

"After."

"After," I said.

"After," she said.

"You're saying Mom drove Misty to the mall after she shot Dad?"

She nodded.

FOUR seconds. TICK TOCK. Sweat beads popped out along my hairline and started sliding down my face.

"You're saying Mom shot Dad and left him lying dead in the kitchen, then loaded Misty in the truck and drove her to the mall?"

"I guess so."

"You're not making sense, Jody. You must be confused. You were only four years old when it happened. And you were in shock. You didn't talk for six months. Do you remember that? Not talking to anybody?"

"I remember."

I paced up and down, my boots making the same futile thuds

that Dad's used to make when he was contemplating a day full of cement.

Three seconds. TICK TOCK.

I knelt down on the porch beside her.

"What did Mom do when she got back from the mall?"

"She got a shovel out of the shed and went in the woods. I thought she was going to bury Daddy."

"Did she bury Misty's shirt?"

She looked at me, curiously. "Why would she do that?"

"Did she have Misty's shirt with her?" I persisted.

"I don't know. It was hard to see. I was in the doghouse."

"Did you see her come back?"

"Yeah."

"What'd she do?"

"She put the shovel away and went in the house. Pretty soon the police cars came. Are you mad at me?"

"Why didn't you tell the police Misty was home when Mom shot Dad?"

"They didn't ask me."

Two seconds. TICK TOCK. Why would they? One of their troopers had just picked her up at the Orange Julius, and Mom had just turned herself in.

"Are you okay, Harley? You look sick. You look like you did when we went to visit Mommy."

"I'm fine," I said, taking a shaky breath, and smiling bravely. One second.

I reached out suddenly and wrapped my arms around her in the nick of time. She hugged me back, and I closed my eyes in relief as I saw Donny on a flaming Zinger intercept Misty in a bloody sunflower shirt and blast her into a million pieces.

chapter ⟨14⟩

Amber didn't come back until Saturday morning. I was out front sawing away at Dad's piece of pipe when one of her girlfriends drove up and dropped her off. She trudged across the yard, lugging her suitcase with both hands, trying not to look at me.

Elvis trotted over to her with his tail waving and gave her a good sniffing. I could smell her from where I was: Sex and Egg McMuffin.

She looked tired and I noticed a small bruise where her jaw met her throat.

"Where's Prince Charming?" I shouted at her.

"Fuck you," she said on her way past.

"I rented your room," I told her. "You're going to have to sleep in one of the doghouses."

She dropped her suitcase on the ground and tripped over it trying to charge at me.

"This is temporary," she yelled, getting up and rubbing at her knee through her torn jeans. "I'm getting out of here as soon as I can make arrangements."

"Jesus, Amber, what is with you?"

I stood up and flexed my sore hands. I hadn't been taking very good care of them. They were swollen and the splinter wounds were festering. I wondered if Callie would suck on them for me.

"If you want to run away from home, I can't stop you. But why now? Why are you so pissed at me?"

"I don't want to live with you anymore. That's all. I want to live with Dylan."

"Dylan." I spit out the name. "How the hell are you going to live with DYLAN? Won't his parents notice an extra body in his bed?"

"He's graduating next week and he and a couple friends went in together and bought a trailer."

"Oh, great. That's just great. You in a trailer with three guys. You going to gang-bang them or will they alternate nights?"

"I hate you."

She went back to her suitcase and picked it up, wincing. I realized she was having a hard time with it because she was hurt. I remembered how I used to feel after one of Dad's beatings. I'd wake up with bruises on parts of my body I never knew he hit.

"What did he do to you?" I shouted at her.

"Nothing."

"Amber . . ."

She stopped and turned around with an exhausted sigh. Even the hummingbird peeking over the back of her hiphugger jeans looked a shade less green today.

"Why do you give yourself to assholes like that?" I said, lowering my voice a little. "You don't even make them work for it."

"They want me," she replied flatly.

"Of course they want you. It doesn't mean they should get you."

"You're one to talk."

"What?"

She went inside, too tired to slam for once. I had a mental flash of her standing naked under the shower, her bruised skin looking like an Impressionist had gone at her with loving strokes

of gray-greens and yellows and rosy purples. I should have wanted
to kill him, but I wanted to kill her. I wanted to break her pretty
neck and end it now like a bad TV show turned off in the middle.

The day was cool. I had worked up a great sweat sawing but
now that I'd stopped, I was shivering. May had been beautiful
which probably meant the first couple weeks of June were going
to be cold and rainy. The sky beyond the hills was turning to
pencil lead.

I got back down on my knees and picked up the saw. Elvis
went back to gnawing on a tree limb he had dragged in from
the woods. It was twice as long as he was.

I didn't look up when I heard the front door open and shut
again. I had a good, strong rhythm going. Once I had the pipe
sawed off as close to the ground as I could get it, I was going to
cover it with dirt and mark it with a rock slab like a grave.

Jody's pink canvas sneakers walked into my field of vision. She
lowered a can of Red Dog down where I could see it.

"Where'd you get this?" I asked after I grabbed it from her.

"Amber has a whole bunch in her suitcase. She told me to
bring you one. You were right," she added, plopping down on
the grass and crossing her legs Indian-style. "He just wanted her
pillow."

I popped the top and gulped down half the can. "How many
did she bring?"

"I don't know. Hundreds, maybe. We're going to have a slumber party tonight. Me and Amber and Misty. Amber said so. We're
going to put sleeping bags on the floor and eat popcorn and
watch TV and tell scary stories and paint our fingernails."

"Misty?" I wondered.

"She's glad Amber's back. She told her running away from
you wasn't going to solve anything."

"What the hell? Did you tell Misty what we talked about the
other night on the porch?"

"What did we talk about?"

"Did you tell her you told me she was home the night Mom and Dad had their big fight?"

"She knows she was home."

"That's not what I mean. Did you tell her you told me?"

"No. Do you want me to?"

"No. I don't want you to."

"Why not?"

"Just don't."

"What if she asks me?"

"Why would she ask you?"

"You asked me."

"Just don't talk to her at all."

"Why not?"

Elvis stopped gnawing and his ears perked up. An engine sounded from down the road. I stood up, wondering if DYLAN would have the nerve to come after her. Or maybe he was coming after his beer.

"That's Esme," Jody announced excitedly. "We're going to the Lick n' Putt."

She ran across the yard, shrieking, waving her arm so hard her whole body jiggled.

I wasn't sure what I should do. I had gone over to Callie's house the day before on my lunch hour and she wasn't there. She hadn't shown up at the Shop Rite either for her Friday night shopping. I was beginning to think she was avoiding me, but she couldn't be if she was taking Jody to the Lick n' Putt. I could go too. We couldn't do anything on a miniature golf course, but she would have to bend over a lot.

Her husband's Grand Cherokee pulled into our driveway, and her husband was driving it.

That was bad enough. My day was shot right there. I had been able to force Callie out of my mind so far today since I knew I couldn't see her until Monday—I was planning on making another lunch hour visit—but now I was thinking about her again. Now I was all keyed up imagining her bending over to help Zack line up a putt. Imagining her licking an ice cream cone. I probably could have handled it though. I probably could have just gone back to what I was doing and sawed through the pipe with a newfound vengeance, but the guy parked his Jeep and opened his door.

My stomach clenched into a knot, and I chugged the rest of my beer. I hoped he knew about us. I could have handled a fist-fight, but I didn't think I could handle discussing the weather with him.

I stayed in the middle of the yard waiting to see if trumpets sounded when he got out, if he was built like Schwarzenegger or had cherubs flying around him like Zeus. He was the man who possessed Callie Mercer. The man who slept in the same bed with her naked body every night. The man who ate her pork chops. In a sense, he was my idol. I expected him to be larger than life.

I took in every detail: the regular features, the short dark hair, the average build. He wasn't tall. He wasn't short. He wasn't old or young. He could have been a dressed-down banker or a dressed-up RED Neck in a pair of palomino-gold hiking boots, new jeans, and a faded red work shirt over a gray T-shirt.

He opened the back door of the Jeep for Jody, and she bounded inside. Then he turned and called to me, "How ya doing?" before giving Elvis a scratch between the ears and a couple thumps on his side.

My feet moved across the grass. I watched them go and felt the rest of my body follow.

He extended a hand.

"You must be Harley," he said, friendly as hell. "I'm Brad Mercer."

I started to reach out my hand, then remembered I had an excuse not to shake. I showed it to him instead.

"Wow. What'd you do? Stick it in a hornet's nest?"

"Splinters," I said.

"Wow." He shook his head. "You might want to get a doctor to look at that."

"No health insurance," I told him. I didn't know why.

"Neither of your jobs give you benefits?"

"One does but it wouldn't leave me with any paycheck."

He shook his head. "That's terrible."

"We can't all be bankers," I said.

He laughed. I was being serious.

"Thank God for that," he said. "Imagine a world full of nothing but bankers."

"Don't you like them?"

"Not particularly."

"But you are one."

"I know."

"You don't like your job?"

I didn't expect him to answer. I was being an asshole. I was trying to get him to say something bitchy about his wife so I could remind him he owed everything to her.

"I wanted to go into teaching," he explained, "but everybody I knew shot down that idea. I added a business minor in school to be safe. Worked in a bank for a couple of years. I was ready to quit and try something else, then I met the boss's daughter coming out of his office, and banking didn't seem so bad anymore."

He had a good smile. What people called a genuine smile. A boyish smile. Women liked those. That was probably what Callie liked about him. And he wanted to be a teacher. That probably meant he was smart and liked books and art. I couldn't tell yet if he had the almighty good sense of humor every beautiful woman in the world said was so damn important even though they all married rich guys with no sense of humor at all.

"You've got a great view up here," he commented.

"We don't own it," I replied immediately.

"Why would you want to?" he said. "Just means you'd have to pay taxes on it. Nobody's going to threaten that land. The coal companies have all pulled out. Who'd want to build on it way out here in the middle of nowhere? You've got a great situation here."

"I thought maybe you owned it. I mean, your wife owned it."

He shook his head. "Callie owns about fifty acres her grandfather willed to her but it's all north of here, on the other side of Black Lick Road."

"She owns it? By herself?"

He nodded, smiling boyishly and genuinely. "I'm just a tenant."

One of the back windows on the Jeep glided down.

"Dad, come on," Esme demanded.

"Come on, come on, come on," Jody and Zack chanted behind her.

"Is it okay with you if we take Jody to the Lick n' Putt?" he asked. "I talked to your sister on the phone this morning. She said you were still asleep but she was sure you wouldn't mind."

"Is your wife at home by herself?"

"No. She's off somewhere. I don't know where. She needs a break from the house and the kids now and then. But I don't get to spend enough time with the kids. I work a lot of late nights. Do a lot of traveling."

"You doing any traveling in the near future?"

"I've got a golf weekend coming up. The last weekend in June, I think it is."

"Daddy!"

"I better get going." He smiled again. "It was good to finally meet you, Harley."

He stuck out his hand again. My instinct was to shake it. I felt an awkward locker room closeness with him. We had been inside the same woman, which was kind of like sharing a wet towel.

"Sorry," he said, lowering his hand and glancing at mine. "Take care of yourself."

"Sure."

He walked to his Jeep.

"Looks like you might get rained out," I called after him.

"If it starts raining we'll just lick instead of putt."

He closed his door, started the engine, and lowered his window.

"You sure you don't know where your wife is?" I asked.

"No. Why? You need her for something?"

"That's okay," I said.

He waved. The kids waved too. Elvis chased after them, and they all went nuts over it. I knew exactly what the inside of the Jeep sounded like, and I was glad I was on the outside because I had a headache from drinking my beer too fast. All of a sudden, they stopped bouncing around and settled into their seats. I was sure Brad Mercer had made them put on their seatbelts. I had a feeling he was one of those caring dads.

My prediction about the sawing came true. I finished in half the time now that I had Callie back in my head and a beer in my bloodstream.

I went to the shed and got the shovel my mom had buried Misty's shirt with and covered what was left of the pipe's ragged rim with dirt. Then I moved the couch back over the spot before going inside.

Amber had her radio on full blast. She had her door closed, but the whole house throbbed to the bass. Misty's door was closed too.

I stopped at Amber's and pounded. I shouted at her to open up. The volume went down, but the door stayed shut.

"I'm going somewhere," I yelled through it, "so make sure you're here when Jody gets back."

Silence. Then the radio turning off completely. Then angry footsteps. Then the door flying open.

She had changed out of her jeans into a big T-shirt and flannel boxers. Her hair was pulled up to the very top of her head in a coppery fountain.

"You sure as hell don't waste any time," she snapped furiously.

I took a step back. "What are you talking about?"

"It's sick and perverted and disgusting and sinful."

"What is?"

"I can't even look at you. You make me want to throw up."

The door slammed shut. I waited a second to see if she was going to add anything. Amber's fits were the closest I would probably ever come to seeing live entertainment. She turned the radio back up, and I turned to leave.

Misty was there in the hall drinking a Mountain Dew; a perfectly normal-looking girl doing nothing out of the ordinary, but she gave me a start. I took a backward step away from her without thinking about it.

"I need to talk to you," she said.

"Huh?"

She stood planted in the hall. "Is this a bad time?" she asked.

I felt funny. I got a bad taste in my mouth. I realized I was afraid, but I didn't know what I was afraid of.

"I was going somewhere but I can talk for a minute," I said.

She raised the metallic green can to her lips and lowered it again. "Are you still mad about the money?" she asked me.

"No."

The can went up and down again and again with excruciating slowness. Her fingernails were painted purple today. In the dim hallway light, they looked like she had caught all ten of them in a slammed door and now they were dead and about to fall off. The stones in the collar around her wrist were clear but dull like dirty ice. I had no more reason to fear her than an artichoke.

"There's something I want to ask you," she continued, "but before I do, I want you to promise you're going to keep an open mind."

"I don't have an open mind."

"Try," she said, and her dark eyes fixed themselves on mine.

Her words were a soothing threat. Maybe she was going to tell me what really happened the night Mom shot Dad. Maybe she was going to tell me what really happened between her and Dad. Maybe she was going to tell me what was going on with Amber.

"I want to get a tattoo."

"What?"

"A tattoo."

"A tattoo?"

"Yes."

Relief rushed through me. This revelation was disgusting in its own right, but it was something I was equipped to deal with.

"No way," I said.

"Come on, Harley. Why not?"

"You're too young."

"I knew you were going to say that," she said, her voice calm but irritated. "That's such a cop-out. Lots of kids in my class have them. There's a place out by the mall that does kids over twelve with parental consent. They do a really good job. Nobody's ever got a disease from it."

"No."

She took a deep breath. "Come on."

It was the closest I had ever heard Misty come to pleading. The needy tone was unnerving.

"Did Amber put you up to this?" I asked her.

"Amber doesn't even know I want one. I don't want her to know."

"Why not?"

"I don't want her to think I'm copying her. I only wanted one because I like the way they look. I thought maybe you'd under-stand that, Mr. Art Institute of Chicago."

I didn't have a chance to say anything else to her. Her face and eyes went blank, and the sociable part of her disappeared with the silent, single-minded menace of a mummy returning to his tomb. She went into her bedroom to be alone, but the act was more symbolic than necessary.

The second her door closed behind her, I headed for my truck. The motor was idling when the front door opened and Amber stepped out on the porch, her face brick-red and her eyes ringed with wet mascara.

"I know where you're going," she screamed.

Then she stepped back inside and slammed the door shut.

I didn't get upset about it. I didn't see how she could know. She hadn't even been home yesterday when I made the call to Betty and asked her to help me get in to see Mom.

chapter (15)

The prison waiting area looked like tryouts for a Little Miss Pedophilia pageant. The kids were mostly girls. I didn't know why. Maybe women prone to criminal acts gave birth to more girls than boys. Maybe there was something viciously female about their hormones that enabled them to kill men in and out of the womb.

Or maybe it was because the adults who brought them here were mostly women and thought the girls could learn something.

I considered both reasons while I stood inside the doorway feeling like a chewed-up piece of gray meat someone had spit out on a plate full of Christmas cookies. I had never seen so many gold bows and pearl buttons and fake jewels together in one place except for the Wal-Mart crafts section where I took Jody every year to buy stuff to make valentines.

Everybody stared at me. Adult conversations stopped. Magazines were lowered. Little ones stopped bouncing on laps. Older ones looked up from coloring last-minute pictures and playing with Game Boys or Polly Pocket sets.

I glanced down at myself to make sure my fly wasn't open or my boots weren't untied. I had grass stains on my jeans and dirt under my fingernails. I couldn't remember when I had shaved last or combed my hair. My days and nights had begun to bleed together into one big sticky puddle.

All the chairs were taken. It was a Saturday. I moved around the perimeter of the room, trying to find a square foot of space that didn't smell like crayons or bubble gum. I ended up standing behind two women who didn't appear to have any children with them. One of them had on pencil-leg jeans, red cowboy boots, and a purple velvet tank top. The other one was dressed like a TV Realtor in a mustard-yellow blazer and sensible shoes. The only place in the world they could have looked okay sitting beside each other was a city bus or a prison waiting room.

I leaned against the wall behind them and assured myself my own wait wouldn't be long. Almost everyone here was in line for a Hug Room. I was going to be doing my visiting through Plexiglas.

I wouldn't have been able to get in at all if it hadn't been for Betty. I had called her Thursday after my talk on the porch with Jody and before my hot dogs and macaroni and cheese.

I didn't give her any details. I told her I had to see my mom. That it was time for CLOSURE. Then I explained that I hadn't been completely honest with her about my other visit with Mom: that I got kind of upset, nothing too weird, sort of the way I acted with her sometimes, and when I came to I was lying on a cot in an office like a school nurse's and a man from Prisoner Relations and a woman shrink talked to me in golf commentator voices and tried to get me to tell them my mom had attacked me. I wouldn't do it. I told them I hadn't been feeling too well lately, but they still decided she shouldn't have any visitors for six months.

When I finished talking, there was a long silence. I thought Betty was going to be pissed at me, but she got pissed at the PRISON. The way she said it reminded me of the loan officer with his scenic wonders calendar talking to me about the BANK and how the BANK couldn't make allowances for me and my sisters but how the BANK wished he could help.

According to Betty, the PRISON should have been aware that I was a teenaged boy under psychiatric care who hadn't seen my mother since the day I watched her leave a courthouse almost two years earlier to start serving a life sentence. The PRISON should have talked to Betty first. The PRISON might have caused me extensive emotional damage and should do everything possible to rectify the situation.

She said she'd take care of it for me, but she made me promise to schedule an appointment with her as soon as possible afterward. She said she'd see me on a weekend or a lunch hour if I couldn't get time off work. I promised to make the appointment. I did not promise to keep it.

I settled back against the wall and closed my eyes. Four more days until I saw Callie again. FOUR. Unless I tried to see her during my lunch break on Monday. Or unless Jody played at their house after Lick n' Putt and Callie drove her home and I casually walked out to the car to thank her and then begged her to meet me at the mining office tonight and to bring the stuff to make s'mores.

FOUR. The number strobed like gunfire against the black in front of my eyes. Watching it made me feel sick to my stomach. Then it stopped and I saw Callie's lips hovering over me, one perfect milky drop clinging to them. She kissed me and I tasted myself.

I didn't respond to her kiss and she drew away, disappointed. She rolled me off the blanket, folded it, and put it in her backpack. She closed up the cooler and stepped into her panties. I wanted to tell her to stay, but I was dead or asleep. She started walking away.

I hadn't done anything for her. Nothing at all. No wonder she had left. I thought about her smile the day we did it on the table. A smile that said, "I'm done."

I opened my eyes and saw the two women.

"I don't know," the one in cowboy boots said. "I have a hard time telling if she's being serious or not."

The one dressed like a Realtor nodded.

"The last time I came to see her she told me prison isn't all that different from married life except she has more free time now and the sex is better."

They both laughed. I watched the room spin and grow dark. My knees buckled, and I sat down on the floor. The women craned their necks over the backs of their chairs.

"Are you okay?" the Realtor asked.

"Yeah," I said, swallowing a couple times.

"You don't look so good, hon," the cowgirl said. "You here with anybody?"

I shook my head.

"Who are you visiting?"

"My mom."

"You poor kid."

"You want my seat?" the Realtor asked, standing up.

"No, thanks," I said. "I better just stay here."

It turned out staying there was the worst thing I could have done because every little kid in the room came over to check me out, and they depressed the hell out me. Some of them walked right up to me, stared for a few silent seconds, and left. Some peered timidly around the cowgirl's chair, giggling or skeptical.

Only one talked to me. She was about Jody's age with brown hair that hadn't been brushed in a while and a face that might have been cute if she ever smiled, but I had a feeling she never did. Her ears were pierced. Her eyelids were smeared with glittery lavender and her lips were neon pink. She had fake tattoos on the tops of her hands and one cheek. The one on her cheek had been a unicorn, but it was flaking off now and looked like a dirt smudge or a bruise. Her little-girl potbelly stuck out between white jeans and an orange shirt the color of a warning sign with the word GROOVY written across it in wavy green letters.

"Why are you sitting on the floor?" she asked me.

"There aren't any chairs," I replied. "Why are you wearing makeup?"

"It makes me look good," she answered immediately.

"Why do you want to look good?"

"I don't know."

"It doesn't make you look good," I told her.

She watched me for a moment to see if I was being serious, then her face fell. She looked really hurt. I was glad. I wanted to hurt her. Making her mad would have just made her go home and put more crap on her face.

"It does too," she said not very convincingly.

"It does not."

I noticed the cowgirl and Realtor were listening.

"It's going to get you in trouble. Do you know what birth control is?"

Both women turned their heads and looked down at me.

"No," the girl said.

"Well, you better learn."

"Excuse me," the Realtor said. "What are you telling this little girl?"

I ignored her.

"What's birth control?" the little girl asked.

"It keeps you from getting pregnant. Do you know what that is?"

"When you get a baby."

"Right. Do you know how you get pregnant?"

The Realtor shot me a furious glare and told me to stop it. She got up from her chair and asked who belonged to this little girl.

"I know you gotta have a boyfriend. Least that's how my mom does it."

"You're a smart kid," I told her.

I was right; she was cute when she smiled.

"If you got a boyfriend, you're bound to get pregnant," I explained.

"What's bound mean?"

"It's going to happen. You can't stop it."

"I thought it meant when you tied somebody up."

"You really are a smart kid," I told her.

She smiled again. "My teacher says I don't use time wisely."

"Next time she tells you that, ask her how wisely she uses all that time she gets off from her job every summer."

"Huh?"

"Jamie, what the hell are you doing?"

A skinny, rat-faced woman with too much hair and too many inalienable rights came stalking toward us. She grabbed the little girl by the arm near her shoulder.

"Get away from him."

"He was telling me how to get pregnant," the girl explained, not even seeming to notice the hand clamped around her arm like a blood pressure cuff.

"Get away from her, you pervert," the woman snapped at me.

"Are you her mom?" I asked.

"It ain't none of your business who I am."

"Are you the one who lets her wear makeup and dress like a slut?"

Her mouth dropped open. She showed as much indignation as possible for a person wearing a Penns Ridge Speedway Demolition Derby T-shirt. This year's slogan had been WHAM! BAM! THANK YOU MAAM!

"You're the pervert," I told her calmly, "for letting her look like that."

"I'm getting a guard," she said.

"He says my makeup don't look good," Jamie mentioned while

standing perfectly still. She seemed to know any movement would make the hand grip tighter.

"Your mom probably wouldn't be in jail right now if she had never worn makeup," I further explained to her.

"Don't listen to him, Jamie. He don't know nothing about you or your mom."

"I know everything about you, Jamie."

When I said her name, she looked at me like I had produced an egg from behind her ear.

"You're going to get pregnant because you think if you fuck guys they'll love you and you want somebody to love you because you think nobody does."

"Shut up," the woman shouted.

"I'll go get a guard for you," the Realtor said.

"The guy who does it to you isn't going to love you either because he's going to be too stupid to realize what you're worth, but you're going to think it's because you're not pretty enough."

"What's he mean, Aunt Kathy?" Jamie asked, looking up at her.

Aunt Kathy gave her arm a yank and started dragging her away.

"The worst thing you can do is marry him," I continued, raising my voice enough so she could still hear me, "but no matter what you do, your life will be over. It's already over if you keep looking like that."

"You mean I'll be dead?" she called, never taking her eyes off me.

"Stop talking to him," Aunt Kathy said with another yank.

"You'll be alive on the outside." I put two fingers beneath my eyes and pulled down so she could see the gross red inside part of the sockets. "And dead on the inside," I finished.

"Like a zombie?"

"Right."

"I don't want to be a zombie."

Aunt Kathy gave her a final hard yank and swatted her behind. "I said stop talking to him."

The door opened and the Realtor walked in, followed by a guard carrying a clipboard. He didn't look much older than me. He had a buzz cut and was wearing reflective black sunglasses indoors. That was always a bad sign.

I stood up. I didn't want to give him any valid reason to put his hands on me.

"Get yourself one of those implants." I kept talking to Jamie. "Get it when you're ten."

The guard positioned himself inside the room. He didn't come after me. He motioned with his hand for me to get my ass out the door.

"My sister got her period when she was eleven," I said walking past her.

Some of the women hugged their girls protectively as I went by but others were unconsciously nodding at my remarks the way they did at Oprah when her show really hit home.

"Move it outside," the guard said.

"You should be locked up for letting her look like that." I made a final announcement to Aunt Kathy at the door. "I mean it. Locked up. The ACLU can take a fucking leap."

"Out," the guard barked.

Once I got out of the room, I started shaking. I folded my arms across my chest and buried my hands under them. They always seemed to shake more than the rest of me, and I didn't want the guard to notice. I took a couple of deep breaths.

He looked me up and down and cleared his throat. "Who are you here to see?" he asked.

"My mom."

He flipped a page over on his clipboard. "What's the prisoner's name?"

"Bonnie Altmyer."

"And you are?"

"Harley."

"I should send your ass packing for that little display in there, Harley."

"I was just trying to be helpful."

He put the clipboard under his arm. "You think telling a little girl to get on birth control when she's ten is helpful?"

"Yes," I said.

He studied me again, but I couldn't tell what he was thinking because of the glasses.

"Come with me," he said finally. "You've got ten minutes."

He led me to a room of gray stalls made of filing cabinet metal. Inside each one, a visitor sat on the edge of a straight-backed chair made of hard gray vinyl. Most of these visitors were men. I couldn't see their expressions, but they were all intently hunched forward and talking in low tones.

I was surprised to find Mom already sitting at my stall. Seeing her behind Plexiglas in her faded yellow uniform waiting expectantly with her hands folded on the counter in front of her, I felt like I should ask for tickets to a matinee.

"Is everything all right at home?" she asked before I could even sit, her voice sounding like she was talking to me from inside a cocoon.

"No one's shot anybody if that's what you mean."

My comment caught her off guard. She looked surprised, then arched her eyebrows as if she meant to scold me. I was her son and her first instinct was to discipline, but I was also the grown man who was raising her children and running her household which put her in my debt.

"Was that supposed to be funny?" she asked.

"Yes," I answered.

"Well, it wasn't."

"Well, I'm sorry. I guess I should have worked on my prison small talk before I got here."

"Harley. Please. What's wrong?"

"Nothing."

"Why are you here?"

I banged out of my seat. "Excuse me for coming."

"Sit down," she said with maternal firmness.

My body instinctively resisted, then instinctively obeyed.

She watched me for a moment, her expression alternating between worry and exasperation.

"I don't want to fight with you," she said finally.

I suddenly realized that I did want to fight. All the secrets and lies came rushing at me. All the abandonment and betrayal. What had been going on between Dad and Misty? What really happened the night he got shot? I had so many questions, big and little, I didn't know where to start.

"You look sick, baby," I heard her say.

She raised her hand without thinking to check my forehead for a fever and hit the glass wall with the startling death thump of a bird flying into a window. We both jerked back at the sound.

"I'm fine," I told her.

"You look like you haven't slept in days. When's the last time you took a shower or even changed your clothes?"

"Recently."

"Are you growing a beard?"

"Stop it, Mom."

I dug my hands into my hair. I thought about ripping it out and presenting it to her along with a prayer like a plea to a stone goddess. Help me, Mom.

I took a shaky breath and brought my hands back down to my sides. My fingers felt greasy from touching my hair.

She was watching me, concerned but no longer sympathetic. She shifted in her chair. Sized me up. Squared off.

We were both thinking the same thing: what happens when someone you love becomes the enemy? Do you destroy him to save yourself? Or do you join him in his hell?

"Why are you here, Harley?"

Her voice was cold. I had never heard her talk like that to me. There were times I had made her angry enough to scream, frustrated enough to cry, depressed enough to sit up all night and eat a Sara Lee cheesecake, but I had never made her dislike me.

What was I doing? I asked myself in a panic. What good was the TRUTH going to do me or anybody else? Was it worth making my mom hate me? Was it worth making me hate my dad?

I could have walked away right then and there. It wasn't too late. I could have been one of those people who survived impact holed up in a bomb shelter and lived the rest of my life in the dark, fully armed, eating canned goods, telling myself everything was fine.

"Did you know Misty took your money?" The words left me before I could stop them. "The thousand dollars you saved up so you could leave Dad? Did you know she was the one who took it?"

The last traces of softness fled from her face. Her mouth clamped shut. She was ready for me.

"She's had it all this time," I went on, uninvited. "Amber found it last week in her closet. Did you know about it?"

Mom weighed her options. I knew she was thinking about lying, but she couldn't deny the actual existence of the cash.

"I thought your dad took that money," she said slowly.

"Well, he didn't, Misty did."

I waited. She started examining her fingernails. She wasn't going to say anything else. I couldn't believe it.

"Mom," I urged. "The money."

She looked up at me. "I suppose it will come in handy," she said.

It was a smart-ass response. My mom had never talked to me that way either.

My absolute aloneness in this world settled over me, and for a moment I was certain I knew what it felt like to die.

I stood up from my chair and said to her, amazingly sane, "Fine. Don't talk to me. But then I'm done taking care of your kids."

"What do you mean?"

"I'm done," I shouted at her. "Done." I shouted again, hitting my side of the glass with the flat of my hand. "I'm packing my shit and driving the fuck away from here. No one can stop me."

Tears burned in my eyes. I tried blinking them away, but they kept coming.

"You know you won't leave the girls," she said, sounding like she was repeating an unremarkable weather forecast.

"Why not? You did it."

"What are you talking about?" she shot back, her own temper starting to flare. "I didn't leave on purpose. Look around you. This isn't exactly the Poconos. I'm in prison."

"You like it here."

"Harley. You're talking stupid."

"I don't love them," I suddenly shouted, hoping to see the words in the air so then they'd be true. "I don't feel any obligation to them. I'm their brother. Not their fucking father. It's not my job."

"You do love them," she argued with me, "but you can love them from a distance. That's not why you stay."

"Why do I stay?"

"Because you know where your place is."

We stared at each other. I tried to figure out if I had just been gravely insulted or paid the highest compliment a man could receive. I couldn't read her face, the only one I had always trusted.

She took a deep breath and blew away her anger. The loss of it seemed to age and cripple her. She lowered herself back into her chair with the trembling delicacy of the very old. She closed her eyes.

"Okay, Harley. Misty took the money. What more do you want

me to tell you? I was saving up to leave your dad. You know that too."

She rubbed her face with her hands like she was trying to wash something stubborn off it.

"I guess it makes sense that Misty was the one who took it. She knew that I was thinking about leaving. I don't know how, but she came to me and told me she knew I wanted to take her away from him. That was the way she said it. It wasn't about the rest of the family. It was just about him and her. She talked like I was the other woman."

She shut up. I could tell by the caution on her face that she was sure she had said too much.

A chill ran through me. I saw the filthy, bloody carcass of a white kitten, its dead green eyes like marbles, lying on the bright spring grass. We had it so briefly I couldn't even remember its name. It had been something preordained. Snowball. Fluffy. Princess.

Mom glanced up at me. PRECIOUS. I saw it etched in silver in her eyes. That was the kitten's name.

I dropped into my chair again. Now I was ready for her. My past had taught me that the strength to face atrocity didn't come from bravery but from reaching a certain level of numbness.

"What was going on between Dad and Misty?" I asked her.

Her eyes turned a sandblasted gray as if she had made them ready for me to carve into them whatever horrible image I chose.

"You owe me," I said.

"Owe you?" Her voice took on a crazy edge; it was almost a laugh. "I don't owe you anything."

"How can you say that? You're my mom."

"So? What does that mean? I owe you love? I owe you myself. You can't give those things on demand. You can only give them willingly."

"What are you saying?" I asked, fear creeping all over me. "You don't want to give those things anymore?"

"I did my best, Harley. Can you try and understand? I did my best to be your mom and I failed."

She stopped and sucked in a pained breath, doubling over like someone had punched her. When she raised her head again, tears were streaming down her face. She tried to smile through them the way I had seen her do so many times after Dad had hurt me, and I felt the same sick, confusing mix of need and loathing I had always felt for her unconditional love and denial.

"What was going on between Dad and Misty?" I pushed harder.

I wanted her to tell me it was true. To tell me she knew about it. To speak the unspeakable. To prove the unbelievable. It would make Dad more deserving of what he got. It would make Mom more justified in what she had done. It would take away some of my own guilt. It would be all Misty's fault now. Mom hadn't killed him because he beat me.

But why would she have kept it a secret? It didn't make sense. I remembered a hushed conversation between lawyers. If only there had been sexual abuse, they argued, she'd get a lighter sentence and then they had both looked at Mom as if she were a piece of pie they wished was slightly bigger.

"I never saw anything," she said in a tear-choked whisper.

"Did you ask Dad?" I said, my own voice breaking in the middle.

She wiped at her cheeks with her fingertips and regarded me blankly. "How do you ask that question, Harley?"

"Did you ask Misty?"

"How do you ask THAT question, Harley?"

I stared straight ahead. Her face dissolved into my own transparent reflection in the Plexiglas.

"Then you never knew anything for sure?"

She stayed silent.

"The only one who knew for sure was Misty," I said.

GROOVY snaked in front of my eyes in wavy fluorescent green letters.

"Misty killed Dad," I said in a flat voice.

Mom didn't answer.

Another chill rippled through me but this time it made me warm. Mom's face came back to me, peacefully lifeless now that she was done crying and the truth was out. I thought of Snow White in her glass coffin. If I outlived Mom, I was going to bury her under Plexiglas.

"Misty killed Dad," I said again.

It was a huge, colossal, momentous revelation but it was a cruel one, not a kind one. It didn't solve anything. It didn't bring back Dad. It didn't bring back Mom. It didn't answer any questions; it posed new ones. It opened a door on a whole new set of betrayals. The fact that I wasn't feeling anything was one of them.

"I don't get it," I said. "You didn't have to take the blame for her. Nothing would have happened to her. She's just a kid."

"Harley, you don't understand."

"Who could blame her for killing him after what he did? The courts wouldn't have done anything to her. She would have got help. She needs help."

"You don't understand," Mom repeated forcefully.

"Were you embarrassed? You didn't want anyone to know what he did to her?"

"Harley. Misty didn't want your father dead. She wanted to be with him."

"Is that why you said you did it? So it wouldn't be on the news?"

"Harley," Mom screamed. "She was aiming at me."

Mom's face changed shape, blurred, and fell away from me into a depthless hole of writhing GROOVYs.

"She was trying to kill me," I heard her explain. "Your dad accidentally got in the way."

I saw the whole thing. Mom at the stove adjusting knobs and stirring pots, talking absentmindedly about us kids. How the girls were driving her crazy after a summer of no school. How she was concerned about me. I didn't seem to have any direction or ambition. Maybe Dad should talk to me about finding a job.

Dad sitting at the kitchen table, his sock-feet propped up on the chair across from him, his head tilted back, eyes closed, trace contentment on his lips.

He gets up suddenly. To go to the refrigerator for a beer? To wash his hands before dinner? To give Mom's rear end a quick feel?

Mom glances over at the sound and catches Misty in the living room with a rifle poised on one shoulder. In that flash of an instant, she understands everything. She gets answers to questions she didn't know needed asking. She suddenly understands all the impossible things Misty is: calm but violent, omniscient but naive, new but ruined, a shadow with substance, a violated child with a mother who missed it.

Mom had her six seconds all right. Dad wouldn't have known anything. Poor Misty. The only thing she thought she was any good at was aiming a gun, and she had fucked up the most important shot she would ever take.

I started laughing. I closed my eyes and saw GROOVY everywhere.

I couldn't stop laughing. It felt great and it felt wrong like sex with a screamer.

A pair of hands clamped down roughly on my shoulders and started to lift me out of my chair. I looked up and saw Mom. She wasn't crying anymore. She should have been crying. A female guard was escorting her away.

"I'm going to get you out," I yelled at her.

I knew she heard me because she shook her head.

"You can't hide from us."

I was pulled back from the glass. I wanted to splatter myself against it like a bug on a windshield.

"Your best wasn't good enough," I screamed. "You're going to have to try again."

"Let's go."

I was yanked and shoved but not too hard. I recognized the voice. It belonged to the young guard with the shades.

"Let's go," he said again.

"My mom didn't do it," I told him urgently over my shoulder. "She took the blame for my sister. My sister killed my dad."

He looked unimpressed. "It happens sometimes."

"I want to get my mom out."

We stopped in the hall. I was breathing heavily and sweat blurred my vision. I figured he'd walk away, but he turned his eyes on me like two shiny black coins.

"Does your mom want out?"

"I don't think so."

"Does your sister want in?"

"She's a kid."

"There's nothing you can do."

"I want my mom back," I said.

"If I were you, your mom's not the one I'd be concerned about," he offered before turning to leave.

His rubber heels made a tiny, piercing squeak like a scared baby rabbit. I had never even known they could make noise until a day last spring when I saw Elvis's teeth snap down on one. It had been no bigger than my fist.

chapter 16

I stopped at every beer distributor I could find and finally, on about the tenth try, I found one that didn't ask me for ID. I was surprised it took that long. I figured my visit with Mom had aged me at least as much as the first time Callie had fucked me, and I woke up from that feeling a hundred years older.

I spent all my money except for two bucks and bought a case of the cheapest shit they sold. I opened my first can before I was even out of barking range for the distributor's dog. After three cans, I let myself think about Misty. After three and a half, I made myself stop thinking about her.

After five, I headed for Uncle Mike's house.

I hadn't been to his house since Dad's funeral. We all went there afterward to eat crusty baked ham and avoid talking to each other. Mike Jr. brought a date.

He lived a forty-minute drive away from our place which was just enough to justify none of us ever seeing each other now, but it had been close enough when Dad was alive for the two of them to hang out together all the time.

His house was perfect; his lawn too. There wasn't a speck of dirt on the white siding, not a flake of rust on the wrought-iron railing leading up the front steps to the polished gold door knocker, not an inch of peeling paint on the green shutters, not a single leaf peeking out from a rain gutter, not a single dandelion or patch of clover or pile of dog shit anywhere in his yard.

When he criticized and advised on the topic of home maintenance, I couldn't ignore him on the grounds that he didn't practice what he preached. I could ignore him for lots of other reasons though.

I took one look at the flawless blacktop driveway and parked my truck on the side of the road. I didn't want to have to come out here later and mop up tire tracks.

I got out, finished my latest beer, crumpled the can, and tossed it in the back of my truck.

I was at a loss trying to decide where I should walk. Which would be worse: getting dirt on their driveway or dirt on their blinding white sidewalk or dirt on their grass? I picked the grass since it grew in dirt, but I wasn't completely sure about their grass so I got down on my knees and checked. Sure enough, dirt. Fine, rich, uniform dirt. Bank calendar dirt.

To look at Uncle Mike, I would've never thought he lived this way. I had never seen his person looking particularly clean or fit. But he was one of those guys who took more pride in what he owned than who he was.

I slowly got to my feet and sort of tiptoed across the yard trying not to bend too many blades of grass. I made a stop at their birdbath. It was cleaner than the mug I drank my coffee out of every morning. I dipped my hand in and slurped up some water.

The mat in front of the door read, WELCOME FRIENDS. I checked my reflection in the knocker and saw a fancy, engraved ALTMYER stamped across my forehead. I remembered Aunt Jan bitching to my mom once about people who actually used the knocker to knock with. I planned to be one of them, but I made sure to wipe my hands off on my coat first. I still left fingerprints.

Aunt Jan took her good old time getting to the door. Apparently, she didn't peek through curtains first because she looked totally stunned to see me.

She put a hand to the collar on her shirt and stared.

"Aunt Jan?" I said, thinking that might help her out.

"Harley," she finally managed to say. "I'm sorry. You gave me a fright. I never realized how much you look like your dad. Especially dressed just like him."

"You thought I was a ghost?"

She gave an edgy laugh. "I suppose so."

She laughed again. I laughed too.

"Is Uncle Mike around?" I asked, after we stopped laughing.

"Yes, he is."

"Do you think I could talk to him?"

She gave the question some thought. "I don't see why not," she said.

"Me either," I said.

She held the door open for me. She always wore a man-style shirt with a pocket over one breast tucked into stiff, inky-blue jeans. Today the shirt was green and yellow checks.

I wiped my feet on the welcome mat, then apologized in case it was the kind I wasn't supposed to use like the knocker. She smiled and said, "That's what welcome mats are for," but I knew the minute I drove away she was going to hose it down and go at it with a scrub brush.

"I won't touch anything or sit on anything," I told her as I stepped inside. "I realize I'm kind of dirty. I was working in the yard earlier."

"That's considerate of you, Harley, but you can sit down," she said. "It's not a museum."

She led me past one of the formal living rooms Mom never had. It was decorated like a little girls' jewelry box in shimmering cream and pink fabrics, frilly lampshades, and fake crystal vases. The reception after Dad's funeral was the only time I had ever seen her allow anybody in it and nobody went.

"How do you like your job?" she asked me, as I followed along behind her.

"Jobs," I said, emphasizing the s.

"How do you like them?"

"I love them. They're great."

I tried to think of something I could ask her about, but I couldn't remember her ever doing anything except brag about Mike Jr. She didn't have any hobbies or interests that I knew of. No clubs or groups. She had never worked, but she didn't need to. Uncle Mike made a good living filling in potholes for PennDOT, and they only had one kid.

She always said the reason why they didn't have another one was because it would have been terrible on a younger sibling having someone as perfect as Mike Jr. for an older brother, always trying to live up to the example he set.

Grandma used to say she never had a second one because she was too goddamned selfish, and Mom used to tell me not to repeat that.

"Your house looks clean," I offered.

"Thank you," she said, a little uncertainly.

I knew she was going to take me to the Mike Jr. shrine, and she didn't disappoint me. It was a sunporch off the kitchen that she innocently ushered her guests into, claiming it was the sunniest, most comfortable room in the house, and then appeared shocked and humbled to find every inch of wall and shelf space covered with her son.

Up until the first time I set foot in it, I had always thought trophy cases were found only in school lobbies.

"I see you're still fond of Mike Junior," I said, glancing around at the framed photos and all the little gold football players striving to break free from their jewel-tone pedestals of red and blue and green.

"He is our son," she said, hesitantly.

"Yeah, well, not everybody likes their kids this much."

They had a picture of him in every imaginable football pose: running with the ball, leaping up and catching the ball, plowing into other players while carrying the ball, staring at the camera cradling the ball like a newborn.

"Look at this," I commented, walking from photo to photo, and pointing. "He can run. Knock people down. Catch a ball."

I came to a photo of him cradling a rifle instead of a ball, standing next to a strung-up buck with its belly slit open.

"Kill," I added.

I turned to the gallery of him posing with all his many prom, Spring Fling, and homecoming dates.

"Have intercourse.

"No wonder you're proud of him," I ended with a big smile.

"I think I'll go get Mike," she said, her face burning.

"Can I use your bathroom?"

"Yes."

I took the leak of a lifetime. There was an extra roll of toilet paper sitting on the back of the toilet wearing a pink crocheted covering with a blond doll head and arms coming out of the top. I figured out the crocheted part was supposed to be her dress. The whole time I pissed, she stared at me with empty blue eyes.

When I got done, I took her off the roll and put her on my dick. I wasn't planning on doing more than that but then I noticed she actually had tits, and her plastic red lips were parted a little, and I kind of liked the way she stared up at me and the way she had her arms thrown out to her sides like someone had just pushed her down. I started moving around inside her dress and her head started bobbing. I gripped tighter and pushed harder and the crocheted part pulled down lower showing more of her tiny tits. I didn't stop until I jerked off inside her.

I thought about taking her with me but I didn't want to be accused of being a thief. I put her back on the roll instead, dripping with my cum.

Uncle Mike was waiting in the shrine when I came back out. He had on working-in-the-yard threadbare jeans and a gray flannel shirt. He was drying his hands on a dish towel.

He gave me a long, thoughtful stare.

"Hi, there, Harley," he said.

"Hi, Uncle Mike."

"This is unexpected. Everything all right at home?"

"Great."

"Something I can do for you?"

He handed the towel to Aunt Jan, who was standing nearby watching me. I tried not to sway.

"I wanted to apologize," I said.

"Apologize for what?"

"The way I acted last time you came by. You tried to do a nice thing and I acted like a smart-ass and I'm sorry."

His expression softened a little. Aunt Jan's didn't.

"You didn't have to drive the whole way up here to say that," he said. "You could have called."

"I don't like phones. You can't be sure people are paying attention to you when you're talking to them."

"That's true."

He took his bill cap off, ran a hand through his hair, and put the cap back on while eyeballing the room. I could have almost sworn he looked nervous.

"Well, apology accepted," he said when his eyes returned to me. "To tell the truth, I had forgotten all about it."

He glanced over at Aunt Jan. She hadn't forgotten all about it.

"Would you like to stay for dinner?"

I gave Aunt Jan a big grin. I wanted to say yes more than anything in the world, but the last thing I wanted to do in the world was eat dinner with her.

"I gotta get home and mow." I tried to sound disappointed.

Uncle Mike smiled back approvingly. "I did mine first thing

this morning. It's been threatening rain all day. You can stay for a beer, can't you?"

Aunt Jan walked over to him and started whispering to him. He leaned his head down. "What?" he asked.

She whispered some more. Little hissing noises.

He looked up frowning and shaking his head. "Your Aunt Jan thinks you're drunk. Are you drunk?"

Aunt Jan gave him an outraged stare.

"No, sir," I answered.

"Satisfied? He's not drunk," he said to her, then he motioned at me to follow him out the back door.

"How are the girls?" he asked, as we crossed the yard to the detached garage.

"They're fine."

"School's out soon?"

"Next week."

"I bet they're looking forward to that."

"Oh, yeah. They love spending as much time as possible hanging around our house."

He had a refrigerator in his garage filled with nothing but beer. This was another thing I planned to have when I got married, along with my lunch hour blow jobs and honey-apple pork chops.

He noticed me looking at his workbench taking up half the floor space.

"Once the warm weather hits I take over the place and start parking the car and truck outside," he explained, handing me a Bud Light. "Drives Jan crazy. But I need this much space to set up my bench and saw table."

He walked over and I followed.

"I'm making a hope chest for Jan to store her mother's quilts in."

"That's beautiful wood," I said, running my hand over its smooth, purple-red surface. "Cherry, right?"

"Right," he said, smiling. "You do any carpentry?"

"No. I just like wood."

I took a couple gulps of my beer, thought about setting it down, but the workbench kept moving away from me.

"I used to think it might be fun to try," I added, "but I would've needed tools and wood and a place to do it. Dad wasn't into the idea."

"I never could get Mike interested in it either," Uncle Mike said. "He was always running off somewhere. That kid had some schedule. Practices. Rallies. Games. Parties."

I nodded sympathetically. "It's not easy being a superstar."

He shot me a stern look. "I can never tell when you're being serious, Harley."

"I'm always serious."

He started picking up tools off the workbench and setting them back down again.

"It is hard being a superstar," he said, examining a drill bit. "I'm happy for him though. He seems cut out for that kind of life. I just hope he can hold onto it."

"What do you mean?"

He put down the bit and picked up a chisel. "There are a helluva lot of kids playing first-string college ball out there and only a handful of pro slots open each year. You don't have to be a genius to do the math. God help me when I point that out to his mother."

The chisel held his interest even less than the bit. He put it back down and took a healthy drink off his can.

"I worry, that's all. He's got the brains to do other things and he's going to have a college degree, but I don't think he could be satisfied having a regular job. I don't think he's got the . . ."

He snapped his fingers in the air, searching for the right words.

"Stomach for it?" I finished for him.

"Why are you really here, Harley?" he asked, staring at me like he was seeing me for the first time. "Not that I doubt the sincerity of your apology, I just don't see you coming out here for that. You haven't been here since your dad's funeral."

"I haven't been invited."

"No, I guess maybe you haven't."

The garage smelled like gas fumes and wood chips, two smells I liked alone, but they were making me sick mixed together with seven beers. I noticed one of the windows was propped open and headed for it, bumping into the saw table and then a Rubbermaid garbage can filled with all kinds of crap: a folded blue tarp, a broken fishing pole, a kite shaped like a shark, two child-sized football helmets encrusted with mud and grass, a Steeler sweatshirt spattered with white paint, three empty Pennzoil cans.

Here was my chance again to walk away. I didn't have to ask him anything. Nothing he could tell me would make my life any better. He could only add one more terrible truth to the other ones piling up inside me like dead sticks waiting for a match.

"I want to know about Dad and Misty," I said, putting my face up to the fresh air coming in the window. "I want to know what you know."

I wasn't going to look at him. Nothing in the world could make me do that. I waited and slowly sipped at my beer and watched a goldfinch perch at the crystal-clear birdbath. The ones at our house were still straw-brown. This one had already turned brilliant yellow.

The garage got so quiet I could hear the refrigerator running and the sound of beer rolling down my throat and echoing inside my empty stomach. I was beginning to think he had left when he said, "I just didn't think it was natural, that's all. Him paying so much attention to her when he had a perfectly good son."

"That's it?" I said.

I turned around laughing, I was so relieved.

"That's it?" I said again. "You're going to accuse a guy of messing around with his daughter based on that? Did you ever see him do anything?"

My relief swelled me with confidence. I walked back toward him, tripping over the star-shaped blades of a rototiller, but catching myself before I fell on the cement floor.

"Why are you asking me about this now?" he said, his expression hardening into something unreadable like a face carved into a mountain. "What do you know?"

"I know a lot of things," I said importantly, wagging my finger at him. "I know you told Mom to leave Dad because you thought he was going to do something to Misty."

"Your Aunt Jan was right. You are drunk. Too drunk to have this conversation anyway."

He set his beer can down on his workbench and started to walk away.

"How can you be too drunk to have this conversation?" I cried out, stumbling after him.

I reached out and caught him by the sleeve. He stopped and grabbed me by the shoulder to help me keep my balance. He hadn't touched me since my dad's funeral. He was the closest blood relation I had to a dad now that my real one was dead, and he hadn't touched me in two years. I remembered the way he had walked away from Mike Jr. at the funeral and put his arm around my shoulders. I remembered walking past the dead baby gravestones.

I started crying.

"Harley."

He shook me to get my attention. I wouldn't look at him.

"Listen to me. I did tell your mom to leave him. I told her some fifteen years ago. I told her the first time I saw him go after you and saw you stand there and take it like a grown man."

"No," I moaned, backing away from him and shaking my head.

The garage flew past me, back and forth, like I was watching its reflection in a shiny clock pendulum.

"Don't blame it on me," I cried.

"I'm not blaming anything on you. You said you wanted to know, Harley, so I'm telling you. I tried to get you kids out of there for a long time and she'd never go. By the time she finally decided to leave, I knew it was too late. I wasn't trying to save anybody anymore. I was just trying to ease my own conscience."

"What about Misty?"

"I had suspicions. That's all they were. Suspicions."

I broke free from him.

"Are you lying to me?" I yelled at him. "I'm sick of everybody lying to me about my own life."

"I'm not lying."

"You never saw him do anything to her?"

"Jesus, Harley. I would have shot him myself."

"Mike? What's going on out here?"

Aunt Jan appeared at the side doorway. I turned my back on her and wiped at my face with Dad's coat sleeve.

"I heard shouting."

"What the hell, Janet?" Uncle Mike bristled. "Can't we have a private conversation?"

"Since when do you have private conversations? I'm always trying to get you to bring Mike Junior out here."

"I think I better go," I said.

"You don't have to go," Uncle Mike practically yelled at me.

"I want to. Can I use your bathroom?" I asked Aunt Jan.

"Well, yes," she said, darting a funny look at Uncle Mike.

They were arguing with each other as I walked jerkily out the door. I kept thinking I was going too slow, then I'd speed up, the garage would start spinning, and I'd slow down again.

Halfway to the house, I thought for sure Aunt Jan had snuck up behind me and was spitting at me, but it turned out to be coming from the sky. I picked up the pace, passed through the shrine, and leaned back against the bathroom door breathing heavily once I closed it behind me.

I got down on my knees in front of the toilet and waited to see if I was going to throw up. I didn't so I stood up and pissed again. The crocheted doll watched me unimpressed.

I grabbed her off the toilet paper and stuffed her in Dad's pocket. She left a glistening smear of cum on the top of the roll. Knowing that eventually Aunt Jan would touch it—even if it was dried by then—made my whole trip worthwhile.

I was hoping I'd be able to get out of the house without running into either one of them, but it had definitely not been my lucky day. They were both waiting for me near the front door, Uncle Mike holding a grocery bag full of food and Aunt Jan holding a small black Bible no bigger than my hand. I suddenly knew what starving Africans felt when they saw us coming, and it wasn't gratitude.

"This is your mother's." Aunt Jan held the Bible out to me.

HOLY BIBLE was stamped in gold across the cracked, black leather cover. I took it and ran my index finger down the outside of the shiny-edged pages the way I used to do as a kid. They still felt like a red satin ribbon. I didn't have to open it to know it was hers.

"Your Aunt Diane gave it to us to return to you. She accidentally took it with her when she packed up your dad's personal things," Aunt Jan explained.

"His effects," I said, nodding.

"Yes."

"Two years ago?"

"I'm sorry but I put it in a drawer and forgot about it. I hope you haven't been looking for it."

"I guess I figured she had it with her in jail. They let you take Bibles in, don't they?"

Uncle Mike shrugged. He had put a chew in and was working it around inside his lower lip. Aunt Jan said, "I wouldn't know."

"I'll walk you out to your truck," Uncle Mike offered, and held open the door.

"Give my best to the girls, Harley," Aunt Jan said.

I thought of that expression, Here's mud in your eye. I gave her my best imitation of a Mike Jr. smile.

Here's cum on your hand, Aunt Jan.

"Sure," I said.

Uncle Mike never gave a second thought to where he walked. He started down the clean white sidewalk, then tromped across the glorious green grass and even spit a stream of tobacco in it.

I walked around to my side of the truck, got in, and leaned over to open the passenger side door so he could slide in the bag of groceries. He closed the door but didn't leave but didn't look at me either. I leaned across the seat and rolled down the window.

"I know I haven't been very good to you and the girls these past couple years," he apologized to the sky, "and I'm sorry about it."

I looked where he looked and saw a speck of a plane flying over. It left a white wispy line in the sky like a smoke signal with nothing left to say.

"Things aren't going to change though, are they?" I said.

"I don't think so," he answered. "I hope you understand. It's nothing personal."

He gave the hood of my truck a thump and started back to his house. Once he disappeared behind the gleaming gold knocker, I took the doll out of Dad's pocket. I stuck my finger inside her to see if she was still gooey, then I tossed her on the floor in the trash with Callie's art book and my mom and dad's wedding picture. Aunt Jan was going to accuse me of stealing her, and Uncle Mike was going to defend me. I took some pleasure in knowing that. I laid the Bible on the seat beside me. I didn't open it to see if the map was still inside.

chapter 17

It poured the whole way home. The rain came down in solid metallic sheets. My wheels spun trying to climb our mud-slick road.

I parked next to a rut filled with water and stepped into it, soaking my jeans halfway up to the knees. I tromped across the yard carrying my case of beer minus a six-pack or so, and my brown bag of groceries with a carnival-striped loaf of Town Talk bread and a little black Bible sticking out of the top. I saw a pair of shiny eyes peering at me from inside the biggest rip in the back of the couch, and a pair of dark, empty ones peeking out between Mom's sheers.

I stopped walking and the dark eyes disappeared. I stood there in the rain and thought about Misty standing on the porch shooting at the turkeys. It had looked like she was aiming at me.

I started shivering. It was the rain, I told myself. But the first thing I was going to do was hide the gun.

Before going inside, I shook on the porch like a wet Elvis. I didn't wipe my mud-caked boots. I didn't have to. It was my fucking house. I wished Mom could have been there to see it because it used to be her house, and I wished Aunt Jan could have been there because it would have given her nightmares.

Elvis met me at the door and went nuts trying to smell the groceries. I pushed him down and took loud clomping steps into the living room where I could hear the TV going. I left a trail of perfectly formed treads behind me and stopped to admire them for a moment like they were art.

All three girls were sitting on the floor in a heap of pillows and dinosaurs, in nightshirts and ponytails, with cotton balls between their toes and bowls of ice cream covered in rainbow sprinkles sitting in their laps.

They all looked up at me with identical, calmly curious expressions on their faces, like I was a bumbling intruder who had accidentally stumbled across their peaceful tribe.

"Hi, Harley," Jody said.

Misty didn't say anything. Amber's face darkened. She was the tribe elder who knew outsiders were never to be trusted even if they came bearing food. Somehow they would eventually ruin your world whether it be with guns, or disease, or a religion whose God had no sense of justice.

"We're having a slumber party," Jody said.

"Isn't it a little early?" I asked.

"Amber said we could start already since it's already dark outside. We had a big lightning bolt and the TV went out for a whole hour so we played Junior Monopoly and I won," she said gleefully. "I even beat Misty."

Misty stared hypnotically at the TV, her blank black eyes reflecting the blue and white flashes, the cheap fake stones around her wrist sparkling fiercely. She glanced up at me dissatisfied but untroubled by my presence.

I felt love and loathing for her at the same time. I wanted to rid my life of her permanently, burn all her belongings and erase all my memories, but I also wanted to hug her. I wanted to give her all the hugs she should have been getting from Mom for the past two years, all the understanding she should have been getting from us, all the counseling she should have been getting

267

from strangers. But anything I could have given to her now would have been too little too late like the bag of groceries I was holding in my aching hands.

She turned back to the TV, and I decided right then and there that I didn't want to know any more TRUTH. I didn't want any more CLOSURE. I wanted beer and blow jobs.

"How was Lick n' Putt?" I asked Jody.

"Great." She beamed at me and bounced on her butt, almost tipping her ice cream out of her lap. "We got to play our whole game before it started raining. Me and Esme did the best. We don't know who won because Esme's dad ate the scorecard at the end. He did!" she said, her eyes getting as big as golf balls. "He ate it because he was so embarrassed by his score. He played terrible. Even worse than Zack and he spent most of the time swinging his club in circles pretending to be a helicopter. Esme's dad picked up the ball once and put it in the hole with his hand and asked us if that was a hole in one. He was serious too. I could tell. And then we went to Esme's house and had potato soup with ham chunks in it."

"Was her mom home?"

"Yeah."

Amber was staring at me furiously.

"What's your problem?" I said to her. "You look like you want to smell me again."

"Fuck you, Harley."

"No, really. If it would make you feel better. Come here. Smell me."

"Go to hell."

"Here, I'll do it for you. I smell like . . ." I sniffed at a shoulder. "I smell pretty bad, actually."

"You smell like beer," she said. "Once you turn twenty-one, you're just going to spend every night for the rest of your life in a bar."

"I hope so," I said, and went into the kitchen.

I set the bag down on the crumb-coated counter and began to unpack it: Mom's Bible, the loaf of bread, a box of elbow macaroni, three cans of soup, a can of green beans.

My hands started shaking so bad, a jar of mayonnaise escaped and went rolling down the length of the counter. I watched it fall into the sink with a dull clang.

I realized I couldn't stay in the same house with Misty. I wasn't afraid of her as much as I was afraid of thinking about her. If I distanced myself from the source, maybe I could avoid the thoughts like I could avoid catching a cold.

I got the mayonnaise and finished unpacking the bag: a can of Crisco, Palmolive dishwashing soap, and a box of Little Debbie Fudge Rounds.

I opened the cakes and left everything else sitting on the counter. When I went to put my own beers away, I found a couple dozen Red Dogs in the fridge. I helped myself to one along with a fudgie and sat down at the table with Mom's Bible.

When I was a kid, I never thought of Mom as religious since we didn't go to church. She liked to tell Bible stories and liked to read from a Bible but as far as I knew, none of that counted with God if a person didn't put on good clothes and go sit in a church for an hour every Sunday. I viewed the Good Book as nothing more than a book until she explained to me that everything in it was true.

After that I wanted her to read from the Bible every night at bedtime instead of my regular books. Curious George's fall from a fire escape and Ping the duck's search for the wise-eyed boat on the Yangtze River no longer held my interest. I wanted plagues of bugs, rivers turning into blood, people turning into salt, God killing babies, floods killing everybody. I wanted giants, demons, and lepers. No matter how many times I asked her, Mom insisted it had all really happened. It was like finding out the Smurfs were real.

I didn't remember exactly when I stopped believing the stories. Sometime after I outgrew Santa Claus and before I stopped liking SpaghettiOs. The fact that Mom never stopped believing always made me feel a little superior to her.

I picked up the Bible by its spine and shook it. A folded square of paper fell onto the tabletop. Relief swept through me. Opening the paper, smoothing it flat, and seeing the little faded yellow house was like a homecoming.

I took my finger and traced the futile black line, gray now from age, and wondered where the intense crayon colors had gone. They weren't rubbed off on the rest of the paper. It was like time had absorbed them.

My hands folded the map without me telling them to and held it in front of my face for an instant before slipping it back in between the satin red pages.

Mom had always believed her line was going to end at nothing, and she believed prison was that nothing. But the child who originally drew the map didn't have a family; the woman sitting in a jail cell did.

I had been wrong. She hadn't ACCEPTED anything. She had FLED to a safe haven. Away from the TRUTH. Away from us. Now I understood why she didn't want to come back here, but I didn't care.

The guard had said there was nothing I could do. If Mom stuck to her story and Misty stuck to hers, it sure seemed that way, but I had the bloody shirt and I had Jody.

I was ready to take the Bible downstairs and put it in my drawer but something made me open the cover first. Inside was Mom's maiden name written in a little girl's handwriting at the top of the page and beneath it all of our names and birthdays written in a grown woman's hand. I stared at my own birthday trying to figure out the significance.

I got up from the chair and walked over to Jody's school lunch menu hanging on the refrigerator. The first week of June had been tacked onto the bottom of May. It ended on Wednesday,

June 3, with the words "NO LUNCH SERVED. EARLY DIS-
MISSAL. HAVE A NICE SUMMER!" I counted back to Saturday, May 30. I double-checked it with the Bible.

Today was my birthday. I was twenty years old.

Twenty years old. I was a man.

I didn't get too excited because I knew I was only becoming
a man in a certain sense. I had already become a man before
in other ways.

Legally I had become a man when I turned eighteen. Spiritually I had become a man the night Callie Mercer fucked me.
Emotionally I had become a man the first time my dad belted
me. Today I was becoming a man chronologically. There would
be no more "teen" after my age.

My first impulse was to go share this information with Amber.
I was no longer a teenager. And for a long eight months, I was
going to be FOUR years older than her, not three. I was twenty;
she was sixteen. FOUR.

But if I told them, Jody would have wanted to have a party
and I wasn't in a party mood. I wouldn't have minded one of
her cards though.

My birthday, I thought to myself. I downed part of my beer,
ripped off half the fudgie in my mouth, and tossed the other half
to Elvis. It had to be worth something.

I took Mom's Bible downstairs and grabbed the gun. I slipped
out the back door and walked straight to the shed with the mud
sucking at my boots and rain pelting my hat.

I left the door open a crack so I could see and hid the gun
in a back corner behind some old two-by-fours, a hoe, and a
snow shovel. The inside of the shed smelled like gas and rotting
wood and leaves, then I detected something clean and perfumed.

A plank of weak gray light fell across the wall in front of me.
I turned around and saw Amber in the doorway, her bare feet
and legs covered in mud, looking like she had just waded through
an oil spill.

"What are you doing?" she asked.

I finished positioning a plastic sled in the corner too.

"What are you doing? would be a better question," I said, giving her a once-over.

She had thrown on a jean jacket over her nightshirt. Ten freshly polished purple toenails stuck out from the ends of her mud-blackened feet like a line of grape jelly beans.

"What are you doing with the gun?" she asked.

"Hiding it."

"From who?"

"The girls."

"Why?"

A brief flicker of insanity sparked through my brain where I considered telling her what I had learned, but I knew I would only be doing it so I would have someone to share the burden with. Amber wouldn't be any help.

"It's dangerous," I told her.

"Dangerous?" she exclaimed. "Misty knows how to handle a gun better than you do, and Jody's too little to pick it up. We should be hiding it from you."

"Maybe," I said, and brushed my hands on my jeans to get the dust and cobwebs off them. "Just don't tell them where I hid it, okay?"

She shrugged her agreement, then her expression turned sullen as she remembered why she had followed me.

"That's why you came out here?" she asked, skeptically.

I paused inside the door, getting ready to run for my truck.

"I'm going out," I answered her.

"I thought so," she fumed at me.

"Where do you get off getting mad at me for going out?" I said roughly, and gave her a sharp look. "Stop keeping tabs on me."

I made a break for it.

"Her dad's home too, you fuckhead," she screamed after me.

I threw open my truck door. I didn't know what she meant but it pissed me off just the same. I gave her the finger. She gave me one back.

Callie's car and Brad's Jeep were parked side by side. The rain had slowed down enough for the dogs to come out of their houses when I walked down the driveway. They ran around in circles, barking their lungs out, stopping every once in a while to shake.

Brad opened the front door and yelled at them to quiet down. I put my hands in my pockets and took my time. I didn't care about the rain.

He was giving me a boyish smile. A scorecard-eating smile. But it faded as I got near. I didn't know what he saw.

"Harley," he announced, and moved halfway out of the door, but he kept one foot planted firmly inside. "Where's your truck? You didn't walk down here?"

They didn't have a porch. They had an open wooden deck in front of the door with two steps leading up to it. He was getting wet.

"I parked it up on the road. I was on my way home from prison and I thought I'd swing by and pick up Jody," I said amiably.

"Prison?" he asked, holding a hand up over his head and blinking water out of his eyes.

"I was visiting my mom."

"Oh, right. I'm sorry. Are you okay?"

"I'm great. Except I don't smell too good."

He moved back inside the door a little bit. "Well, we already took Jody home."

I nodded at him. "Okay," I said, blinking too at the water running off the bill of my cap. "As long as I'm here, could I see your wife?"

"My wife?"

"Yeah. I need to talk to her about something."

"Do you want to come in?"

"You don't want me in your house."

Callie came to the door in her chamois-soft jeans and a red T-shirt with satin trim around the neck.

"Is something wrong?" she asked Brad, without even saying hi to me.

"He says he needs to talk to you."

She flashed me a disbelieving look.

"Could you come out here?" I asked.

"It's raining," she said carefully.

"We could talk in my truck."

Her expression grew more amazed.

"Maybe you should go talk to him," Brad said. "He says he just got back from visiting his mom in prison."

"Oh," she said, suddenly sympathetic.

"And it's my birthday," I added, quickly.

I had her. Right there. That was the clincher. I saw it in her eyes.

She peered into the rain. "Where is your truck?"

"Up on the road."

"Mom!" Esme caroled from inside the house. "Zack wrecked my doctor's office. I had it all set up."

"She threw my ABC bus," Zack yelled too.

"He keeps putting his foot on me."

"I'll take care of it," Brad said to Callie with a sigh. "See you around, Harley," he said to me.

"Right."

"What do you think you're doing?" she asked angrily, the moment he disappeared.

I turned around and started walking to my truck. She splashed after me in her bare feet.

"Harley," she called.

I jogged the rest of the way and got inside and waited for her. She slammed the door behind her and started ripping into me.

"Let's get something straight, Harley. Don't ever come to my house when Brad's around."

"I came to pick up Jody," I said.

"You didn't come here to pick up Jody," she scolded me. "Brad took Jody home hours ago. You came here to make a scene."

She threw herself back against the seat and folded her arms over her breasts. Her shirt was a short one and it rode up enough to show her navel.

"What am I going to tell Brad when he asks me what you wanted to see me about? What could be so urgent that I needed to walk through a downpour and sit in your truck with you? And don't tell me I should tell him the truth."

"Where'd you go today?" I asked, pulling my stare away from her and fixing it on the water rolling down the windshield.

"I did some shopping," she said, "and went to the library. Why?"

"Where'd you go Thursday?"

"Esme's school to help out with a pizza party. What are you doing, Harley? Checking up on me? It's none of your business where I go."

"I wanted to make sure you weren't mad at me."

I felt her looking at me.

"Mad at you for what?"

"You left."

"When? Wednesday night? You know why I had to leave."

"Do you think we could do it sometime when you don't have to leave?"

She was silent.

"Why would I be mad at you?" she asked.

"I didn't do anything."

"What do you mean?"

"I just laid there."

More silence.

She propped her wet, muddy feet up on my dashboard. I

glanced over at her. Her knees were back near her head and she had her hands resting on the insides of her thighs.

The transformation had occurred. She was giving me a smile that reminded me of some dark chocolates my mom gave my dad one Christmas. They had a candy-sweet cherry in the center soaked in a boozy syrup.

I got an instant boner.

"Happy birthday," she said.

"Thanks."

"You don't mind my feet up here, do you?"

"Nope."

"How's your mom?"

"Great."

"How often do you go see her?"

"Twice every life sentence."

She dropped her feet and moved toward me. "Are you okay?"

I nodded.

"I suppose you want a birthday kiss," she said playfully.

"Something like that."

She leaned against me and put her parted lips up to mine. I didn't kiss her right away. I waited until I couldn't tell her breath from mine.

I took my hands out of Dad's pockets and put them around her. We made out for a little bit. It wasn't that long but I didn't have to grope, and I didn't have to stop in the middle and beg. I was making progress.

She was the one who stopped. I could tell she was getting nervous. The rain had slowed down to a comfortable patter. She was going to leave again.

"So, it's your birthday," she remarked, running her finger up and down my leg, while I strained painfully against my jeans. "Have you decided what you want to be when you grow up?"

"Nothing," I answered her. "There's nothing I'm good at," I added.

She lifted her hand and ran her thumb over my lips. "You're good at surviving. That takes talent."

"I'm not good at that either."

Her thumb slipped between my lips when I spoke. She left it there and asked, "Why did you really come here?"

I wouldn't look at her.

"Never mind." She laughed. "Don't tell me."

She got down off the seat into the trash and motioned with her hand for me to move away from the steering wheel. I slid over and she pushed my legs apart and got between them.

"Consider this your present," she said, unzipping my fly.

I laid my head back on the seat and stared out the window at the thick ragged-topped storm clouds spread over her hills like pewter meringue. I didn't bother telling her I considered everything she had ever done for me to be a gift.

chapter 18

I made some calls on Monday. The district attorney's office. The sheriff's department. Mom's attorney whose business card was still stuck to the freezer door with a Laurel Falls Bank magnet between a Halloween snapshot of Jody in a green stegosaurus costume and a school bulletin warning a case of pinkeye had been diagnosed in Misty's classroom.

Getting anyone to talk to me like I wasn't a crackpot was the biggest challenge. The next biggest was getting someone to care. I expected moral outrage that an innocent woman was in jail. I expected them to feel a civic responsibility toward putting the real killer behind bars. Instead I got a lot of Double Jeopardy thrown in my face: once a case has been tried, it can't be tried again. ADJUDICATED, Mom's attorney's paralegal called it. Dad's murder had been ADJUDICATED to the satisfaction of the state of Pennsylvania and even to the satisfaction of the convicted murderer. The DA's office suggested I might be delusional. The sheriff's department told me I watched too much TV. But everyone offered to talk to me in person.

That had been my plan when I started my day Tuesday, but I couldn't get any time off from Barclay's, and no one would see me on their lunch hour. People didn't sacrifice their sandwiches and Cokes for delusional crackpots trying to free convicted murderers who insisted they were guilty. They would on TV. The deputy I talked to was right about that.

As my day wore on, every time I thought about Mom I saw her the way I had seen her behind Plexiglas, drifting away from me into fathomless GROOVY. Then a surging current would bring her back but her features would be gone, her face a smooth, round, white surface permanently shocked clean of all emotion by what she had seen in the depths.

Thinking about Misty was worse. She always disappeared into black and when her face started materializing again, I freaked out. I shook my head, and sang songs, and recited the names of the planets and the Seven Dwarfs and tried to remember the difference between Abstract Expressionism and Surrealism. I couldn't let her come back. I didn't want to see what she knew.

But besides thinking about Mom and Misty, I did okay. They were weighing heaviest on my mind, but I had plenty of other things to distract me. I still had to do something about Dad's piece of pipe.

"I think you'd probably be best off just pouring more cement over it," Bud suggested, reaching for a bunch of bananas while vigorously working a piece of gum on one side of his mouth. "You might stub your toe on it now and then, but you wouldn't have to worry about anybody cutting themself on it."

"I'd feel better if it was completely out of there."

"How deep is the plug?"

I finished with my customer and told her to have a nice night.

"Pretty deep," I told him. "I remember when he dug the hole I was probably about six or seven. He put me in it and all you could see was my head poking out. My mom took a picture of it."

Church looked up from the bench where he was picking at

the bottoms of his gym shoes and flicking tiny pieces of rubber on the floor.

"My mom took a picture of my head once," he called out to us. "I'm not kidding. It's in our house."

"That would be a sonofabitch to try and dig out," Bud continued. "And you can't blast it so close to your well. What about a winch? Find somebody who rips out tree stumps for a living."

He finished with his customer too but when he told his to have a nice night, they launched into a conversation about an estate sale over the weekend near Clarksburg. He went on Saturday. She went on Sunday hoping for better weather, but it rained on Sunday too.

My hands started twitching at my sides. They were feeling a lot better. They no longer burned, just itched a little and they were stiff. The swelling had gone down and the gouges had scabbed over. They reminded me of Jody's little naked back when she got the chicken pox the year before.

"Good night, ladies," I heard Rick say to the cashiers in his oily boss voice.

He was going out with his wife for some special occasion he wouldn't tell us about. Bud said it was to celebrate the zits on his ass finally evolving into calluses.

His fat face stopped next to me. It was full of jiggles and shudders like the surface of a bumped boat of old gravy. There was a film of sweat on his upper lip.

He took a big showy whiff of the air in front of me, then settled his head back into the pillow of flesh where his neck should have been.

"Don't come back to work until you take a bath, Altmyer," he said loudly.

The three cashiers watched me, a little amused and a little afraid, like I was a vicious, spittle-flinging dog on a strong chain that couldn't quite get to them.

They were expecting me to try and kill him. They had been

biding their time for over a year now waiting for the time I finally lost it and the TV reporters showed up to make them famous. I wasn't about to give them the satisfaction.

I politely thanked Rick for his concern for my personal hygiene. I told him it reflected well on his managerial style.

Before he could say anything else, I walked off muttering about stocking the Campbell's soup section with more Chicken and Stars. I made sure he was gone before I came up front again. Church and Bud were busy bagging. My cashier was doing her own bagging, and she shot me a dirty look to rival one of Amber's. I got back to work.

"How ya doing, Harley?" Church asked me.

"I'm good, Church."

"The boss didn't know what he was saying," he said.

"Forget about it."

He shook his head and his eyes rattled around behind his thick glasses. "I told my mom what he said. I told her about the whole thing."

"When?"

"I called her," he explained, smiling big and glancing toward the pay phone. "She said saying that to a nice boy like you was criminal. That means it was a crime like parking in front of a fire hydrant."

"What makes your mom think I'm a nice boy?"

"I told her before. I talk about you, Harley. I'm not kidding. You and Bud. My mom says one of these days she's going to invite you over for dinner because you're so nice to her baby. That's what she calls me sometimes. Her baby. I guess because I still cry at night. She says she's going to do it some night when she's not so tired from her job and she's got time to cook a roast. Would you come?"

"Sure," I said.

"Great," he exclaimed. "I'm going to tell her. Do you like applesauce or pudding?"

"Both."

"Both." He started laughing. "Wow. Both. I never get both. Wait'll I tell Mom you want both."

He put down the two-liter bottle of root beer in his hand and walked off.

"Where are you going?"

"I'm going to call her again," he said, heading toward the phone, "and tell her you want both."

"That's not what I meant," I started to explain, then figured what the hell. I'd eat both.

I finished bagging for him. Once things slowed down again I went and took a seat on the bench, placed my hands on my knees, and watched them jitter. They had been fine earlier while I stocked blocks of mozzarella, and stacked cans of Hungry Jack biscuits, and set up a new display at the end of the snack aisle with cans of Nabisco Easy Cheese and Premium saltine crackers. Another one of Rick's brainstorms: people who eat cheese in a can sometimes eat it on crackers.

I clenched them. They still shook. I laid them out flat across my thighs. They jerked like live wire. I sat on them. I felt vibrations travel up my spine.

I heard the motorized swish of the automatic doors sliding open. I looked over and saw Amber come through. I double-checked because as far as I knew, she hadn't set foot in Shop Rite a single time since I had started working here even though she used to love coming here with Mom when she was little.

The cashiers spotted her immediately and flung dirty looks in her direction. She was wearing cutoffs, and tan cowboy boots, and a guy's long-sleeved shirt that wasn't mine tied in a knot above her belly button. She walked slowly, accentuating every step with a lazy hip thrust, which meant something male was watching her from behind.

She gave me a condescending smirk when she noticed me

sitting on a bench as if she had always suspected I did nothing at my job but sit on my ass.

She stopped directly in front of me with her legs slightly apart, boots planted, and her hands on her hips.

"I was going to leave you a note but I decided this was a big enough deal that I should say good-bye to you in person."

"Who's watching Jody?" I said.

"You fucker," she hissed loud enough for the cashiers to hear. They didn't even pretend to not be listening.

"I'm standing here telling you I'm never going to see you again for the rest of our lives and you want to know who's watching Jody. Misty's watching her, you fuckhead."

"I don't like Misty watching her."

"Well, get used to it 'cause she's all you got anymore."

"Where are you going?"

"I told you. I'm moving in with Dylan."

"DYLAN." I stood up, and made a face at her. "Who the hell is this guy anyway? Where'd you even find him?"

"At school where I find all of them."

"How long have you known him?"

"All my life."

I took the pads of my fingers and rubbed at my eyes. I rubbed so hard, when I took them away I saw nothing but blobs of light.

I revised my question.

"How long have you known him well enough to say hi to him in the halls?"

"I'm serious about him," she snapped at me. "He's different from the other guys."

"Why? Because he hits you?"

She glanced down at me, startled.

"Is that what you want?" I asked.

"He doesn't hit me."

"I know he hits you. I saw the way you were walking. The

only time I ever saw someone walk that way who hadn't been beaten up was Mom in the hospital after Jody was born."

"You were watching me walk?"

I took a frustrated breath and rubbed at my eyes again until she disappeared behind mottled white light and gray nothingness.

"Is that what you want?" I tried again. "You want someone to hit you?"

She stared down at the tips of her boots. They were badly scuffed. If you're going to shack up with someone at least do it with someone who'll buy you new boots, I wanted to tell her, but I knew that wasn't the reason she wanted to move out. I wasn't sure what the reason was. I knew it had something to do with me but I didn't know how.

All I had done these past two years was take care of her, and it wasn't enough. It didn't count. She wanted something more or something else.

"Then what was all that crap over Dad hitting you?" I asked roughly. "You didn't like getting hit back then. Or did you? Were you faking?" I tried to remember exactly what Betty had said about it. "Do you think it's love?"

"You're sick," she said, still staring at her boots.

"Would you stay if I hit you?"

She considered my question. She considered it for a while. I couldn't believe she might actually say yes. I had never felt so let down in my life. Not even when I had to face the price of dog food and funerals.

"Do you want me to hit you?" I tried a different route.

She looked up at me, suddenly defiant. "Only if you want to."

"I don't want to."

"Fine." She whirled away, her hair breezing past my face.

I grabbed for her arm. "You didn't answer my first question. Would you stay if I hit you?"

Everyone stared at us except for Church, who was huddled over the phone receiver talking in conspiratorial whispers.

Amber glanced at my hand on her arm but for once she didn't rip her arm away.

"Do you want me to stay?" she asked.

"Would you stay if I hit you?"

She gave the question more thought, and a sick knot of grief tightened in the pit of my stomach.

"No," Amber finally answered. "Do you want me to stay?"

My grip on her arm dissolved with relief. "Only if you want to," I replied.

"I don't know if I want to."

"Why don't you stay until you figure it out?"

"Are you asking me to stay?"

"Until you figure it out."

"So you're asking me to stay?"

"Until you figure it out."

"Dylan will be mad if I stay."

"For Chrissake, Amber," I growled. "Tell him I won't let you move out."

"Really?" She smiled like a kid. "I can tell him that?"

"Sure," I said. "Just don't tell him here. Tell him you need to get something from home and then tell him once you get there. Otherwise, he might dump you here and I don't get off work for three more hours."

"He's not like that," she assured me, turning to go. She wiggled her fingers at me. "See you at home."

I was trying to figure out what had just happened when Church came up beside me.

"Your girlfriend's pretty," he said. "She's got hair like a new penny."

"She's not my girlfriend. She's my sister."

He laughed and winked. "Right. Right. Your sister."

I looked past him out the store windows and saw Amber standing with her suitcase watching a pickup roar away from her. She turned and gave me a defeated scowl but then she smiled a little. I guessed I must have been smiling at her. I noticed she had got her pillow back.

She hung out for the rest of my shift. We didn't talk in the truck on the way home but for the first time in a long time, the silence between us didn't burn. When we got on Black Lick Road, I let her drive.

Amber went to bed right away. I asked her to check on Jody and Misty first. While she was doing that, I went to the shed to make sure the gun was still hidden. I tightened the lid on the garbage can too.

Amber never came back to report on the girls so I figured they were both still alive. I dug through the refrigerator looking for a snack. I found an open pack of bologna and ate a couple slices.

Jody had left her final report card on the table for me to sign. All pluses except for a section under Gym called Effort. There were a couple work sheets too, a notice to return all library books, a crayon picture of Mickey Mouse beside a blue castle with the words MY VACASHUN DREM written at the top, and a neon orange piece of paper folded into quarters.

I opened the note and recognized Misty's stationery. Amber had bought it for her for her last birthday. It had a border of purple, red, and black prancing unicorns. The first time I saw a sheet of it, I thought they were demons.

Misty had written in the middle of it in small precise letters:

It makes more sense for them to be with each other than to be with strangers. They love each other. Harley will come around.

P.S. There's nothing wrong with their blood mixing. They've got the same blood. Esme's an idiot.

I folded the note. Everything went black. Misty's face came rushing toward me, and I cried out.

I came to in the kitchen with my hands clenched around the back of a chair, feeling like I had traveled hundreds of miles and been gone for years. But Jody's report card was still sitting there and it still said Grade 1.

The note was still there too. Now it had bologna grease fingerprints on it. What would happen if I got caught?

I took Mom's Bible to bed with me, but I never opened it. I figured I'd have a tortured time falling asleep but I only had to stare at my lightbulb for about two minutes before I did. The last thing I remembered was a soft, pale object floating above me and the contented sigh of Elvis lying down next to me. He hadn't slept in my room for a while but tonight he had followed me down the basement stairs, his nails clicking on the cement before he found the square of shag carpet next to my bed.

I didn't dream anymore but I knew the sweet bliss I felt couldn't be real. She was with me. Nurturing me, comforting me, protecting me, feeding me, teaching me, touching me, licking me, creating me. I didn't need to see her to get aroused. Her beauty didn't come from physical form, it came from her loss of self to me. She had not been put here as a helpmate or an equal. She had been sacrificed so we could exist.

I melted into her. Her body was the liquid I breathed. Her fingers were flickers of underwater flame, scorching and soothing my unborn skin. She moaned into my ear. Once. Softly. A silver-pitched gasp. A sound that thrilled and saddened like the bittersweet howling of a penned dog.

I rolled over and took her from Him. She was my gift. Mine. And I was her penance.

Then I remembered, I didn't dream anymore.

Before I could define the horror, I simply felt it. It lifted me up off my bed and smashed me into a wall. My sense of self-preservation told me to run, told me to scrape off my skin, told me to cut off my hands, but I opened my eyes instead.

Amber sat on the floor next to my bed. She was rubbing the back of her head like it hurt. She was naked.

"Oh, God," I moaned.

"You said you wanted me to stay," she said.

I saw Mom's Bible at the foot of my bed. I snatched it up and held it in front of me like a crucifix.

"What's wrong?" she asked groggily. "You were liking it."

I thought I screamed but I couldn't be sure. My brain was suddenly picking up TV static, and domestic squabbles, and radio transmissions from newly formed galaxies. Every word from every language ever written or spoken flashed past my eyes.

I held the Bible up in front of my face.

"Put on some clothes," I screamed.

"What's wrong with you?" I heard her say again.

"Go away," I screamed.

"You thought I was her." Her voice turned savage. "You thought I was her. That's why you were liking it. You thought I was that slut."

She got up from the floor and started toward me. She was still naked.

"I know all about it! I know all about you and her in that shack!"

I opened the Bible and shoved my face inside its red-tinged pages. The smell of my mother made me start crying.

"Did you think I was her? Did you think it was tomorrow night already and you were fucking her?"

"I wasn't fucking you." I sobbed. "I was sleeping."

"She doesn't love you. She could never love you. You're just a body part to her. You're just a big dumb dick she can ride."

I was afraid to try and get past her. I was afraid she'd touch me. I was afraid I'd let her.

"How could you do that to me?" she shrieked.

I closed my eyes and plunged past her like I was running into a wall of fire. Our skin brushed, but I survived. I ran clumsily up the stairs and to the front door where Elvis was trying like crazy to scratch his way out. I made it to the porch railing before I threw up.

I didn't know where to go. For the first time in my life, the woods frightened me. The silhouette of my truck parked in a streak of moonlight didn't strike me as a means of escape; it looked like a means of exile.

I saw the four empty doghouses. I picked one and ran to it and scrambled inside on all fours. I curled up with Mom's Bible and shook, breathing in the heavy scents of dirt and shit and old matted dog hair. I lay there, trying to control my chattering teeth, and listened in terror for her footfalls. They never came.

chapter 19

I never did sleep. I fell into a trance of sorts, clutching my bare legs to my chest, staring through a crack in the doghouse boards, watching the thin strip of sky go from black to rose to blue.

Every sound made me jump. The scratch and skitter of a rodent's feet. The too human call of a whippoorwill. The whisper of a snake's belly. The underground shifting of the Earth's plates. The blood-thump of my own heart.

Then morning sounds. Jody's voice in the kitchen. Cupboards opening and closing. Dishes clacking. Water running. Misty's voice too. No Amber.

The back door opening. Jody calling for Elvis. Jody calling for me. No Amber.

I huddled tighter into a ball and waited. Soon I heard the front door open and close. A set of feet galloped across the porch and another set plodded after.

"Stay, Elvis. Stay," Jody commanded.

In my mind I saw him cock his ears in her direction, then trot happily after her down the road to the bus stop.

The door opened a final time. I pressed my eye against the slit in the doghouse. Amber stepped out on the porch, and I turned my face away fast. She had been fully clothed, but all I had seen was a damp dark triangle and two hard red nipples. She would never be a whole person to me again. She would never be a person.

I bit down on Mom's Bible to keep from laughing or screaming or breathing. I heard her big clunky sandals cross the porch. Amber was going to school. Amber was going on with her life. Amber was fine.

I bit down harder on the Bible until tears squeezed from the corners of my eyes.

I waited until the sound of her crunching down the road faded and I only heard birds. She had the right idea, I told myself. Hanging around the house would have been the worst thing to do. Unless you plan to turn yourself in, get away from the scene of the crime.

I crawled out on all fours and let my eyes adjust to the light. It was going to be a hot, sunny day. I didn't bother standing. I crawled all the way inside the house, and even crawled down the basement stairs which wasn't easy.

I put on some clothes, ran a comb through my hair, checked my bedsheets for nocturnal emissions, and went upstairs for a Pop-Tart.

We only had the watermelon kind. Jody had begged me to buy them for her because of the pink and green frosting and then she hated the taste. So did I.

I grabbed the Frosted Flakes and ate a couple handfuls out of the box, then washed them down with milk and two beers. Elvis started barking outside. I expected to panic. It could have been Amber coming back, but the Red Dogs had taken the edge off. Too much, maybe. I slammed into the corner of the kitchen table as I turned to get Dad's coat off the back of a chair.

I closed my eyes and swore. When I opened them again, Misty was standing inside the back door in baggy denim overalls with a black tube top underneath. Her hair was in a sloppy ponytail. A small purse made of see-through purple plastic hung off one shoulder. Inside it I could see a lipstick, a Little Debbie Zebra Cake, and a pocketknife.

"Are you okay?" she asked.

"Fine," I answered, wincing.

She didn't say anything else or move a muscle. I limped around the table and thought about going out the back way, but it would have meant asking her to move.

"What are you doing here?" I growled, sounding braver than I felt. "Did you miss the bus? Where's Jody?"

"It's the last day of school," she said. "All we're going to do is clean out our lockers and watch a video."

"Something educational, I hope."

"It's based on a book,'" she offered.

"*Moby-Dick?*"

She regarded me blankly. "*Pet Sematary.*"

"My tax dollars hard at work," I said under my breath as I slipped my arms into Dad's coat.

"I heard your fight with Amber last night."

"Yeah, well."

I swallowed hard. I looked all around the room. I emptied Jody's cereal bowl into the sink. I crushed my beer cans and tossed them in the trash. I opened the refrigerator door.

"What'd you hear?" I asked with my head inside.

"You screaming at her to put her clothes on."

I laughed. I laughed a second time. I had to bite my tongue to keep from laughing for the rest of my life.

"You must have heard wrong."

"Why'd you sleep in a doghouse?"

"Purely for kicks."

I pulled out of the refrigerator.

"I don't care what you and Amber do," she said.

It took all my strength not to look at her, but the effort was wasted. I felt the dark, unblinking eyes on me. I felt them reduce me to a boy again and drag me inside with the irresistible lure of black blasted holes in the ground and gutted houses. She meant what she said. Not because she was depraved or forgiving or a victim herself. But because she had lost the ability to be moved, if she had ever possessed it in the first place. She could still care though. She cared by not caring. It was her highest compliment.

"I've gotta get to work," I said.

"How about taking me to get a tattoo?" she suggested. "Since I've already missed the bus and all."

"Forget it. I already told you, you can't get one."

"I thought maybe you'd change your mind."

"Why would I do that?"

She shrugged. Her shrugs conveyed more meaning than most sermons. I thought I knew what she was trying to tell me. I stared back at her in disbelief. Was she trying to blackmail me into letting her get a tattoo because of what she thought she heard going on between me and Amber?

Or maybe she was implying that she'd shoot me?

Another bout of laughter rose to my lips, and I swallowed it back. I had hidden the gun.

"No way."

"Why?"

"It won't ever come off," I said, but even before the words were out of my mouth, I realized how stupid it was to care about a scar on her surface.

I tried again. "You're too young to make a decision that you'll have to live with for the rest of your life, and I don't feel comfortable making it for you."

"Okay."

She walked over to the cupboard and took out a glass.

"Okay?" I echoed.

"I can respect that," she explained, crossing the kitchen to the fridge. "I thought you were going to lecture me on how sleazy it is or maybe try and stop me because you're on a parental power trip, but if that's your reason"—she pulled out a pitcher of blue Kool-Aid—"I guess I understand."

She poured and took a long drink. The band of pink stones around her wrist looked dull and cloudy in sunlight. Only artificial light in a dark room seemed to be able to make them glitter anymore.

"We're not that different, you know," she said to me over the top of her glass. "The way we think."

"Huh?"

"We're both sort of weird. I'm not the way a girl's supposed to be. You're not the way a guy's supposed to be."

"What are you talking about?"

"You don't like football. You don't like to mow. You keep that art book in your truck," she said flatly, taking a loud slurp between each observation.

"Big fucking deal," I said. "Almost all the artists in that book are men. There's nothing wrong with a guy liking art."

"There's nothing wrong with a girl liking to hunt."

"Who said there was?"

"Dad thought there was."

She finished her drink. It left a slight blue tinge to her lips, reminding me of this tiny purple-faced infant hooked to a respirator I had seen in a magazine in Betty's waiting room. The caption warned smokers not to reproduce.

"Dad loved taking you hunting," I reminded her.

"No, he didn't," she said without emotion. "He took me because I wanted to go, but he always wished I was you."

"That's bullshit."

"No, it's not."

"You're saying he didn't like me because I didn't want to go hunting with him, and he didn't like you because you did?"

"Something like that."

Her sullen brown stare fixed vacantly on the bottom of her empty glass. A significant silence passed.

"I tried to make him love me," she said.

The words clanged in my ears like a sprung trap. I wanted to run, but she looked up and her stare stamped down on me like heavy, metal, dull-edged teeth that would only tear if I tried to get away.

"He did love you."

"Not like he loved Mom."

A clammy feeling started in my crotch and climbed up my spine to settle on the top of my crusty scalp.

"That's a different kind of love," I said, trying to keep the rising revulsion out of my voice.

"He never hit her. Did you ever wonder about that? He never hit her. Not a single time. That's probably why she didn't care that he hit us."

And there it was. The final answer. I saw it buried in my sister's muddy eyes: the pain, and confusion, and hatred of someone forsaken.

There had never been any incestuous love she had been willing to kill for. There had never been any deadly loyalty for a daddy who spent quality time with her when he wasn't beating her. Dad had nothing to do with it. The betrayal had occurred between mother and child.

Misty's years of watching animals in the wild had taught her what she could expect and what she was owed. Her own mother had violated the simplest, most fundamental, instinctual law of nature. She had failed to protect her young.

I licked my lips.

And Mom had known that Misty knew her crime. She had known since the day Misty dropped the murdered kitten at her feet and started wearing its collar like a Purple Heart.

The pale speckled face with its Maybelline war paint turned toward the window.

"It's a nice day. I can't believe Amber didn't skip so she could lay out. I bet you're disappointed."

My stomach lurched, and I tasted milky beer in the back of my throat. I swallowed it down. It came up again. I reached for one of the kitchen chairs to steady myself.

Misty was going to terrorize me. Not with the threat of revealing what was going on between Amber and me but with the threat of encouraging it.

I thought about Jody's notes, and I wanted to cry. Misty was teaching her it was okay. They were all going to be on Amber's side.

My teeth started chattering, and I clenched my jaw shut.

I saw my future. I saw Jody's. I had to do something. Then I remembered Misty had her own terrible secret.

"I know what you did," I told her.

She kept staring out the window.

"Did you hear me?"

Nothing.

"Don't you have anything to say to that?"

She slowly pulled her stare away from the window and aimed it at me, pitying my dumb animal fate but savoring my dumb animal fear.

"You're the one who should have done it," she said.

This time when the milk and beer came up, I couldn't hold it back. I lunged for the sink. Misty stepped aside.

Once I started throwing up, I couldn't stop. It was like my body had finally found something it was good at. I stopped to rest at one point and laid my cheek against the cool steel faucet.

In the other room, I heard the TV go on.

I was fine once I got to work. I did well. I calmly took the abuse from my boss at Barclay's. I agreed with him that jobs were hard to come by around here and I was a dumb-ass for risking this one. I told him I understood that I was going to be fired if I was ever late again.

On the road, I was the friendliest son of a bitch who had ever delivered a refrigerator anywhere in the tristate area. I made small talk and chitchat with every housewife and toddler we came across. I even participated in tits-and-ass commentary with Ray. I didn't get upset when various people throughout the day told me I smelled like a barn or asked me why I was wearing a coat.

We were coming back from our last delivery when the big one hit, the one I did not survive. Six seconds was a liberal estimate; I didn't even get two. I didn't get a chance to look up and see the sky explode into a thousand suns. My explosion happened on the inside.

Ray was driving. I wasn't conscious of the way I reacted but it must have been bad because he made me get out of the truck on a busy road on the outskirts of town a good five miles from the store. Once the pain in my head dulled enough for me to catch my breath and my limbs stopped shaking enough for me to move with purpose, I started walking.

I didn't look at the cars and trucks that sped by me. I didn't look at the soft blue sky above me or the long gray line stretching out endlessly at my feet. I found a star in the distance—a green and orange 7-Eleven sign—and set my sights on it.

I went straight to the pay phones attached to the side of the store and called Betty. Her answering machine picked up and said she was at her other office. I could leave a message or call her there. I repeated the number it gave. I started to dial and forgot it. I called her county office again. I repeated the number. I started to dial and forgot it. I called again. I ran out of quarters. I had a dollar in my pocket. I went inside and got quarters. I counted them. FOUR. Four quarters. Good, I told the cashier.

I went outside and called her county office again. I got the number. I hit seven buttons and closed my eyes.

Another answering machine picked up, and I started to cry. Even after the beep, I kept crying. I couldn't think of a better message.

"Hello? Hello?" Betty's real voice came on the other end. "Hello. Who is this? Is something wrong?"

"I need help," I sobbed.

"Who is this?"

"I don't know."

"Harley?"

"Yeah." I stopped, and sniffed, and wiped my nose with the sleeve of Dad's coat. "That sounds right."

"Harley, where are you?"

"I don't know."

"What's wrong? What's happened?"

"I need help."

"What happened?"

"She . . ."

"Who?"

"She . . ."

"She, who?"

A savage pain ripped through my head, obliterating my thoughts, leaving me mute and stupid.

"Harley, where are you?"

I could only cry.

"Are you at home?"

I shook my head at the phone.

"At work?"

"Seven, eleven," I whispered.

"Seven, eleven," she repeated. "You mean the store?"

I nodded at the phone.

"The old one or the new one?"

"The green one." I sniffed.

"Harley." She sounded frustrated. "I'm with a patient right now."

"A real patient," I said.

"Can you get to me? I'm at my office."

"Your real office," I said.

"It's less real than the one I see you at. It's 475 Saltwork Street. Between Maple and Grant. It's a big white house with a bright red door. Do you think you can find it?"

I hung up the phone and started walking again.

I was sweating like a pig by the time I got there. The house wasn't big. It was huge. The ones around it were big.

The floor inside was a dark fathomless wood polished until it looked liquid. A banister of the same wood wound its way up a staircase in front of me. Paintings of pale pink ballerinas and gem-colored gardens hung on the walls papered in cream. Two old-fashioned chairs with striped velvet cushions sat on either side of a doorway I couldn't see into.

Holy shit, I thought to myself.

"Hello," a female voice called. Not Betty's.

I was afraid to step off the plush throw rug onto the floor for fear of drowning.

"Is somebody there?"

A woman came out of the room I couldn't see into. She was smiling politely but then her mouth gaped open a little and her eyes grew wide with concern. "Are you Harley?" she asked.

"Yeah."

"Come in," she said. "Dr. Parks is going to be so relieved to see you."

"Dr. Parks?" I wondered.

"Betty," she explained.

She made a move to touch me, then thought better of it. "Do you want to take off your coat?"

"No, thanks."

She told me to follow her and I did to a room at the end of the hallway. Betty was sitting in it behind a bed-sized Heads of State kind of desk, surrounded by shelves and shelves of books. She was on the phone. She hung up immediately.

"Harley, thank God," she said, and came out from behind the desk.

She had on a respectable skirt the color of toasted coconut, nylons and heels, and a sleeveless cream silk top with pearls. A pair of polished yellow-gold squares on her ears shone through her sterling hair whenever she moved her head.

"It's been almost two hours since you called. How are you?"

"You don't need that government job, do you?" I said.

She followed my gaze around the room. "That depends on what you mean by need," she answered me. "I don't need it for financial reasons. No."

The chairs and the couch in this office were too nice for me to sit on so I stood. Even after she asked me to sit. Even after she said please.

She sat in an overstuffed leather chair like a caramel-dipped marshmallow.

"What happened, Harley? You mentioned a she. You never got back to me after your visit with your mother. How did that go?"

I blinked sweat out of my eyes. Or maybe it wasn't sweat. I remembered eyes are made out of water.

"She . . ." I started up again.

"Yes, Harley," Betty said pleasantly. "She, who?"

"She . . ." I said again. "She . . . she."

"Yes," she urged me. "She."

I licked my lips, swallowed, took a deep breath.

"She . . ."

I shook my head in frustration.

"I used to," I tried.

Betty leaned forward. "Used to what?"

"We used to."

"Used to what?"

I fell to my knees and covered my face with my hands.

Betty joined me on the floor. I felt her hands on my back, I felt them through Dad's coat.

"Who?" she said.

"Amber."

Her name finally left me like a tumor carved from my brain-stem. I could think and speak again.

"Used to touch me. When we were kids. I remember. She used to touch me. In bed. She used to come to my bed and touch me."

"Where did she touch you?" Betty asked.

"You know where," I screamed at her.

"You need to say it."

"No, I don't."

"Yes, you do. You need to say it out loud in order to confront it so it can go away."

"It's not ever going to go away."

"It can fade to almost nothing, Harley. It can. I promise you."

I put my face back in my hands.

"She touched you where?"

I thought about who I was talking to.

"My penis," I said hoarsely.

"Did it give you an erection?"

I didn't answer.

"Did it?"

"Yes."

"Did you ejaculate?"

I buried my face deeper.

"Yes," I sobbed.

"Did you touch her?"

"No," I moaned, and looked up at her. "No. No. I swear I didn't. I never even looked at her. She was behind me. She came into my bed."

"Why did she come into your bed?"

I started crying harder. I couldn't stop shaking. Betty put her arms around me.

"Think about it," she said.

"She was afraid of Dad," I cried into her shoulder.

"And you let her stay?"

I nodded.

"Why?" she asked, rocking me on the floor. "Think about it."

"I was afraid of him too."

"I want you to listen to me very carefully, Harley."

She let go of me and sat back on her heels. She waited for me to look at her.

"You are not a bad person. You're not a freak or a pervert. There's nothing wrong with you or Amber. You were children reacting to debilitating emotional and physical abuse the only way you knew how. By turning to each other for comfort and pleasure."

I tried to cover my face again, but she grabbed my hands and held them in hers.

"What made you remember? Do you know? Did something happen?"

"I can't," I said, shaking my head.

"Yes, you can. What happened?"

She moved away for an instant and came back with a box of Kleenex. She pulled one out and handed it to me.

"She was in bed with me," I began, haltingly. "I was sleeping."

"When?"

"Last night."

"Did she touch you?"

"I don't know. I was sleeping."

I wiped at my eyes and blew my nose.

"She didn't have any clothes on," I volunteered.

"Did you have an erection?"

A shudder traveled from my toes to the top of my head and back again.

"I didn't look," I said.

She sighed again. A weary sigh. I glanced at her. She was sitting on the floor with her legs tucked behind her. I had left wet stains on her silk blouse. I wondered if I had ruined it.

"How did you react?" she asked me.

"What do you mean?" I shouted at her, getting up from the floor and scrambling away from her. "What kind of question is that? I'm not sick."

I backed into the bookshelves.

"I'm not sick."

"I'm not implying that you are."

She stood up too but didn't approach me.

"I'm thinking about Amber now."

"Huh?"

"Amber," she said again. "I'm concerned about how she must be feeling right now."

"Amber?" I shouted. "It was all her idea. She wanted to do it."

"She didn't want to do it, Harley. Try and understand. Your sister isn't the villain here. She's suffering as much as you are. Maybe more."

"More?" I cried out.

"How did you react to her advances?"

"I threw her off me. I screamed at her. I told her to get away. I ran away."

"Where is Amber right now?"

I looked out the window. The sun had fallen halfway down the sky. I was supposed to be somewhere, but I couldn't remember where.

"I don't know," I said. "I think she went to school. Today's the last day. They got out early. What's the matter? She can take care of herself."

Betty didn't look convinced.

"Right now you're feeling repulsion, shame, guilt," she instructed me. "Amber's feeling all that too, but she's also feeling rejection."

She started to the door.

"Please, sit, Harley. I don't think I've ever seen anyone look so tired in my entire life."

She walked out. I stared at the couch. It was the same color as the chair but it was velvety instead of glossy. I went over to it and checked the back of my jeans for filth and sweat. I sat down on the very edge, then stood up to see if my soul had left a stain.

She returned with a Styrofoam cup of water. "Sit," she said, stern this time.

I sat. She handed me the water and I drank it.

"I want you to lie down here and rest," she said.

"I have to be somewhere but I can't remember."

"Work?" she asked.

"Shit," I said, closing my eyes, and falling back against the couch. Its cushions felt like they were stuffed with mist.

"I'm going to get fired from Shop Rite. I'm going to get fired from Barclay's too."

"Don't worry about that. I can talk to your bosses."

"Oh, yeah." I laughed. "That always helps getting a job back. Having your shrink call to say you were too fucked up to come to work today."

"Don't worry about it," she told me again. "Lie down."

"I can't sleep anymore."

"Just a minute."

She left again. I didn't want to listen to her but the couch called to me to throw myself into it the same way fresh snowbanks did when I was a kid. I stretched out on it.

I thought about my dirty boots too late. I had been here ten minutes and already messed up her couch and her blouse. This was why she saw people like me in her other office wearing crappy clothes.

She came back in with a refill on the water.

"Here," she said, handing me a pill too. "It will help you sleep. It's one of my own."

"You take pills?" I asked.

She nodded.

"I thought you were well adjusted."

A small smile passed over her lips. They had red lipstick on them. She never wore lipstick at the other office.

"Define well adjusted," she said.

I didn't like it. It bled into the old-lady cracks around her lips.

She stood up and walked to the door, where she clicked off the light. "Try and get some rest," she said. "I'll be doing some work in another room."

I swallowed the pill. I didn't even think about it.

Enough light came through the window that I could still look around. I had been right about the books. Hundreds of them. A lot of psychology stuff but weird stuff too stuck in between the academic-sounding titles.

The Thousand Recipe Chinese Cookbook. The Art of Walt Disney. What to Expect When You're Expecting. Mass Media Law. Charlie and the Chocolate Factory. The 185th Anniversary History of Laurel Falls. Ulysses. Peterson's *Field Guide to Wildflowers. Black Beauty. In Cold Blood.*

I felt myself dozing off. I threw myself backward into the couch snowdrift and started flapping my arms and legs to make an angel. I kept falling and falling. The snow had no substance then I realized it was a cloud, and the angel I was making was a real one floating along behind me.

She took my hand and we flew to a poor village, tranquil in an endless sea of sand beneath a bright white moon like one of Betty's pearls. We went from home to home, following a stream of crystal light that flew in and out of windows and went from bed to bed.

It took me awhile but I finally figured out it was God cruising for chicks.

I didn't understand. He was God. He knew what lurked in

the hearts of men and women too. He didn't have to search and test for someone willing; He knew.

I asked the angel and she explained that carnal love was the one emotion God couldn't read, an emotion too human for anyone to understand but Man. She left me then at a window where a darkhaired girl lay sleeping naked on a bare cloth mattress with her lips and legs parted and her slender arms extended in a welcome. The moonlight spilled over her, seeping and gushing into every opening, every pore.

Then I was back floating alone in my cloud drift. I couldn't get the girl out of my mind. I felt her fear and her bliss. I felt her regret at lost innocence, but I also felt her need to be ruined.

She was a woman. He was God. He could have blinked and made a son, but He had gone to her instead.

I bet it made her glow from the inside out. I bet it lifted her from the bed, writhing and smiling. I bet threads of silver light shot from her fingertips and toes and every strand of her hair.

I hoped so. I hoped and prayed that it was so. It was her one lousy shot at ecstasy before she became the eternal Virgin, and I hoped she got there.

Betty's office was completely dark when I opened my eyes. It was like waking up inside ink. I rolled off the couch with a thud, then sat frozen on the floor with my heart pounding in my throat. I didn't want her to come back.

She didn't. I stood up slowly and got my bearings. A dim sliver of light came from the hallway behind the cracked door. I went for the window instead. It unlocked easily and quietly.

The moon was high overhead, shining brightly but giving off no light. I stared up at it and knew Callie was staring up at it too thinking it was violent in its perfection like a strong, quick stab with a sharpened stick. She was wondering where I was.

The dream had cleared my head. It was good to dream again. I started walking feeling a slapping rhythmic calm beneath my feet like the tiny waves that finally lap the shore after a distant motorboat has passed by. Betty's rich neighborhood dissolved around me and I found myself walking a gray town sidewalk past uniform shabby houses pushed together in hedgerows of defeat.

I knew where I was. My dad used to point out these houses whenever we drove by them. He always said how glad he was we had our own little spot in the country and didn't have to live like this. I agreed. Isolated failure was easier to bear.

It didn't take me long to get to Barclay's or maybe it did. I had lost my sense of time. I got in my truck and drove away.

The whole way to Black Lick Road, I was only thinking about the release. Not the sex. Sex was too complicated and mental. I was thinking in vague swirling grays of the mindlessness of IN-STINCT and the simple glories of PHYSICAL STIMULI.

I suddenly understood how farm boys could do it with their sheep and daddies could do it with their daughters. They shrugged off their humanness like the shedding of a skin and became something new and raw and beautiful in their own ugly eyes. The only thing separating me from them was the fear that I would find something hideous and mangled under my skin.

I didn't go home first. I left my truck on the side of the road after calculating the straightest shot through the woods to the mining office. I took a couple swats in the face with tree branches and twisted my ankle in a groundhog hole, but I knew she was waiting for me. Worrying about me. I wondered if she had brought the stuff for s'mores.

The light from the useless moon was enough to give a faint glimmer to the rocks around the train tracks. They stretched out like a sill of metal filings.

I thought she might be sitting outside. I expected a flashlight beam or even a fire. I didn't know what time it was. Maybe I was way too late. Maybe she was back home already.

I started walking faster. I broke into a jog. As I neared the of-fice, I saw her backpack and her cooler.

"Callie," I said.

I was breathing a lot heavier than I needed to be.

"Callie," I said again, and stepped up to the door.

The crunch of the gravel crackled inside my head like electrical pops. I peered into the gloom and saw a bare ankle ending in a foot in a woman's white tennis shoe. It lay flat on its side, toe pointed outward, at an angle too uncomfortable for sleep and too unnatural for the living.

I moved an inch farther and saw the tips of her fingers curled up like a bird claw.

INSTINCT dropped me to my knees. Self-preservation kept me from looking any further. Amber's psychos reared their heads all around me. Misty's demonic prancing unicorns filled the sky. Boyish banker Brad: did he do it? What if he had found out about us?

I wasn't there when Mom shot Dad. I had never seen a dead person except for my grandparents who didn't count because they were old and unlovable. Dad's funeral had been closed casket. I never understood why but now that I knew what Uncle Mike thought about him and Misty, I knew he had requested it because he couldn't stand to look at Dad again. It was a shame because Dad had been innocent, and Uncle Mike had lost his brother a second time.

I took a couple deep breathless breaths. She might only be hurt, I told myself.

I couldn't walk in. I stayed on my knees. My closeness to the ground gave me the confidence of a child covering his face with his hands and peeking through his fingers.

"Callie," I whispered. "Please."

I passed through the doorway and waited on all fours, staring at her dead feet. The vomit had already risen to my throat before I looked at the rest of her. I tried to make it outside but threw up next to her. I felt bad about that.

Her face was gone. She didn't have a face. There was part of a jawbone with a couple teeth left and a shattered section of forehead.

My retching turned into dry heaves that I didn't think were going to stop until they turned me inside out. It was dark but I saw bone and flesh and brain and hair. I fixed my stare back on her feet, afraid to see any more, afraid I might see her eyes, whole and unharmed, staring at me from a corner.

I reached out and touched her ankle. It was freezing cold. I moved my hand over to her hand and tried to hold it.

I started to cry then not only out of grief but out of relief too. Now I knew for sure that people had souls. What I felt in her dead hand was much more than a loss of heat and blood. She was gone. She had been more than words and thoughts and feelings. She had been an essence.

She was somewhere else. That was all. And so was Dad. He wasn't over. Maybe there was still a chance for us. I decided to add him to my list of dead people I'd like to meet.

I picked up her hand and held it to my face and cried into it. It smelled like salami and mustard. She had made us sandwiches.

The footsteps outside didn't startle me. I knew they would come eventually. I didn't stop crying or holding Callie's hand.

I knew she would wait for me.

I put the hand down, stood up, and walked to the open door.

Her calm blasted stare settled over me, but she was shivering violently.

"I'm sorry," she said, and began a hacking, tearless sobbing. "I didn't know what else to do."

I made a move like I meant to run at her but nothing happened. My feet started inching forward. I urged them to go faster but they were submerged in a dream or a sea.

I finally arrived and took Uncle Mike's gun from her.

"What about me?" she asked in a broken whisper.

I wanted to tell her she was everything good about me and

everything bad. She was my best intentions mixed with the reality of who I was. She was every promise I couldn't keep. But I couldn't explain it to her. All I could say was "Amber," and nothing else would come.

Her eyes were a bruised violet in the dark. A tranquil fear like the realization of painless death spread through me. All I could give her was what I had left. What I had left was under my skin.

chapter 20

I stop talking to the cops just because I'm tired. I'm pretty sure I'm done anyway. I don't know what time it is. I always thought a police station would be covered with clocks. Time is very important to these guys. They begin all their reports with the TIME. They're always telling hysterical victims to take their TIME. They send criminals off to prison to do TIME. But I can't find a lousy clock anywhere.

I think about asking the sheriff what time it is. He's wearing a nice watch. Not as nice as a banker's watch or a psychiatrist's watch though, and that probably bugs the hell out of him because he knows what he does is more important. More dangerous too. Bankers rarely get their brains blown out. Although sometimes their wives do.

"I want to make a phone call," I think to say, and everybody looks at me like now I'm out of my mind.

"We're not done," the sheriff says from where he's sitting on the edge of his desk. "I want to go over some of this before you sign it, then you can make your call."

Amber doesn't have good aim. That was why Callie got her brains blown out. Standing three feet away from her holding a gun with a high-powered telescopic sight and Amber missed her chest and shot her in the face.

She apologized to me for that during the drive back to our house. She said she would have never done it on purpose. She knew Callie had a husband and kids and family and friends. She also promised me Callie didn't have time to be scared.

"I want to make it now," I say.

Bill, the deputy who belted me in the face earlier, makes another move for me and the sheriff yells at him to back off. The metal-topped table in front of me is covered with balled-up white Kleenex soaked in bright red blood.

"All right," the sheriff says, and looks at his watch. "You've been here two hours. Make your call."

He heaves his couch-smelling bulk off the desk, turns to spit tobacco in an old coffee can the way my grandpa used to spit out the lining of his black lungs, and picks up the phone cradled in a cheap-looking plastic console with a dozen square buttons running down the side of it, some of them flashing red.

He comes over and drops it in front of me.

"Can I have some privacy?" I ask.

"No," he says.

"Doesn't that violate my civil rights or something like that?"

He picks up the receiver and stabs one of the buttons. "Probably," he says.

I take the phone from him, and he walks back to his desk. The other deputies yawn and stretch and go off in search of more coffee, except for Bill. He takes a seat a couple feet away and stares at me like he wants to break more than my nose. He must have known her. Maybe he stopped her for a speeding ticket once and they got to talking about Impressionists.

I dial my number. It rings four times before Uncle Mike answers. He doesn't sound happy to hear from me. I tell myself it's just because I'm calling so late, but tears start rolling down my cheeks anyway.

"I want to talk to Jody."

"Jody?" he says. "Jody's in bed, asleep."

There aren't any female deputies so the sheriff had to dig up a Laurel Falls policewoman to send out to talk to the girls. She told them they had to be put in a shelter overnight until temporary foster care could be worked out for them or they could stay with a relative. Amber called Uncle Mike.

"Can you wake her up?"

"No, I can't," he says tensely. "What are you doing calling here? Since when do the police let people call home from jail?"

"You get one phone call."

"This is your one phone call?"

"Yeah."

There's a long silence.

"Jesus, Harley," he says, his voice all shaky like he might cry. "You might get the death penalty for this."

TRIED AS AN ADULT TRIED AS AN ADULT flashes in front of me like a failing bar sign.

"I know."

"You get one phone call and you call a six-year-old little girl?"

"Right."

More silence.

"I'm sorry," he says, his voice tightening up again. "I can't wake her."

"What about Amber?"

"Everyone's asleep."

"Well," I say slowly, staring at the neon-bright words, wondering when something's going to finally appear there that won't go away. "I just wanted to make sure she's okay."

"She's fine. As fine as she can be." He pauses, then, "You can't keep anything quiet in a small town. Not for a second. People are already driving up here, shouting and throwing things on the yard and it's the middle of the night. Tomorrow should be pretty bad. We're taking the girls back to our house first thing in the morning and getting them away from here."

"What about Elvis?"

"I'm not taking your damn dog."

"You've got to take him," I say. "Who's going to feed him? If he starts roaming around looking for food, someone's going to shoot him. Or he could get hit by a car." My panic starts mounting. "He's been a good dog. He deserves better."

"I don't care what he deserves. He's a dog. And I'm not taking him."

I start crying pretty hard. I don't even care that the sheriff and Deputy Bill are thinking I'm a pussy for doing it.

"You have to get Jody a fortune cookie and a paper umbrella every month," I manage to tell him.

Then I hang up.

The sheriff comes back over, pushes the phone aside, and sits on the table close enough to me that I can see he's got a small reddish-brown stain on the thigh of his gray law-enforcement pants. It could be blood but I'm willing to bet it's salsa.

I reach for one of my bloody tissues since I used up the box they gave me and blow my nose in it before I remember how bad my nose hurts. The pain makes me cry even harder. He's got no sympathy for me. I don't expect him to. He's got heavy-lidded eyes that remind me of a dozing turtle.

"You know much about guns, Harley?" he asks me.

It's the first time he's used my name all night. Usually he calls me "son."

"Some," I say.

"I know you used to go hunting with your dad."

"Not much."

"Enough to know how to handle a gun," he says. "Enough to know how to aim and shoot. Enough to know how powerful a .44 magnum carbine is and what kind of damage it can do at close range."

He gets up and starts walking. I'm glad. I don't like the way he smells or looks. His belt and holster and cheap shoes creak as he paces.

"My question to you is, Why didn't you shoot her from a distance? You've got a nice scope on that Ruger. You don't have to be a good shot with a scope like that. Just aim and pull the trigger."

I don't say anything. He stops, stares at me for a moment, then starts pacing again.

"You could've climbed one of those hills up behind the railroad tracks and shot her in her front yard while she was outside playing with her kids. Or you could've shot her right through all those windows on the front of their house."

He stops again.

"You know her kids, right?" he asks me, even though he knows I do. "Her little girl is friends with that sister of yours you just called, right? It's probably going to be hard for them to be friends from now on, huh?"

I know what he's doing; I just don't understand why he's doing it. Someone's been killed and here I am admitting to it. He's got a murder victim. He's got a murderer. Why mess with that? No one questioned my mom's story.

My hands start shaking again. I sit on them.

"Hell, if you had done it that way, you could've said it was a hunting accident and not gone to jail at all." He starts walking and talking again. "It happens all the time. No one would have suspected anything because nobody knew what was going on between you two. Right? Nobody knew. I know her husband didn't know."

"Did you tell him?" I ask, suddenly feeling queasy.

One of the other deputies comes walking back with two steaming Styrofoam cups of coffee.

"No," the sheriff says, taking a cup from him. "I haven't been out of this room since I found out myself. I talked to him after we recovered the body though, and he was stunned that we had you in custody. He said you liked his wife and that she was fond of you. She felt sorry for you. He said you had come by their house just a couple days ago all upset from visiting your mom in prison on your birthday, and she went out to your truck in the pouring rain and talked to you and made you feel better."

He takes a sip of his coffee.

"Did she make you feel better, Harley?"

I stare at the bloody Kleenex. The smell from his coffee is making me feel sicker.

"I guess she won't be making you feel better anymore."

"Shut up," I shout, surprised by my own words.

I'm also surprised to find myself standing. This time Bill doesn't come after me; the other one does.

He's the one who brought up the death penalty earlier. During my confession, I told them how beautiful she was and he pointed out how killing a beautiful woman, especially a mother of young kids, was the worst crime there was aside from killing the kids. He said I was going to fry for it even though he's a cop so I'm sure he knows Pennsylvania uses lethal injection. What he means is I'll be inoculated for it. I asked him if I'd still get the death penalty if she was fat and ugly, and he said I'd probably only get life. He's also the guy who told me I watch too much TV when I called about my mom. I recognize his voice.

He clamps a big hand on my shoulder and I wince the same way Amber did when I touched her shoulder tonight. When she took her clothes off, she had a bruise there. That Ruger packs a kick.

"I want to go to jail," I cry out to all of them.

The deputy holding me looks over at the sheriff, who nods at him. He lets go.

"I want to go now," I say.

"Okay, fair enough," the sheriff agrees. "I've just got one more question for you, then you can sign your confession and we'll

put you in a cell here and a couple hours from now, when
lawyers and judges start their days, we'll get you to a real jail."

He tells me to sit down. I keep standing.

"Why'd you kill her?" he asks.

"Huh?"

"Why'd you kill her?"

I start feeling panicky again. I think about Elvis and how he's
going to think I've run out on him on purpose and how he's
going to spend the rest of his life thinking he's a bad dog. I think
about Jody and Esme and how the sheriff's right; they can't be
friends anymore. I think about Amber and how she cried and
cried when we were done because it wasn't what she wanted
after all and now she knows.

"What do you mean?" I ask him.

"From everything you've told me so far, I'd say you were in
love with her. Now I'm not saying people don't kill people they
love. That happens around here almost as much as hunting ac-
cidents. But they usually have a pretty good reason for doing it."

I lick my lips.

"I wanted to marry her," I say.

It isn't a lie.

"And . . .?" he urges.

"She wouldn't leave her husband."

"So you killed her?"

"Yeah."

"Okay."

He sits down on his desk again. He takes another drink of his
coffee and places it next to his spit can.

"Let me make sure I've got this straight one last time," he
says, and rubs at his chin like he's an intellectual.

"You're supposed to be meeting her to get fucked and instead
you show up with a gun you know can literally blow her head
off, and you stand there, face to face with the woman you love,
close enough to see the terror in her eyes, and you do it. You

blow her head off. Instead of fucking her. That's what you choose to do. Then you throw up beside her and fold her hands peacefully over her chest. You get in your truck, drive to the police station, turn yourself in, give us a nice neat confession, then call home to see how your dog and baby sister are doing. Is that about right?"

My head aches. My face hurts. My scalp itches. My stomach is heaving. My hands are shaking. The blood is pounding so heavy in my ears, his final words are drowned out by the sound.

"Here's my only problem," he goes on. "One of the people you've described is a cold-blooded, homicidal psychopath. The other is a decent, responsible kid who's had a really shitty life. Can you explain to me how you can be both?"

GROOVY rises up from his spit can like a genie coming out of his lamp. It spreads across the room in pink and purple cloud letters.

"I have a split personality," I tell him, licking my lips some more.

"Is that why you see a shrink?"

"Something like that."

Amber had been wearing watermelon Lip Smacker tonight. The stuff she's worn since she was a kid. I could swear I still tasted it.

"Then she can confirm this? I can ask her. What's her name again? I'd like to talk to her anyway."

I only kissed her once, then I told her I couldn't do it again. I couldn't touch her either. She didn't care. I put my hands in the dirt beneath her.

"I want to go to jail now. You said I could."

"All right, Harley."

He brings me a three-page police report with tons of writing on it. At the very top is the TIME we started. He leans over with a pen and fills in the TIME we ended, then hands the pen to me. He flips to the last page.

"Sign here," he tells me.

He's looking at me differently than anyone's looked at me all night. Not with hatred, outrage, or disgust. Not even with pity or frustration. He's disappointed in me.

I don't like the guy but still I crave understanding from someone.

I had to do it, I want to tell him. I had to give her that one shot at ecstasy. That's what the dream was telling me.

Too bad she didn't get there, but I don't think most people ever do. At least she got the desire out of her system and now she's going to be okay. That's why I don't want her life getting fucked up by going to jail. She's going to be okay now. I'm not, even though I've already blocked out most of it. I don't remember anything except I know I didn't EJACULATE.

The problem with trying to forget about shit is you can't. Time does not heal all wounds. I don't know who was the first guy to say it does, but it couldn't have been Confucius. He would've never said something so stupid.

I sign. A confession's a confession.

The sheriff takes the pen from me, then says something kind of weird.

"I'm sorry, son," he tells me. "I know that you must have loved her."

I don't bother telling him I still do. I'm not going to stop just because she killed someone.

epilogue

This place is not so bad. It has a great view. A bank calendar view. Miles and miles of soft green hills that look like they'd make a great bed if a giant came stumbling through the valley and needed a place to crash.

The food could be better and so could the company, but I'm not very hungry or social these days so it doesn't matter much. I haven't been allowed to have visitors yet, but my new shrink says I should be able to see Jody soon. She's the only person I want to see. Only because I want her to see that I'm okay.

Betty wants to see me, but I don't want to see her. I'm still mad at her for turning in Amber. I know she thought she was doing what was best for all of us but it wasn't her place to make that decision. I had my reason for doing what I did.

I told her this when I saw her in the police station the day after my arrest, and she said she knew I had my reason but it wasn't a good one. I didn't kill Callie Mercer. Choosing to sleep with me may have ultimately, unwittingly led to the circumstances that ended her life, but I did not pull the trigger.

Then she said I would be cheating Amber by taking the blame for her crime. She took a human life. She took a mother from her children. A wife from her husband. A daughter from her parents. She needed to be punished if she was ever going to have CLOSURE.

I have CLOSURE on my wall now. My new shrink told me to write down the words I see in the air. I have a ton of them taped up. We're allowed to have tape in here. We don't have to use tapioca.

I have a ton of Jody's fortunes taped up too. She sent me her whole FORJUNS envelope. Every time I look at one I picture her carefully pulling out the strip of paper as delicately as if she were straightening a fairy's wings, and I feel a little better before I feel really shitty.

She sent me a letter too. I've only been able to read it once, but I'm going to keep it forever because I know how much work she put into it. I've started a dozen letters back to her, and they all begin with how proud I am of her letter. I never get around to finishing them though. Hers says:

DEAR HARLEY,

HOW ARE YOU? I AM FIN. MISTY IS FIN TO.

UNCLE MIKE LET ME BRING ALL MY DINUSORS TO HIS HOWS.

HE SED I CAN GET A NU ONE FOR KRISMIS. I PRAY EVRY NIT FOR YOU AND AMBER AND ESMES MOMS SOWL.

I HOPE YOU WILL CUM HOM SUN. I MISS MY LIF.

YUR SISTER,

JODY

I still have Skip's letter too. I keep it in my one drawer with some other stuff. They're pretty good about letting you keep PERSONAL EFFECTS here as long as they fit in the drawer. Callie's art book wouldn't fit which is okay because I think it was only a loaner.

I've got Mom's Bible and her map in the drawer too, and Mom and Dad's wedding picture. And the crocheted doll. They let me keep her because they don't know what I use her for. I don't think I'm ever going to want a live woman again.

The only other thing in here is a card from Church. I know he picked it out himself because the front is a cartoon dog wearing a party hat shouting, "Congratulations." The inside says, "Way to go! I knew you could do it!" I know his mom would have guided him in a different direction if they had shopped for a card together. I have a feeling Church's mom doesn't think I'm such a nice boy anymore.

I'm not exactly sure what would have led her to that conclusion. Amber's story made the eleven o'clock news, not mine. It turned out I wasn't sent to jail for murder after all and the only reason I'm in here is because I started laughing when they told me Misty was the one who told the police Amber and I had an incestuous relationship. And I couldn't stop laughing. Or maybe I was screaming. I don't remember. The only thing I do remember is shitting myself. Shitting yourself in front of strangers and fucking your sister are two things you don't ever forget.

At least Betty hasn't turned her back on me like Church's mom. Sometimes I think I shouldn't be so hard on her for that reason alone. And to tell the TRUTH, if I'm going to be mad at her for the whole Amber mess I should be mad at Elvis too.

TRUE, Betty was the one who went to the sheriff's department when she heard about my arrest and told them I had been at her office until almost midnight the night before and I couldn't have done it; but on its own, that really wouldn't have meant anything. I still would have had time to kill Callie. I didn't show up at the police station until almost 2 A.M.

She asked them if they had talked to my sister, but that wouldn't have meant anything either. They already had my signed confession.

They decided to go out to the house anyway and the way the sheriff explained it to me was no one was there except for a big shepherd mutt lying on an old, burnt-up couch chewing on a pair of girl's cutoffs spattered in blood.

Amber wasn't any better at burying than she was at aiming.

I was upset all over again when I heard Uncle Mike had really gone through with it and just left Elvis there. Betty wouldn't take him either. I came pretty close to begging. I even asked the sheriff and a couple of the deputies to take him.

Betty did end up finding a home for him though. She told me he's living with a nice family. They live in town so he doesn't have as much space as he's used to but he's still very happy.

Bullshit, I told her. He wakes up every day and looks around him and wonders what terrible thing he did that would make the one person in his life who was supposed to love him unconditionally turn his back on him. That's what he thinks, I told her. I don't care that he's only a dog.

I do a lot of thinking myself these days but only on select topics. I guess that's the way I've always been. My new shrink says that's okay. He says that's not my biggest problem. He says my biggest problem is when I accidentally start thinking about things I don't want to think about, I can't COPE.

EARTH-CROSSERS. I told him that's what I call them. He loved that. He told me it was a brilliant analogy. He's always lying his head off like that. I asked him once if he's got a book with a chapter in it called "Compliment Psychos and They Will Be Your Friends." He laughed and told me I'm very witty and perceptive. I said I was being serious.

I guess some of what he says is TRUE though. I still can't think about Misty without screaming. I can't think about what has become of little Zack and Esme Mercer's lives. I can't think about Jody's notes. I can't think about Callie's six seconds.

I've always figured when a mother sees the big one coming and the sky light up like a thousand suns, she sees her children's faces in every one of them. Callie would have thought about her kids as she faced down Amber. She wouldn't have thought about herself. Not her boyish, banker husband or the grandfather who gave her the hills she loved. Not me or the God she was on her way to see. She would have thought about her kids and how they were going to wake up in the middle of the night, for years to come, calling for her, and she wouldn't be able to get to them.

She's going to hear them too. No matter where she ends up. Heaven. Hell. Or some netherworld in between. She's going to hear them call to her. That's the worst part about the whole thing. Damning Callie and her kids to that fate. They deserved better. Them and Elvis.

The biggest surprise is I CAN think about Amber now. Not everything. But some of it. I try to think positively when I think about her future. It would be nice if she had one of those trials like O.J.'s where everybody knows she did it, but they let her go anyway because they don't like the prosecutor's hairstyle. But that shit only happens on TV.

I can think about our childhood again, and I can even think about her snuggled up against my back in bed at night and how that may have been the only calm she will ever feel in her entire life.

My new shrink says that particular memory isn't healthy for me because I'm only remembering part of it. I'm not remembering the whole TRUTH and he knows how hung up I am on the TRUTH. He's seen my room.

I guess I see TRUTH in the air a lot. I've written it down about a hundred times and taped it to my wall.

"Those who know the TRUTH are not equal to those who love it." Confucius said that. I've written that down too.

I guess I always thought I was someone who loved the TRUTH but constantly had it hidden from me. Now I realize I've always had a lot of TRUTH staring me in the face, but I've ignored it on purpose because I don't love it.

The TRUTH is the TRUTH sucks sometimes. People are the only ones who care about that. The only thing separating me from Elvis isn't my ability to face or deal with or deny it. It's that I let it bother me. I'm trying really hard to stop. Because the TRUTH is I've already wasted so much of my life lying to myself.

The TRUTH is all those times Skip tried to kill his brother, Donny, I thought he was being a real asshole.

READING GROUP GUIDE

BACK ROADS
by
Tawni O'Dell

About this guide: The questions and topics in this guide are intended to generate a thoughtful and lively discussion, and we hope they will enrich your enjoyment of *Back Roads*.

QUESTIONS AND TOPICS FOR DISCUSSION:

1. Harley Altmyer is a complicated figure. He is part saint, part sinner; part child, part man. Discuss these contradictions. Which parts of him do you like? Which do you dislike?

2. How might Harley be different in other circumstances? Could he have had a normal life despite his abusive upbringing if he wasn't caring for his three sisters?

3. Harley sometimes has violent physical fantasies, many of them aimed at women. Do you think his fantasies are worrisome? Normal? To be expected, given his circumstances?

4. There are very few male influences in Harley's life. He obviously grew up in a family with fairly traditional gender roles. Yet Harley was not interested in hunting, sports, or other "manly" pursuits. Do you think this was a subconscious rejection of his father's worst masculine qualities? What effect do you think his father's scorn had on Harley's self-esteem?

5. Discuss why Amber is such a tragic figure. Did you feel that way even before the climax of the book? Why does Amber seek safety and comfort in the arms of all the wrong people? Why does it infuriate Harley? Are the reasons more complex than you initially suspected?

6. Why does Harley's mother take responsibility for the shooting? Do you think she did the wrong thing? In what ways was her false confession further abdication of her maternal responsibilities?

7. Discuss the theme of character as it applies to Misty. Do you think she is beyond redemption? Should Harley's mother have assumed her new role as head of the family and sought help for Misty?

8. Harley's father is as complicated a figure as Harley. In many ways, he is painted as a decent, hardworking, loving man. Does his casual violence negate all that? And how culpable is Harley's mother for overlooking the beatings?

9. Sexual tension between Harley and Amber is evident throughout this story. Is a certain portion of this natural when teens reach puberty? Did you find the violent love/hate relationship between Harley and Amber explained by their semi-incestuous past?

10. Do you think it's significant that Harley's first sexual relationship is with an older married woman who has children? In what ways does Callie mother Harley? Do you find that interesting in relationship to the themes of abandonment and incest that run through the book?

Coal Run

With her eagerly awaited second novel, Tawni O'Dell takes us back to the area where she grew up, the coal-mining country of western Pennsylvania, a territory she renders with such striking authenticity. Filled with the same unflinching honesty and compassion for a place and a way of life that made her first novel, *Back Roads,* such a huge success, *Coal Run* is another stunning example of O'Dell's distinctive style and her ability to find the humor and humanity in the bleakest states.

Coming from Viking in July 2004

J&P COAL COMPANY MINE NO. 9

March 14, 1967

A MEMORY

THE DAY GERTIE BLEW, I WATCHED MY FATHER LEAVE FOR work like I did every morning. It was called morning by the men who worked that shift, but to me it was still night, black and cold and silent except for the far-off rumble of the coke ovens as their doors were thrown open and the infernos inside them roared. I could see them clearly from my bedroom window, strung across a distant hillside, the mouths glowing red, then going dark in a steady rhythm like the blinking of a hundred fiery eyes watching our valley.

I didn't know exactly what it was that woke me. Maybe the squeak of the mattress springs as he got out of bed in the room next door, or his muffled voice along with my mother's as they said their good-byes, or the sound of his steel-toed safety shoes pacing the kitchen floor while he waited for the coffee to brew.

Whatever it was, it had the power to pluck me from my bed and send me stumbling half asleep across the cold, bare floor in my bare feet where I waited at the window to watch him cross our front yard along with the dozens of other men crossing their front yards carrying silver lunch pails the size of toolboxes, their mouths already solemnly working the plugs of tobacco they chewed to lubricate their throats against the gritty coal dust.

They didn't converge in a sudden stream the way they used to when my mother was my age and watched her father and the other men leave the three-room, soot-coated houses in the discarded company town a few miles down the railroad line from here. These days they left one at a time, but still together, in a synchronized solitude.

I always waved at him when he stopped at the car door and looked up at my window, and he always gave me a nod with a scolding half smile that said I should be in bed but what Mom didn't know wouldn't hurt her. It was our secret, one we shared man to man.

It wasn't until the last taillight on the last car or pickup truck winked out of sight around the bend in the road that I went back to bed, but never back to sleep.

I stopped by my bookshelf that my dad had built out of two-by-fours and proudly scanned my small but growing library of alphabet and number books, books about trucks and trains, Little Golden Books and Dr. Seuss books, and a book of Mother Goose nursery rhymes that had belonged to my mother.

At the very end of the row was the copy of *Wonders of Nature* that Santa had left under the tree for me that past Christmas. I took it back to bed with me every morning, along with my flashlight, crawled under my covers, turned to the page about prairie dogs and the diagram of the elaborate underground maze where they lived, and let my mind journey to the place where my dad went every day to do his job.

I didn't know that much about it because my dad and the other miners never talked about their work; they only talked about their fear of losing it. What I did know, I had learned from my mother, who explained to me once that he worked underground in tunnels where he dug coal that was very important to everyone. It gave us energy. It made steel to build buildings. Without coal America would come to a screeching halt.

The part about working underground in tunnels made the biggest impact on me, even bigger than the thought of a colossal shriek of brakes heard around the country and everyone and everything ceasing to move until my dad, and Grandpa, and Uncle Kenny, and Val next door, and my best buddy Steve's dad, and my teacher Miss Finch's boyfriend, and Jess Raynor's dad—who everybody called "Chimp" because one of the other miners once said he'd rather shoot coal with a monkey than be partnered up with Clive Raynor—all went back in the mines and dug some more coal.

The tunnels were what bothered me. I knew certain animals lived underground. Groundhogs and moles and snakes. But I couldn't picture men down there.

The first time I came across the picture of the prairie-dog town was the Christmas morning I got the book. I walked over to my dad, who was sitting in his favorite chair smoking a cigarette, drinking a cup of coffee, and casting glances I didn't understand at my mother, who was sitting on the couch with her bare legs curled up underneath her bathrobe and a short, shiny pink nightgown Santa had brought for her lying across her lap.

He was wearing a bathrobe, too, a gray one over a pair of gray pajamas. The only time I ever saw him wear pajamas was Christmas morning and once when he had the flu and my mom made him miss a day of work. They didn't suit him. He wore them uncomfortably, almost in an embarrassed way, as if he was trying to pull off a disguise.

I stood in front of him holding my new book while he finished looking at Mom through a few wisps of smoke left hanging in the air after the last puff off his cigarette.

I opened the book to the page with the prairie-dog town and asked him if that was what a mine looked like.

He took the book from me and studied it in the serious way he approached all books and all questions, then looked at me with his hooded, brittle blue eyes that were two sparks of startling color in a man otherwise lacking all color.

Sometimes when I watched him in the evening, washing up after work in my mother's green-and-yellow kitchen, stripped to the waist, his arms in black sink water up to his elbows, I thought of him as a person who had been cut out of a black-and-white photo and unknowingly pasted into the real world, and, like the subjects in a black-and- white photo, he seemed to have more clarity to him than people with lots of color.

He was pale skin, black hair, gray stubble, gray work pants, black coal dirt, gray cigarette smoke climbing from between his fingers or his lips, and a blue-gray tattoo etched beneath the dark hair on his hard left forearm, of a glaring man with a bushy mustache nailed to a cross the way Jesus was in church. The man was ugly and frightening but eerily fascinating to me, especially when my dad took me on his lap and traced his outline in his skin and repeated the word "Stalin."

"It's very much close to this," he replied in his broken English. "Except this. See."

At the sound of his command, my sister, Jolene, got up from the play tea set she was arranging on the floor and toddled over to see the book, too, her dozens of new dress-up bracelets and necklaces made of plastic gold and silver beads clicking against each other as she walked.

Dad pointed to the many escape routes the prairie dogs had made from their underground world to the world on top.

"We don't have this," he told us. "We have one way in and one way out."

I had my *Wonders of Nature* book with me at the kitchen table when Gertie blew. I was leafing through its pages while I was eating a late breakfast and might have even been looking at the prairie dogs and thinking of my dad at the precise moment when he would have turned his head toward the roar of the fireball before he was incinerated. Or maybe he never saw it coming. Maybe he was buried instantly by tons of earth without warning. Maybe his bones were broken, his organs crushed, his senses obliterated, his existence erased before he had a chance to understand what was happening. But I doubt it.

He had been a miner his entire adult life, and, like all miners, he understood the language of the coal face. Crackles, hisses, sighs, pops, squeaks, creaks, groans, gurgles—each noise meant something to them: a methane leak that could be ignited, an underground water source that could flood a shaft, a weak section of ceiling that was about to cave in. In response to the slightest tap of a shovel, the wall spoke back to them. I'm sure when it found itself about to be destroyed, it shuddered and screamed in a way they all recognized.

I was in afternoon kindergarten, so I got to spend my mornings at home. I was concentrating on a bowl of Alpha-Bits cereal, trying to spell my name with the sugary letters, being frustrated by the lack of a V. Jolene was in her high chair drawing a picture with her big-girl spoon in the applesauce she had spread all over her tray. She had a cold, and Mom was sneaking up behind her with a bottle of red cough syrup and a teaspoon.

The explosion came first, an enormous underground thunder that shook our house and shattered our windows in a spectacular musical instant with a sound like a million glass bells ringing all at once.

Mom dropped her teaspoon, and it hit the table, where the vibrations bounced it across the Formica leaving a trail of bright red drops like a nosebleed. Her face went ashen as all around us cupboard doors sprang open and dishes fell out, pictures jumped off walls, canned goods tumbled off shelves and rolled across the floor.

Then all movement and all sound ended as abruptly as it had begun. An absolute quiet filled the room that was every bit as loud as the explosion. It made my ears ring, and I clapped my hands over them protectively, somehow understanding that the silence was even worse.

Jolene began to cry. Mom didn't notice. She stared straight ahead at the wall where Dad's most prized possession had hung for my entire life: a portrait of a glowering king with a mustache that drooped to his chin, wearing regal silks and a simple hammered metal crown that looked like a child might have fashioned it out of an old can and some cheap birthstones. It was the only object he had been able to salvage from the remains of his family's farm in Ukraine after the war.

SUPREME SOVEREIGN VOLODYMYR THE GREAT, the little gold plaque at the bottom of the frame read.

"Supreme sovereign of what?" Val asked my mom once.

"Our kitchen," she told him.

Now the portrait lay facedown in the midst of a scattering of glass shards.

I waited to see what Mom's reaction would be. Volodymyr was sacred to Dad, and so was the massive gold frame he had bought with his first paycheck working in the Illinois coalfields years before he came east to Pennsylvania. Her eyes didn't leave the wall, and I realized she wasn't looking at anything. She was paralyzed with fear, waiting for something else.

None of us had ever heard the sound before, but when it finally came, we instinctively knew it meant death. It was a low, moaning wail that rose to a shriek, eerily human yet inhumanly immense, as if the earth itself were crying out in pain.

Mom's eyes filled with tears, and her mouth began to move. I couldn't hear her voice over the scream of the siren, but I could read her lips. She didn't say Dad's name or the name of anyone else she knew working the morning shift. She simply said, "The men."

Before I knew what was happening, she reached out and grabbed me, knocking over my chair. She hoisted Jolene onto her hip and dragged me along behind her by my arm. We went running out the front door, stepping over toppled furniture and crunching through broken window glass spread all over the carpet.

One by one the women of Coal Run joined us. Women I knew well. Women I hardly knew at all. Women my mom liked.

Women she didn't like. Old and young. Fat and thin. Pretty and plain. Some pregnant, some not. Some in housedresses, some wearing jeans and cotton blouses like my mom.

They dashed out of their homes and stopped suddenly as if an invisible door had been slammed shut in front of them. They clutched the shoulders and arms of their children or breakfast dishes they had been washing or laundry they had been folding.

They all stared in the same direction, at a spot two miles distant, impossible to see from our homes, but now it was marked by a thin cloud of black smoke seeping lazily across the blue sky. I searched the tilted faces, and for a moment, all their surface differences were stripped away and they were nothing but the daughters and sisters and wives and mothers of miners.

One woman screamed like a girl in a scary movie. One woman groaned and collapsed to the ground. But these were the only signs of hysteria. The rest rushed with shell-shocked responsibility back inside their toppling homes and came out again with their car keys and purses.

Our next-door neighbor Maxine went running for her car. Val was her son. He had dropped out of high school this past year to start working in Gertie. She shouted at my mom to come with her. Mom ignored her and started running.

Down the side of the road we flew, her grip on my arm like a tourniquet. My legs couldn't keep up with hers. I fell, and she yanked me up. I fell again, and she yanked harder and screamed at me to get up. Jolene sobbed from the pain of being jostled against Mom's hip.

I started crying, too. All around us the world was crumbling. Sections of the road sagged. Halves of houses sank into the ground. I watched a dog disappear with a solitary yelp, his paws scrabbling uselessly at the ground as the weight of the doghouse he was chained to pulled him down. I thought the world was coming to an end. I couldn't know that acres of mine tunnels were collapsing beneath the town.

Mom ignored everything and kept running. Soon I became aware of cars and trucks driving past us. Just a few at first. Then a steady stream. Like blood cells through an artery, they came rumbling up from side roads and back roads, bouncing across fields and crashing through woods. The pickup-truck beds were filled with kids and dogs and old people holding on to gun racks for balance.

Some of the drivers slowed down and shouted at Mom to get in, but she didn't seem to hear or care. We ran the whole way.

By the time we neared Gertie, we were the only ones on the road anymore. Hundreds of people had passed by us in a matter of minutes, but now the roars of the engines and the shouting were gone. I could hear birds chirping and distant dogs barking to each other, along with the sound of Mom's labored breathing and Jolene's quiet, frightened sobs and the blood pounding in my own head. I was in a state of near delirium from exhaustion and the pain in my shoulder where Mom gripped me, and I no longer felt the ground beneath my feet. I seemed to be floating. The only thing real to me was the fierce little glitters of quartz in the road as Mom continued pulling me along.

I fell a final time about a quarter mile from the complex. Gertie was at the top of a hill, like all the other deep shaft mines around here. It loomed at the end of a packed dirt and gravel road, looking like an enclosed village inhabited by a race of people who traveled by chutes and ladders and conveyor belts.

Mom wrapped an arm around my chest and dragged me the rest of the way. My knees were scraped raw, and the skin where she had gripped my arm while we ran had turned purple. Her knuckles were white. Her ponytail had come loose, and her pale gold hair, now dark with sweat, was plastered to the sides of her face. Her bare feet were bloody. She hadn't been wearing shoes when the siren sounded.

She released me and put Jolene down, then bent over, coughing. The air was hard to breathe here. It had a charred stench to

it, like a hundred moms had burned a hundred dinners and re-
fused to open a window.

Emergency vehicles from all over the county had arrived a
while ago. Ambulances, fire trucks, police cars, and the cars and
trucks of regular people had all been hastily abandoned at strange
angles with the doors left open.

Some people stumbled blindly, calling out names. Others
walked around with uncertain purpose, their eyes searching, lips
mouthing names they couldn't bring themselves to say out loud
yet. The rest stood in stiff, silent, immovable rows, like an orchard in winter.

My mom headed off determinedly, as if she knew of a destination that was worth arriving at, but the only destination I saw
was the hillside, and despite having felt the explosion under my
feet and hearing the shriek of the siren and seeing the commo-
tion going on all around me, it was hard to believe anything bad
had happened inside that hill. It didn't look any different than
any other hill.

Where was proof of a catastrophe? I didn't see anything that
resembled the aftermath of explosions I'd seen on TV. No leaping flames. No organized heroics by men in uniforms and badges
hauling people to safety. The miners on the outside, the police
and firefighters, were gathered in big impenetrable knots of grave
discussion.

A sick feeling started in the pit of my stomach as the soft weight
of Jolene's hand snuck into mine.

There were plenty of men around and lots of equipment and
machines meant for digging. Why wasn't anyone doing anything?
Why wasn't anyone saying anything?

The gray wooden faces in the orchard began taking on the
identities of people I knew. Kids from school. Neighbors. My
teacher, Miss Finch, whose boyfriend worked with Dad. Big Dr.
Ed, with his dark crew cut and stance like a conquering warlord,
who had prescribed the red cough syrup for Jolene yesterday. The

lady who drove my school bus. The lady who worked behind the ice cream counter at the Valley Dairy.

I saw my best buddy, Steve, being dragged through the crowd by his mom. I saw the glint of her wedding band on her dirty hand clutching his dirty forearm. He saw me. His eyes were raw from crying.

"Is your dad working?" he shouted at me, his voice high-pitched and shaky. "My dad's working," he said.

I saw our next-door neighbor, Maxine. She was standing on her tiptoes, looking all around her. Suddenly she started pushing her way through people, and I watched her find Val.

Val did everything I aspired to do when I was full-grown. He drove too fast, threw horseshoe ringers, ate Twinkies for breakfast, bagged two bucks every season, wore the same dirty clothes day after day. He could belch the Pledge of Allegiance and throw a football through a tire swing from fifty feet away.

When he wasn't working in the mines, he lived in a backyard world of beer, rock-and-roll anthems, and puddles of motor-oil iridescence. He was always working on his truck, or working on the garage he was building to put the truck in, or working on the description of the girl who was going to sit in the truck when it was running smoothly again. I was his helper. My job was to find the tool he requested in the midst of the dozens of tools spread all over the driveway that led to nowhere, since the garage wasn't finished yet.

Maxine ran to him and threw her arms around his neck. Her weight dragged his head down, and her own head cracked against his helmet. She touched him all over his filthy work clothes, and cupped his blackened face in her hands, and kissed him again and again. I heard her sobs of joy. They should have made me feel good, but they were ugly-sounding things.

I headed toward him, pulling Jolene along behind me. Val would have an answer for me. He'd be able to tell me why everyone was here but no one was doing anything. He had an answer for everything. Not the kind of answers my father gave me that were well thought out and took into account all the knowledge he had accumulated over a lifetime. Val's answers were instantaneous proclamations based on the inconceivability of an alternative.

"Why's the sky blue?" I asked him once.

"'Cause it would look pretty stupid if it was purple," he replied.

We arrived at his side, and I called up to him. He didn't notice us at first; then he finally glanced at me and Jolene, and our presence began to register on his face. I saw a terrible sadness there. It took me a moment to recognize the expression. I'd never seen Val look sad. He got pissed a lot. Anger was his emotion of choice when dealing with tragedy or misfortune. Not rage, but a sort of resigned aggravation that once again life had dealt someone an unfair blow and there was nothing anyone could do about it except swear and have a beer and think about something else.

"Is my dad okay?" I asked him.

I waited for him to say, "It would be pretty stupid if he wasn't."

He knelt in front of me, something he never did. My dad was always crouching down to my level to explain things to me, almost as if he thought we were equals, but Val liked being taller than me. It might have been because he wasn't tall compared to a lot of the other miners.

He clutched me by both arms, and the pain in my shoulder made me jerk away from him, but he held fast. I started to cry. It was the last thing I wanted to do in front of him.

"You be strong for your mom," he said.

"Why?" I screamed the word at him.

"You just do it. Okay?"

I dropped my eyes to the ground. A pair of bare feet appeared in my line of vision. They were filthy and spattered with blood. A few of the pretty pink toenails were cracked. One was ripped off. My mom's feet. She and Dad were going to Miss Finch's wedding tomorrow. She was going to wear high-heeled shoes with her toes sticking out. The night before she had shown my dad a bottle of pink nail polish and a bottle of red, and he had picked pink.

"What's going on, Val?" I heard my mom say.

They began talking in quiet voices, with my mom staring intensely at Val and Val staring intensely at her ruined feet about what was being done and what wasn't being done and why. Val told her we were waiting for a drill rig to be flown in from West Virginia. We didn't have anything here that could drill deep enough. Mom wanted to know why they were drilling instead of trying to go through the mouth. I lost track of the details then except for the numbers. The men were working Left 12. Two miles from the portal. Five hundred feet underground. Val said trying to estimate their whereabouts and drilling from the top was the only way.

"I don't understand," my mom finally said.

She lifted her hands up and covered her face. When she pulled them away again, tears had cut streaks of white through the dirt on her cheeks, but her voice stayed steady and calm.

"What are you saying?"

"It's gone, Mrs. Zoschenko." Val paused and made a strange noise like he was gulping for air. "The shaft. It's gone. It's collapsed. The whole thing."

I heard my dad's voice in my head: one way in, one way out.

I waited to see what my mom would do next. It seemed to me that everyone was watching her. She was the sister, the daughter, and the wife of a miner, and, because of me, it was assumed she would be the mother of one too. Her brother and her father were also working the morning shift in Left 12 along with her husband.

She sat down in the middle of the dirt the same way I'd seen Jolene plop down in the yard about a hundred times while she was learning to walk. When Mom hit the ground, Jolene crawled into her lap. There was nothing on Mom's face. Nothing in her eyes.

She held out one hand like she was waiting for someone to help her up. I walked over to her and took her hand and held it in my own the way I'd seen knights in storybooks kneel and hold a queen's hand.

"Did you wave good-bye to your dad this morning?" she asked me.

I nodded.

"Good," she said.

She pulled me down into her lap along with Jolene.

"We're going to pray," she said.

"Pray for what?" Jolene whispered to me.

"The men," I whispered back.

I clasped my hands together and closed my eyes. I prayed with all my might that my dad was still alive. A couple days later, I would hear my mom praying behind a closed bathroom door that he had died instantly.

Photo by Brian Ende

Tawni O'Dell was born and raised in Indiana, Pennsylvania. She attended college at Northwestern University, where she received a degree in journalism. After spending fourteen years in the Chicago area, she has recently moved back to Pennsylvania, where she lives with her two children.

Back Roads spent nine weeks on *The New York Times* bestseller list in the spring of 2000. An Oprah Book Club pick and a Book-of-the-Month Club Main Selection, it has been translated into five languages and published in ten countries and is soon to be a major motion picture for DreamWorks Pictures.